I0572730

THE GODSTONE DECREE

By : Mitchell Lecoultre

ISBN-13: 979-8-9989447-1-0
Cover design by: Kate Lozovska
Library of Congress Control Number: 2018675309
Printed in the United States of America

Acknowledgements

As anyone with experience knows, no journey is successful without support. Many people have helped me on this road: mentors, teachers, family, friends, and even enemies, but surely that would be too much to write here. Nonetheless, for those of you who have known me—for all my flaws and all my strengths, thank you for your support in this crazy life of ours. Here is to happy reunions and new adventures!

Of course, I would never have made it to the point where I am writing an acknowledgement without the support of my better half, my practical, beautiful, and wonderful wife, Vanessa! You have been there for me through everything from sunshiny days to turbulent storms, and I couldn't ask for a better partner to venture with.

To my mom and dad: No one could have asked for a better childhood. You have given me all the tools I need for success, the wisdom to survive, and a moral compass of immeasurable strength. Truly, I could not have asked for a better set of parents. Thank you!

To my brothers Sean and Ben: Thank you for dealing with a little brother with such patience and showing me how to have fun but also how to navigate this sometimes-rugged life.

To my sister: For the times we shared and the care you gave to me. I hope you are well.

To my friends: Thank you for all the wonderful times together.

Finally, I would like to thank the professionals who helped me complete The Godstone Decree. With a big shout out to Kate Lozovska for the excellent cover art!

Map of the Holliserian Fringe

Note: A glossary to the gods is located within the back of this novel for your reading pleasure.

Part One

Chapter One

Navin

Navin nearly wept. His little baby looked like no more than a ghost—pale and fragile. His wife looked at him, eyes pleading. "Save our boy" was the unspoken cry. Tears begging for him—for anyone—to do something. But what could *he* do? He wasn't a doctor, and he surely wasn't a Keeper. Navin could only look back at her and return the same helpless gaze as he stood in the stuffy, overly hot room. The feeling of impotency heavy as he listened to the sounds of his six-week-old babe, Demetrius, wheeze as he fought for every breath.

"I have given him some ginger and goblin's finger to ease his cough and fight the fever. It will help him rest, but without intervention from the Maiden, I don't … I don't think your son will make it." the apothecarian said. Navin hated the hunch-backed, diminutive man. There was no cause for this hatred, just sullen anger with nowhere to go. He held his tongue as he looked down at the cowed, wrinkled face, eyes downcast so that all Navin saw was a crop of gray hair covering folds of wrinkled skin. Although the elder spoke the truth, the clink of his life savings—two hundred and twenty-four coppers—dropping into the old man's outstretched palm did little to assuage Navin's mounting rage. The frail, bone-thin hand dropped under the weight of the bag, and a smile formed at the edge of his lips which only went to aggravate Navin further.

"Thank you," The older man said. The satchel disappearing into his cloak with a practiced grace. Navin bit the inside of his gum, and before his anger could swell to a crescendo, the apothecarian interrupted, "You must bring him to the clinic day. It's—" The elder's mouth moved as he counted silently. "Eight days. Yes, eight days from now. The Keepers offer their services then, if we can keep the boy's fever and cough down, he has a chance."

Navin studied the grooved face, its crinkled features staring back at him, the head craned like a turtle looking out from its shell. Although the apothecarian's face was impassive, the truth was written in those wrinkled features; Demetrius wouldn't make it that far. This swindler was trying to get Navin to pay for another day of treatment, trying to capitalize on Navin's hope that his son would survive. No, Navin needed a solution now, and although this healer had *technically* helped, it was obvious he was only trying to enrich himself at this point.

To his own surprise, Navin spoke with tempered grace, "Thank you, sir, we will surely bring Demetrius to the clinic day. Now, have a good night." Navin gestured behind him, through the small, scanty living room, to the exit door. The healer, seeing he had not duped the desperate father, sighed and shuffled through the quaint space, making his way past a bench and low table. The wooden home seemed so insignificant, even with such a small man as a sense of scale.

"Ember's breath," Navin cursed. At this late hour, this far from the clinic day, he would have to pay for the blessings of the Maiden herself. An expense only the wealthy could afford.

"What … what did he say? What can we do?" Naomi, Navin's wife, asked in an anxious plea.

Naomi's countenance was unbearable, and he almost burst into tears seeing the anxiety and grief in her eyes. "I … he said that we must make it to clinic day." Navin held up a hand as his wife went to protest. "I know, I know that's too far away." He felt helpless, his boy would most likely die, but he wanted to give Naomi hope. He wanted her to feel there was a chance. "The healer says if we keep his fever and cough down, there is a chance Demetrius will make it. He, um … he will be back in a couple of days to administer another treatment."

A look of relief fell over his wife's face, her spirit latching on to the morsel he had given. "Oh, thank the gods." She reached down and kissed their baby boy on the forehead. "You hear that? You are going to get all better, and when you do … we will laugh and play in the sunshine."

Navin looked away, hiding a tear coursing down his cheek. Choosing not to risk his wife seeing the lie, he resolved to go out into the night. His wife had hope—an escape; he needed to find his. "The healer will need to be paid though. The sooner the better," Navin said while swinging his wool coat over his shoulders. His wife looked up from her matronly pose by the bedside, and with a graven expression, she nodded. He adjusted the coat on his shoulders, "I am going to see if I can rustle up some coins. I'll be back." At this late hour, it could only be from a money lender, but Navin saw Naomi's desperation, and her solemn nod was all the approval he needed.

*

With nowhere to go, he gravitated towards the only place with lights, and life, Minollo's Flagon. Like a small candle, the tavern lay near the center of The Bowl: the natural ridge of hills that ringed Augustia's harbor in a semicircle. It was what made Augustia such a prime location for a seaport, and, as humans tend to do, a diorama of stratification. Its modest nature and location at the start of The Bowl's rise gave it the unique capacity to anonymously serve the rich or the poor. This far into night's embrace, it tended to outlast those taverns which relied on a more regular customer base.

Despite the crowded, rowdy tavern, where drunken patrons shouted over one another and mugs slammed onto tables, Navin wove his way through the chaos. He slipped his way past swaying bodies and overturned chairs until he claimed an empty spot in the shadowy corner. A worn wooden bench produced an exhale of relief.

"What'll it be?" A young woman asked, her dull brown and grey dress stained in a patchwork pattern.

"Uh—"

"The honey ale is a favorite here. It's our house special!" She interrupted him—eager to carry out her duties.

Navin nodded, "Sure … sounds good." He slipped a copper from his weekly wages into the woman's palm. Hopefully it would be the only coin he'd spend here, though it was unlikely.

The young lady was right though, it was a favorite, even for him.

"There ya go!" Patchwork dress said, tossing a mug in front of him. He smelled the earthy tones of the honey infused drink, a concoction unique to Minollo's Flagon. Navin sipped and the rich taste swirled over his tongue. Not yet enough to drown his sorrow, but it was a start. *How did they make it taste like a summer's day?* Navin pondered in-between heavy gulps of the delicious brew.

The alcohol flowed without restraint, warming his veins and loosening his tongue. Before he realized it, he was draining his second mug with unsteady eagerness. The bittersweet liquid sloshed over the rim as he brought it to his lips faster than he cared to admit. It was a stupid decision, but he did not care. Another swig: three heavy gulps tumbling down his throat, the warmth already forming in his belly. Just before dropping his second flagon, he saw over the spine of the vessel, a rather tall, elegant woman approach. "Ember's breath," he muttered before a wash of guilt flooded over him.

Her slender frame was covered in spotless, well-made cloth, and her steps seemed to flutter as they danced towards him. She wore a dark green cloak, its hood shadowing her face. Her appearance, in combination with her bowed head made it obvious she was trying to be discreet. Even then, Navin couldn't help but notice the radiant beauty—masked in shadow. Her manner screamed of the excesses of the upper class, of one from the upper regions of The Bowl.

"Excuse me, sir, may I sit here?" the lady asked pleasantly, like a soft crooning whisper.

Navin, so dumbstruck she had stopped to talk to him, sat with the flagon held in front of his face.

She giggled at his expression. "I heard the mead is quite good here. Apparently, it's *so* good it robs one of speech."

Navin flushed with another pulse of guilty desire. Desperately he tried to wrangle his thoughts back to his family, to Demetrius, but even her laughter was elegant—desirous, he couldn't help himself. A sudden crash from a table of sailors far into their night's drink, jolted him back to reality. He made to stand, stuttering, "Uh, I'm sorry where are muh manners?"

The lady held up a hand, a silver bangle flashing as the cloak's camouflage fell away. "Oh, please don't stand up!" She glanced around nervously before continuing, "I simply wished to have a word with you, sir. So, do you mind?" Her hand drifted down to the chair opposite him.

Navin, halfway between standing and sitting, made an awkward gesture towards the aforementioned chair, "Not at all." He cleared his throat. "Ma'am."

With deft grace, she seemed to float down into her seat. As she arranged herself, she pulled the hood of the cloak away. A golden ponytail, held with silver bands, fell across her shoulder, and the whites of her teeth flashed at Navin in a broad, welcoming smile. His breath was nearly robbed from him, and that small corner of the tavern had become a beacon of light. Before he could gather himself, she spoke.

"So, you may be wondering what a woman like me is doing here, yes?" She raised her brows in question, but not with enough of a gap between speech to respond. "Well, you see I don't normally partake in places like *this*, but I work for someone rather … desperate. Yes, my employer wishes for a simple task. A simple job to be done."

Navin's heart sank, coming to grips with what he already knew. She wasn't there to find love. Of course she wasn't, she was there on business. His guilt surged with a flittering thought of Naomi. He had not even said it aloud in his mind, but his desire had been overwhelming. Somewhere in the secret recesses of his consciousness, a thought had taken root; a fantasy of her approaching him for a night's comfort. His secret hopes dashed, his tone suddenly became gruff, "Oh yeah? What's that then?"

She smiled and produced a small wooden box from beneath the table. She looked around and placed the box down gently. Save for a simple depiction of an oak tree in the center, it was unremarkable. With her delicate hands still placed on the sides of the box, she said "You look like a *capable* man. So, let me be plain." She glanced around again and leaned in closer.

Navin leaned in as well, his heart thumping, the smell of lavender invading his senses.

"I need this box delivered somewhere out of town. Can you do this?" She placed a hand on Navin's own and the delicate touch made a shiver run up his arm. "For me?" A blossoming smile flushed across her face; the blush of her cheeks intense.

Navin's heart raced, and his thoughts swirled between the despair of his child's illness, his wife's grief, and this new fantasy—this new temptation.

"Of course, you would be compensated for your trouble." The lady produced a small bag. The clink of coins barely piercing the din of the tavern as she placed it on the table next to the box. She gently untied the string holding the satchel and exposed its contents to him, inside he could see gleaming Augustian gold marks. His jaw went slack.

A small laugh, like the elegant giggle of before escaped her lips. "There's ten marks in there for you. So, what do ya say?"

Navin was utterly dumbfounded, he felt like he sat there—in silence, his mouth agape—for an eternity. "What … uh … what do you need me to do?" he spluttered.

"That's quite simple. Just take this box here out of town."

"Out of town … where?" he queried. He thought he saw a flash of irritation in the lady's brow at this question, a small tremor on the otherwise pleasant face.

"That information is only for those who wish to be paid."

"Ah, I see." He said, leaning back. He had been ensnared, but there were ten gold marks on the line—more than enough to pay for his son's treatment. *Ember's breath, I could get a better place in the city, somewhere Naomi would be proud of.* A pang of grief at the thought of his wife, coursed through him. She suffered while he flirted with desire. Anger curdled in him, at himself, and looking down at the satchel of coins, he resolved to do better for Naomi, for Demetrius. "Fine, I will take yer bargain. Now where to?"

The lady beamed another smile. "Excellent!" Her eyes swept across the room, darting around as she made sure no one was watching before leaning in. The smell of lavender kissed his senses again and she whispered to him, "I need you to take this to the Broken Stallion Inn. You know the place?"

He nodded.

"Good, take this box there and hand it to the innkeeper. Say it's for someone called—" Her voice dropped even further, and Navin strained to hear. "Bloodeye. You must be on your guard, it is in Argolonian territory. You will also *have* to go tonight. Haste is important, understand?" She pushed the box towards him.

He nodded, grabbing the proffered container. It felt rather weightless, and as he went to put it into his own pockets, she grabbed his hand again. Her eyes—a deep, cerulean blue—a mockery of Naomi's earlier pleading.

The simulacra served to remind him of his oath to his wife. Before she could speak, he knew he had to ask, "I can do this for you, but I need to take these coins to my wife. I need to tell her that I will be gone for a bit. Ya see, my son he … he is sick. 'Sides what man would I be if I just left 'em, with no explanation, in the middle of the night?"

She nodded in understanding, a glint of sadness gracing her eyes. "Aye, I wish I could let you do that. But if you take this bargain and then head home, you'll be putting your family at risk."

"What?" he asked incredulously.

She held up a hand to stifle his indignation, "If you want the coin, you must trust that I can deliver your payment to your wife and child. My assurance is my word, as well as this extra mark for your trouble."

She slid another coin across the wooden tabletop; its metal gleaming in the tavern's heavy candlelight. He still wondered what she had meant, *his family at risk?* This did seem like a rather 'fishy' job, but the amount she was offering was staggering. He'd be a fool to let it slip. Ember's breath, even with just one Augustian mark, he would have made more than a half-year's wages as a dockworker in a single job. "Make it two marks, and I agree to your terms."

The woman's upper lip curled briefly, enough to let him know he had struck a chord. Still, she replied with some courtesy remaining, "Very well, if you *insist.* I will give you another and deliver the rest to your family. Now, where is your home?"

As he told her his address, he calculated how long it would take to get to the Broken Stallion Inn. A week and a half of travel on foot at least. Hopefully, Demetrius would recover in that time, and hopefully his wife would not think too hard when this *lady* showed up to their door in the middle of the night. Oh, the scolding he would get. Yet, it was not unwarranted, for in the recesses of his mind, he wondered if he would see this elegant beauty again.

Chapter Two

Navin

Cool night air brushed past him. The sliver of moonlight at the end of the cluttered alley looked much like the salvation he sought. Yet, Navin knew there would be no respite. Not for a while at least. His legs ached as he leapt over discarded refuse and empty slop buckets; the products of the lower class. Augustia may have marbled halls at the top of The Bowl, but not here, not this close to the Harbor Gate. He shook his head, clearing his thoughts as he pushed forward. Each breath was a strain, each stride a chore, but he would make it. He would get out of the city with this box—whatever its contents—and he would earn those other ten gold marks.

Navin had thought it would be a simple job, albeit a long one. Of course, he knew there would be danger on the roads and alleys in and around Augustia, but this was different. Something, or someone had almost immediately started following him as he left Minollo's Flagon. It was like a prickle on his skin, the hair rising, a feeling of being watched. Now, a quarter mile from the Harbor Gate, he knew it existed. In the shadows around him he had heard echoing footsteps, shuffles betraying a pursuer. Fear had gripped him then, and in desperation he had ducked into an alley.

That had been mere moments ago. Now, as he broke free to the other side of the narrow street, thinking he was free from pursuit, he saw a man veiled in darkness. Something in the stranger's gait warned Navin of danger. He bolted then, ducking into yet another alley; the shadowy figure sprinting after him.

Adrenaline coursed through his veins, his mind whirling at all that had occurred. He leapt over another bucket, and the end of the alley loomed over him. Behind, he heard a crash as the pursuer tripped on some obstacle. *A fool who did not know Augustia's alleys as well as he did.*

A triumphant grin spread across his face at his pursuer's mistake. He exploded from the narrow, oppressive alley into the broad expanse of Harbor Street, the cramped walls giving way to open cobblestones that promised freedom and a clear path ahead. He looked to his left. There, less than a quarter mile away, lay the Harbor Gate. Ironically, his safety would be more secure outside of those gates than in, and they were *so* close. It would be easy to secure his passage out with the signed vellum he had been given by the golden-haired beauty. Whether the document was signed in her name or another's, he did not know. He cursed himself for not asking, it would be nice to at least know her name.

Maybe it wouldn't matter, not with what lay in front of him. As Harbor Street began its descent towards the sea, two figures stood, silhouetted in the moonlight. One pointed directly at him as he skidded to a stop. Navin didn't wait, racing up the street and towards another alley he knew would bring him to the small dirt path that skirted the inner wall.

His breath became hard and heavy now, the physicality he had earned in the Warriors of August long gone, replaced by the decline of age. Still, he pressed on as his legs burned and his chest heaved. Fear drove him, and small flashes of Naomi danced in his mind, driving him to the completion of his task.

He risked a glance behind, and three figures—the original pursuer having caught up—crossed the alley he had used to enter Harbor Street. The three took a moment to regroup before charging after him. With time slipping through his fingers and urgency pounding in his chest, he veered into the narrow side street. His boots skidded over loose gravel while he forced himself into the shadows of the passage he had been aiming for. A short alley his wife's cousin lived on, the thought of his terrible stews flashing in his mind. *Strange how the mind works in such times,* Navin thought while praying the man was asleep. The cousin would only serve as a beacon to the pursuers, and besides, he was not exactly a person Navin would go to in an emergency. Fortunately, Navin did not see any lights on in the high two-story home, or any of the other similar homes. His stride strengthened in hope as he saw he was halfway to the inner wall. The masonry of the high walls shone like silver in the moonlight, and Navin could see the mortar between the gaps of each massive brick. A shout from a nearby doorway frightened him, nearly falling as he turned to see its origin.

An elderly woman stirring a small pot over a low fire stood in wide eyed horror.

"Sorry," Navin muttered breathlessly, waving a conciliatory hand to the victim. He cursed at the noise, knowing his pursuers would be able to pinpoint him from it. Still, he pressed on, breaking out of the alley and nearly colliding with the wall as he turned down the small path. He knew he could be spotted by soldiers on the ramparts, but he did not care. Besides, that would be to his benefit; in fact, he hoped a perceptive guard would see his plight. Unfortunately, no alarm came, no sound of a soldier's challenge. Instead, he was accompanied by his own laborious breaths.

The first large torch that adorned the Harbor Gates became visible around the distant, slowly descending bend. Navin closed his eyes in relief, and he put out a prayer to The Maiden. *Grace us with the boon of your mercy.*

When he reopened them, it was obvious The Maiden and him weren't on speaking terms. A man and a woman slid from the shadows, as if they came from nowhere. He skidded to a stop and, knowing there was no alley close by, turned around. His heart sank as he saw another man blocking his retreat. Unsure of himself, he turned back to the two, his eyes darting back and forth between the two paths.

They closed in on him, like hunters approaching prey. Navin, more instinct than reason, darted towards the single man, hoping he could overpower him. It was only a short jaunt to the blocking figure, but as Navin sprinted towards him, he saw that this man was a brute. At least thirty centimeters taller than him and bound with muscle. He could not turn back. His only hope was the small chance of ducking past the man's grasping blows. With a final burst of speed, Navin rushed forward, ducked to the right, and tried to go low under his grabbing arms. He was not fast enough, a lightning quick trunk of an arm shot out and pushed him towards the wall.

The blow landed with brutal force, slamming into Navin and ripping the momentum from his body as if he'd run headlong into a wall. He struggled to get moving, and he put his leg forward trying to use the small window of escape that remained. A white-hot pain erupted within his consciousness, blinding him. His left arm, flung up in a desperate reflex, gave way with a sickening crack as the bone snapped. Staggering, Navin dropped to one knee, breath ragged and all momentum gone. A massive hand grabbed his short crop of hair and pulled him upright. The brute of a man, his face scarred and malevolent, looked at him with the unthinking barbarism of an animal. With a grunt akin to disgust, the brute flung Navin backwards. His scalp burned in response.

The box he had been entrusted to carry clattered to the scraped-dirt ground.

"Ah, just what we were looking for." Another male voice said, reedy and nonchalant.

Navin tried to grab the box and regain his feet, but a dagger pressed against his throat. Fear lanced through him, death close at hand; a specter that froze him in place.

"What … what do you want?!" He pleaded.

"Hush now," the reedy-voiced man commanded. The dagger wielder swung into view. A woman with a wicked grin winked at him, her features cast ominously in the mixture of torch and moonlight.

Panic started to take hold. "Hel—" Navin tried to yell, but the woman interrupted him with a stiff backhand. The fresh pain throbbing in step with the intensity of his broken arm.

"I said hush, and what do you do? Cry out?!" the owner of the reedy voice now pretending to be offended, like one scorned at a house party. Navin heard the man tut in disappointment as they rounded on him. The sound of boots scraping the dirt slowly centered in front of him, and then a sudden rush of steps came barreling towards him. Navin winced in anticipation, and he felt the big brute's massive hand grasp his hair again. His face yanked upwards, forcing him to look. An elegantly dressed man with a light purple waistcoat stood before him, his hands clasped behind him. "Why do people never listen? Why do they always think that *they* don't have to listen!?" The man said, his voice building in anger. With a heavy breath, he composed himself almost theatrically. "So, who sent you?"

"I ... I don't know. Some woman at a tavern." Navin said meekly. Another flash of pain erupted as the dagger-wielder backhanded him again.

The thin man stooped to Navin, his voice hardening, "Think *harder.*"

Navin's mind was a whirl of pain and fear. Instinct and an inclination to live overrode everything else, and owing no loyalty to the beauty who paid him, he divulged all. "I don't know her name, but it was at Minollo's Flagon, she had a dark green cloak and a golden ponytail with silver bands holding it together!"

Nothing happened for a moment, until slowly the thin man's lips curled into a wicked grin. He reached out and patted Navin on the cheek, his hand cold. "Very good. Yes, very good. Kill him!"

"What ... *no* I—" Navin's voice failed him as the dagger was drawn across his throat. He felt his strength drain, the heat of his own blood coursed down his neck onto his chest, leaving his limbs heavy and unresponsive. The big brute let his hair go, and Navin drooped gently to the ground. The weight of Telaea pulled him as close to her embrace as it could. He lay there shocked, spluttering as blood erupted from his mouth. The warmth of it feeling like a balm against the night chill.

"Soon it will be alright dear," he heard the woman say gently. She crouched over him, dominating his view, her eyes glossed in what could only be empathy.

Slowly, his eyes glazed over, and the sensations of the outside world dwindled away. He thought of Naomi cradling Demetrius in their home. He thought of the warmth of the sun, the caress of his wife's lips, her dress flowing in the sea breeze. He thought of his mother's smile, his father's laugh. He thought of his son's wheezing breath and hoped the coins would buy him life. Then he thought no more.

Chapter Three

Sophia

"Yeah, looks like they scooped his eyes right out! Gruesome stuff I tells ya," Sergeant Conrad said in the all-knowing manner of one used to seeing it all. "But," He sucked in a breath through clenched teeth. "On the Lower Bowl it's like that sometimes."

Sophia couldn't help but notice the man was rather enthusiastic about the whole affair; a brutal murder where the victim appeared to have been robbed, his throat cut, his eyes gouged out, and his body left to rot. The only remainder of their missing organs were hollow sockets with speckles of viscera. "And why do you think they would do that, sergeant?" Sophia queried.

"Well, I don't know, Keeper. Sometimes people is just cruel I guess." The sergeant replied with a shrug.

"Maybe so." Sophia bent to investigate the body further. He was a middle-aged man with a short crop of black hair, tousled in a way that indicated it had been roughly pulled. A wool coat lay tattered behind him, stained with the blood that came from a grievous neck wound, and his arm was bent unnaturally at the elbow. Sophia knew this had been more than a robbery, at the very least there was some sort of revenge motive. "What time was the body found?"

"Shortly before dawn, Keeper. Wall-guard spotted him laying there," the sergeant replied.

"And how long do think this fellow has been dead?"

"Well, at the time we found him he was still warm an' all, but he did start showing some purpling round his backside. So, at that time it would've been 'round one … maybe two hours after death. It's hard to tell for sure, Keeper, but my best guess is this happened 'bout six hours ago."

Sophia smiled, appreciating the sergeant's knowledge, and the accuracy of his statements. His enthusiasm mired in the eagerness of practicing a craft they knew well. She stood and faced the sergeant, the sunburst tendrils of his Warriors of August heraldry near blinding in the bright morning sun. "Thank you, sergeant. You have been very *thorough*. Give me a moment to contemplate on this and then we will discuss, agreed?"

The sergeant smiled in response. "Of course, Keeper. I will be nearby if you needs me."

She nodded again to the sergeant as he smartly turned and headed off a respectful distance. He stood with another of his guardsmen, nearly touching the side wall of a cluster of high wooden homes. It was one of many such clusters that lay between the inner wall's dirt path and the cobblestone Harbor Street, looking like spires of scaffolding against the masonry of the wall. The clutter accompanied a slight tint of raw sewage. A sensation always on the edge of perception down here by the docks. The smell and the sights brought on a tinge of guilt. The dichotomy between the Lower and Upper Bowl fueling it, especially since her own lodging, a small room in the Keeper's Bastion, was at the crown of hills that ringed Augustia.

It felt strange to be living there again, like she was a fresh-faced novice still. Well, she was a novice … just not a fresh-faced one. It had been three years there now; three years away from Elgion, away from her sisters. Those two lovable miscreants still lived in that far away settlement across the sea; meanwhile, she was back here, in Augustia, and she still hadn't quite reconciled her new position. After all, she had been a Keeper of means—of power. Elected as the senior Keeper of the Stones for Elgion, she had been the primary conduit of the godstones will and voice. In that position she had prospered, using her scholarly prowess and god-granted magic to enhance the logistical, arcane, and productive capacities of Elgion's holdings. Now she was relegated to *this*; investigations, clinic days, transcription of manuscripts, and more. All busywork for a novice who had once been more. It was hard not to feel anger at the sting of demotion, but to be fair, it wasn't like she hadn't earned it.

Sophia turned to see Olivia, a stalwart friend from far away Elgion and smiled. She figured the gesture would look rather gruesome against the backdrop of such a crime scene, but she struggled not to feel happiness at the sight of the former laundress. After all, they had been soldiers, side-by-side in a gruesome battle against overwhelming odds. A fateful encounter that had all started with a corrupt miller and had ended in fire. *Two fires in fact*, Sophia thought wryly.

The first of which had been a mistake; the culmination of dealings with a man skimming off the top, and—now that she looked back on it—a rather insane addiction to a particular godstone. That potent combination had found her using her embershard amulet to launch a fireball into the miller's eldest son's shoulder. A mistake that had ultimately cost her the title of senior Keeper.

Fortunately—or perhaps unfortunately—that son, whose name was Dunkeath, had survived. Not only had he survived, but to everyone's surprise, he had become one of Sophia's most stalwart companions. "Well, if she's going and you're going … I'm going too. 'Sides someone needs to keep yer temper in check," he had told them before she and Olivia had shipped out to Augustia. With that, it had been decided, and now he was here—just as loyal and robust a friend as Olivia ever was. Of course, his friendship had also started in the fires of war. Hard to break bonds that are forged against the anvil of death.

She glanced over at that eldest son, curious as to whether he had insight into their situation. *Not yet,* she thought, *soon though*. Dunkeath was doing what he always did—talk. He had cornered one of the guards and was assailing them with his nonsense. In time that *talk* would bear fruit, but as always with Dunkeath, she would have to let him work.

She looked away from the lanky man before he noticed her staring. To be caught was to invite conversation, and she wasn't sure she could handle his affable, albeit rather crass manner at the moment. Even in the three years they had been working together, she hadn't quite gotten used to some of his more … colorful turns of phrase. Or maybe she had some innate bias towards the man. Some animal instinct left over from their first encounter, or at least, the first encounter she *remembered* of him.

It had been not far from the mill his father owned, in a grove where pilfered grain had been temporarily stored. Dunkeath had tried his best that day to manifest a dagger into Sophia's chest by the sheer malice in his stare. The dagger never appeared, but something rather unexpected did. Alexa, Sophia's oldest sister, had stumbled out from the trees injured and weak. Her wounds which had left her near death had been obtained during her patrol as a ranger, a Warden of the Wilds. That was what made her remember that day so often, not Dunkeath's malice. Unfortunately for him, those malicious glares happened to be the anchor point for that memory. She sighed as she recalled the chain of events that followed.

Bella, her youngest sister, brash and headstrong, had charged off into the wilds to discover why Alexa had been so threatened. Of course, Sophia privately thought it had been some attempt at revenge. Regardless of the motivation, Bella did in fact discover the threat—orcs.

Called by Magdris, that bloody god of war, to the distant shores of the new world, an orcish horde had assaulted Elgion herself. Their goal? To pillage all humanity had made and bathe it in the blood of their barbaric rituals—fuel for Magdris's designs. Fortunately for humanity, the Vollimosa sisters had been there, and together they had rallied the defenders of Elgion to hold fast against that storm. It had been a hard battle, and for Sophia, it had become a personal one. A battle of wits and wills against the very gods themselves. That was where the second fire had come into play. Her hand tingled; an unbidden desire creeping up her nerves.

"Keeper! You alright?" Olivia asked.

Sophia shook her head, so lost in her reverie she had drawn concern from the former laundress. "Yes, yes, I am fine." She blinked away the past and bent back to the task at hand; a victim of a gruesome murder.

The hollows of his gouged-out eyes were still difficult to look at. The throat had been horribly mangled, cut so deep the head appeared to be on a hinge. Her eye, being intensely drawn to such a macabre sight, couldn't help but notice something in the lines of cuts on the neck.

She stooped again to the corpse's side, peering at the cut patterns. They were from a well-honed blade, most likely a dagger, and there was more than one set. Like the victim had been cut on two separate occasions. A shallower line curved slightly at the end, a product of some swift practiced stroke. While the deeper cuts were straight, methodical, like a butcher making a cut of meat. She wondered why someone would take the time to simply cut the neck even further when a revelation popped into her mind. A fragment of learning garnered from the rather well-used tome of *Keeper Maldis's Reflections on Crime and Human Nature.*

> *The truly savvy criminal has learned to severe the lines of communi-cation, even after death ... Perhaps a Keeper was able to get a reani-mate to blink a message or even write one? Without the use of eyes, one would struggle to do either.*

She glanced up at the eyes, the black hollow sockets sending a shiver up her spine. Those too seemed to have been done more methodically and with little struggle, the victim having been dead long before the criminals removed them.

Olivia asked "So, what do we gots here?"

"Well, it looks like someone didn't want this fellow to divulge what he knew," Sophia said.

"I mean ... wouldn't the being dead part be enough?" Olivia asked with some light humor.

Sophia chuckled wryly, "Yes, one would think that, but when a Keeper can summon the dead back for questions … people tend to be more thorough."

Olivia furrowed her brows at this, not understanding what Sophia had meant. She may have been a faithful companion, but the intricacies of Keeper life always seemed to be a mystery to her, even though the woman was quite capable of recalling the histories and back stories of the various gods.

Sophia sighed and explained, "Necrostone, my dear. I could, if I so chose, question this man after death with the use of Necrostone. Mosyneta does not forget, and their memory of events can be acquired with a little coaxing of his stone."

"That's right, the ol' bugger doesn't leave well enough alone," Dunkeath said suddenly. *How did he hear us so well when he was already in conversation?* Sophia wondered as she watched him approach, a small nod from him to the previously cornered guard. "I am assuming you mean that we can't use the ol' stone cause this fella couldn't tell us anything. Well, on account of his … um, missing bits?"

Sophia responded, bemused, "Yes, Dunkeath. This fellow is unable to answer questions even in the afterlife. Now, we must ask what answers did he have?" She turned again to the sergeant and yelled, "Sergeant! Did any of your men or anyone you questioned give any leads on suspects?"

Sergeant Conrad shuffled over smartly, "Unfortunately, no, Keeper. Everyone's been quiet as mice, and muh guards only ever saw him dead here." He kicked at a stone in the dirt, obviously uncomfortable, before coming to his own defense, "Whoever did this must 'ave been rather practiced. If'n you catch muh meaning."

She did, and she agreed wholeheartedly. Although it was rare practice for a Keeper to use Necrostone, on account of its dubious legality and its questionable efficacy. These folks didn't take chances, and they did the job well. No doubt they were professionals, which seemed rather odd for what could only be described as your typical, common man. "I do, sergeant. Well, keep your eyes open and your ears out, ok?"

The sergeant nodded and opened his mouth to speak but was interrupted by a sudden shout.

"Sergeant! Sergeant … I," A young woman had raced from the nearby alley and skidded to a stop near them, struggling for breath. "The-there … has be—"

"Catch your breath soldier. Calm is control," Sergeant Conrad said with a bit more iron in his voice than Sophia had heard earlier.

The young soldier nodded and panted heavily for a few breaths. "There has been another murder, sergeant. This time in the Upper Bowl."

Sergeant Conrad glanced at Sophia, who was still stooped by the corpse. A look of worried confusion on his brows, and with some hesitation requested of the reporting soldier, "Well, details then."

"Well, it's at some estate. The wife of a rather well-off member of the Chosen. Looking a lot like that fellow there."

Sophia stood abruptly, slightly off balance from the cumbersome Keeper's robes she was forced to wear. With her curiosity piqued, she asked, "What do you mean? The injuries are the same?"

The soldier looked at Sophia and then to the sergeant, looking for permission to speak to this unknown person. Sergeant Conrad gave it, "'Tis alright Gilda, this here is a Keeper."

Gilda nodded and replied to Sophia, "Yes, um, Keeper. Same cuts and everything."

Once again, the sergeant looked at Sophia, obviously wondering what she was thinking. She bit her lip in thought. Two murders in such a fashion on the same night were likely connected. Not that murder was uncommon in the streets of Augustia, but two murders avoiding the interference of a

Keeper, were worrisome. She would have to investigate—immediately.

"Well, sergeant, I guess we better be off then."

Chapter Four

Sophia

Lady Aliana Lupern looked like a child who had been put to bed, tucked in nice and neat under the covers. If not for the twin hollow sockets, Sophia could almost believe she was sleeping. The thick fur blankets covered what surely was another grievous neck wound, and her head, which rested atop a goose down pillow, was all that was visible. An elegant canopy of silver and gold drodang silk—a luxury acquired from bipedal herbivores farmed in the Palosian Swamps to the south—veiled the scene in an air of mystery. It looked like something from one of the horror stories at the amphitheater; the producer having used the artifice of silk to give the hollow sockets a ghostly appearance.

It didn't help that the lady's two hand servants were propped against the wall, the nearby window open to allow the rapidly increasing stench of death escape. Their eyes gouged out and their necks cut in the same double manner as before. The care for their bodies consisting of no more than convenience for the killers, and their rigid, rigor mortis-induced posture made them look like puppets ready to serve their master, even in death. Regardless of the horror of the image, the opulence was truly an affront to the meagre holdings Sophia had just seen in the Lower Bowl.

Yet, even in this house of Augustia's elite, she stared at a victim who had fallen prey to the same fate as one who had nearly nothing. Sophia couldn't help but feel there was a lesson there, but she did not have time to reflect on human nature and its societal moorings. She crossed the room, the sound of groaning wood startling everyone. Their gazes had been glossed over; the scene had enthralled them all. Olivia even shook her head in an almost comical fashion, evidently trying to break free of the trauma.

Sophia approached the bedside, brushing the gossamer aside and feeling the delicate fibers against the backs of her fingers. Kneeling beside Lady Aliana's head, she slowly rolled back the fur blanket, exposing another double cut neck. *One wound to kill and one to sever the vocal cords.* The only difference was in the obvious care the killers had used. Tucking this poor woman back into bed was a sign of respect, especially in comparison to the cast aside corpse lying on the inner wall's dirt path. Still, they had *murdered* her, and in almost all cases, no amount of respect for the dead can forgive that crime.

Sophia placed the back of her hand against the lady's cheek, and although it was cool, there were still traces of the heat of life. The skin of the cheek also remained firm as she pressed against it. Sophia lifted one side of the blanket slightly, enough to let the candlelight in. A vast purple bruising covered the exposed skin, livor mortis in near textbook fashion.

"I would say this lady has been dead for at least eight hours … maybe more. Would you agree, sergeant?" Sophia asked the guardsman who had been so knowledgeable before.

Sergeant Conrad approached the opposite side of the bed and mimicked her actions. After a short while, he nodded to her from over the body of Lady Aliana. "Her arms is also stiff and that don't go away till at least a day. It also don't start till about half a day. So … yes, Keeper, I think I agree."

"And the other two? Same timeframe?" Sophia asked

Sergeant Conrad nodded.

She blew out an exasperated breath "Well, why in *Ember's breath* did four people die in the same manner in the same night?"

Sergeant Conrad shook his head, puffing his cheeks as he expressed his uncertainty.

Seconds passed in silence, the metallic clop of horseshoes on cobbles from the open window marking the slow, deliberate march of time. The monotonous sound seemed to drone on for an uncomfortable length. Yet, as the clip-clop of the hooves began to fade, Sophia heard another board of the hardwood floor creak.

"The man by the Harbor Gate could've been working for this here lady, and, well, the servants … they knew too much. Best to just kill 'em," Olivia said with the meekness of one afraid of being wrong.

"Perhaps, that *would* be the most logical explanation. Coincidence is a factor, but from the similarities and timing of these deaths … I would concur." Sophia looked towards Sergeant Conrad.

He was kneeling by the bedside like herself, gazing up at Lady Aliana's stiffened face. The soldier slowly looked back at Sophia and gave a curt nod in agreement.

She stood, the drodang silk sliding over her head as she backed away from its embrace. It was pleasant and made her shudder as her skin tingled, an odd sensation in such a place. "Good thinking, Olivia."

Olivia beamed as her face blushed with pride and then looked to the floor like one who did not know how to handle compliments.

Then to the whole room, Sophia spoke with more gravity to her voice, "Have we found any evidence? Have your people searched the place?"

Gilda replied for her sergeant, "Uh … we have … um, my lad—Keeper I mean … uh, sorry. But, well, we haven't found much of anything and the lord of this here estate is rather *difficult.*"

"Nothing? Not even a scrap of paper or a drop of blood leading away?"

"Well, I mean, yes. It's obvious they used the columns behind us here to scale up to the second floor and through the windows. This wasn't opened by us." Gilda, who was standing near the opened window patted the sill. The action drew Sophia's eye to the dead servants once again. Even with death so close at hand, the cleanliness of the air—in comparison to the Lower Bowl—was noticeable.

Gilda continued, the stuttering, brought on by her inability to properly address a Keeper, now absent, "There is also one in the study that was opened. Looks like they got in there, did the deed proper, found two servants who were rather *displeased* with the manner of their lady's treatment, and then the group, because surely it had to be, propped up these poor folks for the display we are given here." Gilda waved a hand across the room. "Now, blood drops and scrapes on the paint show that, sure as day, but any other tracks get lost in the grit of the cobbles, either coming or going. Even as white as those stones are; they don't show any trackable signs."

Sophia wished then that Alexa had been the first to this scene. Her Rangemaster sister, a true Warden of the Wilds, would have been able to discern a track, even in such difficult conditions. As it stood now, too much time had passed for even a talented tracker to make any headway. With a sigh, Sophia replied to Gilda's report, "Very well, thank you for your investigations. Let's keep looking though shall we? You said there was a master of the house?"

Gilda replied, the stutter returned, "Yes lady … sorry, Keeper."

"Where might I find him?"

As if on cue, a booming voice could be heard on the lower floor. "The gods will know what to make of this!"

"Well, that would be him," Gilda replied with a smirk.

"Sir, you … uh, don't want to—" the voice of a different guardswoman could be heard trying to waylay him.

The sounds of heavy footsteps rushing up wooden stairs told Sophia how successful that guardswoman was. The booming voice replied, "This is my house, and I will know what that messenger has to say. I have a right thing to say to Ember about this!"

Sophia, knowing to interact with this man, especially a member of the Chosen, in front of his brutalized wife would be difficult. She moved quickly towards the threshold of the room and, as she left, she couldn't help but notice the wealth on display. The luxurious estate had a long bracket-shaped landing fronting four rooms, one of which was the bedroom Sophia had departed. A large wooden staircase with gilded railing lay central to the main foyer. She could see thick red carpet gracing the floor below. Stark, white marble statues on elegantly carved wooden plinths gave a beautiful contrast to the rich red fabric.

Her eyes were pulled to a chandelier with a multitude of candles that dazzled her senses. Sophia wondered how much time it took just to keep those candles lit and replaced. As if to answer her question, in the shadows of the landing she saw a servant on one side of the bracket, a long pole and other items of their craft placed about them. She also noticed a similar panoply of items on the other side. No servant stood on that side. *Perhaps they now lay cold.*

She clicked the heavy oak door in place as the man, a rather portly fellow, mounted the landing of the stairs. She went to firm her Keeper's vest but realizing she was forced to wear the interminable robe of her order, settled on smoothing the thick gray linen in irritation.

Holding the finial of the stair railing, the man, having a wispy red and yellow beard, breathed heavily. He was bent over slightly, displaying a rather sad looking crop of combed-over blonde hair. Sophia heard the strain of his leather trousers as he held the recovery pose, and the tunic and light blue vest he wore looked like they were about to burst at the seams. The normal accommodation for his stomach's girth gone as he tried to compose himself. Sophia felt some small agitation rise within her. Still, she gave him time to catch his breath, and listened to his lungs fill and exhale with heavy gasps. "You must be Master Falris Lupern."

He closed his eyes, exhaled one last breath, and stood. The vest crumpled at the top of his stomach, and he smoothed it with practiced grace, apparently used to that sort of issue. "That would be me, and you …" He paused a moment as he fixed Sophia with a raised eyebrow. There was some small wit in those eyes, albeit not one of concern. The man continued, "You must be the Keeper?"

"Yes sir, that is correct. I am … the messenger." She replied, repeating the word he had chosen to yell throughout the house.

"Good! I have a few things to tell you—"

She interrupted him impetuously by pulling out her Embershard amulet from beneath her linen robe. The red-orange jewel hung about her neck on a silver chain and seemed to pulse as it was exposed to the light. "And *what* did you have to say to Ember?"

Master Falris's head cocked back in shock, displaying the folds of his chin. "Well, I—"

"It's alright Master Falris, *I* am here to answer your questions." She smiled and tucked the amulet away. The impertinence of the man was brushed away by her display, and she knew she would have a much calmer and humbler victim to question. *Or perhaps a suspect,* Sophia thought wryly.

He relaxed at her words. "I'm sorry Keeper. I just … my wife—" He trailed off for a moment. Traces of pain writ in the lines around his eyes. "She was a beauty," he said suddenly, the last word coming out like an exasperated breath.

Sophia could see tears welling in his eyes and decided a small ounce of comfort may help. "She was, and I heard she was the epitome of grace," Sophia said without knowing much of anything about the Lady. A touch of flattery, even if it was a lie, could go a long way in this situation.

"Aye, that she was—" He trailed off again, his eyes glazing over as he was lost in memory.

Sophia noted the man truly did seem at a loss, but figured the love may have grown slightly cold. His manner was grief-filled, but not like the wailing lamentations she had seen on clinic days. Not like the despondent look of those who had lost their *everything*. Of course, he could have some hidden reserve, some stoic nature that forced him to hold his sorrow closer to himself. She waited until his eyes came back into focus and then pressed on, "I'm sorry to ask this right now Master Falris, but what can you tell me about last night?"

He nodded in understanding, "It's alright, Keeper. I know what you must do. I came back to the house in the late evening, maybe seven or eight or so. I had been held up with some dealings at the harbor. Anyways, I got in last night, and since I didn't see Aliana, I assumed she would be in her study." He pointed to another room in front of the stairs.

Might be the room with the other open window, she figured.

"Not wanting to bother her while she worked on the ledgers," Master Falris stopped and smiled to himself. "She was a right wizard with that. Numbers, I mean. Much more than I ever was, and she saved me from myself on many occasions when she found an error in my accounting."

The man seemed lost in thought again, and Sophia gave a brief moment before she pressed the interrogation forward, "Master Falris, are you saying she was involved in your business?"

He furrowed his brows but answered politely, "Yes … I mean, she helped me with all the ledgers and accounts. Things of that sort. On many occasions she helped me seal deals with other traders." A thought struck him, for he stopped and with his pride threatened, puffed his chest slightly, "Of course, it's in the Lupern name that I am a wolf myself! Not just on the battlefield, but at the negotiation table as well!"

Sophia permitted herself a wry smile at the man, not wanting to offend him. However, she could see in his eyes the truth, Lady Aliana seemed to be the brains of their operations, and he … the name. A fool Master Falris is, but so far, an innocent fool. She pressed him with a few simple words, "I am sure you are sir, *but* the lady?"

"Ah, yes, sorry," he shook his head, and a slight flush of embarrassment graced his cheeks. "Anyways, I got home, figured she was in her study, and sat down for some food. It was … seared goose breast, grilled asparagus, and some honey-drizzled laepous legs." He said with relish and looked upwards as if thinking of the meal.

Sophia knew of the delicacy known as laepous legs, and even her mouth watered slightly at the thought of the tender, fat meat that accompanied the furry hindquarters of the small mammal. Still, it agitated her that he distracted himself with the thought of food. She only had to raise her brow to prod him forward.

"Ah, yes, sorry! So, I ate and then I sat by the fire for a while with a glass of wine, fine stuff from Augustia herself. Well, I must have dozed off because I was woken by one of my servants. I quite didn't realize I had fallen asleep! Ol' Trelio lets me sleep in my chair if the fire is nice and warm." Master Falris dipped his head to the side and towards a servant who stood a few steps down and a respectful distance away. "Well, as I woke in the morning, I went up to my quarters to refresh myself, then check on my wife. Before I could even get to my room, I heard a terrible wail. There, in my wife's room, one of her maids was all in a fit, and there … there, lying like a babe, was my wife." His voice became cold and distant, "Her eyes gone, her beautiful green eyes *plucked* away—"

"How did none of your servants come upon the lady earlier? How did no one hear this commotion?" Sophia asked, even though she knew two servants were dead. *Information is sometimes gathered by asking the obvious.*

Master Falris looked rather offended at this question and raised himself with impertinence. "I hope you are not implyi—" He interrupted himself before trying another approach. "I am a member of the Chosen's Wisdom! And, well, you saw for yourself *Keeper* what happened to her hand maids! The other servants would have either been asleep or doing what they are paid for, not checking on the lady randomly. As for me, well, I-I didn't hear a thing!"

As Master Falris's anger swelled, Sophia decided, although he was still a suspect himself, she would not press him as such. "Oh! Good sir, I didn't mean to offend." She held up a hand in placation.

He bit the inside of his lip and some of the red in his cheeks faded. He grabbed the lapels of his vest, gave an audible harumph, and spoke, "If you *must* know! My wife's study has been dampened from outside noise and is connected to her bedroom. From what your colleagues have told me, the killers—those vicious dogs—got in through the window. Wouldn't be hard to scale I suppose. I never knew it was so … vulnerable." Suddenly, he stopped, firmed his brow, and spoke in annoyance, "Now the rest of *how* is up to you, not me!"

Sophia couldn't help but agree with that statement and had to stifle a smirk at the comment. The man was indeed difficult, but under the circumstances, who wouldn't be? She decided that little more could be gained from this line of questioning. "Thank you, Master Falris. I am so sorry about your wife. If you would permit me and my colleagues, I would like to set up in Lady Aliana's study. I find it best when investigating such things to start at the beginning."

Master Falris's chest visibly fell, the threatened posture diminishing. "Yes, that would be alright, Keeper. Trelio! Show the Keeper and her *friends* into the study. Get them what they need."

Chapter Five
Sophia

Sophia leaned back in a leather chair, the black walnut desk in front of her holding command over the study. As she eased into the chair's plush embrace, she couldn't help but take in the thoughtful elegance of the Lady's décor. Directly to her left was a shuttered window, the very same window used by the murderers, now closed to minimize distractions. Sophia fancied herself enjoying a cup of tea or coffee while she glanced out to the city below. *Perhaps the Lady had done the same?*

The rest of the study was inhabited by Sergeant Conrad, Olivia, Dunkeath, and Trelio, all looking like a group of disappointed children. Nothing had come from their search. Even the neutral Trelio; a man who seemed to blend into the dark furniture of the background, seemed rather … dejected.

It was best to avoid eye contact for now, and she chose to scan the room once more. *What had they missed?* The outer walls were lined with bookshelves. Their wooden lines holding a myriad of business accounts for the Lupern family, a neat quill and inkpot on Lady Aliana's desk showed their origin. Behind Sophia was a heavy oak wooden door that led back into the bedroom, discreetly designed like it was mimicking its intent; an escape. At the front of the room was a high table with two clay pitchers, some silver rimmed goblets, a tray of grapes, and some stark white cloths. *A refreshment station?*

Around the room was a hint of golden glitter spread about like dust settling on old furniture. It was quite an odd choice for such an astute woman, the sparkling gold catching the light whenever she looked around. *We all have our vices,* Sophia allowed, as a pang of unbidden jealousy crept its way into her heart.

She looked up at the ceiling to distract herself from the luxury of the room, and, even there, she couldn't escape the opulence. An array of sconces with flickering candles were placed about, their wicks relit by the pole-wielding servant from the landing. With renewed flame, the candles danced almost joyfully, casting shadows onto the dark wooden slats overhead. It was a mimicry of the room's mood, a dour aura brought on by the lack of evidence. Sophia blew out an exasperated breath towards those dancing candles and leaned forward, placing her elbows on the desk. A flash caught her eye, and forced her focus to a small mirror. It was beautifully wrought, a silver frame adorned with emerald studs dotted equidistant around an oval. Not only was the mirror an imported luxury from Xeeland itself, but the artisanal design must have made it more expensive than the houses of the Lower Bowl. Setting aside the extravagance of the accessory, it did its job; reflecting an image.

A lock of her autumnal red hair hung over her eye, contrasting a green-tinged, hazel iris. She blinked and the lock fell away, revealing slightly freckled skin that still held the luster of youth. As far as looks were concerned, she knew she was luckier than most. Although, she did maintain a skincare routine which consisted of applying a mixture of lanolin, orange juice, honey, and ground mint—the last for smell—daily. All to combat the whispers of age that were just now making themselves known. A flash of Keeper Gilbert— a nervous, but quite handsome black-haired man— came to her mind, especially the moment they had stolen in the Bastion's library; it still fluttered across her lips in memory.

She wondered if the younger man noticed the quiet lines on her face, that unstoppable march of time. At twenty-six years of age, they were nigh imperceptible, but maybe …

No, she could hardly see them now, and she was in a well-lit room with the best mirror money could buy. Still, they *were* there, no matter how minute, and all her routines and tricks seemed to do little to slow their stolid tread. Of course, it hadn't been easy since she was taken away from Elgion and demoted. The punishment confirmed with a single line from Grand Keeper Chalepos: "This decision had been made in light of her *misuse* of the gifts of Ember."

The right bastard had smiled that day as he handed down the judgement. Now she suffered, as he, who constantly thought of her as no more than a fool, gave her every job of undesirable standing. The man had not needed to take her as a ward, not when he was a Grand Keeper, but he had felt it was his personal responsibility to 'rectify' her course. Still, as insufferable as it all was, they were right to punish her so. *But why all the condescension?*

Yeah, she had royally screwed up, but she wasn't an idiot. Now, like so many times before, she found solace in the same thought; the Grand Keeper didn't know the Vollimosa sisters, they never backed down from a challenge. The image of Alexa's stalwart stoicism and of Bella's wiry tenacity made her smile wolfishly. A rather ironic gesture as her gaze rested on Dunkeath; the man she had brutalized with 'Ember's gifts', the man whose posture now favored one shoulder, and the man who made her nearly jump out of the leather seat as he barked out, "Trelio! Any of the house's servants missing, well, beyond those two in the other room?"

Trelio, who stood at the high table near the front door, stiffened as he was asked the question. Without moving his head, he replied indignantly, "No, *sir.* All are accounted for."

"Hmmm," Dunkeath said as he took a step further along the length of the bookshelf, picked up a book almost absent-mindedly, flipped it over, investigated the space left behind, and then shoved the book back into place. "So, did the lady have any dealings with the sort of unsavory types that would do something like this?" Dunkeath asked while still searching the bookshelf. *Good questions,* Sophia thought.

"Not that I am aware of, *sir.*" Trelio responded. Apparently, the butler did not like having to deal with such a man from the lower classes.

Ember's breath, the elite were always full of arrogant fools.

Dunkeath stopped what he was doing and shot his glance towards the chief servant, eyebrows raised in dramatic fashion. "That you are aware of? What ya mean? Aren't you head of the servants, the big leader? *Or* is there someone else I should talk to?"

Trelio's lip curled slightly before regaining his practiced poise. The man breathed heavily through his nose, "Sir, Lady Aliana's maids would have been more privy to any dealings she would have had. I am not one of those maids, and, unfortunately for us all, they have shared the same fate as their master."

Dunkeath nodded his head and clicked his cheek. He returned to shuffling through the bookshelf and called out in finality, "Thank you, Trelio. Good man!"

The chief servant showed no more response than a slight dip in his brows. *Yet another dead end,* Sophia thought. She recognized, though the servant was arrogant and brash, he didn't appear to be lying. Frankly, she didn't know what to do. It was clear whoever committed this atrocity didn't want their victims to divulge their secrets to a Keeper. That probably meant they had some evidence, beyond the killer's faces, that could incriminate someone. Likely a bit of political intrigue or perhaps some trader's deal gone wrong. Yet, without evidence, Sophia knew she could only cast a net into a wide dark sea of possibilities. She rapped her fingers against the walnut desk and the rhythmic thudding drew Trelio's eye, a flicker of annoyance held within.

Sophia was about to smirk back at the man when his normally placid face showed genuine astonishment, but not at her. His eyes were cast slightly above her head, and in a feeling of mystery and slight fear, Sophia tilted her gaze upwards.

Floating gently down from the rafters, an eight-centimeter-tall figure with butterfly wings drifted towards her. Like a miniature lamp, it cast a nearly pure white light from a central core. The luminosity was near blinding, making the feminine form of the creature barely discernible. Naked and unabashed, the graceful character mimicked a human woman in design, only without the organs needed for reproduction. The rest was a mimicry of humanity; either a trick of the gods, or some strange evolutionary path that led to its current form. In place of those few features, there was marble smooth skin that glowed with the white luster of its light. Sophia thought it had an uncanny resemblance to the faeries drawn in the more fantastical illustrations of Augustia's art community.

Then, with sudden horrific realization, Sophia recognized the creature, *a nocturne*! She involuntarily retreated, leaning back in the chair as far as she could manage. Though beautiful, these creatures held a malevolent secret; a symbiotic relationship that had doomed many young women to an early grave.

Keeper Kaldin's Agricultural Primer: Keeper's Stones and Living Things had described the Nocturne's method of survival. Find a willing host, convince them they needed eternal beauty, give that to the willing supplicant for a number of years, and then slowly suck the life force away to feed themselves. This relationship would eventually lead to the creation of a new nocturne, or in the case of a particular strong woman, two new nocturnes. The cost? An early demise from a vampiric beauty that preyed on a woman's desire. Nocturnes always left their human partner cold and in the grave. Sometimes before forty years of age yet with the tragic appearance of a twenty-year-old taken from this world too early.

Everyone else, though Sophia did not look at them, stood stark still, the absence of idle movement either by rustle or shuffle told her they were just as entranced. Slowly, the Nocturne floated down, just past the desk's edge and at eye level with Sophia, hanging in the air in front of her. A sudden movement from her left; Dunkeath moved with a book in hand, ready to swat the little creature.

"Stop!" Sergeant Conrad bellowed. Dunkeath froze in place.

"I've seen't this before in other houses of wealthy ladies. Always appearing when I am called to bring the bodies out. One sorry soul tried to do what you're doing, and well … they and a bunch of others went blind. I would've too if it weren't for the distractions of a pretty maid." Sergeant Conrad took a moment to smile in memory of whoever that maid must have been. "What I and probably the Keeper here would say, is that *thing* could make our lives miserable if'n you did that." Throughout the sergeant's hasty debrief on the nocturne's penchant for blinding, the faerie-like creature bobbed back and forth with tiny wings keeping it aloft.

Dunkeath looked to Sophia for confirmation. She nodded, and he backed away, bringing the book away from its readied position. She had no idea how to handle such a creature, but she knew swatting it was not the way. Suddenly, the Nocturne did a little circle in the air and waved with its delicate arm at her. With a shocking speed, it dashed in front of the emerald-studded mirror; surprisingly, no new reflections appeared. Sophia felt the whispers of the gods, ones unknown to her, pervading the air. She clutched at her Embershard amulet before a reflected image of herself faded into a *younger*, happier version.

Sophia stood, upsetting the leather chair which fell backwards, its leather muffling the sound of its fall. Her heart thudded in place, and she felt sweat break out on her brow.

The Nocturne flew upwards, allowing the mirage wrought on the mirror to fade and then levelled itself with Sophia's face. Sophia clutched her amulet tighter, internally reciting the litany of Ember's might, *Never again will we allow your strength to falter. Never again will we allow the dark to overtake your light.*

The Nocturne, probably sensing the rising influence of Ember, shook her head and waved both hands as if she meant no harm. With another whimsical circle in the air, the tiny figure darted towards a corner of the room. A nondescript step stool sat veiled in shadow. Sergeant Conrad, the closest of them all, grabbed the stool. The Nocturne flew to the center of the bookshelf Dunkeath stood near, and he retreated from her approach—book held upright as if it were a shield. The faerie-like creature did another circle then flew towards the wooden slats of the study's ceiling.

Sergeant Conrad looked at Sophia hesitantly. She could only shrug in response. The man chewed his lip, looked up at the Nocturne, whose radiant light cast wide shadows on the ceiling, and back down to the stool. Apparently deciding his curiosity was worth following, he placed the stool in front of the indicated bookshelf. Sophia watched as he clambered up the stool, found a conveniently placed grip, and brought himself to eye level with the Nocturne.

The Nocturne's dance intensified, and Sophia's eyes started to hurt as the creature's light flared. Sergeant Conrad, squinting with his own eyes, pushed the small slat upwards. Surprisingly, no dust floated away at the disturbance. The Nocturne raced into the black void and pushed a small leather tube within Sophia's view. Sergeant Conrad grabbed the tube and clambered down to the floor. Delicately, the sergeant opened the stopper from one end of the tube and pulled out a rolled piece of vellum alongside a linen sheet filled with writing. With the linen sheet unrolled, he squinted and mouthed words to himself. With a look of confusion, he handed the document to Sophia, stating; "It's just nonsense. Is this … Xetemian?"

Sophia grabbed the proffered linen, feeling its coarse edges on her skin.

Hj tld jlzf kind zjiintj. Bnzj dqwi agkxfwd nbs mfwbt xflle dl Mflpjb Idnkkwlb. Twcj dl wbbpjjxjf nbs inv wd'I elf Mkllsjvj. We bjjs mj, alzj dl gi. Hj hwkk xfldjad.

It truly was nonsense and definitely not a language she knew, but as she unrolled the vellum alongside the paper, her heart skipped with excitement.

"No sergeant, this is not Xetemian. Fortunately for us, dear Lady Aliana was quite a novice at spycraft it seems. For in this vellum, is a cipher!"

Sophia held the treated animal skin up for all to see, and they nodded even though no one could see what was written on the precious material.

Olivia called out with rising excitement, "You mean like a secret code?!"

"Exactly like a secret code!" Sophia replied with a smile.

Dunkeath scoffed and shook his head, "Ya wealthy types are awful weird."

"Oh, and you would want all yer business known when ya got a pair of peeping eyes 'round every corner?" Olivia replied sternly.

Dunkeath bit his lip, mulling over the question. Evidently, he conceded the point because he raised his eyebrows and nodded as if to show he understood her meaning.

Sophia unrolled the two documents, holding them down with lead weights already placed for such a thing on the desk. She peered at the vellum.

$$c^1 \; n^2 \; v^3 \; t^4 \; f^5 \; r^6 \; u^7 \; w^8 \; s^9 \; e^{10} \; l^{11} \; o^{12} \; b^{13} \; a^{14} \; q^{15} \; k^{16} \; h^{17} \; x^{18} \; d^{19} \; g^{20} \; z^{21}$$
$$y^{22} \; i^{23} \; p^{24} \; j^{25} \; m^{26}$$

With a distracted tone she called out into the room, "I will need some time to decipher what is written here. Surely, something the victim had done already. She probably burned it, which is smart. Hopefully, this will get us somewhere! Give me a few minutes. It's not a complex cipher, but it is enough to deter peering eyes and nosy servants."

It was quick to understand how to use the cipher. Each letter within the original message simply translated to another based on its numeric order within the alphabet. Once again, it wasn't complex, and Sophia assumed Lady Aliana was not a trained agent. Instead, she was a contact the writers had developed and were trying to glean information from. Simple ciphers like this were easy to use and did much to dissuade all but the most curious. Unfortunately, she grimaced, it may not have been enough this time.

For several minutes, she scratched out the true message on a piece of linen paper retrieved from one of the desk's drawers. As she finished her work, she felt a rush of adrenaline. She would *have* to tell Bella and Alexa about this! *Sophia the codebreaker.* With a smile to herself, she held her deciphered message and read.

> *We got your last message. Name this culprit and bring proof to Broken Stallion. Give to innkeeper and say it's for Bloodeye. If need be, come to us. We will protect.*

Sophia's mind raced at possibilities. The victim near the Harbor Gate was definitely linked to Lady Aliana, and the intrigue behind this case increased in intensity.

The Nocturne flew down to Sophia once more. The small faerie waved and smiled at her with a shocking charm. Sophia suddenly felt a pang of sorrow at her lost youth, and the Nocturne tilted its head slightly, like a dog curious what its master had to say. They, both human and Nocturne, held each other's gaze for a moment. Suddenly, the faerie-like creature shook its head sorrowfully, waved at Sophia, and zoomed up and into the now open ceiling. There was a sudden flash of light from the shadowed attic, and then it disappeared completely.

"And thus, she disappears, back to whatever realm she resides in. Perhaps, that will be the last we see of her," Sophia said, unable to keep the awe from her voice.

As the group slowly collected themselves, Sophia wondered what the missive meant. She pondered the questions it brought forth, but could not answer them with confidence. However, she did know one thing. They needed to go to The Broken Stallion, an inn along The August Highway.

"Dunkeath, Olivia, we need to pack our things. We have somewhere to visit! But first, I must write a letter to my sisters."

Chapter Six

Alexa

Alexa looked upon the okenavis, an ocean-going vessel, its carvel-built strakes exposed as it lay tilted in the sand. The two beams of its fore and main mast pierced the sky and although they were unadorned with sails, they were crisscrossed with a myriad of hemp ropes. From her vantage point within a stand of hawthorn trees, Alexa saw two—maybe three—figures moving atop the deck, while fifty or so men and women gathered on the beach below. The deck-bound figures had their balance askew as they dealt with the tilt of their ship; a product of the design changes that were slowly increasing the okenavis' ability to withstand the sea crossing. The normal flat-bottomed keel giving way to a narrower design with each new iteration. Alexa had even heard of a new Xeelander ship that had no flat bottom at all; instead, it flaunted an arch design that supposedly gave the vessel better handling in the rough seas.

Although the ship before her still had the remnants of a flat, cog-style bottom, it was obviously Xeelander in origin. Alexa could see it in the gaudiness of its design, railings that had unnecessary curves and decorations, stained glass windows dotting the rear cabin, and a large wooden carving of Melleas, the god of the sea on the figurehead. Yet, the majority of the individuals below appeared Argolonian in their manner. Frustratingly, there were no flags or symbols indicating which city-state they hailed from, but whoever they were, they had risked crossing the Sea of Melleas. That large angry body of water between this new world and the old, and she had no idea why.

The unflagged ship had been spotted by fishermen in the Bay of Elgion as it made its way north. The alarm had sent Alexa, Bella, Elira, Matthias, and Hislock—their sentient reptilian friend—north from Elgion to investigate. That lizard man's fiery temperament and staunch loyalty to his tribe had helped save them all, and had delivered them from a grisly fate at the hands of a brutal orcish warchief. It was nearly three years now, but Alexa still remembered those days like they were yesterday. A brutal wound from an iktomid, a haunting discovery of orcish influence from the north, a scouting foray that led to the death of her old Rangemaster, and finally a climactic battle for the fate of Elgion.

It had been the first test of her command as Rangemaster, and through her leadership she knew they had prevailed, but not without help. If it weren't for Sophia overcoming her struggles with the godstones, they would never have made it. Even then, if it weren't the timely intervention of Hislock and Bella with the saurian raptor riders, they would all have fallen to the orc's onslaught. Now—three years later—the saurians continued to render the people of Elgion aid, and Alexa couldn't be happier for it, especially since Hislock, the twitchy Gecko-like male, was the ambassador of that aid. They could say 'male' now, before it had been a mystery, but through Bella's close association with the saurian tribes, they had learned a little of saurian culture. Like how to determine gender or courtesy, and at the cost of Alexa's tortured muscles, how to traverse the Forest of Mossgrave at blinding speed.

Even Bella, now an ambassador to the saurians, struggled to maintain Hislock's grueling pace through the trees. Her raptor mount only lending her so much aid against the skill set of another, intelligent species. Yet, Bella was tough, and that struggle was only perceivable by the tiniest of changes in her voice; a deeper vibrato that grew with her exhaustion. This newest trill made Bella's current whisper seem foreign, distant, "Now what do we have here?"

"I don't know" Alexa replied. "They look like Argolonians by the way they carry themselves, and from the shields strapped to the railing. *But* that's a Xeelander ship if I ever saw one."

She could see Bella nod slightly; her scrappy sister having chosen to stay with her as they scouted ahead. Their quarry had been discovered by the enhanced senses of their raptor mounts—a scent on the wind—and Alexa had ordered the others to hang back a couple of kilometers. She would hate for a horse's whinny or the screeching hiss common to the raptors to give them away.

"I see three above and fifty below. You?" Bella asked.

Alexa only nodded. Her silence partly to prevent exposure and partly because this ship's landing worried her tremendously. They all knew that the other city-states would come in force as the secrets of travelling to the new world became known, but this … this was a warship from the looks of it. *Why did it land so far north?* She could only think of one answer. That the captain of this ship wanted to stay hidden. So, they had sailed well north of Elgion, landing on the first safe beach that put the hills and forests of Eukaria, the formal name of Mossgrave, between them and the Augustian settlement. *But why?*

As if in answer to her internal questions, one man, who appeared the leader of the group shouted. If they were Argolonians, *that* would be their strategos. The words were indiscernible from this distance, but it was clear that he was braying out commands. He swirled his arm in a circle above his head, and the group on the sand formed up into smart ranks. Three lines of sixteen soldiers coalesced into a formidable force, impressing Alexa with their speed and discipline. The leader, glittering in bronze, paced back and forth in front of the group. She could see the hallmark armament of an Argolonian strategos. A large round shield—its rim cast in bronze—was flanked by twin javelins, either of which could be slung from over the shoulder with speed. Strapped to his left hip was a short scabbard, a finely decorated hilt reflecting the sunlight. On the opposing hip, a long-handled mace hung loosely on his belt. The panoply of war displayed upon that man made her stomach tense.

"Ember's breath, the goofy bastards still use bronze," Bella whispered.

Alexa replied, "They got iron underneath. As rigid and traditional as they are, they aren't stupid."

"Still." Bella said, her voice bitter with scorn.

Alexa wondered if it was all just a foolish tradition, or if some sort of utility was gained from the stubborn use of bronze when iron had been shown to be better in so many ways. Maybe, maybe not, after all it had only been about one hundred years since humanity was able to make a fire hot enough to melt and work iron. True, one could have always used Ember, but that god was temperamental, and no smith could do what was needed with the short erratic bursts of flame that Keepers could wield. The recent advent of ironworking had made the voyages across Melleas's sea possible. For the tools and implements to build such sturdy ships required the strength of iron, vessels that were quickly outperforming the triremes and biremes of old. Now, with the secrets of iron unlocked, humanity spread across the world. Tools of their own design opening doors to realms unknown. With an inward sigh she pushed her self-reflective thoughts away, because regardless of the strategos's choice of metal, he was still a sight to behold—a terrifying sight.

The strategos stopped and took an iron helm he had couched within his arm and slid it over his head. Jet black raven feathers crested the head piece and swayed slightly in the breeze. *The one place they had not compromised for tradition*, Alexa recognized. With crisp motion, the strategos turned about and began marching inland, his company following behind.

"They don't all have the same regalia," Bella said with the inflection she affected whenever she recognized something of value.

"True, mercenaries?" Alexa asked.

"That would be my bet, especially since, as block headed as the Argolonians are, they wouldn't just land a ship here. It would be a diplomatic disaster." Bella responded, in an uncanny mimicry of her own thoughts.

Alexa and Bella watched as the company disappeared into the short, hawthorn-covered hills that ringed the small beach. The glint of iron or bronze ceasing altogether as the last of them vanished behind the hill's rise. They marched east into the vast plains north of the Eukarian Forest. That vast sea of grass where Bella had discovered an orc encampment three years ago. An unbidden thought of the eyeless orcish god-talker, that bloody thrall of Magdris who had brought the malevolent magic of the Crimson King upon them, entered her mind's eye. Only thanks to Sophia had they survived that encounter, and now, in a sort of morbid memoriam of those brutes, did Sophia name the plain that lay before them, Magdris's Calling.

"We need to get back to the others." Alexa said, her eyes on the three figures who stood guard atop the beached ship. They probably could overwhelm the guards, but until she knew what these folks were up to, she would not risk open war.

Bella nodded in response.

They crept slowly out of the hawthorn they had been in; its southern vantage point lay just below the hill's crest. Before long, Bella and Alexa were able to jog at speed without risk of discovery. After about a kilometer and a half, and with only a slight tinge of exertion upon her breath, Alexa reached the companions she had left behind. Alexa's horse Scout, a spirited beast lent to her by Blythe, whinnied at the sight of her.

Elira raised her eyebrow at Alexa. "Well, Rangemaster, what's the verdict?"

Alexa took one long breath and replied, "Elira, Matthias, I am going to need you two to shadow a company of forty-nine. They appear Argolonian but they have no marks stating they are such, beyond their manner and gear. I will take Bella and Hislock back to Elgion and prepare a force that can match their strength. Report to me when you have something of value."

Elira clicked her cheek while nodding. "Yes, Rangemaster. Do you know what they are after?"

Alexa shook her head. "No, but they headed off east over Magdris's Calling. They should be easy to track, they didn't bother trying to be discreet. Careful though, the boat is guarded."

"By how many?" Matthias asked, causing Elira to grin maliciously.

Alexa sighed, a humorous, knowing sigh. "Don't start any wars, ok? Just follow them."

"Yes, Rangemaster." Elira replied, the grin still showing her stark white teeth.

With the orders given, the two groups split apart, one headed east to track the mysterious company over the plains and the other headed south back to Elgion.

Chapter Seven

Alexa

It was mid spring and Alexa's office felt—as it always had in that verdant season—rather cramped. Outside lay the bounty of Telaea's gifts, but instead of being amongst those natural wonders, she was confined to the stuffy room. True, it was a nice office, which held a sturdy pine desk and chair, a shelf full of books and missives important to her order and herself, and two more pine chairs that sat opposite her own. It was the office of the Rangemaster, a true honor that had been granted to her in dire circumstances. An honor that had been confirmed three years ago by the Chosen's Wisdom; the formal name of the elected branch of Augustia's government. "Now, if they could only honor me with a more comfortable chair," she murmured to herself.

She shifted and contorted, trying to find at least one spot that didn't feel like sitting on a tree trunk, but her efforts proved fruitless. Finally, she surrendered and bent to read the letter from Sophia that had arrived yesterday. Carried by one of the many okenavis that dared the ocean for trade, it had waited upon her desk until her return, its seal unbroken.

Alexa and Bella,

I hope you all are well. Know that I am. My duties here as Keeper progress, and I am never without things to do. In some ways, it's a blessing to be so busy, but it leaves little time for me to explore my scholarly interests. Did you know that the Xetem Empire was once ruled by a Caprix? The scandal was what broke them apart, and some say that Augustia herself was built on the bones of a Xetem settlement—

Alexa's reading was interrupted by a mix of joy and sadness. On one hand, she chuckled inwardly seeing her sister's lust for knowledge in written form, while on the other, she missed her terribly. She firmed her lips and continued to read the letter which had just outlined how a Caprix, the sentient goatmen of the Central Spine, had somehow managed to rule the ancient Xetem Empire.

> *I have some correspondence with a Keeper in Xeeland, note the similarity in name, that might get me some documents on the matter! Those stuffy aristocrats that squat over the Palosian swamps and remains of the Xetem Empire simply sneer and hoard their ancient knowledge. But I digress.*
>
> *I may have stumbled onto something troubling. A bit of intrigue between power players that may spill out into something greater. How I wish you all were here to help me! Maybe soon. Maybe the Grand Keeper and the Seniors will reinstate me soon. Still, I have no way of knowing the scope of this 'trouble', but I have a bad feeling about it. I will write more as I know more, but, for now, you two keep your eyes open for any suspicious activity over there. There might be a game afoot.*
>
> *With Love,*
>
> *Sophia Vollimosa*
>
> *Keeper of the Stones*
>
> *Augustia's Bastion*

She placed the letter down, the wash of natural light from the open window to her left now served to shadow the words that lie within the curved parchment. With a sigh she leaned back, prompting yet another groan from her damned chair, and reflected on the letter's contents.

"What game do you think, sister?" She asked aloud as she considered the world around her, hoping to parse out some clue to the ominous warning.

Elira and Matthias had been gone for nearly two weeks while her other charges were either training or out on the range. The rangers of Elgion were constantly trying to preserve *The Balance*, her order's most sacred charge, for the surrounding lands and for the people of her community. She looked out the window and a light drizzle blanketed the streets. It was near midday and the streets were filled with citizens looking for wares and food at the lunchtime market. The cobbles laid upon Main and Hook Street made the roads, even in wet conditions, much more manageable. She recognized it was one of the better decisions the ruling council of Elgion—which included herself—had made, although at an enormous cost. Costs that more than paid for themselves. Even now, Alexa could see two carts with logs from Mossgrave easily make their way south down Main Street.

The clang of the blacksmith's hammer—that jolly old fellow—rang out across the street, pounding in time to the rhythm of the people. Even from here, Alexa could see colorful hats jumping near the forge's heat. The little gnomes that had allied themselves with Elgion had taken a particular liking to the smith, and one could never visit the man without seeing the myriad colors of the gnomes' characteristic hats. It was no secret their defense, and possibly their magic, had helped bolster Elgion's food stores to a level that hunger was rarely an issue. Such food security had helped Elgion grow quickly from both immigration and natural growth.

Yes, Elgion had expanded nicely, filling the space between the palisade with homes and businesses; the old stables that once lay at the north edge of town were now surrounded by the squat wooden homes of pioneers. She looked upon one such home, its backfield of cabbage coming in nicely, and the comfortable rain-cast view made her mind wander.

An image flashed across her mind's eye, that strapping young Warrior of August who had arrived in Elgion one year after the orcish raid. Amilicus was his name, and his shortly cropped black hair had capped off a tall muscular frame that looked ready to spring into action at the drop of a pin. She still remembered the smile he had dared to show to her, accentuating brown eyes that seemed to sparkle when they had been introduced. The man had risked chastisement for such a scandalous grin towards a superior, but Alexa couldn't deny that it was rather charming. Now, two years since that day, they had become friends … and more.

A surge of anger rose in her as she remembered how long it took for Amilicus to even approach her. *Ember's breath*! The man had spent a whole year in awkward flirtation. Until finally he had asked to accompany her on a walk to the port. There he had let his feelings known. Even then he had only offered a promise of future encounters. No, it wasn't until six months ago when Alexa spotted the man walking home at night from guard duty that they were able to finally act on their feelings. From that moment, it had been the sort of whirlwind romance you only ever heard about. Love—or lust—in all its glory. In some ways, it reminded her of the plays put on by the troubadours of the Augustian amphitheater.

Every chance they got they managed to sneak in quiet moments together, and truly it had been an exciting time for her. The young man had shown her something she had not known she needed, a partner, and save for a brief stint of romance back in Augustia, she trod on unfamiliar ground. As uncertain as that prospect was, she couldn't be happier. Her daydreams brought contented sighs, and the thought of his dashing smile, alongside the drizzling rain, stirred a pleasant passion within her.

That was until an all-intrusive call came crashing in, *I gotta piss!* Her fanciful daydreams were interrupted, as she set about solving her body's complaints, and although she could simply use the buckets dotted throughout the Ranger's Hall, she knew a walk, however short, would help jog her mental muscles. She *was* meant to be pondering Sophia's warning and not her love affair with Amilicus after all!

She slid a small dagger into her boot, and with no mirror in sight she rubbed her face, hoping no streak of grime or dirt would remain. With practiced speed, she undid her ponytail allowing her shoulder length brown hair to flare out. She then set about rebinding it, aiming to attain the tighter, sleeker look she enjoyed. "Must keep up appearances," she sighed.

Satisfied she would at least look halfway decent, she made her way down the stairs, out of the Hall, and onto Main Street, heading north. She passed the small corral that fronted the Ranger's Hall. There, Scout, the horse she had used for their expedition north was being brushed by Blythe. With Bella's guidance as Stablemaster, Blythe had maintained high quality mounts for the rangers, going so far as to lending his favored horse to them on many occasions. The big man turned from his task and beamed at her. She waved at him, and he nodded in return. That gentle giant remained a stalwart companion to her and Bella, never faltering, even during the battle for Elgion so long ago.

Just north of the Ranger's Hall, a small alley cut between a leather worker's shop and the hall itself. She darted west up the alley, knowing one of the fouler buildings of Elgion lay down the way; a latrine pit. One of many such constructions dotted strategically around the community. This one was optimally placed, because the tanners, who desired the ammonia from urine, fronted the establishment. Thankful the field immediately behind the Ranger's Hall had been turned into a cow pasture and not the latrine pit, she passed north behind the tanner's hut, the smell of urine and feces becoming overwhelming.

With the comforting touch of the dagger in her boot, she mounted the artificial rise and entered one of the simple thatch huts. Within the privacy of the latrine, she conducted her business, and although the smell was intense, she considered the contents of Sophia's letter. Already, there had been 'suspicious activity' as Sophia had warned them, but that could be coincidental. Although when dealing with Sophia, coincidence rarely played a part. No, this okenavis, potentially filled with mercenaries from Argolon or Xeeland, could be bringing about trouble. Ember's breath, these cutthroats could have been hired by Kyros or Lucidicus, both city-states determined to compete against Augustian might. It was impossible to know how they were linked to the greater world, and a multitude of possibilities swirled through her head.

A sudden gallop of hooves on cobbles jarred her thoughts, and a jolt of worry bounced through her. The clatter of their tread was that of urgency, and, for an instant, she wondered if they carried some dire fate for Elira and Matthias in their haste. Wrapping up her business at the latrine, she rushed back down the alley to the wider Main Street.

She saw both Elira and Matthias, their mounts frothed in white sweat. *Thank the gods,* she prayed internally. Blythe was already there to greet the two, his concern for the over-worked horses forcing him to abandon his normal, gentle tone, "Ya could've killed 'em! Oh, Incatus, Roland … my poor boys. What have they done to you?" The big man beckoned swiftly for Elira and Matthias to dismount, taking the reins to slowly walk the horses, cooling them down after such a flight. Alexa winced slightly at the chastisement, and wondered if Epidus, the god of beasts, would forgive them.

Alexa looked upon Elira, who looked nearly as ragged as her mount, and spoke formally, "Report."

Elira nodded. "Yes, Rangemaster. Those *fiends* will soon be heading back to their ship. Their job done." Elira paused and looked around at the gathering crowds of people. "I think it best if we talk about this somewhere more privately."

Alexa nodded solemnly, wondering what dire tidings her ranger had brought. In the crowd, she spotted Guard-Captain Alexander Vitrusian, his height making him obvious. She cocked her head back towards the Ranger's Hall, and he understood what she meant, pushing his way through. The man's insight was always a boon. After they had barred the doors to curious onlookers, Alexa brought them to the mess hall, centrally located in the building, and they sat or lounged on the assortment of chairs and tables used by her rangers for communal meals. The space looked rather sad without its full complement of occupants.

However, she had no time to worry about her other charges and pressed Elira to her full report. "So, ranger, what have you learned?"

"Those bastards slaughtered innocents!" Matthias cried out suddenly. His face red with indignation. Elira glanced at her range-mate, but Alexa did not see chastisement. Instead, she saw a mixture of sadness—an uncommon emotion for Elira—and anger swirl upon that slender face. Elira looked back at Alexa and nodded in confirmation. Matthias, cowed by the loss of his own discipline, simply hung his head. Alexa prompted Elira to continue.

The ranger blew out a heavy breath, as if she was going to unburden herself of tremendous trauma. "We tracked them for five days across the plains until they came upon an encampment of what we think were Xeelanders. They waited until nightfall, and, in a sudden rush, ambushed the hapless fools. They didn't stand a chance, an-and …" Elira's voice faltered. Her eyes instantly glazed over with whatever horror she had witnessed. Slowly, almost monotonously, Elira continued, "And we are pretty sure their leader used Bloodstone. We could taste it in the air, just like the day those orcs attacked, but this time it felt more directed; more personal." Her voice waned in time with eyes that were squeezed shut. Elira shook her head and mouthed something to herself. "It was that foul taste of metal. Ya know the one? Well, the bastards butchered anyone unlucky enough to face them. Taking their lives one by one no matter their age or cries for mercy. They-the—"

Guard-Captain Alexander Vitrusian moved to the traumatized ranger and placed a calming hand on her shoulder, any sign of his old injury, a broken arm earned in the Battle for Elgion, absent. "It's alright, Elira, you are amongst friends. Tell it all, and your heart will feel less burden for it. Trust me." For a moment the two looked into one another's eyes and Alexa could see some resolve return to Elira's countenance.

The ranger continued, "They strung the dead up onto poles. They cut them in a sort of ritualistic looking ladder pattern and then wiped the blood about themselves. They might as well have been worshipping ol' Magdris just like the orcs … No one survived."

"Berserkers?" The Guard-Captain asked. When no one seemed to recognize what he meant, he clarified, "I have heard of this. Once before in a book I lent to your sister." He nodded at Alexa, and she knew he meant Sophia. "Whenever a human ingests, interacts, or even just tastes Blood-stone on the air long enough, they go berserk. The blood rage overwhelms them, and normally they just … die, either from their suicidal actions or from the body's rebellion. But it seems our elusive visitors have found a way to harness Magdris's power. Or at least we can assume that, what with the similarities in blood obsession and stringing up victims. After all, the orcs had a whole totem dedicated to the practice." The Guard-Captain shook his head in disbelief. "We *must* put a stop to this. I don't know how, but we can't let a danger like that go unchecked." Alexander Vitrusian looked up at Alexa holding her in his intense gaze.

Alexa returned the look and knew he was right. "Are their numbers diminished at all?"

"They lost one man to a brave Xeelander but otherwise, no."

"Do you think they are back at their ship yet?" Alexa interrogated further.

"No, we rode hard. Nearly killed our mounts, but we rode day and night for three days. Last we knew of these … bastards, was that they were gathering up some stone. A rose gold crystal, looked like a godstone lode—

possibly Minollo's. It was a damn big one too. Probably what the Xeelanders were there for. Still, with the worship of Magdris and the work they looked to be doing, I would say they probably were going to stay for a while. We have time to head them off, if we are quick."

Alexander interjected, "We should take one of the triremes. It would be faster. If the wind is on our side, we could be there in less than two days' time."

Alexa bowed her head in thought, considering his request. "I'm sorry Guard-Captain but we cannot. We need surprise on our side, and the beach we are heading to commands a wide view of the sea. If they fled inland with or without their full force, we may never find them. I must ask that we go overland and attempt an ambush." Alexa tensed. He did, after all, hold authority in this matter.

The Guard-Captain chewed his lip. "Very well, Rangemaster, but we better be quick."

Some small relief flooded her, even three years into being Rangemaster she still wished to avoid the ire of the man, he could be *intense*. Without further delay, she outlined her plan firmly and with measured haste. "I have eight rangers in training here. I can muster them by tonight and we can leave as a group. Guard-Captain can you muster a company of your own? This force is about fifty strong, and they seem well trained."

Alexander clicked his tongue and stared off into space, obviously calculating the numbers for a requisite force. "Yes … yes it could be done. I can pull some guards from the port to shore up the missing force here in Elgion. I could muster—" He mouthed numbers to himself. "Sixty, fit to fight."

A sudden flash of worry coursed through her, and she wondered if the Guard-Captain would include Amilicus in that group of sixty. After all, he was *fit* enough. She grunted to hide her discomfort at the thought. "Very good. Elira, Matthias. I know I ask a lot of you, but you are rangers, and damn good ones. I need you to take Weston and Parius with you and stalk this company. You should find those two out back. Me and the Guard-Captain will head straight to their landing site with the sixty guards and the other six rangers that are still here. If they stray from their course, or sense our coming, send someone to warn us. You will be our eyes."

Elira stood to attention briefly, an uncommon action for her, and replied, "Yes, Rangemaster!"

Alexa knew that Elira and Matthias had ridden hard and fast; she knew they would be exhausted, but there were few so reliable—so capable. After all, Elira had been a stalwart second in command ever since the death of the previous Rangemaster, Erin Apararius, and time and time again Alexa found herself relying on the near-malicious zealotry of her old friend. A reliance she needed to count on once more. Elira must have sensed Alexa's thoughts, for she suddenly flashed her characteristic grin. Stark white teeth showing that familiar tenacious spark.

Alexa finished her orders, "We will make them suffer for what they did. We won't let them leave without answering for their crimes. Go now and see it done. We will be shortly behind."

Elira, dazzling grin in tow, nodded once again to Alexa and then to Matthias and just as they set off to do her will, Alexa spoke spontaneously. The thoughts of the mutilated Xeelanders swelling her with a sudden anger, "And Elira, don't let them leave without us."

Chapter Eight

Alexa

Sixty guardsmen and women, one Guard-Captain, seven rangers, including herself, Bella, and Hislock set out north. Their goal? The landing site of the mystery ship and its unknown crew. A force that had committed an atrocity at their very doorstep, and the brave men and women of Elgion set out to right that wrong. All of them ready for war; all of them ready for a fight. Even Godfrey, who was shy his left arm, had begged to come with his trusty ax, "I ain't gonna let no missing arm keep me from a good scrap."

But the Guard-Captain had refused, instead sending him, and the twin saurian guards that normally accompanied Hislock, to the saurian village in case trouble came their way.

It was the sort of pioneer attitude that Alexa had come to expect from those she dealt with in Elgion, and Godfrey was as stalwart as any pioneer. Thankfully, Godfrey and Bella's ambassadorial duties to the saurian peoples were paying off, and the expeditionary force was blessed with Hislock as their guide.

That sentient reptile held large black eyes full of hidden wisdom, ones that would widen whenever they divulged the secrets of his people. A wordless gesture to help with tracking, a calming hand on errant livestock, or a delicious mixture of herbs, roots, and mushrooms—all gathered from the forest floor. These were just a few of the tricks he held within. She wondered how many more secrets his people reserved for themselves. Maybe she could ask Bella, after all, her, Godfrey, and Hislock had spent the last couple years travelling to and from the various outposts and farmsteads of their peoples, human and saurian alike. To the point that a steadfast alliance was taking root, even Orator Malfias had drafted a preliminary document outlining a partnership between Augustia and the saurians. Alas, those were all things for another day, she thought.

For now, she was content with the hidden trails and paths Hislock led them through. In just four days, they found themselves descending the foothills of Eukaria's Range, a blazing speed only matched by their earlier journey to this same spot. Though, this sojourn was made all the more impressive by the increased company size. Surprisingly, the momentum was not at the cost of safety, and their company made it through the far north unscathed. Even amidst the possibility of the arachnid horrors known as iktomids. That fearful thought made her shoulder ache in memory, but fortunately, with Hislock around, they never seemed to encounter the spider-like fiends. Of course, the size of their company would deter any iktomid attack, but it was still nice to avoid their horrific visage altogether. Sure, they did stumble upon the occasional track or trail of the creatures, but it was only ever in passing.

Now the group found themselves within a few kilometers from the beach. Hopefully, it had been fast enough. No message or sign of Elira's group had been discovered, and she could only assume that all still went to plan. Yet, inside of her, a worm of doubt wriggled within.

An urge pulled at her and, for what was likely the tenth time that day, she found herself risking a glance behind. Amilicus walked on resolutely, the mail of his iron coat so polished that flashes of sunlight flickered back at her. He had indeed been one of the guardsmen chosen by Alexander, and Alexa could see why. He looked the very image of a soldier. His tunic with its sunburst tendrils gleamed, and the iron that bound his shield sparkled with each step, light pulsing in time with the hefty blade of his ax. The malicious looking weapon brought thoughts of battle to her mind, and a sudden image of his face broken and bloody, troubled her thoughts. She

prayed to the Maiden and to Ember that they would see this through together. Sensing her gaze, Amilicus, like every time she had glanced back at
him thus far, winked and smiled at her.

The gesture ripped a wry smile from her in return and, feeling somewhat abashed and somewhat happier for it, she turned forward once more.
Scout's saddle creaked as her weight shifted, but the discipline of Blythe's
favored mount did not waver, and he trotted on unphased as they led from
the front of the column. The two commanders—Rangemaster and Guard-
Captain—had decided to split their oversight, and it had been an easy
choice for who should be at the head. Rangers were primarily scouts after
all, and a Rangemaster was essentially the master of scouts, especially in a
war time environment.

So, she plodded along; her emotions battling against mounting nerves
as they marched in a single file line down the hill. They passed hardy moun-
tain scrub, and the stragglers of Mossgrave's forest, which consisted of no
more than a few lone pines scattered across the hillside. There were tall
stalks of once dormant grass waking up from spring's warmth, and dazzling wildflowers—purple, yellow, and pink in their splendor. To her left
was a wide view of the Sea of Melleas, small whitecaps dotted the dark blue
waters until they disappeared into a distant horizon. It felt as if she was
going to fall off the edge of the world staring into that distant curving line,
and she found her breath stolen just as much by the wind as the sights
before her. Every little glance filled her with awe. It didn't help that somewhere over that turbulent ocean lie Augustia, and markets filled with curiosities and treasures, gleaming halls and pillared bastions, civilization in all
its splendor; not to mention her mom, dad, and … Sophia. She clicked her
cheek in somber memory.

The wind whipped a flurry of scent, a combination of sea salt and
wildflower. Coupled with Amilicus's smile, she felt her anxieties quell ever
so slightly.

"Must you be so obvious," Bella whispered to her.

Alexa blinked in surprise. "What?"

Her sister was mounted, but on the scaly skin of a raptor. The height of the mounts discordant so Bella had to look up at Alexa. Even with the disadvantage, Bella still managed to make her raised brows look terribly dramatic. "Come now, you know what I mean."

Alexa felt her heart thump. Apparently, her attentions on Amilicus were more obvious than she would have hoped.

Bella must have sensed her concerns. "Oh, I think your secret is safe with me. And well, the Guard-Captain. That man doesn't miss a thing."

Alexa couldn't help but open her mouth in horror, which earned a giggle from her red-haired sister. Her mount huffed a reptilian hiss in response to the stablemaster's vibrations, which drew Alexa's eye to power-ful *crushing* jaws. Its mouth hung slack, threatening anyone who dared come close with the glint of savage teeth. The image stole her breath, but not wanting to be made a fool, she shook her head and retorted angrily, "I don't know what you're talkin' about!"

"Sure, sure. We all need to stretch our necks on occasion. Some just do it seven, maybe eight times a day. Weird though. I never come back from my stretches with a smile. You *must* tell me your secret," Bella said with a mischievous grin.

Alexa sighed, there was no convincing that woman of anything other than the truth, and quite honestly the thought of unburdening herself was more than a little appealing. The secret romance was exhilarating but, with-out a doubt, tiresome. Other than the fear of having such a flagrant vul-nerability exposed, there was no reason to hide the relationship from the world, and the concealment had started to chaff. Maybe it would be nice to finally share her interests after all, especially if it were her sister.

"Rangemaster, look," a guardswoman called out, interrupting any re-sponse she could make. Coming up the hill was one of the scouting pairs of rangers she had combing the ground around them. Their forest green cloaks and hooded appearance made them look like moving bushes. Living foliage emerging from the ever-thickening hawthorn, juniper, and crabapple trees. They marched on for another fifty paces before the pair rendezvoused with their leader.

She gave them a few moments to collect themselves and although she was anxious for news of Elira, she forced her voice to stay calm. "Gaston, Menias, report."

The pair blinked at one another, and, with an unspoken agreement, Gaston turned to his Rangemaster to deliver their news, "Rangemaster, enemy 'as been spotted. Thirty minutes to 'der boat, group of forty-four strong. Three guards on the okenavis."

"Any sign of Elira or Matthias?"

Gaston shook his head. "No, Rangemaster."

A sudden coldness gripped her heart as curiosity bit at her. "You said forty-four?"

Gaston looked at Menias with uncertainty, and his range-mate nodded an affirmation, prompting the ranger to response. "Uh, yes Rangemaster. I was certain. Did the count twice. Jus' like you taught us."

She knew Gaston, and he was no fool. The man would not have miscounted. So, somehow this group had lost five soldiers. A raw gnawing sensation clawed at her gut, and she wondered where in Ember's breath Elira was.

The gallop of hooves accompanied Guard Captain Vitrusian's voice, "What have we learned?"

"Our *friends* have been spotted. With your permission commander I think it's time to act." Alexa replied, giving deference to the senior commander on the field.

Alexander nodded in response with a small twitch on his upper lip, the only betrayal of emotion. He turned his mount around, circling his hand and pointing to the ground near him; a signal for the Warriors of August to form into battle lines. With practiced discipline, the company smartly locked into three ranks of twenty each. Alexa saw Amilicus in the second rank, his ax a weapon to tear down shields. It was small consolation for her worried heart, and she felt a pang of guilt as she remembered him begging her to practice swordcraft with him. She hadn't wanted him to be good enough to be in the front rank, not yet.

The Guard-Captain brought his arm up swiftly, and, as one, the company rolled shields off their backs. A wall of pine and iron now faced Alexa and Bella, and she heard Hislock hiss in excitement. The raptor-riding saurian came to Bella's side and from over her sister's mount she could see the two exchange a glance, obvious friendship held within.

"Bring in the scouts, Rangemaster," Alexander said, almost as a formality.

"Gaston, head west one mile, get Dillon and Reisha. Menias, west three kilometers, get Lucius and Erin. Go!" Alexa barked out to the waiting rangers. The two raced off in opposite directions, knowing how best to find their comrades.

The group made their way to the beginnings of the hawthorn trees. She strung her bow, taking a moment to appreciate the small pink and white crabapple blooms that broke up the monotony. Bees danced merrily around the sweet-smelling blossoms. *Perhaps the last good thing I'll see*, she mused.

Guard-Captain Vitrusian roared, "Right, warriors! break up into groups of four. Let's get through these trees with at least some grace. Rangemaster, take the lead and let us know if this bit of nature is going to kill us before it does. Perry, take three others and stay behind with the horses and baggage."

His company, who had so beautifully trotted to the woods edge in formation, were now being forced to navigate the thorny thickness of a coastal tree line. As the warriors partnered into small contingents, Alexa saw Hislock and Bella dismount and hand the reins over to Perry's group. Even the forest dwelling raptors would not be able to navigate the brambles with ease, and the four rearguard soldiers led the mounts up a sea cliff that flanked their destination.

It was only a half mile or so to the descending slope that led to the beach, a small, sandy patch nestled between long stretches of treacherous rock. Alexa winced with every snap and crack of branch or twig, but to be fair to them, it was nigh impossible to prevent such noises from an armored infantry company. Even a group of rangers, trained for such movement, would struggle to remain fully quiet here. Their only advantage would be speed, and she set a brutal pace. The company obeyed her unspoken command with only a few curses and grunts, trusting the Rangemaster of Elgion to guide them through the trees, a skillset mastered by her order.

To her left, just past the furthest group of warriors, she saw Gaston return with Dillon and Reisha. As the rangers made their way towards Alexa, Dillon, a ranger from before the death of the previous Rangemaster, nodded at her, telling her his report was unnecessary. A thorn scraped her arm, and the pain snapped her attention forward once more. The low hanging branches made for difficult travel, but the pioneers of Elgion would endure.

Suddenly, a scream pierced the air, a mile or so to their north where the beach lay. The thudding of her chest quickened, and she gritted her teeth as she pushed her way through a particularly troublesome bramble. Her caution falling away as speed became more paramount. Then, almost without warning, she broke free of the trees and stood atop a slope dotted with brush.

All around her, the crash of armored soldiers breaking free of bramble and tree could be heard. They were too late; the enemy was already preparing to board. Only a few crates, some of which were already roped and ready for transport, remained on the beach. Their leader wanted to make a quick exit, and she could only assume they had immediately prepared for departure when they hit the beach. It must have been an hour since Gaston had reported to her, giving the enemy one, maybe two hours, on the beach before her group arrived. A horn sounded; the wielder easy to spot for the brass of their instrument shone brightly in the sunlight.

"Form up!" Alexander called, accompanied by the rasping tones of his sword leaving its scabbard.

His call to action forced Alexa to her own. "Dillon be ready to assist the Guard-Captain. Gaston and Reisha stay with me, and we will rain down fury."

Gaston grinned with pleasure. The horn cried out once more and there she saw their leader standing just a few paces from the horn blower, the shining bronze of his breastplate and the raven feathers of his helm, marking him as the one she saw just a week before. He wiped his face with his hand, almost ritualistically, and Alexa saw that his cheek was now marred red. With rapid short barks he dispensed orders, urging his company to hasten their departure. And as the Warriors of August marched quick time down the slope, thirty or more of his men and women were already pushing the okenavis free of its mooring. Ten remained behind with the leader, forming a shallow line, a bulwark against the forces of Augustia.

"Gaston, Reisha! It's our time." Alexa shouted as she raced in front of the right flank. *One hundred and fifty meters.* She drew, aimed in an arc, judged the distance and wind, and fired. It would be a difficult shot, but time was running out. Gaston and Reisha's arrows followed shortly behind, and the three shafts whistled through the air. Alexa's arrow was dodged at the last minute by the leader and buried itself into the sand just behind. Gaston's own slammed into a shield of the enemy line while Reisha's buried itself in the sand in front. They moved forward keeping the Warriors of August on their left flank.

One hundred meters. The leader held up his vicious looking mace, pointed it directly at Alexa, and grinned. It was a bone-chilling look, and just as she strung her bow to fire again, he turned and trotted away to the ship. The ten strong group left behind, a distraction to hold them at bay. Alexa fired the arrow, hoping to catch the enemy commander in the back, but the distance made her accuracy falter and the shot went wide. Alexa watched Reisha and Gaston's arrows fall onto the enemy line. One shuddered as it hit a shield and the other fell between two bronze rims. Save for a small quiver of one shield no response was given.

Fifty meters. Alexa could see Bella and Hislock jogging along with Dillon, ready to support where needed. Their presence in the infantry company would only serve to hinder the tightly practiced formation. Years of practice and drill allowed the Warriors of August to march down that slope at a slow jog while holding shield and blade. She nocked another arrow aiming at the enemy line.

Small targets; small misses she thought to herself and aimed at an exposed neck. Her shot flew straight, the distance no longer an issue, and buried into flesh. That victim broke away from the formation, stumbling backwards with a look of confusion until the loss of blood forced them to drop to their knees and out of view. Another arrow from her rangers was rewarded with a cry of pain as it pierced a shield. Another simply quivered, buried in sturdy pine with its stark, white goose feathers somehow out-of-place in the bloodshed to come.

Twenty-five meters. Alexa tasted iron in her breath. She watched in horror as two of their own soldiers charged ahead of their comrades, bellowing in incoherent rage. The enemy line, finally allowed to hit back at their enemy, roared in challenge. Yet, they held their ground and let the two soldiers charge onto them.

"Ember's breath! Charge! Shields together, now!" Guard-Captain Vitrusian shouted in dismay, as he watched the two errant soldiers get hacked to pieces. Their impotent charge, as filled with rage as it was, was broken on enemy shields. The mercenaries flung a volley of spears into the Warriors of August. Save for one poor soul, the shields of her countrymen held firm. Then the two forces met with a clash, Alexa knew she could help that fight no more. Bella moved with Hislock and Dillon to wrap around the opposing force. Their spears would deliver grievous wounds to the rear of the enemy. As brave as the foe was, they would not stand long, and she wondered what enemy they faced to so willingly sacrifice themselves.

Yet, there was no time for such questions, and she turned her focus to the okenavis. The angled portion of its hull now fully submerged, and one could see the furrow in the sand on which it had rested. The mercenary company heaved against the boat and in a few seconds they would be free.

A sudden pulse of anger washed over her, more than she had felt in battles before. She charged towards the departing boat, and only in afterthought did she yell over her shoulder, "Gaston, Reisha! Take down those still pushing!" She skidded to a stop one hundred meters from the boat and fired. Her arrow lost from focus as a rapid swishing sound frightened her. With nothing but a short grunt, Gaston, who had just found his place by her side, fell to the sand of the beach, a red gash in his skull.

It was as if he was struck by the gods, and she desperately scanned around for the source. The swishing started again and just as she felt panic swell, her assailants were found. Two Caprix, the hardy goatmen of the Central Spine, had taken up league with these mercenaries. *A strange company indeed, to have such mixed forces.* The one and a half meter tall goatmen brought their cloth slings into a whirling frenzy, and Alexa knew they were about to loose once more. On instinct she dove to her left and into a combat roll; her reward was the sound of stones hitting sand. Alexa thanked the Maiden the Caprix had not targeted Reisha; the novice ranger still stood with her mouth agape at the sight of Gaston's prostrate body.

She hadn't the time to deal with the traumatized ranger and knew her best option was to try and keep the enemy slingers from firing. Alexa's draw was sluggish, as she had forced her body to extreme exertion. She puffed out air and brought her mind to focus with her comforting mantra. *Small targets, small misses.* She fired towards the goatmen, trying to take the left most one at central mass. A sudden lurch of the boat spoiled her shot, and the arrow clattered off its rear planks. Her target nearly falling to the sands below in the commotion. The only thing saving them was their instinct. An evolutionary advantage of their species formed from years in the mountains. An advantage that made the Caprix leap backwards with uncanny speed and distance.

With the small seconds granted to them by the slinger's recovery, Alexa turned to the stunned Reisha and commanded, "Reisha! See to his wounds. He could still yet live."

Reisha shook her head slightly, breaking from their trauma and focusing on her leader. A priceless second passed as Alexa held her charge's gaze, allowing the novice to process the order. One that made itself worthwhile as Reisha nodded curtly, dashing off to the injured Gaston.

"Come on now, we got them!" She heard the crash of iron shod boots on the sand to her left. The Warriors of August, having won their contest, now pushed on towards the departing foe.

They were in disarray; overcome with victory.

"No!" Alexa cried out, even though another surge of anger made her want to follow them in their reckless charge. Only a few mercenaries were still on the beach, up to their chests in water as they waited to clamber up the net like ropes on the stern of the ship. Her company had failed to stop the mercenaries, and, though she felt a sort of rage, Alexa did not want to see another fall with a stone cracking their skull.

"Halt!" She shouted again, and most of the company reluctantly staggered to a stop, accompanied by grunts of frustrated anger. Still, a few guardsmen and women pressed on, unaware of her order or just lost in bloodlust. The rapid swishing noise whirled up again and a guardswoman, her blade held upright in challenge, suddenly lost control of her legs. She fell face first into the sand. Another guard to the woman's left grunted in pain as their shoulder was ripped violently backwards.

"Ember's breath! Halt, damn you. Halt!" Alexander Vitrusian said, a tinge of uncommon malevolence in his voice.

There was only a little delay and she heard the slings winding up once again. The relentless assault could only be thwarted with return fire, and she nocked an arrow to fire rapidly. The arrow lanced towards the departing boat; now firmly in the waters. At almost two hundred meters, it was becoming difficult to make out, but she saw the silhouette of a caprix as they ducked. The other—unhindered—let loose. A sudden flash of emerald-green darted up the beach and slammed into the back of the furthest soldier, a stone skipping harmlessly behind. Hislock understood the threat, using his short bursts of reptilian speed to close the distance. Rolling off the top of the soldier he had just saved, Hislock hissed in command at what few remained. Something in his manner finally halted the impetus of bloodlust, their charge bringing them to the edge of the water.

"Get back here, and reform the line! Shields!" The Guard-Captain roared.

Alexa watched as the two guards, that had charged forward and were lucky enough to still be standing, came to a halt. Their weapons held loosely at their sides. Both turned and looked back at their comrades in confusion. Alexa watched as one's mouth exploded with blood. A stone cracked into the back of the guardswoman's helmet. Alexa grunted in anger at the okenavis, the slinger's accuracy was brutal even at this distance. She watched the sail drop, yanking the vessel forward, and knew that she could not hit them in return.

Bella, slower than Hislock, had still charged forward with her friend, "Hislock, get your scaly ass out of there!" Bella grunted as the stricken guardswoman collapsed onto her, saved a further fall by Bella's timely intervention.

"Dillon! Let's get them off the beach!" Alexa shouted as she sprinted to help her sister. She closed the distance; Bella dragged the soldier just a few paces forward. A splash in the water rippled behind them. Alexa closed her eyes in thanks; the slingers were finally out of range. Out on the okenavis, oars and sails pulled her quarry away, and she cursed herself for not bringing one of Elgion's galleys. An oath that was impotent for even with the war galley, they would have been hard pressed to catch the faster vessel. Okenavis emphasized sail and speed. Yet, she thought maliciously, if they did catch them, the galley's gleaming bronze ram would have ripped them apart.

The red-marred leader stood at the stern, and she saw the glint of his mace as he held it high, almost in mock salute. It was a long way off, but he bellowed a single word, "Magdris!"

Her heart nearly stopped at the sound.

Bella, apparently unconcerned with the imposing enemy commander, yelled, "Are you going to help with her or just stand there!"

Time swirled back into normalcy, and she shook her head before grabbing the opposing shoulder of the guardswoman. Together they dragged her rapidly up the beach. The Warriors of August, alongside Dillon and Hislock, had dragged all the wounded together naught but ten meters from where the enemy line had once stood. Mangled bodies of the enemy were mixed with four of their own, now five, as they brought the guardswoman gently to the ground.

The Guard-Captain shouted curses as he directed the healing efforts of the wounded, his normal calm demeanor gone. "You dumb bastards! Get a cloth on that head wound. Why in all the gods would you charge into ranged fire? Perdicus, get pressure on that wound!" The man was a torrent of fury and command, but Alexa knew it was wrong. She knew something held the usually reserved commander in its grasp.

"Ember's breath! Where's a Keeper when you need one? Get our healing her—"

He stopped abruptly as Alexa placed a hand on his shoulder, stopping his frantic pacing. He was breathing heavily, *angrily* and with a force of will he kept himself rooted to her firm grasp. Alexa saw the discipline of his years force him to try and regain control. Slowly, Guard-Captain Alexander Vitrusian looked around and saw the worried faces of his soldiers. They had never seen him command like that, like a tyrant. He closed his eyes and whispered, "Berserkers."

A sudden cry of utter anguish pierced the air. Almost inhuman in its agony.

"Al-Ale-Alexa! what in the gods is that!?" Bella yelled out in fear, pointing to four staked figures near the smoldering remains of campfires. She knew now where the leader got his red mark from and felt ice course through her veins.

Chapter Nine

Bella

Bella stood; her mouth agape. The question she had asked subconsciously fresh on her lips. Her arm pointed towards a sight her mind refused to fully comprehend. No matter how hard she tried, it would not coalesce into a solid thought, like shadows falling away from candlelight. All she knew was something was horrifically wrong. A trauma so intense her mind buried itself away from the terror; protection from scars that would remain for years.

She did not pull her eyes away, nor did she drop her arm from its outstretched position. Instead, she simply heard Alexa run, the soft patter of her sister's leather boots pounding the sand. Even the hardy ranger had not run towards the sight immediately, but now as Bella stood frozen, her sister acted—her cloak billowing in the breeze. Bella still could not move, could not wrangle her thoughts together into a usable pattern. She simply was stuck in space as time flowed over her.

Unbidden thoughts of the past swirled into being. The widened eyes of her orcish tormentor, the brutal war chief who had caged and tortured her three years ago, pulsed within her thoughts. His final moments barging its way into her psyche. It was the only time she had power over him, and it was ever so brief. She had plunged her spear into his shoulder, an impact so intense that it remained a phantom to this day. Yet, as always, that memory fell away to the touch of his oversized finger. The moment *he* had power over *her*, the moment—or moments—in which she had been caged and at his mercy. In her mind's eye, his brutal tongue would coarsely form a single word, "Good ..." The memory vivid and lucid enough to carry the sensation of his touch; the wicked caress of her cheek with his cal-loused finger. Her face trembled, a whisper within her muscles, a twitch coming from the recesses of her darkest thoughts.

She flinched as Hislock placed a scaled hand on her elbow. His natural stoop and body proportions making it difficult to reach up to her shoulder. The saurian must have seen the pain in her. He must have known what lay on the beach in front of them threatened to overwhelm her. She looked into his black eyes, and although his face was so alien, so different from hers, she felt the sympathy coming from him. They stared at one another, slight panting in their breaths from the battle they had just fought. Simply soaking in the comfort of another, a friend.

Finally, her thoughts converged, and she blinked as the surge of emo-tion from unprocessed thoughts washed over her. She nodded slowly to Hislock and without a word began walking towards the horror.

"Elira? No! Elira! No … No … No!" Alexa screamed.

Bella started jogging, and spat heavily to the sand beneath, trying to clear the heavy taste of blood in her mouth. She heard Hislock's padded footsteps behind.

"What in the gods is this? Wha-what did they do to you?" Alexa asked, her voice frantic and broken.

Bella was nearly there, and shouts could be heard from behind. The rest of the company becoming fully aware of what shook their Rangemas-ter.

Alexa fell to her knees, grasping at the body that caused her such mis-ery.

Bella stopped just five meters away from her sister, who now fell into an utter grief, sobbing in an uncontrolled torrent. There, in front of Bella, were four heavy wooden poles staked into the ground, each standing nearly three meters high. On each was a body, their arms pulled over their heads, the wrists bound tightly at the apex of each stake. Their ankles and waist wrapped in thick rope so that their bodies were firmly strapped to the poles. It must have been a necessary measure for what had been done to them.

Bella's vision finally cleared and like sunlight washing over veiled shadows, she saw in perfect clarity what lay before her. The bodies had been stripped of their clothes, and a patchwork of cuts interlaced the flesh. The position of each cut was methodical and ritualistic. Twin slices, each a hands breath apart, looked like the bloody rungs of a ladder stepping its way down. The symmetry of it all was sickening, and Bella could see that each gash served to funnel blood down the center line of the body. A pool at the base of each stake evidence of its success.

Every cut was done in a way that wouldn't kill instantly, instead opting for slow pulses of blood to pour forth until the life was finally snuffed out. Oddly, the skin of the face, neck, and scalp remained untouched, although the hair had been shaven off. On three of the stakes the bodies were desiccated, with only a red stain marking the path that their blood had drained down. The horrific act having been done at some earlier time. Bella recognized one immediately. It was Matthias, his face sallow and graven. Life had left him long ago. The others were rangers from Alexa's company, and Bella could not recall their names.

She did not need to recognize the middle figure, for Alexa mumbled their name over and over. *Elira, poor Elira.* Blood glistened as it poured from the fresh butchery. *Perhaps she was the source of the screams?* Bella postulated as her head started to shake involuntarily. She had to bite down to bear the pain she witnessed. Anger and horror mixed in a turbulent concoction. Even Hislock, whose own tongue was so different to their own Holliserian language that he often chose to remain silent, couldn't help but mutter. The rasping hiss of a reverential prayer was obvious in his intonation. The saurian repeatedly dipped his head to the ground and then in a jerking motion raised it to the sky.

Alexa suddenly cried out, "I will … I will kill them for this!" Bella's sister scooted on her knees even closer to the stake. Her trousers and cloak soaking in the blood that pooled at Elira's feet. "Do you hear me, Elira?! I will find them and … and make them pay for this! In Ember's name I will rip them from this world!" The Rangemaster pounded at the stake with a fist and held her hand to Elira's bound ankles.

A groan issued forth. Alexa looked up in sudden horror at the sound. The groan turned into a sob of pain. The Rangemaster stood suddenly, and Bella watched her sister grasp Elira as high as she could reach. The height of the pole only allowed her to reach the upper part of Elira's arm. "Elira? Elira, do you hear me?"

The tortured ranger only formed an agonized moan in response. The exsanguination having stripped her of consciousness, or at least Bella hoped it had.

Alexa's brown eyes, full of helpless, angry grief, suddenly snapped towards her, and Bella took a deep breath in preparation for what must be done. Alexa broke into a sob and bowed her head.

They had to end Elira's suffering. There was no way they could save her, not even if the Maiden themselves came to Telaea. There were too many wounds, and too much blood loss. Bella planted her spear into the sand and pulled one of her long daggers—its hardened edge tempered in the very forges of Elgion—free from the sheath at her waist.

Alexa, her head still bowed, inched her gaze upwards. Staring deeply into her sister's eyes, Bella asked as calm as she could, "Do you want *me* to do this?"

Fresh tears, and Alexa struggled not to collapse from the grief. From Bella's periphery, Amilicus, the guardsmen Alexa had so often looked upon, came to her sister's side. The man placed a hand on her back, and the Rangemaster latched onto the comfort. She fell into his embrace, allowing his offer of solace to consume her, even if just for a moment.

"Look … look at what they did to her." Alexa said between sobs.

"I know, I see," Amilicus replied as he tightened his hold even more.

Another moan escaped Elira's mouth, and Bella knew they should hurry to release Elira from the pain. "We need to give her mercy, Alexa. I-I can do this for you."

"No! It should be me," Alexa barked suddenly. She pushed Amilicus away and turned to the task. Abruptly snatching the dagger away, and with sudden coldness, she said, "It *must* be me." The Rangemaster did not hesitate any longer, and—with grace—used the bound ankles as a foothold while grasping the pole with her free hand. She brought herself eye to eye with the brutalized victim, the blood from Elira's body mingling between the two in sticky strands.

"May the Maiden take you," Alexa said and slashed the dagger quickly across Elira's throat. She dropped down as the remaining life drained away. Like it was held by the tortured soul, the taste of blood dissipated. It had been a sensation she had felt since they had broken free from the hawthorn trees. *Magdris is gone from here … for now,* Bella realized.

Snapping to attention, and with a sudden authority to her voice, Alexa spoke, "She goes now to that Far Range. That place where we all must go. She was our sister, our companion. She was a Warden of the Wilds. She was a guardian against the unknown. She was a watcher in the woods. Here we remember her, but here is not where she stays. We *will* see her again on that Far Range … goodbye."

"Goodbye," a chorus of voices replied. Bella looked to see their origins and four rangers stood at attention, in obvious reverence. Dillon, who had helped her skewer the holding force from behind, she recognized, for he was one of the rangers that had survived the Battle for Elgion three years prior. The other three had missed *this* battle, but sometime in the recent commotion arrived unnoticed only to witness such horror.

Alexa stepped back and repeated the ranger's hymn for each of her fallen charges; Matthias, Weston, Parius. With each completion, the surviving rangers echoed the goodbyes of their leader.

As the reverential practice ended, Alexa turned and walked towards the sea. No one followed her. Bella walked over to Amilicus who stood alone and unsure. "Thank you," Bella said as she placed a hand on his wrist.

The young man looked up at her, his eyes full of uncertainty. Bella could only conjure small sympathy, "Just … give it some time. Ok?"

Amilicus nodded and walked away. He looked up at Elira's body again and jogged off towards the makeshift hospital where his company was being healed. Many of the Warriors of August, including the Guard-Captain, stood in a semi-circle around the scene. Bella had no idea how long they had watched; how long it had taken for them to end Elira's suffering. All the faces looking upon her suddenly became too much, and anger surged through her.

She grunted in irritation and then she too found herself moving away from the crowd. She rushed up the beach, aiming to find her mount, the simplicity of her animal companions always a balm for the soul.

Suddenly, the totem from that orc encampment in which she had been imprisoned so long ago overrode her thoughts. Tears began to threaten as the thought of Godwin, Godfrey's now dead nephew, impaled upon those malicious spikes forced their way into her psyche. She ran on, trying to break free of the horrible images, but they only increased in intensity. Every moment of her captivity now playing out in vivid detail. She could not escape, she could not flee. Blindly crashing into hawthorn with tears streaming freely down her face. She lost herself in the memories, allowing her legs to carry her forward without thought of her destination.

She jogged on in a trance through the coastal tree line until she broke free onto the grassy hill. The buzzing of bees droned lazily, and a light spring breeze carried the sweet scent of crabapple blossoms. The stark change in sensation forced her to stop, and without knowing why, she looked down upon her arms. They were lacerated with many cuts from thorn and branch, she wondered how she had not felt the pain at first.

"Ma'am?" the sudden question broke her free of her daze, and she looked up to see Perry, the man who had taken the mounts. "Are you alright?"

At first, Bella could only form an utterance with no semblance of words. Perry looked on expectantly as she mumbled for a few seconds, until finally she came back into herself, finding her voice. "Yes, yes I am fine."

"We won then?" He asked apprehensively.

She had not realized she appeared to have been running from the battle. In a way, she had been, but not from the physicality of it. Quickly, she spoke to assuage his fears, "Yes, we won … But we didn't get what we wanted. The company's alive, 'though a bit battered."

Perry took in a stuttered breath and while closing his eyes, exhaled. The relief was dramatically plain, and it made Bella wish that Blythe or even Godfrey, those stalwart friends, were there. Unfortunately, Godfrey had been denied accompanying them on account of his missing arm; a wound she still felt somewhat responsible for. After all, he had been with her when he lost the appendage, following her as she charged foolishly into the unknown. Whereas Blythe had spent more and more time remaining in Elgion, he was not a warrior, unless in absolute necessity.

Blythe's insistence on watching the stables was, in some ironic way, her fault as well. They had bonded over animals and her passion for all beasts had increased Blythe's own. Now, every time Bella left to deal with the burgeoning relationship between the saurians and Elgion, or the ever-increasing demands for a beast master outside of the settlement, Blythe would stay behind. In some ways he *was* still helping her, because she never had to worry about Elgion's stables when he was there to mind them. *What have I done to earn such friends?*

Hislock came bursting from the trees, his own scaled flesh unmarked. The saurian raced over to her, looking up into her eyes almost angrily. Perry backed away subconsciously, as most of Elgion's citizens still did around saurians. Fear of the unknown was a powerful mistress.

The gecko-like lizard spoke some of the Holliserrian words he had learned, "Belllaaa, why runnn? Baaad, down on beasshh. We want runnnn too, but no runnn. Warrior." Hislock finished, slamming his spear to his chest in salute.

"I know Hislock. I know, I'm sorry, alright?" She wanted to say more, but the words would not come.

Perry grunted awkwardly as the two, human and saurian, looked at one another. Hislock twitched his head to the side in a manner character-istic of himself. "Belllaaa, we know. Pain. Youuu feeeel pain."

Bella closed her eyes, and the tears broke free from under her eyelids. "Perry, me and Hislock here will take care of the mounts. Best you and your group head on down to the beach. They need all the help they can get."

"Yes, ma'am," Perry raced off, obviously glad to be away from the intimacy between the two species. She hoped that in time they would un-derstand that friendship could be shared across even this unique divide. After all, the saurians, like all creatures, had desires, hopes, and pains, just like themselves.

"Come on, Hislock, let's check on our friends." Bella cocked her head up the hill to the mounts. They passed by Perry's contingent who—jogging after their leader—risked nervous glances at the two. Hislock and Bella crested the small hill that overlooked the sea. The horses, who cropped at the rich spring grass, were leashed to stakes planted in the ground, while the raptors were chained to a makeshift hitching post. A precaution El-gion's citizens requested whenever the raptors visited the human settlement. Bella walked towards her raptor, knowing the heavy iron chain chaffed at him.

"It's alright, friend," she said as she unhooked the chain from its clasp on the collar. The heavy leather collar fastened with an iron link, being the only other addition requested by humanity for the care of raptors. *At least the only other one, so far*, she thought grimly. Hislock did the same to his own mount, hissing in agitation at the concept of chaining his companion. The saurians did no such thing with their own beasts of burden, but to be fair, the saurian mounts were far more intelligent than even the best of horses. A brief memory of her previous mount flashed within her mind. Precious, a faithful steed who died to the orcish menace years ago. *That* had been a good horse, and she sighed in memory. But, like all things, it must pass, and her time with Precious had ended. Now she held a bond with a new beast, and frankly it was quickly becoming one to rival even Precious's place of honor.

Rex, it was such a simple name for such an elegant creature. Yet, somehow, it fit. After all, he did seem the king of beasts.

Rex batted their head into Bella a few times, prodding her to pet him. "Alright, alright. Don't get hasty now," Bella said chuckling. She placed her hand on his head and stroked gently downwards in between the ridges of his eye bones. The raptor vibrated with the motion; almost like a cat purring. "That's a good boy. That's a *good* boy."

Bella looked up and out towards the distant horizon. The vast dark blue sea below stretched on for what seemed like forever. Sea birds whirled overhead; their constant shrieking accompanied the roar of waves crashing into the rocks below. To the south, seaside cliffs battered by the white froth of Melleas's tempestuous waters, stretched endlessly onwards as the mountains and hills of Eukaria made for few safe landings. It wasn't until you rounded Huckleberry Mount before one could find a decent mooring.

While to the north, hawthorn forests strung along the twisting coastline. Bella knew many beaches lay that way, but one would be hard pressed to find another such sheltered landing, like the one the mercenaries had used. Since it was shifting to low tide, they could just make out the edge of the beach, the sands repeatedly washed over by the relentless waves.

It had been terrible timing, she thought. The mercenaries had escaped right at the end of high tide, and now looking out at the sea, she spotted the lone okenavis. Twin white sails against the dark blue of the sea made it easy to spot. The tempestuous winds near Melleas's Wroth, a storm-wracked strait that bridged the old and new world, speeding their escape. Already the enemy vessel looked to be kilometers south of the beach. Whoever they were, they had succeeded in their mission and now headed back to whatever foul hole they came from. The only comfort to Bella was that she knew their strength was not enough to threaten Eligon itself. The galleys in her harbor would make short work of the lone okenavis. *Too bad they will probably just scuttle on home,* she bemoaned.

Hislock hissed irritably and she knew he too looked upon the enemy ship.

"We will find them Hislock," Bella said, trying to comfort her friend.

Hislock twitched his head over in the snappy motions of his kind, "Nooo. Youuu not readddeee. Musssst heal."

She looked at him and saw he pointed at his head.

Hislock then pointed towards her own head, and he repeated himself, "Heal. Youuuu come to home." Hislock said as he pointed to his chest. "Heal." He nodded knowingly.

She smiled at the saurian and was amazed at the kinship she felt towards this foreign figure. Never in her wildest dreams did she think she would call a sentient reptile friend, but now she wondered if he was her best friend. Godfrey may rival him for the title, and he, as the human ambassador to the reptilian folk, was also at Hislock's village. A trade he was rather good at. Although he grumbled at not being able to be in the fighting line, Bella knew Godfrey enjoyed his new ambassadorial role. After all, he was a natural at it. Maybe it *would* be good for her to have some time with the simpler lifestyle of the saurians.

"Ok, but first I need to speak to Alexa. What she saw … might break her."

Hislock narrowed his eyes and nodded in understanding.

"Come on, let's see if we can get these mounts down to the beach," Bella said.

As they prepared the mounts for travel, she shuddered as the thought of Elira's exposed tissue slammed into her consciousness.

Chapter Ten

Sophia

"And what then will we do when the children become thieves and vagabonds on the streets?" Master Eamon Salferesis asked the assembled members of the Chosen's Wisdom. "How will we keep them out of the street gangs that grow every year? How will we grow our great city of Augustia, if we do not spend the aforementioned funds on a new orphanage?"

"You speak in hypotheticals!" Master Kylos retorted. Her curly black hair bobbed with her abrupt stand. Her supporters, other members of the Chosen who seated themselves around her, murmured in support.

Master Eamon smiled and held his hands out to the side of him. Powerful arms slid out from under his chasuble, "What is life but a game of best guesses?"

Sophia couldn't help but smile at the charismatic response. She was not alone for several of the Chosen laughed.

"Once again you play games with us Master Eamon, but this is the Hall of the Chosen. The People's Will elected us to lead, not enjoin you on your farcical fantasies!" Master Kylos replied, her tone irritated and troubled while Master Eamon seemed at ease. It was as if he was having a simple discussion over the dinner table with friends and family, and Sophia, even though she tried to remain unbiased, felt her will bend to his.

Her spot in the gallery allowed her and any other citizen who could vote in the People's Will attend the meetings of the Chosen. Although, on heavily debated topics, the capacity of one hundred persons became a privilege you would have to pay for. While on the Day of Choice, it became an impossibility, with people waiting outside of the hall for word on who would be their next Chosen. A sea of bodies would stream down from the marble steps of the hall and into the forum that fronted the building. For there, in the center of Augustia, just as the climb of the Upper Bowl began, lay the Chosen's Hall. It was a massive building of marbled columns and clay tiled roofs. It's grandeur like a rock in a stream, as Grange Street—the main thoroughfare for the Upper Bowl—was pierced by its foundations.

Fortunately, today was not one of those days and although the gallery was nearly full, she had found a perfect vantage point. One that looked down upon Master Eamon who let his arms glide back into his chasuble; the robes the elected must adorn when entering the Chosen's Hall. He looked magnificent, with a neatly trimmed black beard and dark brown hair that stood atop a tall and rather muscular frame. His chasuble was a stark white cloak beautifully adorned with red and gold trim, and she couldn't help but feel that the garment and its wearer struck a rather handsome figure. Of course, it helped that he positioned himself right in the center of the Augustian sunburst heraldry; a mural painstakingly etched into the marble floor of the amphitheater's center. The suspiciously coincidental placement of his feet made her wonder how many of his actions were intentional or just circumstance.

"Master Kylos, must we exchange these insults?" Eamon dipped his head and raised his brows like a father questioning an errant child. "Yes, the People's Will elected us to lead, and that is what I am trying to do. Your idea to spend the new trade incomes is a sound one. Who would say that charting the northern coastline of the new world, that glorious Continens Hyclepius, wouldn't be a good thing? We would all benefit from such a venture, even if just from the keels of the new okenavis we would need to build."

Master Eamon paused, allowing magnanimity to draw in the Chosen. "And we *will* do that but first let's care for our own. Yes, the people want us to lead, but will those same people still thank us if we forget about the children left behind? Will they forgive us if we tell them that we could not care for our children this year, that we could not care for the next genera-tion?" Master Eamon let the rhetorical question hang in the air, like he dared anyone to deny its validity. Even Master Kylos, who still stood, re-mained silent.

Master Eamon's smile fell quickly, and he dropped his voice like he was imparting a secret. Everyone leaned in to hear, Sophia included. "Chil-dren will not wait; they grow old and bitter. We all have seen one …" He paused, allowing his voice to trail off, seemingly lost in some bitter memory.

Sophia's heart sank as she watched the man, feeling empathy for a life she had little knowledge of. Suddenly, he erupted into speech again, his familiar smile beaming out to them all. The sudden change in the volume of his voice caused many to jump slightly in their seat. "While coastlines are much more immutable! I spoke to a mother yesterday who told me she looked after three kids from other unions! Not one, not two, but three! Children who had all lost their parents. Is it not fair that we should try and provide a place for those who are not so fortunate? I suggest we use all five hundred marks to fund the construction of a new orphanage. There is space near the Hill Gate and the people are willing. So, my only question, are the Chosen willing?"

A pregnant pause stole the breath from the air as he finished. The sounds of merchants hawking their wares in the forum outside the only sound. Then, seemingly as one, the people in the gallery roared in appreci-ation. Sophia too had stood, unconsciously at the same time as the others. She did not cheer but just stood overwhelmed with the power of the speech. She glanced at Master Kylos who attempted a response, but the time for words was over and Kylos had lost any ability to argue back. Ev-idently, the words had gripped even the Chosen, now upended into a ca-cophony of chaos as they cheered, jeered, or argued from their seats in the amphitheater. Almost all cheered for Master Eamon. Sophia smiled at the display. She loved the democracy of Augustia, and she loved watching the debates when her time allowed.

Her lunch of honeyed bread and beef stuffed cabbage wraps had brought her to the forum, where—if she fancied—she could attend the meetings of the Chosen. It was a lunchtime practice she applied whenever possible. One that allowed her to watch many debates in the three years she had lived in Augustia, and, like the other citizens of the city, she had learned to appreciate Master Eamon's rhetorical abilities.

Regardless, she needed to get back up the Bowl—to the Keeper's Bastion. Grand Keeper Chalepos had demanded she finish copying his letters in triplicate and she had not even started on the droll document he wrote to his sister in Argentios. The man was a tyrant, and he had taken a distinct dislike to her. She sighed, and alongside the buzzing attendees of the gallery, made her way to the marbled staircase that would take them to the floor and exit below.

Whatever Chalepos's demands, she was in no particular hurry. Meanwhile, the rest of the gallery's attendees rushed down the stairs, their excited conversations forcing their gait to match their enthusiasm. By the time she reached the floor of the hall, she was amongst only a few, preferring to daydream as she walked instead of engaging in the excited banter that danced out the door.

"Ah, Keeper! I have been meaning to speak to you."

She recognized the voice as Master Eamon, and her heart quickened. She froze in place but kept her head bowed. She knew that there were no other Keepers in attendance that day. *Why would he want to talk to her?*

A chuckle was followed by a rather amicable follow-up, "Yes, I do speak to you Keeper. Unlike some of your *leaders* I recognize talent. The work you did for poor Lady Aliana, remarkable!"

Sophia finally looked up; her anxiety overcome. Master Eamon looked about fifteen centimeters taller than her, and she herself rivalled some men in height at about one hundred and seventy-five centimeters. His gait was strong and confident, and Sophia felt a trickle of sweat break out on her brow. She chewed the inside of her lip, her heart racing as her mind went blank.

Eamon stopped just steps away, well within arm's reach. Sophia looked up at him and wondered if her breath had been freshened with mint that morning. The thought was accompanied by the smell of healthy sweat, a musk that blew in seemingly from the man's force alone.

He smiled at her, and as if she had not made the interaction awkward by her silence, continued, "All of us in my house felt better when we heard your reports. We said, *ah* there's a capable sort. She! She will get to the bottom of this! Quite shocking about the Nocturne though." He stopped and held her gaze.

Sophia could only muster a shy smile, and with a quick grin Eamon continued. "Yea, Nocturnes are a cruel mistress. Little vampires they are. I know that is not what killed Lady Aliana, but still … Ah well, those with wealth are always doing the strangest things. Sure, she seemed a good sort, but one can't help but wonder if she forgot what was truly important. Yes?" Master Eamon beamed at her as his eyebrows slightly raised in question.

Her nerves trembled as she forced out a meek response, "Um, yes."

His toothy smile turned to a knowing grin, and he spoke once more, "Yes indeed! Beauty is grand …" he cocked his head towards her like he was using his eye to point at her. Sophia felt passionate heat radiate from her cheeks, but Eamon continued unabashed, "…but what about beauty mixed in with knowledge and good deeds? Now there is where I think you and I lie. Neither of us grew up in the excess of the Upper Bowl. You may not have needed to fight for *every* scrap of food, like myself, but you did have to make your own way. So, we know."

Master Eamon Salferesis clasped his hands behind his back, exposing the tunic that covered his midriff. She couldn't help but glance. She saw that it too was adorned with ornate trim, albeit this was silver and platinum in color. She realized that he had stopped speaking and curiosity drove her to ask, "What do we know Master Eamon?"

"Well, that's simple!" He tutted sarcastically. "Keeper, you disappoint me. We know what it is like to struggle. To become something greater than ourselves. To achieve! And thus, we strive for greatness. You in the manner that you address your work. I might have said it already but *fine work* on Lady Aliana's murder by the way. While *I* strive for greatness here on the floor of the Chosen's Hall and out there in the trade of nations!"

His words were intoxicating; her emotions overwhelmed and giddy. Sure, she wasn't keeping up with every nuance of this man's speech, but she didn't mind. It was like she indulged in a play put on just for her. Still, she had to maintain her humility. "I, well, I haven't solved Lady Aliana's murder. I would hardly say good work yet, Master Eamon."

"Please, just call me Eamon," he smiled and shuffled a step closer. He placed a large hand on her shoulder, and the smell of cinnamon and Epidus blossom, that rare yellow flower that carried an earthy musk to it, hit her.

A pang of guilt stabbed at her, as another flush graced her cheeks. Keeper Gilbert would not enjoy this interaction. She swallowed, chewing her lip as she wrestled with strong emotion. *Yeah, Gilbert wouldn't like this exchange, but he wasn't here. What's wrong with a little flirtation?* With a shy smile, she replied, "Very well, *Eamon*. You can call me—"

"Sophia! I know, I already know. Anyone of intelligence knows of Keeper Sophia. You handled Dolocius, that malign god, and won! Few can say that, Keeper." Master Eamon interrupted and pulled his hand away so as to use it in his expressive body language.

Her shoulder almost tingled at the absence. "That's … very kind of you, Eamon. Still, I wish I could have remained in Elgion with my sisters."

"Hmm, I understand. Family *is* everything. That little hiccup with Ember won't hold you back for long."

Sophia was shocked he knew the details of her departure.

A seemingly obvious emotion, for Eamon let out a hearty bark of laughter, speaking loudly over his own levity, "What? You didn't think I knew? I am Master Eamon Salferesis, and it is my job to know things!" Eamon patted at the air. "Don't worry, don't worry. No judgements here and I don't plan on using that knowledge against you … yet." He winked as he said the last.

With a hint of mischief in her voice, she replied, "Well, even if you did, I believe the damage done and not much could be gained from a lowly Keeper like myself."

"Lowly? *Lowly!?* You mustn't talk so! You are Sophia, Keeper of the Stones and destroyer of devils!"

It was impossible not to grin like a beaming fool at the over-the-top compliment, and her cheeks hurt at the strain of her muscles. It had been a while since she felt so *alive.*

"That's more like it! Anyways, do not fret overmuch. In time it will pass, and you will achieve great things and go wherever you wish, Elgion included. *But!* I did not wish to just praise you. Although the praise is well earned. I simply wished to speak to you, no requests no ulterior motives just a desire to become *closer.* To become friends." Eamon leaned in, "Would you like that?"

Sophia's heart thudded; her face afire. "Yes. Yes, I would."

He drew back and, with a smile to light up the night, clapped his hands together. "Great! Well, I must be going. Lots to do, lots to do. *But* you are always welcome at my estate. I may have grown up in poverty, but I believe I have earned *some* comforts." He raised his eyebrows in quick succession, causing a small giggle to erupt. Eamon carried on relentlessly, "I live on the western edge of the Upper Bowl near the inner wall. There is a large marble lion adorning my gate, you can't miss it! Do come and visit, and who knows, I may come calling for yourself at the Bastion. Although I enjoyed you coming to see me perform, we *must* find a less droll venue the next time."

His words ran like honey over freshly baked bread. Truly, she was enthralled and found herself giggling as she offered a short reply, "Yes, we must."

"Alright then, have a good day, Keeper." He suddenly clapped her on the shoulder, "Sorry, Sophia. I near forgot we are friends now!"

She giggled once again as he smiled and winked at her. He walked away; his confident stride taking him towards a group of three heavily armed guards and a man in a purple waistcoat. *His aide and some former Warriors of August by the looks of them*, Sophia reckoned. Together the five strode out of the Chosen's Hall and into the forum below. Sophia immediately heard Eamon's booming voice yell out a greeting to some other lucky individual.

She stood there for a time, giddy from the riveting conversation. She wondered what he meant, for the word friends could mean a lot of things. His smile was intoxicating, and she allowed her fancies to stroll around the upper bounds.

"Keeper? We must close the hall."

Sophia started at the strange voice and turned to see a thin man standing there. His poise was immaculate.

"Ah, yes. I am sorry, sir." Sophia replied.

The man simply smiled and with a gentle gesture motioned towards the nearest exit. Sophia walked out of one of the two double door exits of the hall, swimming in the conversation she had just had with Master Eamon.

Chapter Eleven

Sophia

"A little jealous, are we?" Sophia asked jokingly.

"No! I'm just saying that the man is a little *suspicious* is all." Keeper Gilbert replied.

Sophia could see the truth written on his face. His dark eyebrows furrowed in consternation while his slightly crooked nose wrinkled in anger. She had never asked how he had broken it, but now, as the shadows of the candlelight danced around its large curves, she had never been more curious.

Sensing her gaze upon him, he felt the need to elaborate, "I'm not jealous!"

"Of course, of course," Sophia mocked.

He looked up suddenly and slammed the last book he had been carrying on top of a little stack he had made. Sophia could see a hint of anger flash in his eyes, but as he recognized her smile his own features softened. "That's not fair."

She chuckled, "What's not fair?"

He grabbed the stack and swung towards the rows behind him. All around were shelves upon shelves, containing thousands of books. Even amidst the vaulted ceiling, the library sometimes felt small and cramped. A tapestry of stories, tomes, and aspirations interwoven amidst a multitude of bookcases; sturdy constructions wrought from expensive, Lucidican oak. Ladders that reached four meters high were scattered about, allowing those hungry for knowledge or an escape to reach the top shelves for that *perfect* find. Like so many times before, Sophia realized that here in the library of the Keeper's Bastion, nearly any book written in Telaea, at least by human hands, could be found.

Over his shoulder, Gilbert replied in a pouting but playful manner, "You are making me jealous."

"Only if to see you pout!" Sophia shouted as he disappeared into the nearest row of shelves. Fortunately, the two Keepers had the library's reading area to themselves, otherwise such conversation would be met with harsh glares and, if not ceased, the dreaded shushing. She still remembered the first time he had nervously approached her. His fumbling attempt was met with a dramatic shush from a nearby Keeper. It was, after all, a place for knowledge and contemplation, not flirtation.

Still, the two had made it so, and within that space that consisted of twelve large tables, a stone fireplace, and many—*many*—bookcases, her and Gilbert conducted an awkward dance over several months. The first time she saw him, he appeared so small over the plethora of parchment that surrounded him. Under the light from the sky dome above and the candlelight that flickered from the tables below, he had not struck an impressive figure. Yet, with each new encounter she became more and more curious.

Over a course of months, the two became closer with each rendezvous in the library. Small actions, like setting up at a table closer to one another or simply muttering, "Good day," formed the basis of their clumsy flirtations. The excuse to 'meditate' or 'research' in the library became a sort of truth over the months, and now Sophia found herself there more and more often; for love and for the treasure-trove of knowledge held within. She wasn't complaining, it *was* a beautiful space after all. The primary proponent of that beauty being the sky dome above; exorbitantly expensive Xeelander glass cut into curved patterns, allowed for sunlight to fall through.

Although the library's domed and arched combination roof stood tall enough to avoid the shade of surrounding structures, the design of the dome never allowed the full rays of the sun make it through. Instead, a pool of light would refract off into the recesses of the ceiling, mimicking a large but rather weak lamplight. Regardless of its intensity, it was enough to see your surroundings whenever the sun was out, but never enough to read from. Thus, the Keeper's Bastion, in their demand for candle wax, kept not only their own beehives happily productive but also those apiaries of the surrounding farmlands.

"Still, I wonder what he meant, what *thing* had Lady Aliana forgotten that was 'truly important'," Gilbert interrupted her thoughts.

Gilbert spoke of her conversation with Master Eamon, particularly the remarks on the now dead lady. She replied, "Honestly, I wonder about that myself."

"It seemed like he knew *a lot* about you."

"Yes, I am sure he is preparing for our first date," Sophia teased with a wink. Gilbert furrowed his brows playfully, but, before he could talk, Sophia spoke over her own, light laughter, "It was also a little *disconcerting* that he knew about the Nocturne. Reports, like the one I did for this murder investigation, would be reserved for those that *need* to know. Yes, any commoner would know some of the gruesome details of the murder, but that Nocturne … that was reserved knowledge."

Gilbert nodded like he already knew Eamon's gambit, and Sophia felt a tinge of anger swell within. *Was Gilbert allowing some emotion to guide his judgements?* It was innocent enough for now but dangerous if allowed to grow. She mastered herself and spoke, "I don't know, maybe he *needed* to know."

"Maybe …" Gilbert replied distantly as he opened a new book he had retrieved. "Let's see if *Rykker's Bestiary* has anything shall we?"

"You are not going to find anything of use in there," Sophia replied as she heard the name of the book. It was a fantastical work riddled with wild assumptions and shaky suppositions. When Gilbert only made a light harumph sound but continued to read from the tome, Sophia asked, "What are you looking for?"

"Knowledge on Nocturnes of course! Wouldn't want you turning into a vampire. Would make for a *nasty* surprise."

Sophia felt her heart quicken at the response. *He looked for knowledge for her.* It was rather charming, but there was little time to wile away in a realm of charms. She stood and walked around the table to him. "You would find more from *Keeper's Stones and Living Things*."

He nodded, "I know, but it sometimes helps to get wide perspectives. After all, legends and myths sometimes come true. Rykker here is a master of myths!"

She stopped just centimeters from him, and she could see him swallow nervously. With a smile she reached out a hand and cupped his cheek in her palm, "Thank you, that is … sweet."

Gilbert reached up, grabbing her wrist, "I just am worried is all. Studying what scares me helps me survive."

She couldn't help but look into his eyes then; time becoming more of a suggestion than an interminable march. *Not now, they had more to do.* Almost at a whisper, she spoke, "I have to see Chalepos."

Gilbert replied with much more volume, "That ol' fool? He may be the leader of the Bastion, but why couldn't you have had someone like Senior Keeper Matthias?"

Sophia let her hand fall to her side and pursed her lips. Both were aware of the tense relationship that Sophia had with the Grand Keeper, and both were aware how blissful it would be to share wardens. Alas, that was not the case, and so Sophia filled the silence that was starting to grow, "I wonder that myself. Still, I need to ask him for something, and I cannot imagine it going well. It never does with him."

"One day he will see what I see. What we all see. Just … just give it time." Gilbert said reassuringly, his dark brown eyes full of empathy.

The words were like water to a parched throat, and she felt her heart swell. Surprising even herself, she suddenly wrapped the young man in her arms and squeezed. "Thank you, Gilbert," She whispered.

"Oh, oh my. Uh, I mean it though," Gilbert's muffled voice consoled her.

"I know, I know you do. But I must go," They pulled away from one another and she bit her lip, wondering if she—

He lanced forward, grabbing her cheek in his hand, and kissed her deeply. All thought disappeared and she surrendered to the whims of passion. Time seemed to surrender; unhurried and blissful. Slowly, he broke away and looked into her eyes. His own eyes cast in glistening compassion. "I understand, same time tomorrow?"

She laughed, not quite sure how to respond to the—once again—surprising young Keeper. She composed herself, tucking an errant lock of her red hair back into place. "Sure," she managed to say and with a shy smile she turned towards the exit.

Two massive wooden doors set in a stone arch led to the outdoor courtyard of the Bastion. She pushed one door open just enough to give her passage through. Instantly, a warmth that had been absent within the library embraced her. It was the end of spring, and the days became warmer and warmer with each passing sunrise, a truth that felt delicious on what little of her skin was exposed. The massive stone space of the library had never been a warm area, and many Keepers would hide within it when the summer heat became too much. Yet, in the colder months, even with the fireplace roaring, there was a permanent chill in the room. Sure, it was good for the preservation of the books within, but it was debatable whether the permanent coolness of the space was intentional or just a fallacy in the design.

She moved towards the courtyard, stepping upon the first of the large stone slabs that had been painstakingly carved to a smooth surface. The beauty of their design became rather dangerous whenever a small skim of ice or snow graced them. Surely, those in the tower would have a grand time as they watched hapless novices crossing the icebound stones. She couldn't think of another reason for such a foolish building choice. After all, she had nearly cracked her own skull open the first time she tried to hurry over them in winter. She could hear it now, Grand Keeper Chalepos alongside Senior Keeper Ramsey guffawing in their uptight manner.

The imagined insult made her glance up to the looming tower. It had taken her breath away when she first looked upon it, and even now she felt a catch in her throat. Hawks circled around the forty-one-meter-tall tower. They nested in the tower's eaves and crevices, unaware, or uncaring of the humans that inhabited the nine separate stories held within. Truly, it was a marvel in engineering, and Sophia could find little fault in its design.

After all, the whole complex had been designed by their founder, Grand Keeper Erica. Her statue, a bronze coated hunk of marble that stood upon a raised marble platform in the center of the compound. At Erica's feet lay small flower beds holding lilies, tulips, hyacinths, and even Epidus Blossom of varying shades and hues. The flower beds were atop 'arms' that pointed in each cardinal direction. The library to the west, the gates of the bastion to the south, the quarters and other living accoutrements to the east, and the tower, looming over it all, to the north.

Within the shadow of such grandeur, Sophia wondered if the legends were true. Whether an avatar of Olkanestus, the god of craftsmen, and Grand Keeper Erica sat around a campfire and planned the city that lay before them. The thought of a god in the flesh, whether avatar or not, made her chuckle. An odd juxtaposition since she *had* talked to the gods, but it was like talking to someone through a mirror, a reflection of a thought not a genuine entity. In the years of humanity's rise, never had the gods been made flesh. No, those supernatural beings were dead, and all that was left were their echoes.

For Sophia, the success of Augustia was attributed to the rare intelligence of Grand Keeper Erica. Sure, the Keeper may have invoked the power of the stones, but it was *her* hands that did the work. Forming the concrete of the structures into designs that would stand the test of time. Not just any concrete, but a type that—unlike the earlier designs from the Xetem empire— held strong over decades or even centuries. The supposed trick was in the stone they used in the aggregate, and to the west, along the coast, massive concrete works fronted limestone quarries. The bounty of which, when mixed with sand, water, and ash produced an immensely strong and resilient building material. Maybe it was a combination of things then. One part genius builder; another fortunate geography.

Whatever the case, she had a mission and thus she turned north towards the tower. Towards Grand Keeper Chalepos and the unlikely possibility he would grant permission to investigate the Broken Stallion Inn. The location of her last and only clue to Lady Aliana's murder. Unfortunately, Grand Keeper Chalepos never gave anything lightly. Still, she had to ask.

Chapter Twelve

Sophia

With the same resolve she had used to face down Dolocius, that god of deceit, Sophia entered the tower. She was greeted by an open planned lobby, where Monique, a pleasant Keeper, sat behind a desk.

"Hey, Sophia! What brings you here today?" A bubbly voice greeted her.

"Hi, Monique. Hope all is well," Sophia said with a matched giddiness.

"Oh, it is. It is. I just about solved this puzzle," With clasped hands, Monique gestured to the puzzle in question. It was just one of many the steward of the Keepers would spend her time on. Of course, Sophia couldn't see it from behind the desk, but still she could imagine the small pieces of wood in their jigsaw pattern scattered about the workspace.

"Ooooh, that sounds fun!' Sophia responded.

"Truly, it is. So, I know you didn't come here just to see me. Although you are welcome to it. What can I do ya for?"

Sophia's smile dropped as she thought of the task ahead. "I need to see Grand Keeper Chalepos."

Monique stood quickly, her girth not hindering her body from matching her enthusiasm. The portly woman, drenched in the woolen robes of their order and clinking with stones, made her way to the locked door that would allow Sophia access to the staircase. There was no need for a guard, for although Monique was an exceptionally pleasant individual, she had a particular knack for the icy gifts Melleas could grant, a rarity since Melleas was well known for being rather *obtuse*. The warped wood beneath their feet evidence of the few occasions which Monique had curried the fickle gods favor.

"Well, he is in a rare sort today. Best if you keep whatever you got to say … brief." Monique said as she unlocked the door and pulled it open.

"When is he not in a rare sort?"

Monique chuckled lightly, "Best of luck, Sophia." With a wink, the bubbly woman closed the door, and Sophia was engulfed in the gloom of the stairwell.

Only the sparse light from small windows lit her way. She sighed and pulled up the hem of her robes, a necessity for the arduous climb up the marble stairs. Sconces with candles lined the walls, serving as a remedy to nightfall. As she stepped up the stairs with as much grace as she could muster, she sighed to herself, *Of course, Chalepos would be on the seventh floor.*

The bastard enjoyed making those who called upon him suffer the climb. It was an irritating request, seeing she just passed the second floor, a level specifically designed for those who wished to meet with either the four Senior Keepers, the Grand Keeper, or all the leadership of Augustia's Bastion.

"Ember's breath," she muttered. The third floor, which stored various odds and ends for the messengers of the gods had a clark's desk that could be used. Still, that did not sway Chalepos from forcing meetings within his quarters. Save for the rare circumstance in which the four Seniors and the Grand Keeper of the Bastion had to convene, the wiry old man would remain in his rooms, studying or experimenting from texts and oddities.

Finally, she dragged her way to the landing of the seventh floor. The sweat on her brow soaked into the heavy cloth of her sleeve, and a wisp of her red hair dangled in front of her eye. She licked her hand to try firm out the rebellious locks. With a heavy sigh, she firmed her robe, causing a jingle sound to emanate from the stones within. She brought her hand to her Embershard amulet and sent a small prayer to the dragon god, the leader of all the others. *They would know how to handle Chalepos*, she mused.

Since she was *not* the dragon god, she resorted to simply knocking heavily on the wooden door. The rapping sound echoed within the hollow chamber of the stairwell. She heard some small movement within, but as was Chalepos's custom, she waited on the landing for what felt like forever. Eventually, she heard the shuffle of his robe as he made his way to the door. The sounds of bars and locks becoming disengaged pierced the quiet of the stairwell, like ghosts being freed from their mooring. The door swung open, and a tall thin man with a wiry mustache—grey as old ashes— stood before her.

"Ah, Sophia." He said in his reedy voice, obvious disdain in the notes as he sized her up.

"Grand Keeper Chalepos, thank you for taking my meeting request," she said politely with no emotion, hoping the Grand Keeper's messenger, one that she had paid, emphasized the importance of her request.

For several seconds, he said nothing, but instead allowed an uncomfortable silence to fall over the two. Without warning, he pushed his way through the door, locking it behind him with a large brass key. "Let's move up to the observation floor, shall we?"

"Certainly, Keeper," Sophia replied formally, and as Chalepos moved up the stairs, she fell in behind. *Even more damn stairs,* she thought with barely contained rage. She bit her tongue knowing her 'punishments' would only get worse with disobedience.

When they reached the final upper landing, he pushed the door open, and they were both greeted by the wash of sunlight. The observation room was the smallest room, a quality that was a necessity due to the design of the tower. Still, it was large enough to hold a large oak table with a map of the known world carved upon it; a commission of immense cost done several years ago and updated at regular intervals. Truly, it was one of the most prized possessions of the Bastion, and, at times, elite individuals ranging from generals to the hallowed regents of The Mandate's Justice would come to view the map, planning for some campaign or stratagem in the interests of Augustia.

Chalepos shuffled past the oak table to stand with his hands clasped behind his back overlooking the view from the northern end of the room. All around them were marble columns that supported the roof of the tower, with a concrete wall ringing the outside. The wall itself held massive windows cut from the clearest glass that could be bought from the artisans of Xeeland. In all directions, one could see out to the distant horizon, and though Sophia was always amazed when looking up at the tower, the view from the top was breathtaking. It wasn't the first time she had been here, in fact one of the first lessons her and other Keepers received was from this very gallery. The concept of Telaea's immensity was much easier to impress from such a vantage point after all.

The tower itself stood atop the bowl of hills that ringed Augustia, those hills dropped steeply to a plain below. Twin rivers, almost equidistantly spaced to the east and west coursed their way between rolling gold green hills as they made their way to the sea. Their design granting them the name, The Arms of Olkanestus, though they were commonly referred to as just The Arms. The sparkle of their blue green waters glittered between thick groves of trees that drank in the natural irrigation of the river. Even from here, Sophia could see flocks of birds darting to and fro over the rich fields that carpeted the gently rolling hills and plains. Massive farmlands had been carved from the rich soil there and it was obvious from that view why some instances of Augustian heraldry held a sheaf of golden wheat within.

With his grating voice, Chalepos suddenly asked, "What do we look upon?"

Sophia furrowed her brows in confusion, sensing a trap in the question. She could not figure out what that trap was, and so replied practically,

"We look upon the northern hills and farms of Augustia watered by the Arms of Olkanestus."

"Yes, that is correct." He turned to her, his expression dour. "What lies beyond our view here?"

She delayed her response, but the inevitability of being made a fool of was impossible to stop. "I don't know. I guess the August Highway; Argent Bay?"

He looked at her and wrinkled his nose in disgust. With a sigh he responded, "Both of those are correct. So, *Keeper*, tell me where either of those leads."

She discovered the trap then but knowing that she would gain nothing by trying to foil it played along. "I suppose the highway leads to Argentios and beyond while the bay can lead to just about anywhere."

A menacing smile crossed his lips. "Once again, correct!" Chalepos turned his gaze back to the horizon. "With that in mind, tell me, who controls Argentios at present?"

"Currently, Argolon holds that honor, Keeper," Sophia replied.

"Once again, you are right!" Suddenly his voice grew hard with irritation, "So, why in Ember's breath would I send a Keeper to this Broken Stallion Inn? A place figuratively in control of Argolon, the very city-state that took the place from us last time?! Do you want to provoke those brutes? Do you want a war on your hands?"

Sophia bowed her head. Of course, he spoke of the Five Points War that saw Argolon victorious over Augustia, Xeeland, and Vidrosia in one of the bloodiest conflicts in recorded history. The only thing holding the peace was how utterly devastating those wars were, death happened in droves and not even the most ambitious wished for a return to the tensions. Yet, memories fade, and the ever-closer borders were beginning to broil in simmering tensions. "No, Keeper," she said, defeat in her voice.

"Of course not! You buffoon. What goes on in that mind of yours? You were once so promising, now you squander your gifts on wild flights of fancy. For shame, Keeper!"

Sophia's embarrassment raged within her, forcing anger to rise in equal measure. She could not hold back without some form of defense. "Sir, these murders are linked and I beli—"

Chalepos shot up a hand, silencing her by its violent abruptness. "Not … another … word. You are lucky to still be wearing that Shard of Ember. Do not tempt me into taking that away! These *murders* are no more than unfortunate circumstances. Now, let that be the end of it!"

She closed her eyes, mastering herself. She thought of her mother and father down the Bowl to hold her heart steady, and she exhaled with some semblance of calm back in her veins. "Yes, Keeper."

"Good! Now, I need these documents copied. In triplicate!" He produced three parchments from within his robes and shoved them towards Sophia.

She grabbed the proffered documents and without another word took her leave, closing the oak door behind her and on the view of Augustia's riches.

Chapter Thirteen

Sophia

Sophia rolled the remains of her biscuit in her palm. Small crumbs dropped from the drying bread and either remained static upon the wooden table in front of her or bounced and bobbed until they fell to the flat stone floor. The broken morsels almost always finding their way into the tiny, grout-filled crevices between each stone. The image brought back warm childhood memories.

"Twenty-six years old and you still play with your food!" Mira Vollimosa barked.

Sophia sighed at the light mannered criticism and put the tattered biscuit down on a small ceramic plate. The rejection from Keeper Chalepos weighed heavily on her and her appetite, even for her mother's own cooking, was virtually absent. "Sorry, mom. I'm just … not hungry is all."

"Well, your friends don't seem to share that problem!" Mira exclaimed but with the tone of a mother content to be feeding those she cared for. Dunkeath, Olivia, Gilbert, and Sophia's father, Skorin, were arrayed around the dining table of Sophia's childhood home. It was a place of warmth and happiness for her, and after such harsh words from her warden, she needed the safety its refuge brought.

Dunkeath looked up from his bowl of peppered cabbage and bacon, gulping down a spoonful. He grinned. "Ah, Misses Vollimosa! I see now why Sophia became a Keeper."

From behind the stone island that she was working upon, Mira looked up at Dunkeath, fixing him with a stern look. She slapped down a ladleful of batter onto a thin iron sheet pan, and with a dramatic gesture rested her wrist onto her hip with the spoon still in hand. "And why is that?"

"Well, it's simple ma'am. Ya see? This here food is blessed by the gods, and if I ate like this every day, I only imagine I'd be blessed muhself." Dunkeath's sarcastic manner made the words flow with ease. Her dad let slip a small chuckle at the comment, and as Sophia glanced at her father, she saw him quickly purse his lips in an attempt to stay neutral in whatever was about to occur. *He always was a bad liar.* Over the years, his manner had remained much the same; save for the new wrinkles that were wrought upon his face. At least they were etched in the way someone accustomed to happiness would have.

Her mom laughed suddenly. "Oh, what a charmer!" she said as she placed the spoon down and grabbed the iron pan; the craftsmanship of which was superb. The cookware reminded Sophia that her parents, while not wealthy enough to live on the hills of the Upper Bowl, were well off enough to afford some of the finer things of life. Mira swiveled to the stone oven behind her and placed the pan in the flat space inside, the biscuit batter glistening in the low firelight.

The smell of the sweet honey wafting into the room made her mouth water as she thought of the treat to come, even with her diminished appetite. Those honey butter biscuits had been her mother's go to for times of happiness and sadness for years. They were a treat made with such care that they became an enhancement for any party, or a balm for the soul in darker times. The thought that her mother had made them specifically now, when Sophia was feeling so dejected, did not escape her.

All these small morsels of her home life—the access to small luxuries, the caring mother, and a father with wrinkles marked in happiness—made her realize how fortunate she was. How fortunate all of them were, for without such capacities, neither she nor her sisters could have pursued their desires. A fact Sophia felt most acutely as she looked at Dunkeath and felt a tug of guilt at her own upbringing in comparison to his. While he had not been poor, she remembered how his father had been stealing flour from Elgion to try and fund their livelihood. The pity soured as he slurped down another spoonful with ill manners.

Gilbert spoke suddenly, his voice seeming timid against the backdrop of Dunkeath's soupy escapades, "This is great misses Vollimosa, thank you." This *outburst* prompted yet another glare from her father, who grunted as he fixed Gilbert with narrowed eyes and obvious disdain. Sophia had to hold back laughter as she watched her special guest bow his head as if he hadn't spoken at all.

"Oh, thank you, dear!" her mother replied, swinging around the stone island and finding her seat. As she sat, she glared at her husband with disapproving eyes.

Her dad, apparently sensing the admonition, slowly inched his head up to meet the cold look. "Yea, it's great!" He said hurriedly before bowing his own head in a mirror of Gilbert's own cowed look.

Mira harumphed audibly and let the icy glare linger for a few seconds before swinging her eyes towards Olivia. "Olivia, how are you liking the new place? It sure is nice having you and Dunkeath so close by. I just wish I could say the same for *my* daughter."

"Mom, we've been over this," Sophia replied as her mom affected an exaggerated eye roll.

Sensing that no more was to be said on the matter, Olivia piped up, "Oh, its grand. Sight better than that ratty place we had before. Although, it still has Dunkeath."

"Hey!" Dunkeath exclaimed over a mouthful of cabbage.

"Well, that's lovely. Nice having a plumbed toilet innit? I remember the first time we could afford a house with plumbing. No more of those stinkin' buckets for me!" Mira exclaimed.

Olivia chuckled, her face warm with happiness. It was a sight that occurred often when she was around Mira; almost as if they had adopted one another. Of course, this was not out of the ordinary for Sophia's mother, who always seemed to take on broken things. Never quite getting her fill whilst working as an apothecarian and healer.

Sophia could recall them on their first meeting, an encounter in which the cause for Olivia's parents' death had come to light. Apparently, they had fallen prey to a fever inducing flu, one that could have been easily prevented by a trip to the free clinic days provided by the Keepers Bastion. Mira had groaned and cursed at the news. She may have been an ardent user and supporter of herbal remedies, but she was the first to admit; sometimes a Keeper's touch was warranted.

Instead, Olivia's parents had refused, believing the medicine provided by Keepers were unnatural. Their stubbornness cost them their lives, and Mira had sensed the utter contempt oozing off Olivia, a scorn born from her parents' stupidity. It was no wonder Sophia's mom had taken an instant liking to the former laundress, who was not only broken, but also rather enthusiastic when hearing about either apothecarial knowledge or the mystical teachings of the Keepers. This bond, at times, seemed stronger than her own with Olivia; sometimes finding the two swapping stories and jokes that Sophia had never heard of. It was hard not to feel a twinge of jealousy, after all, she had fought alongside the woman against towering orcish brutes.

"Yes, it is nice to simply … go. Without the hassle 'dat is," Olivia interrupted Sophia's reflections. The former laundress's brows then furrowed in concentration. "Keeper, do ya have plumbing in the Bastion?"

If it weren't for the earnestness of the question, Sophia would have laughed at the almost childlike wonder in Olivia's voice. "Yes, Olivia, we have toilets."

Apparently unsatisfied with the answer, Olivia muttered, "Oh … good." The curly-haired woman took a small nibble of her table biscuit and abruptly snapped her fingers as if she had just come onto a great idea. Sophia knew this trick; asking an innocuous question and pretending the answer brought your mind to a new revelatory question. With little subtlety, Olivia had used the ruse many times over the last few years. It was effective, if not frustratingly simple. "So, why now can't we go to this inn?"

Thankfully, Gilbert replied in her stead, "Well, Sophia's warden denied the request. And since we can be stripped of our Embershard amulet and thus our rank for disobeying our warden, she cannot go."

Skorin grunted irritably, prompting a nervous glance from Gilbert, making his eyes even wider than before. The table's occupants all awkwardly bent back to their food, not wanting to poke the ire of their host.

"You have something to say?" Mira asked unabashed.

Her dad, drinking the remnants of his meal from the bowl like it was a cup, placed the wooden vessel down gently and with eyes nearly as wide as Gilbert's gulped. His wife did not relent and even cocked her brow towards him. It made her look even more menacing than Sophia thought possible. Her father was doomed, and Sophia knew he would not escape this prod.

Skorin sighed and mumbled, "What's the right thing to do?"

She was taken aback by the question. One he had asked before when indecision plagued any of his daughters. Her shock only allowed her a meek reply. "Uh, what?"

Her dad sat up straighter, taking on an authoritative air that normally lay dormant. "I said, what is the right thing to do?"

Dunkeath offered, "Well, we—"

Skorin's hands shot up, silencing Dunkeath. With blue eyes, her father bore into Sophia. Now *he* would not relent.

Sophia took a deep breath, knowing what he meant. "It would be to go and investigate the murders. It's our only clue and those people deserve justice."

Her dad nodded, turned to look at Mira—who also nodded—and then gave Gilbert an angry glance for good measure. *What a chain of support,*

Sophia thought with bemusement before adding, "Still, if I go, I will most definitely *lose* everything."

"Well, it's simple 'den isn't it?" Dunkeath asked rhetorically. "Why don't me and Olivia go and look for you? We may be in your employ but we ain't tied to the Bastion. 'Sides we could make it look like we were on holiday or something."

She leaned back in her chair, clasping her chin in thought. That could work, but she worried what they would find there. Whoever was responsible was well versed in the power of the stones, and there was a good chance the killers employed a Keeper themselves. Also, if Keeper Chalepos's fears of provoking Argolon were true, then that Keeper could be trained professionally. A grim prospect, even more so than facing some hopped-up whisperer, those unsanctioned, god-talking mercenaries.

As if answering Sophia's request, Gilbert spoke with unexpected confidence, "I can go as well. Keeper Chalepos is not my warden and besides, I have family on the northern farms. I am owed a holiday."

Dunkeath grinned. "There ya go! Now we only needs to lie *just slightly* about our leaving and all."

Gilbert must have been overwhelmed by the intensity of his proclamation, because Sophia watched his face go red. Her heart trembled at the gesture, and she wanted to scoop him up in her embrace. Unfortunately, she was in her father's home and his overprotective nature may not approve of such an action. She decided to save that embrace until after dinner. However, Skorin did look upon the young man, and this time his gaze was slightly less disdainful. With intense will, Gilbert, obviously overcoming frayed nerves, returned the look. In compensation, he received a slight nod. The smallest of gestures, but huge in its importance. Not able to bear it any longer, Gilbert bowed his head once more, awkwardly swirling his spoon in his barely touched soup. *He had earned some favor there*, she mused.

The idea quickly flourished within her; it did address her concerns, while solving the very real issue of 'the right thing' her dad had presented. "That could work, but you three will need to be discreet. Keeper Chalepos is right, we *could* provoke Argolon with a sanctioned mission to the inn. It is *putatively* in their control, after all. So, you will have to make it look like you are simple travelers. Merchants or the like."

The gathered company all pondered the quandary for a few moments, before Skorin offered. "I have some letters that need to make their way to some of my colleagues in Xeeland. You could take those to the inn and have them delivered to Argentios. If they don't make it, it's not a big worry, but I know that the couriers stop there at The Broken Stallion. Half the reason the place exists." Skorin's voice had taken on the lighter tone he adopted when speaking of his work. For years he had been sort of an ill-defined professional, working primarily as a tutor for wealthy sons and daughters. Yet, he also had taken advisory roles with many of the Chosen's Wisdom and had even assisted in the drafting of some decrees straight from the Mandated. Whenever asked, Sophia's father would simply state he was a scholar, but she knew there was more to it than that.

"Gilbert," Sophia said and as he glanced up at her, she froze. She didn't expect the intensity of Gilbert's eyes to be so *entrancing*.

Seconds passed in awkward silence around the table until Skorin grunted irritably.

She cleared her throat in embarrassment, "You, um, you will have to hide your Keeper's vestments. Take your Embershard amulet with you but hide it. They cannot know you went on my behalf. They would disband you from the order."

"I know," he said reassuringly. "I'll be fine, besides Keeper Matthias owes me a vacation. So, I can't imagine him denying it; meanwhile we *know* that Chalepos would strip you of your amulet if you tried to leave. Don't worry." Gilbert allowed a small sideways smile creep up his face at the risk of Skorin's ire.

Mira giggled, and before Skorin could become more enraged, spoke, "Well, it's settled then! Looks like I will be needing to give you guys some food for your journey." Mira stood abruptly. "Let's start with some of my honey butter biscuits." It was as if she had timed the baking to coincide with the conversation, and with practiced grace, fished the iron pan out of the oven. Mira drizzled honey on the golden-brown tops of the biscuits, and the whole of the table watched with hungry eyes. With a beaming smile, she hand-delivered a biscuit to each of the table's occupants, and Sophia blew on her still cooling treat, eager to bite in.

Dunkeath didn't have the patience, and he desperately blew around the bite he had taken with steam pouring from his mouth.

"Patience, ya fool, you literally watched me pull it out the oven!" her mom said.

Over the pain of his scalded mouth, Dunkeath replied, "Blessed ma'am. Truly blessed."

The table, even Skorin, burst into laughter at the exchange. Then with joy in their hearts, they all eagerly dove into their own biscuits, speaking excitedly between delicious mouthfuls. Sophia savored her first bite and, for a time, forgot about the worries of her day.

Chapter Fourteen

Dunkeath

Dunkeath shifted his sore buttocks in the saddle, his back stiff from three hard days of riding. Olivia or himself had ordered stops to eat or sleep only when it had become too dark; pressing on until the edge of night in the necessity of urgency. The new boy, or Keeper—or whatever—must have agreed because although he spoke little, he did not complain about the brutal pace. Dunkeath was glad, because the oddity of growing up not far from here had put him on edge. The memories of the past welling up inside, and fragments of those long-gone days flickered within his mind's eye; even the day his father had taken them to Elgion—across the sea.

He remembered it as a terribly boring place. Of course, it was pretty and all; with rolling green and gold hills filled with bounteous wheat, barley, and rye. There were even immaculate orchards of apple, pear, and walnut trees that clung to the banks of The Arms. Sure, those groves only ever found themselves on the lands of the rich sops that built oversized homes, but it was all quite majestic—all quite quaint. Looking back at the places of his past, he figured his memory served quite well.

Still, it had been a backbreaking lifestyle that only ever rewarded you with barely enough food to fill your belly. He was glad to be away from it, either here or back in Elgion. It still was funny to think of his new boss, Sophia, and her utter astonishment when he said he would accompany her back to The August City. That had happened right after she had been ordered back there, evidently, to be stripped of her senior rank; punishment for the wee fireball she had hurled at him. It was a shame really; she deserved better than that. So, when he had offered his services to her, he didn't think it would be all that surprising.

What did she expect? They had fought together, they had nearly died together, and when she had ignited the power of a god in front of him, he knew Sophia was someone to follow. Someone that would take him from his boring meagre life as a miller or as a farmer; someone to show him the mysteries and magic his mother told him and his brothers in her better moments.

Although this new life contained a lot of time dealing with endless parchments, scrolls, books, missives, and other nameless documents, it *had* been far more exciting. Never in a thousand years would he imagine himself investigating a double murder as a miller's son, now here he was tracking down clues for just such an act. *The price to entry?* Dunkeath mused, *The scar on his shoulder.* A charred mess that, although he could use with little impediment, pulsed with chronic pain; a wound he would bear for life. Some people wondered if he regretted working for her, but Keeper or not, she had proven herself to be a person of high quality. Besides, he had been an ass the day she called Ember down on him. Now, he prayed to that god of gods every day for he knew how much that bastard could hurt.

So, when the problem of investigating the inn came into discussion, he took on the duty without a second thought. They had set out the next morning, provisioned heartily by Sophia's mother, Mira. That tall, powerfully built woman made him smile in memory. Jokingly, he wondered to himself what it would be like to be Skorin, Sophia's father. *I bet she drizzles honey on more than just travel biscuits …*

He chuckled to himself, of course, he would never know. A woman like that only drizzled her honey on one fella, and it weren't him. Then he shut his eyes to try and escape the steadily more vivid image of the two elderly people covered in honey out of his mind.

When he had managed to tuck the wicked wonderings away, he resolved he would be content with teasing the ol' battle axe. Something he suspected she secretly enjoyed.

And that enjoyment saw them well stocked to set out north and west along the August Highway. Now, three days in on their journey, they trotted into a late afternoon sun sore as Magdris's Teeth. Luckily, as recollection and the words of a kind farmer along the road would have it, they were only a few kilometers away from their goal. It had been a brutal pace and a trip that would normally take five days had been done in three.

That speed had been made possible by Mira's delicious provisions and the effective use of quick rest stops for their horses. Packs full of delicious honey biscuits as well as some cabbage, dried meat, and healthy portions of peppermint to chew on for a refreshing burst of energy, alongside oats and clear well water for their mounts. With food and drink not an issue, Dunkeath had reveled in the hard ride and, admittedly, had enjoyed sitting atop a horse as he passed farmers and millers that reminded him of his old life. They had looked upon him as if he were something more, something greater, and he had struggled not to grin at every one of them as they passed by.

One, a voluptuous farmer's girl, had trotted to the side of the road to see the strangers near her land, to feel the excitement. She had stared at him from beneath a bonnet, locks of blonde hair cascading down her face. Whether her cheeks were flushed from her exertions, or her *desires* was difficult to tell, because she had stared at Dunkeath as if he were the only man she had ever seen. His mouth still hurt from the stupidly wide smile he had beamed at her. Not for the first time since he saw her, he cursed himself for not stopping to chat with the buxom woman. *Maybe she would be there on their way back.*

The pleasant and somewhat torturous thought pulled his attention back to the company and he twisted in his saddle to look at Olivia. There too he felt the bite of desire, one not as raw and straightforward as the roadside farmer's girl, but something deeper, more in tune with his very self. He couldn't understand it, and at times he didn't want to. Sometimes he just let his mind run rampant over the emotion, and, looking upon her now, he knew this was one of those times.

Olivia, although coming from the same frontier life as Dunkeath, had only ever lived within the confines of human settlements, and this countryside trip produced a persistent awed expression on her full red lips. Her short and somewhat pudgy frame gripped the saddle well and he watched for a moment as her brown locks, fashioned into a curly bob, bounced upon her head. He wondered if this would be one of those drunken nights in which they would become more *familiar*. A luxury she allowed only when she weren't sober. It was a strange relationship, and now that they lived together in the same home—without others—he dreamed of where it would lead.

"What you lookin' at?" Olivia asked in irritation.

He cursed inwardly, knowing he had been staring too long. "Not sure … But I wonders if that horse ya ride is a cousin of yours. Face looks similar." Dunkeath heard a shocked gasp from Gilbert. The man had been riding with them for three days. *When would he realize that this was how they were?* That they teased one another constantly. Someone had to, for most of the people he was around took life *far* too seriously.

Olivia narrowed her eyes at Dunkeath, "Aye, well from where I am sitting, I sometimes get confused."

"Yea, that's common enough wit' ya." Dunkeath interjected quickly.

Olivia pressed on undeterred, "I gets confused because I don't know where to look when I am speaking to ya. Is it da horse's ass or is it coming from the even uglier thing on top? Both sound and smell the same."

Clever, Dunkeath allowed as he smiled at the retort. Gilbert, the buffoon he was, laughed as if he had never heard a joke before. Unfortunately for the rather naive Keeper, the former laundress was having none of it, and turned to Gilbert with the same stern expression, "Oh, hush ya fidgety lout. You ain't much a sight better. Don't know what the Keeper sees in ya."

Gilbert's face turned bright red. The odd colors clashing with the orange glow of the setting sun, especially since much of his skin was now laid bare. They had given him a cloak along with a simple tunic and breeches, but it still failed to hide the starkness of his flesh. Hopefully, no one would take a keen interest in the Keeper. A sharp mind would quickly sus out he weren't a courier; that job belonged to people who had gotten lots of sun. Dunkeath sighed and knew there was little they could do about that now. Instead, he wondered at the common sight of flushed embarrassment upon the man. *Did he have any courage at all? Did Sophia see something in him they didn't?*

"We-well, I do—" Gilbert started to protest.

"Oh, hush man. She's only teasing."

"I know I—"

Dunkeath pressed on over his stuttering reply, "It's alright lad. Don't put no stock in the words. It's just a game. One you fancy folk never understood. Keeps ya humble it does."

"Well, it hasn't worked on you. 'Course I don't know if anything gets into that thick skull of yours." Olivia teased expertly.

Dunkeath laughed. "Ya see? *Completely* untrue but she says it anyways to show me she cares. Don't want me getting too big for muhself ya see?"

Olivia snorted in exasperation, but he noticed the beginnings of a smile creasing her cheeks into dimples.

She loved the game just like him. With a wink at her, he turned to look back at Gilbert, who sat his horse rather dumbfounded. Dunkeath had to ask, "This whole time we been jibing one another, and you haven't picked up on the fact it's a game?"

"I have …" Gilbert replied sheepishly.

"Right, so stop leaving your jaw so slack every time we play and be glad you gots included. It means we accept ya. If it were all, *please* and *thank you* then ya should be worried. Understand?"

"Oh, um, ok. I-I think so," Gilbert said with furrowed brows, obviously thinking hard because his gaze was locked onto the mane of his horse. Satisfied with his lesson being understood, Dunkeath twisted forward once more. Yet, just as he was settling in for the final leg of the journey, Gilbert blurted out, "I believe I met your mother once, Dunkeath."

Curiosity forced him to turn back to the Keeper, and with more confidence than Dunkeath was accustomed to, Gilbert looked up from the saddle, grinning at him. Suspicion grew within, but Dunkeath couldn't help but ask, "Oh yea?"

"Yeah, she came down from The Spine, all anger and fury, a *lot* of hair too."

Olivia snickered, and Dunkeath narrowed his eyes, knowing he was now the target for this fool's first attempt at the game. With gritted teeth, he allowed the farce to continue, "Oh really?"

"Yea, ya see they called me in after a troll tore up a village, and well when I got there, she was frothing at the mouth, all savage and *hair*. I mean …" Gilbert swallowed, the first sign of nerves slowing his progress. Still, the man pressed on; resolute. "I see the resemblance now." Gilbert looked him up and down in an exaggerated manner. "I can't believe I didn't remember it until now! Do send my regards the next time ya meet."

Olivia burst into laughter, reveling in the clumsy but successful tease. Between fits of giggles she added, "Bet they smelled the same too!"

Gilbert, thoroughly pleased with himself, flashed his teeth and like he was an old hand at the game, sniffed the air loudly. After a few snorts he looked at Dunkeath, waved his hand as if he stunk, and stated sarcastically, "Ya got that right!"

Olivia nearly fell out of the saddle as she vibrated from laughter. Apparently, he had underestimated the fidgety Keeper and regretted ever explaining to him. "Ah, that's a good one alright. I mean to be fair to dear 'ol mum she was just trying to escape the incessant braying of yer own mother. Those Caprix never know when to shut up." He paused to see the effect at his own rebuttal but was sorely disappointed when it fell flat. Any chance at recompense was gone now, drowned out by raucous laughter.

Gilbert, glowing in his triumph, was oblivious to Dunkeath's words and Olivia was struggling to stay in the saddle over her bouts of laughter. A spike of anger, and—oddly enough—jealousy swelled in him. The sight of Olivia so pleased at the Keeper's barb did not sit well with him, and not wanting to endure the feeling any longer he clicked his cheek, digging his heels into his mount.

*

The Broken Stallion Inn sat atop a small hill. Rich green grass wove itself between stands of knotty pines and slender poplars. Thick green leaves flashed their grey undersides as they danced in the sea breeze. A pleasant salt-kissed wind swept down from the Bay of Silver—still kilometers away. The ballet of nature, with its flashing colors, looked like small silver scales in the late afternoon sun. Dunkeath was reminded of the fat trout that swam the Farney River back in Elgion, and he smiled wryly at the display. This innkeeper must have been mighty smart to plant these poplars; their silver looking leaves would be like a beacon to travelers already heading to Argentios. That city of silver setting their minds to riches so that any hint of the precious metal would be an irresistible lure.

And, like all hoards of riches, this inn was protected. The grey and green leaves were hiding behind a palisade that ringed the hill, forcing any would be attackers to fight uphill. From above the gate, Dunkeath could see the flash of a spearpoint, and from a tower that lorded over it all, he could make out two figures peering into the lands around. It was no surprise such an establishment—though it was only a day's ride from Argentios—had developed such defenses. Bandits and the more sentient beasts, like the hideous troll, were known to raid homesteads for their riches or food, and an inn, no matter how popular it was, was *not* immune to such raids.

Dunkeath could see several carts and horses stabled for the night around the inn, showing this place was a frequently used establishment. The number of guests surely lent a hand in warding off attacks; an indirect defense of the most effective kind—prevention. No matter how crowded it was, Dunkeath was glad to finally see the place; this goal of theirs. His heart quickened knowing warm food and cold beer were moments away.

"State your business stranger," A cheery guard called out from the top of the palisade.

Dunkeath looked up, having to guard his eyes against the setting sun that lay to his right. "We're jus' travelers, sir. Headin' to Argentios." Dunkeath jerked his hand backwards and pointed a thumb towards Gilbert. "This one here got a message to deliver as well." Remembering his Keeper companion looked like he barely spent time outdoors, Dunkeath quickly added, "He's new to 'dis line of work and I'll be glad to stop smelling his stench for a minute."

The guard barked out a laugh. "Aye, the travels of the road make us all smell like toads!" The cheery guard paused, letting the rhyme, which he seemed accustomed to, hang in the air.

Does he want us to laugh at that? Dunkeath wondered.

When there was nothing but silence, the man continued, "Alright, you can come in, but we will need to search you here. No weapons allowed in the premises, but as right as rain I will give them back to you. When you leave of course. On my honor."

It was a common enough request, and the company dismounted as the wooden gate was disbarred and three guards dressed in mail and plate in the typical Argolonian fashion stepped out. Two of them held menacing clubs, while the other approached them to conduct the search. Dunkeath could see they all had a shield strapped to their back, and the two that held the clubs also had wicked-looking short swords at their hips. *No javelins on these fellas … not exactly good fare for guard duty at an inn I suppose,* Dunkeath noted to himself.

Their dour expressions were in stark contrast to the cheery guardsmen that had greeted them. Once again, this innkeeper showed their smarts by hiring such fearsome gate guards countered by a happy-go-lucky greeter. It was the cherry-on-top, reminding Dunkeath this was a business, and the innkeeper probably learned that nothing but swords and grim expressions could turn away even the most desperate customers.

The searching guard pushed Dunkeath's arms up and away from his body and ran his hands over him efficiently. The guard was used to such a motion, and carried it out with deft grace; quickly finding the long dagger at his hip and the shorter knife he kept in his boot. Satisfied Dunkeath held no more weapons, he swatted his shoulder. With speed the man crossed to Olivia; likewise pushing her arms up and away in the practiced manner of one who has done this for a *long* time.

"Oh, yer quite the charmer, ain't ya?" Olivia said as the man reached behind her, the action making him look like he went for a hug.

He paused and stared up at her for a moment.

Olivia smiled sarcastically and with a cheerful tone said, "Though I'd recommend a bit of mint." She bent her head closer to him and speaking just as loudly as before made her voice sound like she was attempting to whisper. "Ya know, for the breath." She brought her head back up and winked at the guard.

To the barely stifled chuckles of Gilbert, the man grunted and bent back to his task. Within seconds, he produced a short spear from behind Olivia's back and his eyes widened in curiosity.

"Oh, that there is Bertha. She helps me ward off the *undesirables*."

She loves that gods damned spear. Dunkeath couldn't blame her; it *was* the one she had bloodied in the orcish attack on Elgion years ago. Now, that very same weapon, albeit heavily upgraded, was a constant companion of the former laundress. Well, that and the sarcasm. One day her tongue would doom them all, and Dunkeath wished she would just bear the uncomfortable situation in silence. But, wishing for that was like wishing for Drodang silk.

The man dropped to a knee to search her legs, prompting another barb. "Not you of course. *Definitely*, not you. Truly, one to sweep ya off yer feet you are." The man stood—emotionless—and held the bootstrap knife she kept in her boot. "That's a good lad. Good lads ya got here," she said to no one in particular.

Dunkeath noticed the club-wielding guards were seemingly unaffected by her goads, and he assumed they might be accustomed to loud-mouthed merchants and travelers. With a grunt, the search guard tossed her knife onto the pile, not showing the care he had done for the other weapons. The man moved on, pretending not to hear Olivia's protest at the maltreatment of her blade. *Small compensation for your foolishness,* Dunkeath tutted to himself.

Her brown eyes looked at Dunkeath, recognizing his annoyance. She shrugged whilst raising her eyebrows. All he could was simply shake his head; the interminable woman laughed at his displeasure. Though, he had to admit, he couldn't help but feel the infectious lightness of her mood and a smile forced its way across his lips. He looked back at her to see laugh-reddened cheeks, and as she recognized his smile, she winked. *The woman was a tempest.*

Distracted, Dunkeath did not witness Gilbert's frisking. From the silence behind him, something was wrong. A sudden surge of panic coursed through as he wondered what these hardened guards would think of a bag full of Stones. *Why had he not coached Gilbert earlier? Perhaps the lout had put the god shards in the saddle bags?*

Slowly, Dunkeath turned to look at the cause of the silence. The search guard handed a bundle of letters back to 'the courier,' and Dunkeath thanked the gods Skorin had given them the alibi. What wasn't an action to be grateful for was the guards display of empty palms. Obvious disbelief at an unarmed traveler. Dunkeath groaned inwardly, cursing Gilbert for not having at least a bootstrap knife to sell the lie. *Maybe they thought that like his un-weathered skin he was a novice at this trade?*

But where was that small leather pouch of stones that Gilbert carried? He had watched the young Keeper stuff his Embershard amulet inside the pouch at the beginning of their journey. He had pushed it into the recesses of that small satchel alongside an assortment of other stones, making the whole lot disappear into some interior pocket of his tunic. Yet the guard, who had been so thorough, now stood empty handed. *Perhaps Gilbert had a trick or two up his sleeve?* Of course, his stupidity at not even giving the guard something to find could endanger them all. It was a classic mistake of those trying to hide something, and Dunkeath learned long ago you had to give the guards something. If'n you didn't, suspicions would arise.

For several seconds of tension, Dunkeath felt unspoken words between the three guards. Their neutral eyes communicating a world of information that was anyone's guess. Abruptly, the search guard stood to the side and waved his hand to show they were clear to proceed. Dunkeath had to bite the inside of his lip so as to not show his relief.

The cheery guardsmen piped back up, accustomed to his silent friends, "Alright then, looks like you folks are clear. Come, I'll show you where you can park your mounts for the night."

As the three companions grabbed the reins of their horses and followed the guard who chattered ceaselessly, Dunkeath relaxed. Yet, the tension would not fall away completely, because something in the manner of the guards—some shadow of doubt—lingered within his private thoughts. He wondered what they knew and vowed to warn the others when they were given a moment of privacy.

Chapter Fifteen

Bella

Red torchlight burned in her eyes, unnervingly bright for their flickering flames. Scattered beacons in an all-consuming darkness, and the only thing Bella could see. She felt an all-too-familiar fear as loud sniffing grunts pierced the darkness. She strained to see their source, but no matter how hard she tried to penetrate that shadowy veil, she couldn't make out anything, save for the brightly burning torches. She squeezed the lids of her eyes closed, a trick to help refocus a tired mind. When she reopened them, thick iron bars blocked her view. Though she could easily reach her arm through, she was trapped behind their crude design.

Utter despair from a despondent soul blanketed her thoughts as she realized her situation. Her heart increased in tempo, emotions swelling within. She was trapped; she had been captured once again. Death and agony hung over her like a heavy fog. In the echoing vault of the space, the loud sniffing returned, but she still could not locate the source. Her breath caught at the noise; her eyes fixed on the pure darkness. Nothing but silence replied, and her senses were inundated by its power. Not even the torches made a sound. A croaking whisper came from behind her, "Ma'am … w-we are in it now."

She looked behind herself, and Godfrey lay there with his arm broken beyond repair. She gasped in horror, but he did not seem to notice. "Th-they … are … coming."

Frozen in fear, she could not reply to the ghostly emanations. A massive spike caked in blood protruded from Godfrey's chest—a feature she swore hadn't been there before. His sallow skin was that of one long gone, and he spoke through death. Terror ripped through her heart. A sudden piercing sound echoed behind her, the sniffing grunts of her captors, and with tense nerves she spun to look behind. Nothing lay in that pitch black even though she swore it was right in her ear.

As she twisted back towards Godfrey, the man had disappeared, and Godwin had taken his place. Recreating the very image of the dead soldier who had been impaled in front of her so long ago. Her mouth lay open in terror, all while Godwin was raised to the sky, taken aloft on the crude totem of the orcs. Their malign altar to their malicious god. Corpses—more than there had ever been—drooped from an unfathomable myriad of spikes, and still the totem rose with more and more victims adorned upon it.

Overwhelmed, she fell to the ground and started to hyperventilate. Yet to her utter terror, an even worse feeling emerged. The coarse touch of a massive finger graced her cheek. She turned to see this new sensation. There, with a mouth full of sharp, jagged teeth, was the grinning face of the orcish warchief; his massive finger caressing her cheek. With his ragged tongue, he crooned at her, "Good."

Closing her eyes again, she willed the thoughts away … *Silence …*

She reopened her eyes, there was nothing save the blackness of the void. Not even the torchlight remained, and her heart slowed to a calmer pace. She dared to hope the dark thoughts had passed and blinked. Suddenly, her vision was wrapped in the sight of the warchief's head, all-encompassing, in front of her. Her heart quickened uncontrollably, and she gripped at her chest, the thumping beats too fast to control.

"Good," The oversized head boomed, and his eyes dripped red with blood. She felt her chest tighten and dizziness started to overwhelm her. Death had come for her and her heart raced away. Suddenly the mouth opened …

*

Drenched in sweat, she woke with a jerk. Her torso upright and her hand clutching her rapidly beating chest. The fear of her nightmare still had a hold on her psyche. Fortunately, some cool night air wafted over her, and its mild touch soothed her frayed nerves. Her breath stabilized, and she concentrated on the sounds around her. A fox's cry whispered in the distance, an unfortunate creature that either cried in loneliness or in defense. An owl hooted in triplicate calling into the forest with its mysteries. All sounds that belonged; all sounds that were safe. She forced a slow respiration and dropped her hand to the hide blanket that covered her. There was no light, but it did not matter because she knew where she was.

It was a simple wooden hut nestled against a massive moss-covered cedar tree. Her home away from home, and a gift granted to her by the saurians who viewed her as friend. It did not go unnoticed that such generous lodgings and amenities—one for her and Godfrey—were commonplace luxuries whenever she visited the saurian village within the trees. The generosity of these people made it even harder to resist the village's allure. The raw simplicity of it beckoned to Bella, and at times, she yearned to shed the responsibilities of Elgion and just immerse herself in such a quaint lifestyle.

That could never be, she relented. Still, she could use her time amongst the saurians as a balm to the soul. A tool she had used quite frequently in the years since the orcish attack on Elgion, jumping at the slightest opportunity to visit the humble villages of the reptilian kind. Some 'jumps' were wild stretches of the term *necessity*, even for her beleaguered soul. *But where else can my troubled mind go?*

She pulled the covers away; the night air washed over her now bare legs. It was cool but pleasantly so, summer was nearly there, and Bella reveled in this time of year. Life springing up in abundance to prosper in the rapidly approaching summer days. The thought pushed the last ill remnants of her nightmare away, and she swung herself off the cot. In the center of the hut was a fireplace, situated below a smoke hole, and combined with the design of the airy leaf-and-needle bound roof, smoke was rarely an issue within the confines of the home. She felt for her flint and iron striker in the darkness, and her fingers retracted instinctively once they felt the sharp edges of the flint tucked within a leather pouch. It was an item she never travelled without, and though the saurians had their own fire strikers, Bella preferred her own.

She secured the striker pouch and grasped around for the small bundles of tinder wrapped in le'kwii, a simulacra of hemp the saurians used. It lacked the scratchy fuzziness of hemp and honestly seemed sturdier than hemp ever could be. It was only a matter of time before humanity adopted its usage.

Tiny pricks of wood and thatch tickled her palm as her probing hand pushed into a bundle lying upon the dirt floor. She placed the le'kwii bound bundle, no larger than her hand, in the center of the fireplace, and unstrung the leather pouch that held her fire strikers. She wrapped the iron in her left hand, and the bow of the metal acted like a second set of knuckles. With her right hand, she gripped the flint tightly and as far back from the sharpened edge as she could. Even with years of practice, mistakes could still happen.

She inhaled before bringing the flint down upon the iron. A spark illuminated her surroundings, and she saw the bundle nestled between two thin branches. She struck again and the world flashed around her, but still no spark graced the tinder. She breathed in again and brought her iron-bound hand closer to the tinder. With another forceful blow, she struck. This time her aim was true. The sudden flash dissipated, but the light did not completely fade because the tinder grabbed onto the smallest morsel of flame.

With gentle breaths she blew, feeding the tiny light the oxygen it craved. It flared to life and as she continued to blow upon it, she gathered small sticks and kindling that lay around the fireplace, placing them into a tented mound behind the tinder. For minutes, she fed that small flame until the kindling comfortably held onto its burning state. Finally, she was able to place a larger log upon the fire, and, as the log became wreathed in flame, she sat backwards on the dirt floor; just watching the embers caress the wood. She sat there for a long time, lost in her thoughts; images of her past flashing in and out of existence, scars and all.

All the work she had done to overcome the trauma of her captivity felt wasted. All of it undone by the horror of recent events. Sleep had been … difficult to say the least. In her quiet times, her thoughts would filter through the same images; the malevolent eyes of the orcish warchief, the fear of being chased, Godwin's unnaturally stretched face as he lay with an ax in his back, and now Elira with her skin cut to look like a bloody ladder. All of it flickered over and *over* and *OVER* in her mind, no matter how hard she tried to focus on something, anything else. With sudden rage she slapped her forehead, angry at it all; at the whole damned mess.

Godfrey, Alexa, Sophia, and even Hislock had told her it wasn't her fault, but in her private thoughts she knew the truth. If it wasn't for her, Godwin would have survived; if it wasn't for her, they would have never been captured; if it wasn't for her … maybe things would be different for them—for everyone.

Now a new death stained her mind, and though it was not her fault, Bella felt vulnerable in its shadow. All of her failings were being brought back into the light, and as the surge of emotion swelled over her, she was overcome. She slapped her forehead again … and again. The sting jarred her thoughts, breaking away from the mental agony; if only for a moment.

When she had finally pushed past the self-loathing, she jumped to aid the near-exhausted flame. *How long had it been?* After giving the fire new life, she saw a grey dawn light peeped through the hole above her. It was time for some breakfast.

A mix of morels, oyster, and chanterelle mushrooms sat in a large basin nearby, but what was most tantalizing was a bowl of fresh kwamin, a hardy fruit known only to the new world. Its pleasantly sweet taste and smooth texture was quickly becoming a highly prized luxury and even in her dour mood she couldn't help but salivate at the thought of the delectable treat. She had learned that when mixed with cinnamon—another wonderful new world discovery—and milk, the kwamin made for a delicious breakfast.

Ember's breath! It made for a good meal any time of the day. Unfortunately, there wasn't any milk or cinnamon present, so she settled on popping a couple slices of the soft fruit in her mouth. The taste was smooth and delicate, reminding her of laying on the grass during warm summer days, a light breeze gently caressing her skin. In stark contrast to her darker thoughts of the pre-dawn hours, it was a much better way to start her day, and she resolved to bring back some of the dried kwamin the saurians used for long journeys.

Though her hosts did not farm on the scale of humanity, they did cultivate some crops, and kwamin and oyster mushrooms were a constant in the saurian diet. Swathes of meadow, tilled with squash, beans, and lentils, lie not far from the village and were ringed with kwamin trees. Trees that served as fence posts, a layer of compost, which grew succulent oyster mushrooms, at their feet.

Morels were a delicacy; never farmed, only foraged around this time of year. Bella's mouth, still reeling from the succulent taste of the kwamin, craved the heartier taste of the mushroom as she poured a bowl of them—sliced into bite size bits—into a cooking pot. Not far from the iron pot was a bucket filled with water. Filling the pot with water made her own thirst rise even with the small hydration she gleaned from the kwamin.

Quickly, she placed the pot on the campfire to boil and found the large deerskin bladder that held her own drinking water. She released the stopper and took a swig. Though there was little water left, the few mouthfuls revitalized her senses and washed away the dreariness of sleep. Not wanting to leave her breakfast, and the fire unattended, she set to work sharpening her daggers while she waited for the water to boil.

In poetic fashion, the final nicks disappeared as the sound of boiling water could be heard. She put aside her daggers and ladled the mushroom mixture into a wooden bowl. It was not an overly flavorful meal, and she nearly scalded her tongue in her haste. Nevertheless, she felt the heat fill her belly and the warmth gave her some courage to face the day.

The pot had sufficiently cooled after finishing her meal, and she poured the rest of the water on the low burning fire. Sudden smoke and steam filled the hut, and she coughed at the enveloping mixture. *It was time to get some fresh air.* She dressed herself in a woolen undershirt and tunic along with some trousers, and with her boots properly laced, headed out the door to the village beyond.

Chapter Sixteen
Bella

The grey wolf light of dawn washed over the village and colors were just making themselves visible in the wane light. The vibrant greens of lichen and moss were splashed everywhere, hugging the trunks of large cedar and pine which soared into the sky above. Odd protrusions jutted from the base of those towering giants, and only in the knowing did Bella recognize them as the camouflaged homes of the saurian peoples. All about her, there were huts, lodges, workshops, and storage places scattered to and fro, and—save for the hide-flap door—they blended seamlessly with the forest they inhabited. She breathed in appreciatively at the sight of it all and moved down the path towards their water source.

The road, if you could call it that, seemed no more than an animal trail, but Bella learned it was indeed an intentional construction that led to the various locales the saurians desired. She walked north and east on a slight decline, comfortable in solitude and guided by a light roaring noise in the distance. The village was silent at this early hour with most of the saurian people still inside, using the fires of their huts to warm their blood, a necessity amongst their kind.

The image of scaled flesh being warmed in fire reminded her of a most treasured secret. One she had mulled over for months as she decided its fate. One that in the years since her and Godfrey had saturated themselves in saurian culture, *they* had discovered. A secret that, even amongst all the other awe-inspiring aspects of the sentient reptiles, was one that could change the world in its telling. Whether that change would be chaos and calamity or celebration and progress was unknown, and Bella loathed to think on it. That secret lay with the gods themselves, and Bella now knew that these saurians—these lizard folk—were innately attuned with one god in particular, the lord of all the others, Ember.

It had shocked her when Hislock showed her the small red-orange stones, small tokens given to the nighttime guards to keep them warm and active through the night. When that secret was unveiled, it was like she saw a whole other world. Small bits of Ember's gifts were strewn everywhere. Not turned into jewelry and trinkets like humanity had done, but instead weaved into the fabric of their lives—like a tool. *Perhaps in the way that it was meant to be*, she mused. A small spark of flame here; a prayer to the heavens; a charm to ward off predators, these were just some of the small ways in which Ember's boon was distributed, and Bella was flabbergasted at the almost casual use of the Shards of Ember. Especially when Hislock had demonstrated the near blasphemous use of the stone by rubbing an activated shard against his arm, almost in ritual, right before the slaughter of a large boar for a tribal feast. He had simply said, "warmer bloood clossser to them. Clossser to Great Saurussss."

These were the secrets she and Godfrey had been shown, and somehow, she felt like they should stay that way. Maybe in time she could tell Sophia, for she trusted her absolutely. But, for now, she would hold onto this little morsel of the far away saurians and let its magic linger for just a little longer.

The conundrum echoed in her mind as she weaved her way through trees and huts. She passed the only easily visible mark of civilization, a flat stone platform which had room for a large fire in its center. Even then, this tribal gathering spot appeared to be no more than the ruins of the past as moss and roots snaked their way through the cracks and crevices of smaller—but still quite large—flat stones. There wasn't a feast or a reason to dawdle so she pressed on until the sound of a waterfall could be heard plainly.

A lattice of tripwire and traps bordered the village, and she carefully dropped down a steep embankment, one that ringed the whole of the village, rising it up on a natural platform. After dropping down, she couldn't help but look behind her. All around were the remnants of iktomid, bear, troll, and even orc corpses, though the orc bits were virtually unrecognizable due to their age. Still, bits and pieces of the vicious predators were strung up to make clear their fate. She gritted her teeth as she rested her eyes upon an arachnid fang, and the three inches of death belonging to some unlucky iktomid brought bad memories to the fore.

On a few occasions, Hislock had taken her on an iktomid hunt, showing her the poisons and medicines that they could produce from the abrasive hairs of the beasts. Yet they were not always the predators, and once they had endured a terrifying ambush. She would call it luck that they survived with no injuries, but Hislock and his companions were more than used to dealing with the monstrous spiders, dispatching them with relative ease. A surge of empathy washed over her as she thought of Alexa's own near-death experience with the iktomids. The blackened shoulder, healed now, was still stuck in Bella's memory like a bad taste in the mouth.

Her survey of the trees was broken as she saw a slight red glow flash in the treetops. Unmoving and staring at her, a gecko-like saurian perched upon a branch. *Even the saurians are accustomed to war.* She nodded, and the sentry returned the gesture. Her curiosity sated, she turned back to her task.

Much like the first time she saw it, her breath caught in her throat. Water roared down from moss covered stones, a cliffside bracketed against the steadily rising peaks to the east. The range of wet rock—thick with vegetation—stretched south as far as Bella could see, disappearing as trees masked its departure. To the north, the cliffs abruptly jutted west and just as they were about to vanish from sight, back north. The geography left a cozy little nook for which the rushing waters could gather until they were strong enough to flow south. It was a stream humanity had yet to discover and the saurians simply called "Mantou".

She walked to the edge of Mantou, feeling flecks of cool mist kiss her skin. Small fish darted away as she knelt, their silver scales reflecting the early morning light. A whole cavalcade of life lay within these clear waters, and it soothed her soul when she looked upon it. Slowly, she submerged her bucket beneath the water, watching the rushing liquid fill the void of the vessel. She held it there for a few seconds; the wood turning dark brown, and she wondered if the saurians would appreciate clay products. *They'd leak less often.*

"I figured you would be up already!" A familiar voice called out.

Bella had been so wrapped up in her thoughts that the sudden sound of speech made her jump.

Obviously, the newcomer saw the small bit of fright and between a chuckle stated, "Oh, I got ya good this time! Ya know, you *really* should pay attention."

Bella, feeling the slightest spike of irritation, gripped the bucket handle tightly to calm herself. Pulling the bucket out and standing up simultaneously, she turned to see this, sometimes rather rude, individual. Godfrey, a one-armed man with tousled grey hair, stood beaming at her, and his mood—which was always rather infectious—weaseled its way into her heart. A smile of her own crept across her face, "And you shouldn't be sneaking up on people so early!"

Godfrey, his own bucket in hand, nodded and, while moving to the water's edge, replied, "Oi, I can't help it. I'm just a deadly assassin type ya know?"

"Sure," Bella rolled her eyes.

Godfrey made a mock scoffing sound, as if his feelings were hurt, and knelt by the pool. He placed the bucket by his side and with a rapid motion splashed water on his face, soaking a grey beard and mustache that ringed his face. The absence of an arm did not seem to slow the man, and Bella was happy to see the vibrancy within. He seemed to thrive here in the saurian village better than he ever did in Elgion; even after the loss of Godwin.

"I will have you know that the Warriors of August once called me … The Snake." Godfrey said with a hint of mystery. His one hand fluttered away from him to accentuate the title.

"Because of the lying?"

Godfrey, who had been staring up at the waterfall and dramatically holding a pose that looked as if he were lost in memories, sharply turned to her and narrowed his eyes. "No, 'cause just like your hippity hoppity self I made folks jump whenever I approached. Not a one heard me a coming. Ember's breath! I was like a snake in the grass. Always ready to ambush." Godfrey swiveled his head back and forth, evidently trying to imitate his former namesake.

Looking at his face, Bella wondered if it was true. Like so many of his stories, no matter how fantastical, he made it easy to believe. A skill that made him a huge favorite amongst the saurian peoples, and messages, asking for his return, would reach Elgion whenever the ambassador spent more than a week away from the saurian village. She relented on her teasing and allowed the man his tale, whether false or not. "Ok, *Snake*, why you *slithering* up beside me?"

An easy grin came to his face, and while plunging his own bucket beneath the water he stated matter-of-factly, "Get some water of course!"

She chuckled, his mannerisms always light and playful, so much so they made her heart feel light. It gave her a sort of joy, like fond memories of childhood in which her days felt carefree.

With a sudden seriousness to his voice, Godfrey spoke again, "You alright today, ma'am?" He did not look directly at her, but just put the question out over the clear pool.

She froze. The question so sudden but so necessary. *Oh, how he knew her mind.*

"Ya know … Hislock came to see me yesterday. That lizard is awfully worried about you, and though I still can't understand all what he says it was pretty plain that he thinks … no he *knows* you're hurting." Godfrey looked at her, and she still could not move. He continued with empathy full on his lips, "By the Maiden, I would be too. What you saw there, what you have seen …" His voice trailed off and he turned once again to look towards the waterfall. This time it wasn't just for dramatic effect.

The pause was enough for Bella to overcome her paralysis, and she looked on Godfrey. This man, this friend of hers looked suddenly older, as if the years abruptly dropped their weight upon him. The wrinkles of his skin sagged under heavily furrowed brows. Distantly, and almost at a whisper, he murmured, "Well, those kinds of sights would weigh heavily on anyone's soul." He turned to her and his brown eyes searched her own, probing at her soul.

She trembled slightly under the inspection.

Godfrey continued, "*I* worry about you. So, once again—and I know you are as tough as they come—I am gonna ask: You alright today, ma'am?"

Tears threatened and she abruptly looked away. The question pierced her defenses, breaking through the barriers she had placed within her mind. She closed her eyes and felt a tear escape past her lids. Hiding within the refuge of her mind gave her enough safety to dare a reply. So she did, with the only reply she knew. "No, I am not ok, Godfrey. I-I … I don't think I've been for a while."

"I know it ma'am. It's our time with those foul pigmen, it's the death of … Godwin, and now this newest horror. That *mutilation* on the beach, ain't it?"

She opened her eyes, letting the tears fall freely now, and nodded at him.

He scooted closer to her, moving to sit instead of kneel and then he crossed himself with his good arm to place it on her shoulder. "Aye, I know. I know."

Bella breathed in and out, letting the emotions wash over her. She smiled at Godfrey, and whilst moving to a sitting position herself, placed a hand on his own. *She would be ok, at least for today.*

He let his hand drop, and together they sat beside the pool of the Mantou River for several minutes just looking out over the beauty of nature's design. Two veterans of past terrors consoling themselves against the horrors within their minds.

"Welp!" Godfrey said while slapping his knee with his hand. The sudden outburst made her jump again, and he laughed. His usual light manner returning in a flash. "See? Like a snake!" His hand mimicked a striking snake.

She shook her head in disbelief. Not to mock him, but at how resilient he was. One moment so serious, another so light.

Godfrey did not let her linger on such thoughts and continued, "So, I told ol' Hislock that I would get you geared up for a hunt today. He thinks it would do you some good to get out there in the woods, and I agree."

Godfrey stood abruptly, surprising Bella with his grace and speed for a man his age. He reached out his hand and with the warmth of a friend's voice demanded, "Come on then. Let's seize the day."

Chapter Seventeen

Bella

She breathed slow and methodical; her heart pounding at the recent flurry of activity. Alongside Hislock, Bella had raced to a vantage point, silent as the wind. Years of training allowed her to maintain calm exhalations. Just fifty meters away, the wiry reddish-brown fur of a boar could be seen, and the beast rooted at the base of a moss-laden cedar—unaware of any danger. Within moments, Godfrey would charge from behind and hopefully drive their prey straight into Bella and Hislock's long boar spears. It was a standard hunting technique of the saurians and she reveled in the game.

A last recovery breath, heightened senses, and adrenaline swam in her veins. The hunt was going perfectly; her silent traipse to the front of the boar's position awarded with a grin to herself. Hislock did not move, but only glared at their target, his hunter's focus absolute. Her heart skipped a beat as the boar grunted and jerked its head upwards. It was a massive specimen, a lone male that must have weighed around one hundred and eighty kilograms. The boar sniffed the air several times in rapid succession, and, satisfied with its survey, trotted a few paces to a fallen log to begin rooting once more. Bella breathed out slowly in relief.

Hislock looked at her and cocked his head to the side and towards their next location. They would need to get to the flat ground a few meters away, and the most obvious path the boar would take in flight. With a creature like this, it was best to face it head on, though hopefully with a shaft or two in its side already. She nodded, and with utter grace the pair crouch-walked until they were squatting behind a stand of cedar and pine directly in front of the boar. The sounds of grunting and birdsong still echoed in the forest canopy, and Bella bit the inside of her lip in grim satisfaction at their success. Everything was in place. Now the thrill of the fight to come was all that lay before her.

The two waited amongst the grunting sounds of the boar as it rooted ever closer to their position. Like Hislock had shown her, she focused on long deep breaths to calm her adrenaline-soaked heart. In all things, the saurians tried to maintain an inner reserve of calm, a skill Bella had sorely lacked. Now, here in the northern ranges of the Eukarian forest—and from lessons of the past—she felt a glimpse of that inner peace as her mind pushed away all thought. She was utterly wrapped within the moment, and as she fell into the deep rhythms of her long breaths, peace enveloped her soul. She was ready.

A sudden panicked grunt pierced the air, and the birdsong died abruptly. The boar, not yet startled into running, sensed—like the rest of the forest—that a predator lurked. Godfrey was making his move. There was always the risk that the boar would gather its courage and charge at the lone predator. *Eh, what was life without a little danger?*

The tension in the air rose as Bella saw—almost felt—the boar's muscles prep for the flight to come. Then, nearly making her jump in fright herself, Godfrey roared meters away from the boar. His challenge was echoed by a clean throw of his spear into the boar's side, a strike that would serve well to weaken the animal. She saw where he had gotten his nickname.

The boar immediately darted away, terrified by the pain and the sudden appearance of a predator. It charged directly at them. *Thirty meters.* Hislock glanced at Bella and the two bared their teeth. She gripped her long boar spear tightly, taking comfort from the ash wood shaft. *Twenty meters.* The boars squealing barreled closer. Bella's heart raced even against the attempt at meditative calm. *Ten meters … Now!* She sprang out to the right of the trees, her spear held ready. Hislock took the left, leaving the boar with nowhere to run but into their blades.

A squeal of panic but the charge continued. The boar bowed its head and committed to its path, straight towards Bella. She braced herself. The animal's gait was slightly off, its rear left leg muscles torn from Godfrey's spear, and she shifted centimeters to the right to take the charge from its weaker side. She felt her left calf tense in anticipation, the leg anchored behind her. With a roaring squeal, the boar leapt towards her, hoping to break the threat in front of it. She had practiced for such a move, and she was ready. With calm determination she thrust her spear forward, striking true into the animal's chest. The sudden jarring weight reverberated up the shaft, and her shoulder quaked from the impact.

She leaned back, the boar's weight forcing her feet to skid on the dirt. The natural motion pushed the spear butt into the ground, setting it against the force of the charge. Together the two—boar and woman—shuffled several centimeters until the spear bit into the ground, arresting the charge completely. It was perfectly executed and save for the unnatural bend of the spear's shaft, the hunter remained unharmed. She let out a breath, exultant in success.

The boar squealed in terror, but its life force was draining away. Hislock raced towards the animal and with sudden speed lanced his own spear into its neck. Blood poured freely from the wound and the animal's cries quickly faded to the rattling tones of death. She looked into the animal's eyes, and her heart went out to the beast. It was nature's course and the saurians would feed well on their gifts. Still, as the adrenaline of the hunt faded alongside the life within the boar's eyes, she felt the death as keenly as any other.

She did not regret her actions, but as Hislock murmured a prayer of his own, she allowed solemnity to wash over her. Only here in nature could one understand the circle of life, the sacrifices necessary to keep the machine of existence running. Unlike the brutality of what she had witnessed on the beach, this was part of something greater, something necessary. The death of the boar was the fuel to keep those mechanisms of life turning as they always had. She swore, as she was sure Hislock did himself, they would not let his sacrifice go to waste.

"Woo! Atta girl!" Godfrey whooped in delight.

A breath, she didn't know she held, released at the sound of Godfrey's celebration. The reverential mood fading and her tension eased. A new delectable calm overtook her, and she couldn't help but grin as the old man capered over to them.

"Bella the boar slayer! Bella, the gods damn magnificent I tell ya!"

Godfrey's exuberant celebrations were so infectious, that Hislock even broke from his requiem to flash a rather wicked set of teeth. She had come to know that particular look as being close to a smile as you could approximate on her reptilian friend. Canines fronting the whole of a wide, saurian mouth with molars and bicuspids hidden behind. Spontaneously, she clapped Hislock on his shoulder and shook him vigorously, still energized from the thrill of the hunt, "Ember's breath! That was something else, wasn't it?"

Hislock let out a hissing roar, caught up in the jubilant mood of his friends. Together, they took a moment within the woods to unleash a torrent of emotion. Their stresses unburdened within the embrace of nature's absolution. Slowly, as the cheerful mood faded, the team set about preparing the boar's body for travel. They harvested the major organs quickly, throwing them in salted le'kwii wraps. With every removed piece, they splashed a smattering of salt within the empty cavity. Hislock shoved the intestines in a large deerskin satchel alongside the stomach, all pieces that can be used in either cordage or food preservation. They had tracked this beast through the late afternoon, and now as the sun was setting, they were hard pressed to finish the field dressing quickly. But they were skilled at this kind of work and, before long, they had fashioned a makeshift sled to drag the corpse and all its trappings back to the village.

Satisfied the job had been done properly, Hislock moved to take the first turn on the haul. "Belllaaa, great hountear. NO, carr—" Hislock's praise was cut short. In the distance, the group could hear the unmistakable sound of a foreign voice, deep and low with a boom to every syllable. They all strained to hear.

"No, I told ya its ours!"

"No, it's mine!"

"You idget! We both are mine!" An abrupt pause interrupted the pair of voices, both distinctly different but oddly similar. A thudding crash boomed through the trees.

The trio looked at each other, and Bella was sure she mimicked the look of bemused curiosity that rippled through their expressions. Without a word, they set off towards the disturbance, even though the delay would find them walking home in the dark. This new development was far too intriguing to miss. Besides, the kill had been field-dressed and the preservation methods they used were meant to last for at least a day of travel.

Another thunderous crash sliced through the air, followed by the booming voice. "You little brats … this ours!"

"I said! Mine!"

A large cedar was shaken violently. Several of its needles broke free from their moorings to drop to the ground below. She could not make out what shook the tree, a small hill blocking their view. They fell onto the earthen mound and crawled to its precipice.

"You dumb. We both are mine! I told you. Ah, stupid spider!"

Bella heard a whooshing sound followed by the unmistakable sound of an iktomid's cry. She hurried to peek her head over the berm, overwhelmed with curiosity to see what caused such a commotion.

There, standing with its back propped against the previously shaken cedar, was a monstrous two-headed ogre. Immediately, Bella grimaced, knowing that the only way such a fiend could grace Telaea's firmament was through the union of a cambyad, the seductive changeling cousin of the nocturne, and a man. Their offspring were giant dimwitted brutes that held onto only small vestiges of their humanity. Through the immense strength of their brood, the cambyads used these offspring to make guards for their realms. *Someone in Elgion had been busy,* she mused.

At least five Iktomids surrounded the ogre, clinging from branches or scurrying around its feet. The ogre smashed the ground with a wooden club more fit to be a log than a tool. The twin heads, which were given a healthy separation by the ogre's massive shoulders, roared in triumphal unison as their weapon crushed an iktomid who had ventured too close. Blue viscera scattered about the scene, splashing the surrounding brush— as well as the ogre's own body—in an unnatural hue. The light blue blood contrasted poorly against the ogre's patchwork of fur and bare skin. The erratic clumps unkempt and wild: another malformation of the cursed coupling, as if nature did not know what to cover and what to lay bare. Another iktomid leapt from an overhead branch and plunged its fangs within just such a patch.

The monstrous oversized man roared and plucked the spider free, slamming it to the ground with contempt. The fangs must have missed their mark only to bury impotently in fur. No blood or other signs of damage could be seen. A huge bare foot crushed through the spider's chitinous abdomen with a sickly squelch. There were only three iktomids left; all of which were wary of the brutality of their foe. *What drove the creatures to such a frenzy,* Bella wondered

Iktomids were normally ambush predators and left larger *dangerous* prey alone. Then she saw it, or at least what she could only infer was the cause of their madness. Draped over a fallen log was a young man, probably a teenager, who's head lolled with the obvious sign of a concussion.

The creatures fought over a meal, and this blundering behemoth declared his dominance. The ogre swung the club in a wide clumsy arc, fending off an iktomid who reared in preparation to leap. The creature relied solely on strength, and his awkward swings belied a lack of martial experience. With his arm overextended, the two iktomids struck in unison, leaving behind a flurry of leaves and forest debris. A roar of pain reminded Bella of the abrasive hairs that could poison flesh. As the ogre stumbled backwards, the third iktomid dropped from its overhead perch landing perfectly on the top of one of the skulls.

"No, no, no, no!" the threatened head roared in terror. The second head, still free from danger, looked aghast at his brother. The fangs of the iktomid plunged into the bald scalp, and the ogre went berserk. The head-bound iktomid scrabbled for purchase, but the flurry of activity dislodged the beast. The ogre twisted, slamming into trees and brush without control.

"Argh! It hurts; it hurts!"

"Brother, calm!"

"Ember's breath! You, shut up! It hurts!" The punctured head cried out; its previously mellow voice frantic with fear. The rampaging abomination threatened to rip through the unconscious teenager and Bella started to stand.

Before she could lift herself more than a few centimeters, Godfrey placed a hand on her shoulder. She looked over at the veteran soldier and he shook his head, "Not this one ma'am."

She had to admit that the ogre—even injured—was too great a threat for them. She looked back at the turmoil, anxious for the stranger on the log. Fortunately, the lumbering behemoth slammed into a large pine tree before he could come close, toppling immature green cones to the ground. One iktomid who was clinging to a patch of fur was squished as the ogre collided with the pine tree, its lifeless body left behind as the ogre rampaged on. The last iktomid was ripped free of its anchorage from the violent actions of the ogre, and the sound of scurrying footsteps fled north, into the trees. Their meal forgotten.

"Broth—" The uninjured head tried for calm, but his breath was knocked free as they tripped on a root and slammed into the ground. The ogre's massive chest rose and fell with huge heaving breaths, exhausted from the flurry of activity.

Hislock glanced at Bella, wondering what they should do. She had no answers for him so simply raised an eyebrow and shrugged. Suddenly, the ogre punched a fist into the thick blanket of moss and decaying plant matter below and leveraged himself onto his back. For a time, the oversized man recovered, sucking in huge mouthfuls of air. All the while the unconscious teenager rolled his head in the first stirrings of consciousness.

Bella was frozen in indecision. They were at least seventy-five meters from the unconscious young man and the ogre lay naught but ten meters away from the log on which the stranger was propped. There would be no way, even for the stealthy nature of Hislock, to approach without alerting the already heightened perceptions of the ogre.

Slowly, the brute sat up, scratching at skin that looked raw and red. "Brother. You alright?" The unthreatened head asked in genuine concern.

The fang-punctured head poured blood from its scalp but to Bella's astonishment he replied with little effort, "Yea. Magdris' Teeth! It bloody hurts! I tell ya, It hurts!"

"Uh … yea, yea. But why you act stupid?"

The bleeding head turned to his twin and, even from this distance, Bella could see his face curl into a rictus of malice. "Me, stupid! You, stupid! Why you swing when no one there?"

"Me not swing. You swing," The uninjured head replied in rising anger. Together the twin heads stood and stared at one another. Sibling rivalry apparent in their standoff. *But how would this play out when they shared a body?* Bella wondered.

With incredible speed the arms of the ogre struck out towards the opposing heads. It was like two boxers trying to strike a blow on an unprotected face. In unison, the blows struck true, and the ogre staggered at its own flagellation. Slowly, the twin heads lolled, their massive body rocking backwards and forwards. The ogre tried to stay upright but the twin blows had been too much for his consciousness and he crashed back to Telaea.

Bella's mouth lay open, shocked at the absurdity of this new development.

"Welp, that solves that," Godfrey said while rubbing his hand against his tunic, like he was satisfied with a job well done. "Best we gets a move on though. That bugger is tough as nails and I just saw that chest rise."

Neither Bella or Hislock argued, and together the three hastily jogged in a crouched manner towards the unconscious man. Bella's heart raced as they passed by the dozing behemoth. She looked over at the punctured head and saw a disturbing fate in store for the ogre. Already, a mesh of veins—ones that were normally present within the scalp—were turning black with the corruption of the iktomid venom. It was a solemn reminder of a similar wound Alexa had taken so many years ago.

The bare skin of the ogre had developed a raw red rash that was already blistered in places. It was true the ogre may survive for now, but chances were the iktomids would be feeding on his flesh before long. Of course, a creature that could punch itself with a neck-cracking blow and survive may be more resilient than she could imagine. Not to mention the fact its mother was a cambyad and were known for their knowledge and understanding of nature's mysteries.

Somehow, Bella felt empathy towards this behemoth as it lay motionless, and she sent a small prayer to the Maiden to keep the brothers together. She prayed they would save the injured head. Like that benevolent god had kept Alexa alive years ago despite a similar fate. A wave of uncanny introspection hit her, *not all things foreign must die; not all things unknown, no matter their threat to us, must disappear. They would never find peace between ogre and humanity, but maybe they could endure the harmonious cycles of nature. Cycles that allowed for predator and prey to share the same realms.*

Her thoughts were interrupted by the young man, looking no more than thirteen or fourteen years old, as he groaned; a sound pulled forth by Hislock's forceful hoisting. With Godfrey and Bella's help, Hislock placed the teenager onto his back, and Bella was once again surprised at the saurian's strength. Of course, it was evening and Hislock's blood, although not at its peak, was still primed from the hunt and the summer sun. As Godfrey and Hislock—young boy worn like a backpack—raced back towards the slaughtered boar, Bella spotted a simple leather satchel. She fished it from the ground before following her friends. The sound of scurrying footsteps filling in the silence behind her. Her nerves trembled in empathy.

Chapter Eighteen

Bella

At first, the young man had not understood where he was or what had happened to him. His eyes constantly widened in fear or confusion. It didn't help that Grace, Godfrey's old friend and healer, shambled over to him as soon as he stirred. One of her protruding chameleon-like eyes fixed, while the other telescoped around in a survey of the healer's hut. Bella thought it looked rather comical; the teenager's mouth agape in response to her inspection of him. Grace checked the salves on his lacerated ribs, and the teenager tried to follow the chameleon-healer as she ambled back over to her cooking pot. A firm slap on his wrist by the whip of Grace's tail, turned the look of awe into one bordering on betrayal.

"Aye, I know the feeling, lad," Godfrey said. Bella struggled not to laugh as the combination of Godfrey's reminiscence and the teenager's young face mixed in a rather amusing manner.

"That there is Grace. She may be a sour ol' bag, but she is a wickedly good healer," Godfrey finished.

Leave it to Godfrey to have the sense to try and reassure the lad, Bella thought as she approached the boy. Memories of her own similar recovery years ago bright in her mind. She held her hands up in placation, and—eventually—the boy understood there were no enemies in the room. Without warning, the young man let loose his story in an awful torrent of words. A deluge pouring forth from a traumatized youth. Of course, Bella couldn't understand much of it because his language was that of Xetem. Though there were some similarities, she could only understand fragments.

Ogre. Xeeland. Ember. Minollo. All words common enough. They listened patiently as the teenager told his story in his native tongue, until the realization that he wasn't understood dawned on him. Bella saw him try his best to compose himself after the disappointment, but failing that, he started over in frustration.

"Sidon … Sidon … Sidon." He repeated as he pointed to himself. Clearly, he was used to travel and to people not knowing his language.

Godfrey chimed in with his normal empathy, "Godfrey, son. Sorry we don't understand ya, but please … we wants to help."

The boy repeated what he thought was Godfrey's name, "'odfeyson?"

Godfrey laughed, "No, no. It's Godfrey. *Godfrey.*"

The boy nodded and repeated the name, though the strong consonants were softer than they should have been, "'ahdfey."

"Bella … Bella." Bella said as she pointed at herself.

Once again, the boy nodded and with a little more success repeated the name, "Bella." His cheeks flushed, suddenly made shy after looking into her eyes. Apparently, the concept of talking to a woman was a bit much for him, even after experiencing whatever trauma had befallen him. He was, after all, at an age, and Bella allowed a smile to ease the boy's troubled temperament.

With the introductions completed, Bella and Godfrey looked at Sidon with expectant eyes. Sidon looked back at Bella sheepishly, he nodded and launched into his story. This time with just enough of Bella and Godfrey's Holliserian tongue for them to understand the general concepts, and with excessive body language to fill in the details.

He had been a part of some expedition. All of them were apparently lost or dead. The boy's eyes were full of excitement as he made stabbing and swinging motions, vividly indicating what had happened to each of his former comrades. Yet, as he fell into a reverie of names, his eyes turned from thrill to sorrow and slowly tears formed. One in particular, Ramnios, made him stop his story entirely, and they had to sit in respectful silence as he sobbed at the memory of whoever owned that name. Even without the teenager's obvious use of the word 'Argolonian,' it was plain that the mercenaries they had failed to capture on the beach were responsible. She had to grit her teeth as a broiling anger consumed her.

Sidon demonstrated how he hid, though to the consternation of Grace who had to whack him once again. An action she had done four or five times already, a consequence for his wilder reenactments.

And, like before, he would apologize, "Surret." The rapport between the chameleon-like healer and the young man went some way to prevent Bella's rage, and Godfrey was beaming with delight, calming her even further. The old veteran loved Grace and her mannerisms, and every time he met with her, even though she hardly spoke, he wore a look of utter bliss.

As the chastisement faded, Sidon continued, "After death of Xeelanders, and Argolonian leave, I went south. Ogre caught me … um … gulmavarm." Plainly he did not know the Holliserrian word and rubbed his stomach while mimicking an eating action.

Godfrey barked out in understanding, "Hungry!"

Sidon's face lit up and he continued, "Yes, yes. Hunnnree. Ogre hunnree. Took me in … um, yebam, uh, dark. Took me and uh—" Sidon slapped his head twice, which was rewarded with another whip of Grace's tail.

"Surret. Um, hurt me. Ogre hurt me. And I, uh, um …" The boy, at a loss for the proper word, put his hands together almost as if in prayer and laid his head upon them like they were a makeshift pillow.

Godfrey, who was quickly learning to enjoy the little translation game they played, blurted out, "Sleep!"

Sidon, thanks in large part to Godfrey's own enthusiasm, was obviously starting to enjoy himself. "Yes, yes! Ogre hurt me. Make me sleep. I woke in … yebam to ogre making fire. He would … uh, eat me. Hunnnger. Before finish, big, um, mukhri come and attack!" The boy drove his hand from on high down into his palm, showing the sort of diving ambush an iktomid would pull off. "Ogre threw me. I fell sleep 'gain. Woke here.

Woke to 'ahdfey and Bella." The boy smiled, capping off his retelling with a bit of a flourish.

Godfrey spoke first, "I'm sorry that happened lad, I mean, Sidon. We will, well Grace'll take care of you. You need anything ya just ask, alright?"

"Yes, we are here to help," Bella added with a smile. Sidon's cheeks flushed, and Bella felt a trickle of anger as she was made to feel awkward by the teenager's obvious attraction. Hurriedly, she spoke to hide her frustration, "Well, Godfrey we have a lot to talk about … you care to join me outside?" Bella fixed Godfrey with a look of desperate appeal.

He was always one to understand social cues and with ease replied, "Sure, sure. Sidon you take care of yerself."

Sidon nodded to Godfrey and held his hands up in a prayer like gesture while saying, "Shukop, shukop."

Before they left, Godfrey turned to his friend and healer. "Grace, charmed as always by yer gentle touch." He bowed dramatically, but in his posture, there was only respect.

This old dog really does like her, Bella grinned.

Grace stood and her telescoping eyes suddenly pinpointed Godfrey in their sights. It was unnerving when both twitching eyeballs stopped to fix themselves on one target. Grace let out a low non-threatening hiss and her head cocked downwards in something akin to a bow.

Apparently, that respect was shared. With a smile as wide as the Sea of Melleas, Godfrey headed out the door. Bella followed him quickly, glad to get away from the awkward glances of Sidon.

The saurian village was a bustle of activity as reptilian peoples made their way through nature bound paths. Three crocodilian-snouted saurians darted in front of them, two of which were no taller than human children. The small ones hissed in delight as they chased each other, and a taller, matronly sort was forced to snap irritably at them. Godfrey had to step back lest he collide with the pair.

"Sa'as," Godfrey said to the taller crocodilian while bowing his head.

They turned to him, comfortable with his presence, and a flash of white teeth could be seen. "Sa'as," they replied and then hissed to their children to carry on.

"You really are the right one for this job," Bella said as Godfrey looked on at the little family.

"What ya mean?"

"Well, they all know who you are. They respect ya, and you seem to have taken to the job better than anyone could. I mean what does 'sa'as' even mean?"

The left side of Godfrey's lips curled in a weak smile. "Ah, that means excuse. Saurians are big on respect and honor I found, and best to be polite in such a crowd."

"You realize you are the only human on all of Telaea that probably knows that?!"

Godfrey waved his hand like the compliment was unwarranted.

"No, I am serious! You amaze me Godfrey, truly," Bella finished.

"Fine, fine. I am, as always, *amazing*. But enough 'bout me. What's up? That boy, Sidon, making ya feel strange with his ... um, developing curiosities?"

It must have been obvious then. She shook her head more in disbelief than in disagreement. She gestured to him to walk away from the hut, and together they strolled along the paths of the saurian village. The smell of roasted boar, carried aloft on a gentle breeze, tingled in Bella's nose. "Hislock has been busy," Bella said with a smile.

"I smell it to. Gods that's gonna be good!"

They walked past a pair of gecko-like saurians who seemed very close for just friends and Godfrey's "sa'as" seemed to fall on deaf ears. *Young love seems to blind all; no matter if they have scales or skin,* Bella mused.

Feeling comfortable with the distance from the hut, Bella spoke, "We *have* to get that boy back to Elgion. Whatever happened at his camp; whatever is in that satchel we found; whatever happened on that damned beach, verges on the political. War, Godfrey, war could be in the cards."

Godfrey's smile he had worn throughout their jaunt disappeared. "Aye, I know … Argolonians were always bloodthirsty bastards. Still, they might just be mercenaries, but who hired them? Who stands to gain besides Argolon?" Sudden malice and anger overrode Godfrey's normally bemused features. "Ember's breath! They have gone too far this time!" He breathed in steadily for a few exhalations. "I mean, Argolon sits pretty after the Five Points. The City of Silver in 'der hands an' all. It'd be hard to get a Chosen or even a Mandated to act upon this. Fear of Argolon's might is a real problem. Frankly, I think the Chosen and all the others may *choose* to ignore this."

"Maybe so, but it's our duty to let them know, nonetheless. Alexa would skin me alive if she knew I held this back."

Godfrey laughed in response, "Aye, she would. So, two … maybe three days an' that boy will be fit to travel. Ya want to leave then?"

Bella nodded at him. "As soon as possible my friend. As soon as possible."

"Great! That gives us plenty of time to see what in all the gods Hislock has done to that boar to make it smell *so* delicious!" Godfrey clapped in excitement, making a chameleon like saurian, who had been sitting on a stump fashioning a le'kwii-bound rope, jump. "Sa'as! Sa'as." Godfrey said, clasping his hands together in furious apology.

Bella chuckled, forgetting the troubles that lay ahead with her friend's delightful manner. Together the pair headed towards the delicious smell of roasted boar.

Chapter Nineteen

Bella

Bella watched Godfrey's normally cheerful disposition fade into sour resentment. His once bold proclamation, "The lad can ride with me!" becoming a cursed oath Godfrey wore with ill-concealed regret. Before Sidon ended up on the wrong side of the veteran's good arm, Bella offered to take the fidgety bundle. Though the boy probably deserved a good walloping, he was vulnerable, and Bella wanted to give him as much freedom to talk as possible. In so doing, Bella hoped he would reveal any clues to this Argolonian mystery they now faced, and, she had to admit, her heart went out to the young boy.

Within the hour, she was starting to regret that decision. Sidon asked about every little thing, and his body would tremble and fidget as he did so. It took all of Bella's riding skill to keep Rex on task, and several times the raptor hissed in irritation at his passengers. For what felt like *hundreds* of times, Bella would correct the raptor's course and then offer some variation of, "Please, stop moving so damn much."

"Surret," would come the reply, but it was a hollow apology. The boy would immediately fall back into his energetic—near manic—style of conversation.

How could this boy who had travelled to a new continent already, still be so full of wonder? Bella wondered rhetorically; the answer was known, and the only reason they all tolerated his annoyances.

Like the surety of thirst after a long day in the sun, Bella understood this teenage boy must have lost hope. In the mercy of their care, he had caught sight of that elusive emotion once more, and he chased that heady feeling of promise. The recipe for the sporadic spunkiness of an interminable youth.

So, as they meandered through the trails and paths of southern Mossgrave, they were *entertained* by Sidon's performance. A woodpecker rapping the bark of a tree; the remains of a deer punctured in the neck by iktomid fangs; patches of goblin's finger mushroom—their 'fingers' so similar to their namesake, and the rustling of a thimble berry bush were just some of the things that stirred his excitable curiosity. All the while he was accompanied by melodic bird song, as if nature itself accepted his eccentricities as one of their own.

Near the end of the day, they passed lumber camps and the hearty hails of happy loggers. The practical woodsmen knew Bella and Hislock and the role they played in preventing a grisly fate at the hands of orcish brutes. Taking a bundle of fresh-looking venison from one old lad, they pressed on. Even though the loggers insisted the group stay with them at their camp, the group was worried the boy may let slip too much. In so doing, rumor would burn like wildfire across the holdings of Augustia and beyond.

Avoiding that possibility, they found themselves camping along the cliffs at the end of Mossgrave. The sun was still well overhead, a product of the steadily increasing days, and Hislock wasted no time. The saurian stalked over to Sidon, handed him a small hatchet, mimicked cutting branches for firewood, and hissed at him to head off for the chore. She couldn't remember ever seeing him more agitated. As the boy walked away, Bella looked at her gecko-like friend with a barely disguised grin.

"GahdFRey tell me annoying," Hislock said in his halting grasp of the Holliserian tongue. "He annoying!" He pointed his short spear at the now out-of-earshot lad.

Bella burst into laughter, nodding in agreement at the appraisal. "I know, Hislock. I know," she managed to say after catching her breath. Yet, something inside of her disagreed, albeit slightly. At first, the boy's incessant chatter grated on her nerves heavily, but after a time she let her pre-dispositions fall away and let the current of his manic behavior carry her. It was somehow comforting and irritating all at the same time because be-hind the annoyances was an abundance of life. In the recesses of her mind, she wondered if she could grab onto that exuberance ever again.

Godfrey interrupted her thoughts, "I thought he would never … shut … up." He slammed his pack down rifling through the contents for his camping gear.

Hislock hissed in agreement and went to retrieve his own pack, which held very similar items to Godfrey's. The saurians liked the human-made camp craft materials and had adopted the kit as their own in many respects. Apparently, centuries with a culture that honored wilderness loving groups like the rangers produced skills that could match and even sometimes ex-ceed those who lived within the very trees themselves.

The three set about making their shelters and Godfrey was well ahead of the others by the time they had retrieved their own gear, even with the handicap of just one arm. Bella grabbed her pack from the packhorse's saddlebags. She found a spot near her friends and after ensuring no ant nests or other such pests were nearby, she set about building her own tent. She started by tying a deerskin hide, which would make up the floor, to several holes at the edges of a large leather sheet. She inserted flexible wooden poles into pouches along the outer length of the leather sheet, and the poles converged near the center. As she propped the bottoms of the poles into the ground in a circular fashion, she fixed strong le'kwii rope—the primary contribution to the kit by the saurians—to the end of each pole. On the ground, she used a small wooden mallet that came with the kit to hammer iron stakes into loops at the end of each taut rope and the base of each pole.

The physics of the construction kept the frame strong against the wind and rain, stabilizing the structure in place. With the tent upright and sturdy, Bella rolled a precut flap up and tied it together with a bundle of le'kwii rope, exposing the inside of the tent which held enough room for two sleeping people. She grabbed the bulkiest item in the kit, a heavy wool blanket, and rolled it out nicely on top of the deerskin floor. With her shelter complete, she turned to the sounds of Godfrey trying to ignite his tinder. Bella did not reach for her own fire striker, which made up a crucial component of the camping gear, but instead grabbed the final piece of that kit, a large tin cup. Hers was horribly deformed from hard travel, and with some force she smoothed out the rougher dents and bends within the cup's surface as she knelt beside Godfrey.

Hislock was still finishing his own tent, taking longer than the others, because as always, he struggled with tying the floor and walls together.

Godfrey grunted with effort as he struck the edge of the flint. His missing arm forcing him to keep the flint in place by sandwiching it between his knee and a flat stone. *Tenacious as you ever were,* Bella mused.

Sparks flew, but none caught even though the tinder had been kept dry in a box within the camping gear. He struck once more, missing entirely as his action shifted the position of the flint. His course corrected, he looked up at her.

She knew this look; he was gauging whether there was mockery in her eyes. So, she smiled at him as if he were a person she passed on the road. It was a lesson learned from the first few times watching him struggle, knowing to best serve her friend's feelings was letting him be useful.

Three more strikes on the flint; each failed to catch the tinder. Godfrey wiped his brow and took a centering breath. With a look of determined ferocity, he struck again and *finally* the tinder caught flame. As old as he was, he dropped smoothly to a prostrate position and blew the fire to life. Bella cracked some sticks nearby and held the small pieces out as he fed the fire to a sustainable burn.

Hislock came to their side when the fire was nearly built and set about rounding out the pit with stones from around the grove. Bella thanked the gods for Godfrey's success. His damnable pride would have smarted in front of the saurian.

Within a few minutes, the fire was built and the three companions sat about the comforting blaze. Bella looked around for Sidon. "Ya know, he's gonna be back soon."

With a sigh Godfrey replied, "I know …"

Bella chuckled, "Oh, he's not that bad. Just young is all."

Godfrey looked at her with raised brows and a look of astonishment, "You feelin' alright?"

She grinned at his sarcastic question. "Yes, I'm fine." They let the humor hang over the crackling fire, and she broke the silence by tossing the last of their tinder onto the hungry flames. "Well, he has to sleep some-where …"

"Ember's breath! Are you saying he needs to sleep with me?" Godfrey asked in exasperation.

"Well, he can't sleep with me. Wouldn't be proper for a *developing* lad," she replied.

Hislock laughed in his throaty hissing rasp, enjoying Godfrey's dis-comfort.

Godfrey looked up at the reptilian and barked out, "Well, he can sleep with Hislock."

Bella looked at him like a teacher with a wayward student. "Come now. Me and you *know* Hislock and the saurians. But him? He would be terrified to sleep. Sorry, Hislock."

Hislock blinked in understanding. His scaled hand waved to show he was not offended.

Godfrey chimed in, "Ugh, I guess yer right, 'specially since he makes an awful racket when he sleeps." Hislock looked at Godfrey in confusion, forcing the veteran to elaborate, "What!? It's true, it's a wonder how yer lot can hunt anything with that hissing, rattlin' snore of yours."

Bella laughed, and Hislock clicked his teeth together, a common response from the saurian whenever he was annoyed. With some effort, the lizard man responded, "Better than you. *Old* man."

This plain response made her laugh even louder.

"What funny?" Sidon asked as he appeared, seemingly out of nowhere. Godfrey jumped at the boy's sudden appearance, and Bella struggled not to add to the volume of her already cacophonous laugh.

"Magdris' teeth lad. Don't just sneak up on me like that," Godfrey chastised the boy.

"Surret, surret," Sidon said as he dropped a massive bundle of wood near the fire. Truly it was an impressive amount, and Hislock's eyes widened slightly at the success. The boy did not seem to notice and launched into speech with his normal excited tone, "So, we stay here, um, yebam?"

"Yebam means night don't it?" Bella asked and pointed to the setting sun.

"No, not sun. Um, dark … luna."

Bella smiled wryly at the response, and answered his question, "Yes, lad, we are staying here, and Godfrey here is *thrilled* to share his tent with you!"

Godfrey growled, "Yes, I am *so* excited!"

Both Bella and Hislock laughed, much to the confusion of Sidon. He responded in kind, "You are all … um, kilal … joyful."

"Yea, were a regular bunch of comedians," Godfrey said sarcastically.

"I'm sorry, Sidon," Bella said between chuckles.

"Sorry? Surret? No, need for you and 'ahdfey to say such word. You both big help. You and um …" he gulped as he nodded at Hislock. "Um, your friend save me. No need for surret."

The sudden seriousness of the boy made her laughter cease, and she looked at him with a more mature lens.

"Until you. Sidon felt scared … felt taksan. You laugh and be kilal. Makes me forget." The boy's eyes dropped, and his stare faded into the fire. All three adults were silent then, knowing he thought of those he had lost. Bella felt a surge of empathy, a sort of kinship with this young Xeelander. Her own struggles with trauma giving her compassion she did not know she had.

She scooted closer to him and with a gentle touch, she laid her palm on his shoulder. "It's alright now, Sidon. You are safe."

He looked up at her and tears threatened his eyes. "Truly? You will protect me?"

She gulped hard at the question. The weight of responsibility he laid at her feet nearly overwhelming. With resolve she replied, "Yes. I will protect you." The boy fell onto her then, embracing her as his tears unleashed. She hugged him in return, letting the young lad vent his emotions.

Godfrey came around and knelt on his other side while laying a calming hand on Sidon's back. "We *all* will protect you lad."

Hislock let out a loud hiss while nodding affirmation of his own resolve to the promise.

Sidon couldn't help but look at the saurian. He cuffed his face with his wrist and asked, "Does that mean yes?"

Hislock replied, "Yesss."

The boy's eyes went wide as they always did at hearing the saurian speak, and both Godfrey and Bella laughed at the change in expression. Bella ruffled the boy's hair and gently pushed him upright so he would not overstay his embrace. Slow chuckles rippled through the group until they fell into genuine laughter, and Bella felt better than she had in days.

Chapter Twenty

Dunkeath

After a long march on the road, Dunkeath welcomed the warming effect of the beer. The light amber ale sloshed into his stomach, biting deliciously as the carbonation sizzled and popped. The drink settled and slowly a warmth radiated up until he felt a warm flush on his cheeks. Olivia gulped noisily on her own flagon, looking at Dunkeath from over the vessel. His heartbeat increased slightly, and he chose to hide his face in his own mug under the intensity of implication.

It truly was a delicious drink, and the innkeeper would have no trouble selling this particular brew. A fact that was evidenced by the throngs of people gathered around the dining hall. Dunkeath had counted at least twenty long wooden tables that could fit six to eight people a piece, and from what he could tell, they were all nearly full. The clamor of voices—in various states of inebriation—roared within the vaulted hall. A staccato backdrop of wooden bowls and flagons scraping on countertops and tables made it difficult to hear anything but a yell. It was a lively place, and Dunkeath would have been happy if it weren't for the sensation of danger.

Ever since they left the guards by the gate, Dunkeath knew something was amiss. At first, he dismissed it as simple paranoia, but the fear grew. Something in the way those three Argolonian mercenaries carried themselves wasn't right. Something that went beyond the normal hazard of ruthless men and women. There was a promise there; some command that would carry them further than simple gate guards.

Still, he did not know what to do about such a revelation. Therefore, he sat at the table, hidden in the anonymity of the crowded dining hall, and thought of his options, which was made difficult by his friends.

"So, lovely place ay?" Olivia asked, her voice carrying well in its enthusiasm, even over the racket around them.

He took another sip of his beer and leaned in, "I wouldn't be so sure …"

"Oooh, mysterious. I like a mystery man," Olivia responded with a wink. The blatant flirtation making Gilbert groan aloud.

"Olivia, much as I would like to drink and … um, play with you all night, I think we are in danger," Dunkeath responded.

Her red flushed cheeks—creased in a smile—dropped slightly, sensing his seriousness. "Alright, I guess fun can wait. We are on business after all."

Dunkeath nodded to her and placed his hand on the table palm up. She pouted her full red lips in confusion and slowly, like he would bite her, she put her own hand in his.

"Don't worry love, we can always mix business with pleasure. I will be sure to leave time for me, you, and the hay!"

Olivia yanked her hand away and slapped his own with more than a little force. "Ember's breath! You really are the worst!" And though she spoke with a hint of venom in her voice, there was also something more. Something … hungry. She bit the inside of her lip, an action she performed whenever they *mingled*. His heart thumped in his chest.

"Oh, can you two stop!" Gilbert interrupted with a yell. The sound was muffled by his hands which rubbed at his face, once again flushed red with embarrassment. "Now I am not naive enough to think *this* is a game. We literally have a room, well a barn stall, you two should probably use it. Get out your *desires* before I *too* have to sleep there."

Dunkeath grinned as Olivia laughed aloud, her face lighting up delightfully. The roundness of her frame and cheeks gave her a warm appeal, one Dunkeath couldn't help but admire. She truly was a lovely woman— full of life, and he hoped a hay rustling was in the near future. Yet, even through the excitement of that thought, danger overrode his psyche. He took another drink and spoke with a little more gravity, "Aye I would love that Gilbert, but um, I thinks we need to all go to the stall here soon. Something ain't right here."

Through a barely suppressed chuckle Olivia asked, "*Oh*, the both of ya?" She took a final swig from her flagon and slammed the mug down. "I doubt you two could handle it!"

Gilbert groaned audibly, much to the delight of a cackling Olivia. It was a piercing laugh that drew some attention from the surrounding customers. Though the place was full of noise and laughter, Olivia had that effect, being as full of life as she was. They needed to leave soon or risk unwanted attention, especially with a drunken Olivia. Through a forced chuckle, he spoke, "Nah, I'm serious. I'm gonna settle up with the innkeeper and meet y'all in the stables."

"Alright, alright," Olivia said as she wiped the remnants of her beer from her mouth. "Tell him the stew was terrible, but the beer? The beer was delicious! Come on now Gilbert, let's see if we can't make ourselves *comfortable*." She said with a wink to the young Keeper, who rolled his eyes.

Dunkeath felt a tinge of jealousy even though he knew that was simply her manner; a friend to everyone. It's what made her so appealing. His two companions stood, and Gilbert, being the wholesome soul he was, stacked the three wooden stew bowls together in the center of the table. Dunkeath looked at him in bemusement and Gilbert simply shrugged. Not wanting to tease the man any further and encourage Olivia to another outburst, he decided not to press it. Instead, he spoke curtly as he stood himself, "Alright, I'll meet you two outside."

He weaved his way through the crowd until he got to a wooden bar top at the far side of the hall. Spills and bits of food scattered along its length. A woman in a plain white bonnet was visibly sweating as she scrubbed at wooden bowls and flagons in a tub of soapy water. Dunkeath nonchalantly leaned his elbow on the countertop, trying to let the innkeep know he wanted a word without being pushy. The staff here were overworked and hastiness in a customer would do him no favors.

The innkeeper was one of those fellows who looked overweight at first, but at second glance, one could see his stocky and tall frame held some strength in its girthy exterior. With that in mind, he was easy to spot. His build was complimented by a heavy, yet well-rounded face that held a thick black mustache and no other hair. Dunkeath thought the man was born to be an innkeeper from his appearance, especially in the way he carried himself. He always seemed to be in a hurry but not rushed, and he seemed—at least for the time Dunkeath knew him—always cheerful. Even now as he dealt with three young men who were obviously 'far into their cups,' the man smiled as he listened to their drunken ranting.

With a tiny nod, the innkeeper let Dunkeath know he would be right with him. Then with a series of gestures and words Dunkeath couldn't hear over the bustle of the crowds, the innkeeper had all three lads roaring in laughter.

One of the young men placed a coin on the countertop and slid it towards the innkeeper. They then headed off to find a seat with their new round of drinks, the contents nearly empty already.

The innkeeper made the coin disappear with deft hands; never taking his eyes off the departing lads. When the young men had sat down, he briskly walked towards Dunkeath. "What can I do ya for?"

"Just want to settle our tab," Dunkeath replied.

The innkeeper smiled with a big toothy grin, making Dunkeath feel strangely at ease. "Alright then. Let's see … you were the three Augustians right? Came in with some rather nice-looking horses if I remember?"

Dunkeath nodded, though he felt rather uncomfortable having his dealings so loudly proclaimed.

The innkeeper noticed his discomfort and leaned in a little closer. "Look, sir … oh, never mind."

Dunkeath looked at him with confusion, furrowing his brows. Yet, before Dunkeath could ask, the innkeeper jolted back up from the countertop and carried on with his conversation.

"Right, that will be one silver coin. Augustian or otherwise is fine with me. I even take Xetemian, but I will need two silvers there. Just none of that Vidrosian stuff."

Dunkeath scoffed at the sum.

The innkeeper laughed in reply, "That there is with the discount sir. You and your mates ate and drank for free. Room and board is what costs, and I charge what is necessary."

With regret at his unwarranted gesture, Dunkeath pulled a silver coin out of his leather satchel and handed it over. "Thank you. Oh, and my friend said the beer was delicious."

The innkeeper beamed, "Why, tell them thank you!"

As he took the outstretched coin, Dunkeath thought the innkeeper would speak again. Like he held a secret he wished to divulge but decided against it. Instead, he simply took the coin, smiled cheerfully, and with a nod and a clap of his hands he sauntered off to deal with his thriving business. He left Dunkeath mystified as to what might have been said.

*

Outside, in the stables, the three gathered at the back of the barn alongside their horses which shared a neighboring stall. The company was given cloth mats on which they could lay amongst the straw. Frankly, the barn was plenty warm. One could even call it cozy, and not uncomfortably so, unlike the rapidly growing heat inside the inn. Two other groups also shared the barn with them; one was drinking heavily inside and the other— an old man and his son—were already tucked in and out of sight. For all intents and purposes, they had the place to themselves, as long as they didn't scream their business out into the void.

"So, what is it then? What's got ya all bothered?" Olivia asked tersely.

He couldn't reply at first, choosing instead to pace back and forth, disturbing the loose straw that lay about the barn floor. His thoughts were solidly on his strange interaction with the innkeeper moments before. *What had that man wanted to say?*

"I swear it's like talking to a brick wall sometimes," Olivia pouted. Her grievances were aired in the general direction of Gilbert, who just nodded, not wanting to get involved in any dispute. "Hello? What's got ya bothered!"

Her shout finally broke him free of his thoughts and he stopped his frantic pacing. She looked rather short with him, and he figured he should air his concerns, "I-I dunno. I can't be certain, but this whole place feels off. From the guards at the gate—not the cheery bastard—to the conversation I just had with the innkeeper. It all screams *danger.*"

Olivia did not laugh or mock him this time. No, she simply nodded her head. Years of association with Dunkeath had taught her to trust his instincts. "How dangerous we talking?"

"Like I said, can't be sure, but I would reckon that we should sleep with one eye open tonight," he replied.

The admission silenced Olivia for a few moments, and all that could be heard were the soft snorts of a horse as it ate. Dunkeath was ready to start pacing again, not having any other outlet to unleash his anxiety, until Olivia broke the quiet, "Well, what're we gonna do 'bout it?"

He bit his finger, a nervous tick, "I have no idea, maybe …"

"I do," Gilbert interrupted calmly, shocking them both. When no one spoke, but just stared, the Keeper clarified, "You see, us Keepers all have a thing. A certain god that we talk to more *intimately.* Mine just so happens to be this." The Keeper pulled out a bundle of smooth rose gold rods from beneath his tunic, seemingly out of nowhere.

Dunkeath blurted out, "How did you do that!"

Gilbert's face rocked back in shock at the sudden outburst, "Do what?"

"Pull the stones out," Dunkeath stopped, realizing he was talking too loudly and shuffled closer to Gilbert, "I mean, how did you just pull that stone out from nowhere? How did you hide it from the guards … they was thorough."

Gilbert smiled then, a beaming, triumphant countenance, "That sir, is a secret. But to sate your curiosity let's just say me and gnomes may have had similar conversations with Hercurius."

"Hercurius? That's the one who likes to move fast and all innit?" Olivia asked, surprising Dunkeath with her knowledge.

"That's right!" Gilbert said like a teacher would to a student who impressed them, it was a bit sickening. "Hercurius has a few more tricks than that up his sleeve though." Gilbert paused, evidently to try and make his words more impactful.

Dunkeath hated when people did that, *just say what you got to say.* "So, you hide it then?" Dunkeath asked plainly, and Gilbert's beaming smile dropped away. He couldn't help but think back to the frisking that had so worried him, and he now realized how this seemingly naive Keeper had managed. The little bastard was using gnomish magic to do what took him years to learn. Frankly, he felt a little miffed the Keeper was able to cheat the system so easily and he didn't mind bursting his bubble. Dunkeath pressed on, "Just like them gnomes. Little buggers disappear and reappear all the time. I tell ya, when Sophia made that deal with them in Elgion, I swore they was just everywhere. But ol' Dunkeath figured it out," he said while tapping the side of his head.

When he—accidentally mimicking the very dramatic pause he despised—did not elaborate right away, Olivia interjected, "Oh, you ain't figured out nothin'. All talk you are. So, how can you help, Gilbert?"

"Right," Gilbert held the smooth stone up, rotating it so they could all see. Its edges were sharp, contrasting well with the smooth faces that shone in the lamplight of the barn. The color was wonderful, and it seemed like all shades and hues of pink danced just beneath the stone's surface. Dunkeath could feel a tug; a pull that beckoned him, and he subconsciously shuffled forward a few steps. It was *such* a beautiful stone; he had the sensation he would be swallowed up whole—he almost welcomed it. Before the sensation became a reality, Gilbert interrupted, "This here is Artstone, or if you're so inclined, Slivers of Truth."

"Why they call it that?" Olivia asked eagerly.

Gilbert clicked his cheek, and while still staring at the small rose gold rods of godstone, sat up straighter, "Well, it's simple. Artstone represents love, beauty … emotion. And, well, what is more beautiful than the truth?"

Dunkeath—not one to be swept up in such dramaticisms—felt a chill run up his arm. *What is more beautiful than the truth?* What a little morsel to reflect upon, a gem for those quiet moments.

With his silent audience enraptured by the stone, Gilbert continued, "The prettier you shape these particular stones, the better they work. Notice the smooth edges?" Gilbert twirled the godstone; the gemstones faces each more radiant than the last. "Anyways, like I was saying, all Keepers have a sort of *patron* if you will, and this god here is mine."

"Minollo?" Olivia asked sheepishly.

Gilbert looked at her again and smiled, "Once again, correct! Boy, you *have* learned a thing or two from Sophia."

Olivia blushed heavily and her button face turned a deep red.

Gilbert—satisfied his impromptu pupil was appropriately rewarded—turned his gaze back to the stone. "She is the best …" The Keeper did not elaborate.

Dunkeath did not want to be trapped by the beauty of the stone again and looked at the dirt floor below. He kicked some loose straw and grunted loudly, prompting the Keeper.

Gilbert shook his head roughly, and his eyes seemed to refocus. "Right! Anyways, um, I can tell you if something dangerous is coming. Well, I can *probably* tell you." Gilbert winced and tucked his head between his shoulders like a man afraid of reprisal.

Dunkeath chuckled at the gesture, "No questions here, Keeper. If you say you can do it, well, I have seen some rather crazy things from my boss, and I have learned to take you Keepers at yer word." His heart quickened as he saw Olivia flash him a smile. Apparently, he had said the right thing.

"Uh … wow, um, thank you," Gilbert stammered. Suddenly, Gilbert stood and walked forward still staring at the outstretched stone. Without prompting, the Keeper elaborated on his plan, "So, I'm going to go … somewhere. I will need you two to watch me. I'm probably going to start convulsing rather *violently*. You'll have to keep me steady, and if it seems like I'm not going to come out of it. I need you to pull me out. Slap, kick, pinch me, whatever it takes. Understand?" Gilbert pivoted on his feet and looked back and forth between the two.

"How will we know that ya ain't gonna come out of it?" Olivia asked.

Gilbert pursed his lips, "Change in tempo—expression? I can't say for certain, but it should be obvious," With his cryptic instructions delivered, he looked around the barn. "Ok, I will need a more comfortable seat. I can't have my focus break by sitting in itchy straw. Ah, there we go!" Gilbert raced over to a stool and picked it up. He plopped it down near where Olivia was still sitting. He then turned to Dunkeath, "You think it's the guards at the gate or the innkeeper that's most dangerous?"

Dunkeath, stunned by the Keeper's sudden energy, stammered. He hadn't made that conclusion yet, but his gut told him the truth. "The guards; definitely them guards."

With a curt nod, the Keeper started muttering to himself, rubbing the stone between his palms. Dunkeath swore he saw flecks of pink and gold dance above the stone, like mini fireworks. Gilbert sat with a plop, not even looking to ensure his seat was still there. The Keeper's eyes were closed and the sound of his muttering increased in volume, "Minollo, come to me once more and show me your light; your truth. MINOLLO, come to me once more and show me your *light*; *YOUR TRUTH.*"

Over and over Gilbert repeated the phrase as he rubbed the stone. Dunkeath saw with certainty this time, tiny, dancing lights that made a menagerie of color above the god fragment. Olivia took up a kneeling position near the Keeper, ready to 'pull' him out as he requested. Dunkeath was several centimeters away and he remained standing, too entranced by the proceedings to move. Suddenly, Gilbert's head rocked back, and he stared straight up towards the ceiling. Dunkeath could see the whites of his eyes and felt a sympathetic pain in his neck as he saw the Keeper bend his neck heavily backwards. It was like he was looking somewhere that did not exist.

Gilbert started trembling, and his mouth moved silently. The tremble grew in intensity and the Keeper shook all over, like every muscle in his body was convulsing, save for his arms which were glued to the stone in front of him. They no longer rubbed but instead were clasped like vice grips. The shard pulsed, and Olivia was forced to steady the man as his trembles became strong enough to nearly vibrate him out of the stool. With a glance, Olivia prompted Dunkeath to take up a position on the other side.

He fell to his knees near the Keeper and placed a steady hand on the man's back. He could feel the intensity of this latest magic. Not only was Gilbert's every muscle quivering, but also an emanation of energy coursed through Dunkeath's veins, and his heart raced in exhilaration. Olivia looked at him from over the Keeper's lap and he could see worry plainly wrought on her face.

Then—as suddenly as it began—Gilbert's head rocked forward, and his muscles collapsed. Dunkeath, alongside Olivia, was forced to snatch the Keeper's tunic to prevent him from falling. He maneuvered in a way to shoulder the man's weight more easily, but he was like an inanimate stone. With as much grace as they could muster, they eased him backwards into the straw.

Gilbert's eyes opened, and as if he were a person on his deathbed, his lips quivered with a mockery of final words. At first, they were wordless intonations but slowly he found his voice, "They … are … coming … *now!*"

The warning was plain enough, and its starkness chilled Dunkeath to the core. Yet, they did not delay in their response. Olivia and him had seen too much by now to be crippled by fear. He leapt to his feet and ran to the barn door, staring out into the night to see if he could spot anything. Save for the torchlight of the inn, there was nothing but shadows, and he imagined all sorts of monsters hidden in that deep dark. He shuddered as he pulled the heavy twin doors shut. With them fastened, he threw the crossbar into place. There was a smaller entrance to the left, but this would prevent the enemy from knowing what happened inside the barn. It would also keep them from being turned into porcupines by some distant projectile.

When he had turned around, Olivia had managed to get Gilbert to his feet, and the Keeper swayed unsteadily before holding himself upright with a post. Dunkeath jogged back to his friends, and watched Olivia rip a pitchfork she had hidden from underneath a pile of hay. He grinned at her as she pulled bits of straw from it. The action reminded him of the knife he had managed to secure as soon as they had entered the tavern earlier in the day. His years in Augustia, looking for criminals and other such oddities, gave him the skills to *borrow* what was necessary. He pulled the knife out from under his belt and ran a finger along the edge. It was no more than a kitchen knife, but it was sharp and seemed sturdy, though he wondered if it would withstand an intense conflict. Regardless, it was comforting to have at least *some* sort of weapon to face the threat that approached.

"Ya gonna prick 'em with that?" Olivia asked jokingly as she dragged Dunkeath's stallion out of its stall.

"Aye, best I could do. I see you made out alright—as always."

Olivia jerked her head back towards Gilbert, "Best see to our friend."

He nodded and took comfort from the grin she gave him before dashing over to Gilbert, who swayed slightly.

He skidded to a stop near the Keeper, "Alright, boss, how ya feelin'?"

The young man looked at him, and to Dunkeath's surprise, Gilbert grinned, "Right as rain. Right … as … rain."

He laughed and clapped the ever-more-surprising Keeper on the back, which nearly made him fall forward, "Woah, sorry about that. Um, so can you elaborate on *what* is coming?"

The Keeper shook his head, "It doesn't work like that. I am only able to read their thoughts. With practice, I can choose whose mind to read in the sea of souls that surround me." Gilbert rolled his neck and stretched his back muscles out, clearly regaining some of his composure. With some effort he continued, "Most people use it just to see a 'truth' they find more enjoyable. I use it for more *practical* purposes. In so doing I found one of those guards, and sure enough they were thinking of us; thinking of death."

He nodded at Gilbert but held back the shiver the Keeper's dire warnings had produced. Not knowing what else to say, he simply added, "Well, I hope you got some more tricks up your sleeve."

Gilbert winked, and Dunkeath realized he was starting to like the young man. His tousled black hair gave him a more rugged look than his normal, scholarly appearance, and Dunkeath wondered how much further this man's character went. He sure wasn't as shallow of a personality as he originally thought. Unfortunately, he had to abandon that train of thought because the small door that led into the barn flung open.

Chapter Twenty-One
Dunkeath

The side door slammed into the wall, and a reverberation stunned even the horses into silence. The man that had bunked with his son was peeping over their closed stall when three Argolonians appeared. The man darted back into the darkness of his 'room' after the front man of the Argolonian group glanced at him. The three guards centered themselves in the main lane of the barn.

All three wore an iron helm which had a wide slit down the middle and cutouts for the eyes. It gave them a shadowed, deeply unpleasant appearance. They also wore a bronze chest plate, greaves, and bracers over an iron link mail coat. *Some traditions are hard to break*, Dunkeath thought as he struggled to not focus on his own lack of armor. All three had wooden shields rimmed in bronze on their backs and two of them held short, punching swords in their hands. The front man of the group held a mace with iron studs on its surface. Clearly, the Argolonians were not so foolish as to let tradition deny them the use of iron.

For a time, the two groups just stared at one another, and the mace-wielding Argolonian pierced the silence by methodically slapping the mace head into the palm of his hand.

"Ya leave now, and we won't kill the lot of ya!" Olivia yelled defiantly.

The mace-wielder chortled, "You're rather brave … stupid though."

It was obvious he was the leader, and Dunkeath wondered if they could incapacitate him quickly enough to make the other two falter. It was doubtful, these people looked like those born to war, and Dunkeath's heart sank as he felt his own death rapidly approaching.

"We were told to look out fer *Keepers*," the mace wielder said with a malevolent grin that made itself known even from underneath the iron face plate. "And here … you … are," The man punctuated each word with a slap on the mace.

Dunkeath felt a prickle on his neck, like winter's chill. The leader stepped forward a few paces and his companions followed.

Olivia brandished her pitchfork, stopping them briefly. "Ember's breath! What do you want?"

"That's simple, girl, we want what our boss wants," the leader did not elaborate, and Dunkeath could hear his companions chuckle malevolently. The three started forward again in a stolid march. It was the moment Olivia had been waiting for. She slapped the rump of the stallion which whinnied in fright and charged. The massive horse barreled down on the guards who were paces away. Dunkeath watched the leader's eyes widen as he saw the threat coming. One guard dove and the other twisted deftly out of harm's way, but the leader was only able to spin before he was bowled over by the horse's charge. Dunkeath saw the man's leg twist unnaturally.

"Just like I thought," Olivia said smugly. The stallion reared up and slammed the door with its hooves, but to no avail. Frustrated, the horse bucked to and fro at the front of the barn, acting as a barrier to anyone trying to escape. *Hopefully, that horse won't charge back and kill us all,* Dunkeath worried.

The standing guard recovered and with a glance back at the raging horse, marched forward once more. Dunkeath's heart raced in panic; death—that ever-present specter—a breath away. The chill intensified and a sudden breeze whipped up from behind him, forcing him to look back.

Gilbert stepped forward, haloed in a blue pale light, his cloak was dancing in an artificial breeze of his own design. In Gilbert's hand was an ugly lump of cerulean godstone, shaped like the tempestuous waters it represented. There were no words to whatever spell Gilbert worked on, and Dunkeath wondered if the god he beseeched heeded the cries of humanity as the others did. His thoughts swirled at what was to come, as Gilbert lanced out his arm, prompting the guard who had been aiming at Dunkeath to charge. They had recognized the threat.

Dunkeath counter charged the man, slamming into the Argolonian, narrowly saving Gilbert's outstretched arm from the blade. As the two fell to Telaea, Dunkeath managed to glance at Gilbert. From the Keeper's hand, a bolt of ice—sharp as any blade—issued forth, but Dunkeath could not witness its outcome because he was slammed into the ground. The air was knocked out of him and his body bounced off the armor of his enemy.

Clumsily, Dunkeath took the dominant kneeling position over his foe, to the sounds of an agonizing cry from Gilbert. There was no time to look at his companion; the guard in between his legs reached up to grab his tunic. Dunkeath lunged his knife towards the man's face, but his wrist was gripped by the enemy's free hand. The hold was like iron and Dunkeath's wrist throbbed in agony. The man, using the leverage of his tunic, brought Dunkeath's head downwards and headbutted him. The force of the blow, accentuated by the iron of the helm, stunned him. All he could see were stars as he felt his own knife—one he had dropped after the headbutt—bury itself into his shoulder blade. *Gods the man was good.*

Dunkeath felt himself spin to the ground, and the weight of the armor-encased guard bore down on him. His eyes refocused and he saw the guard grinning at him. They held their short sword ready for a plunging blow. Dunkeath braced for the end.

Suddenly, a wailing cry from Olivia could be heard. Her pitchfork lanced towards the man's face. Two of the tines scraped off the top of his helm, but not before knocking it askew. The guard was temporarily blinded by his own armor, and before he could react, Olivia brought the pitchfork around in a sweeping blow. It was just enough to knock the man aside, and Dunkeath rolled away.

He tried to prop himself up, but the lancing pain in his shoulder forced him to drop to the ground. Slowly, he rolled on his side with his good shoulder and watched as the man who nearly killed him stood, his helmet righted. He grinned wickedly and charged Olivia. Dunkeath strained to sit upright, and his head swirled in agony as he heard blow after blow connect with wood. Olivia's grunting replies to the strikes becoming more desperate with each thud.

Dunkeath regained a sitting position. All he could do was watch as Olivia's pitchfork snapped in two and the guard backhanded her heavily. She fell to the ground with a cry, her pitchfork discarded in a useless pile. "Olivia!" He cried out, but his voice was a hoarse whisper. She looked at him with fear in her eyes, and he reached out towards her.

"Hey!" A new voice boomed.

They all looked at this new development. There, with the barn doors wide open—freeing the panicking horse—stood the innkeeper, alongside the cheery gate guard from before. The innkeeper held a large axe in his hand and wore simple leather armor. The man looked rather imposing as he rolled his shoulders, "I knew you three weren't right. Now, stop trying to kill my customers and *walk* away."

By now the leader of the Argolonian guards had found his feet; although, he favored one leg heavily. The leader scoffed, "Not before we do what we need to." With that he limped towards Gilbert. The Keeper held the wrist of his left hand, his mouth open in silent agony, and Dunkeath could see at least two of Gilbert's fingers were blackened and shriveled.

Gilbert fell backwards as he looked at the clumsily approaching leader. The Keeper's injured hand was still in his own grasp, and Gilbert whimpered as he closed his eyes and prepared to meet his fate. As the man brought his mace up to crush Gilbert's skull, a thrumming whoosh interrupted the action. A small axe buried itself into the enemy leader's throat. It was an expert throw, and stunned by the suddenness of it all, the leader looked at the innkeeper in amazement then back at his own bloody hand which had touched the lodged axe blade. Finally, he looked back at Gilbert before falling to his knees, his face full of confusion. He slumped over onto his side; his bronze armor rising once more as he heaved a final breath that rattled out of him.

The remaining guard, who had so nearly killed Olivia, looked around at the situation and chose to flee, running past the innkeeper who did not bar his way.

"And don't come back!" The innkeeper roared after him.

Though Dunkeath loathed to think who that guard would report to, it somehow felt right to not kill unnecessarily. It was a small solace in the face of the grim fate they had nearly endured. A fate that had come at them quickly, and he struggled to fully comprehend all that had occurred. He glanced around through vision blurred by pain, and he could see the third Argolonian lying cold on the ground. A jagged sliver of ice had pierced their throat. His mind registered the threats were gone, and he felt suddenly weary with exhaustion.

"Hey, hey! Don't you go to sleep on me!" He felt Olivia grab his shoulders as he fell back to the ground. "He took a nasty blow to the head. I think he's got a concussion."

Dunkeath tried to keep his eyes open, but the lids forced themselves closed.

He heard another voice, a strong baritone that seemed to engulf him in its command. "Right! I got some salts that will keep him awake. Crassus! Run to the bar, look under the top and to the left of the wash basin, there's a small satchel of the stuff there."

Dunkeath felt another strong hand lift his head and a soft material placed underneath.

"Well, don't just stand there. Go!" The baritone voice yelled.

It all seemed so distant, the pain throbbed all over, but it felt like a far-off memory. He was able to briefly flick his eyes open and he glimpsed a warm face, one he knew. He felt himself smile, not entirely knowing why.

"Oh, ya big lummox! Don't you be smiling at me like that. Come on now, stay awake!"

He tried to heed the command, even as he felt a series of hands poke and prod at him, he could not summon the strength to obey.

*

Sudden wretched smells assaulted his senses, and his beleaguered mind roared into life. *Something poisonous. Near him. Need to get away!*

A lancing pain shot through his shoulder as he abruptly sat up. He could feel himself roaring, not in rage, but in raw survival. *Who was he?* He did not know, but all around him were hands trying to subdue him.

"Oh, thank the Maiden!" One bubbly voice cried out.

"Alright lad! It's alright." Another followed suit, but with a bass that demanded to be heard.

Where was he? Who was he? His mind swirled in confusion as he thrashed about himself desperate to know safety.

"Alright, it's alright," the bass-filled voice repeated.

On his right he could hear the faint sound of crying. His nostrils were clearing the poisonous scent. A mixture of ammonia and … and salt. It was like the smells he had endured whenever he was forced to clean out the family latrine back in Elgion. *There;* there was a fragment of his memory—a sense of himself—swirling back into life. Sudden spikes of pain shot through his skull, and he felt his stomach sour with bile. As he twisted to the side, his shoulder burned in agony, but he couldn't stop. His body convulsed, retching up a stream of vomit, but through the bombardment of pain his name came back to him, *Dunkeath.*

"Oh, Ember's breath! You sure know how to charm 'em." A familiar voice said. *Olivia.* As he finished hurling up his stomach, his eyes refocused, and there in front of him was the button faced lass who he found so endearing. She beamed at him, "There you are!"

Dunkeath fell onto her. She caught him and let his head lay within her lap. Her hand calmly brushing his hair. In the solace of her embrace, all his life came swimming back into focus. From what he remembered, it wasn't so bad, especially the parts with Olivia in it. A gentle sob forced its way out, brought on by the overwhelming intensity of recent events.

Through tears of her own, he heard Olivia croon, "That's a good lad. We're gonna be alright. That's right, we're gonna be just … fine."

He didn't know how long it took before the innkeeper could wait no more, but the large man's voice seemed eager—impatient. Like he couldn't wait for Dunkeath's little recovery session to finish. "I knew I should have said something. I knew it in my gut! Something weren't right and I shoulda listened."

With a wince of pain, Dunkeath's shoulder quivered. He put a hand to the pulsing torment and felt wet cloth swaddling the wound. He glanced at the medical intervention and saw a slowly growing patch of red in the center. *They got me pretty deep*, he mused as he sat upright.

The burly innkeeper pulled their throwing ax free from the neck of the now dead Argolonian. "Y'know I told muhself, 'Now Bertrand, don't go a trustin these folks.'" The innkeeper wiped the axe blade clean on the dead man's trousers. "They look *mighty* shifty!" He then rubbed his thumb along the axe blade to test its edge, "And what did I do? I trusted 'em … Damn fool I am! Jus' look at 'em though! They were mighty fierce looking and wit' the rumors of bandits and trolls about. I wanted … reassurances." The bald man stood and let his throwing axe slide into a hoop on his hip.

Gilbert groaned and the innkeeper's face lit up, recognition of him being needed plain on the happy-go-lucky features. Another squirm, and the girthy innkeeper raced over to kneel at Gilbert's side. In a friendly, almost soothing way, the innkeeper spoke "I'm sorry lad. I had to take the fingers off. The rotten flesh can quickly turn septic and, well …" He trailed off and batted an imaginary worry away with his hand. "Eh, doesn't matter.

Anyways, just trust me! Being in my line of work you see all kinds of things. And yes, that includes frostbite. You tried using that dirty ol' sea god didn't ya? Bastard never delivers without exactin' a heavy price." The innkeeper checked a bandage that looked freshly applied, and once satisfied, stood once more with an easy grace. The big man walked over to Dunkeath and Olivia. "Name's Bertrand by the way. I don't think we formally met!" The innkeeper held out a massive hand, one that looked more bear than man.

Dunkeath straightened a little, feeling his shoulder complain at the movement, and took Bertrand's hand in his own. The grip was like iron, and Bertrand shook vigorously. The motion sent slivers of pain shooting up his shoulder.

Bertrand glanced towards Olivia, blanched, and quickly spoke, "Oh, right the shoulder! Sorry about that! Just get a little friendly is all." He pulled his hand back and shuffled awkwardly for a moment.

Only a few seconds passed before the silence appeared too much for the dear old innkeeper, and he spoke with nervous energy, "Well, I wanted to say something to ya earlier. You folks coming from Augustia right?"

Olivia nodded.

"Well, there used to be a fella here. An Argolonian."

Olivia interjected sarcastically, "Seems to be a lot of those around here."

The innkeeper chuckled, "Right, but this one, ya see, was not just any Argolonian but he did *work* for Argolon. If'n ya catch my meaning. Well, he roomed with us for a long while and then one day he just up and vanishes. But not before he left me with'n this here message." Bertrand produced a metal tube from behind him and held it up in the torchlight of the barn. "Yeah, he gave it to me and he said, 'Now Bertrand I want you to give this to any Augustian's that come looking for me.'" Bertrand stopped suddenly, his body going rigid. Quickly, he hid the metal tube once more and with apprehension souring his friendly tone he asked, "What brings you folks out here anyways?"

Dunkeath glanced at Olivia who shrugged at him. It would be up to him to decide if they could trust this eccentric innkeeper. From what he could tell, the man seemed genuine enough and frankly Bertrand had saved their life. The decision was easy to make. "We're here to try and find someone named, *Bloodeye.*"

Relief flooded Bertrand's face, and he pulled the tube out once more, "See I ain't no good at all this … cloak and dagger stuff. I nearly gave up the goat without even knowin' if'n you were the ones to give it to!" Bertrand opened the metal tube and pulled out a sheet of rolled crinkled parchment. "Well, I did take a look at the thing, but I figure it must be something special 'cause I can't for the life of me figure it out. And since Bloodeye told me to give it to the first Augustian's looking for him. Well, ones that—and he was very clear about this—ones that if they call him by any other name … well, no sirree do not give, ya know what I mean?"

Dunkeath struggled to keep up with the rapid speech of the innkeeper, especially in light of his throbbing head.

Bertrand, on the other hand, didn't seem to notice his audience was on death's door and continued undeterred, "But if they use the 'ol name Bloodeye you show them this here paper. So, here we are." Bertrand shuffled over to Olivia holding the delicate parchment out.

Olivia eyed Bertrand suspiciously, and then delicately grabbed the parchment, unrolling it to read what lay within. She simply stared at the document for a moment, until a grin formed. She looked at Dunkeath with mischief wrought on her face and handed the parchment to him. He felt it crackle under his fingers, and with forced slowness, he gently unrolled the parchment, revealing the full missive.

We ylg sjawxqjf dqwi, ylg zgid mj Ngtgidwnb nbs pblh nblgd zy kwddkj mwfs. Hj algks hlfp dltjdqjf. Ngtgidwn qni ilzjlbj dfywbt dl znbgenadgfj hnf dl ijagfj mlblxlky lb dqj iqnfsi, zlid gftjbd. We wbdjfjidjs, kjncj zjüntj gbsjf mfistj lgdwisj le Qnfmlf Tndj. W hwkk ewbd ylg.

-Mkllsjvj

Dunkeath frowned, "It's gibberish."

Olivia sighed, and with a patient tone corrected him, "Nah, think about that letter we found at the Lady Aliana's house."

Slowly, he understood what she meant. This was another ciphered missive. *Exactly* what Sophia would be looking for.

"Yeah? Innit just like that?" Olivia asked.

He nodded at her, allowing the excitement to build. The pain was still fresh, and he knew they couldn't just up and leave yet, but somehow getting a hold of the very type of evidence Sophia would be looking for filled him with glee. "We have to get back to Augustia. Soph—The Keeper will *need* to see this!"

"I agree," Olivia said, rising to her feet and dusting her trousers.

"Now, hold on, now! You folks are gonna need at least a few moments rest!" Bertrand chimed in. He was rewarded with a scornful glare. Bertrand decided it would be best to elaborate, "On the house of course! 'Sides I need better light to make sure yer bandages are right."

Dunkeath glanced at Olivia, who nodded with a chuckle. "I think we better take the man up on the offer. You look even worse than normal. 'Sides we have some letters from a friend of ours that need delivering. Mayhaps you could take 'em to Argentios for us?"

Bertrand nodded, "Certainly!"

With that, Dunkeath let out a wry chuckle and with little reluctance, accepted Bertrand's offer. After all, he had been rather rudely awakened.

Chapter Twenty-Two

Alexa

"Row! Ember's breath, row you filthy dogs! You want to be food for the lizards? Row!" Sergeant Prinius had a particular talent for inspiring the crew of the bireme. A long career within the Warriors of August had given him a broad lexicon of insults that seemed more humorous than hurtful. Alongside the gravelly bellow he had nurtured over the years, Alexa had no problem hearing him. A truth even over the wind and splash of salt water as he stormed up and down the center strake.

"We have no time for yer idle fancies! Put yer backs into it! Lyra! You want me to console your grieving mother? No? Then row! Gravin! You wipe that smirk off yer face and row ya bastard! Penelope, Magdris's teeth, do you not hear? Row to the beat!"

Barely stifling a grin at the man's exaggerations, Alexa resisted the urge to laugh. If she did, the crew would most certainly join her. So, she bared her teeth and continued to row. Her oar partner Roderick, who went by Ro, had yet to find a suitable range-mate replacement. Like Rangemaster Apararius had done with her years ago, she used him as her proxy partner until a solution could be found. At present, that partnership consisted of helping her with the twelve-meter-long oar.

One hundred and ten men and women made up the crew of the bireme named The Malegost, and it needed every soul to perform as expected. Many of them had helped build the ships they now crewed. After all, Augustia couldn't send war galleys over the sea; no one could. War galleys couldn't handle an ocean voyage, and thus, Elgion's homemade navy was born. Three galleys built with stout timbers straight from the Eukarian Forest. Each galley had two banks of twelve oars on each side which required two rowers per oar, and with that many rowers, a trierarch, a drummer, some scouts, and Sergeant Prinius, one hundred and ten crew was the bare minimum.

"Row! Row! Row!" Sergeant Prinius timed his shouts to the beat of the drum.

He loves this, Alexa smiled. She was glad he did, because they needed speed, especially now. They were bait, and capture was not optional. So, she let herself fall into the steady rhythm of the drum.

Boom! She heaved, and her thoughts drifted like so many times before in recent days. *Boom!* Unbidden, she saw Elira, stripped, stabbed—mutilated. *Boom!* It had been her order—her fault. *Boom!* Elira was dead because of her. *Boom!* Alexa tightened her grip on the oar and pulled with all her might. *Boom!* She roared along with the salt spray as she heaved away the guilt. *Boom! It* ... would not ... go.

"Come on crew! We are nearly there! Thirty more seconds, Row!" Sergeant Prinius commanded his marine contingent of the Warriors of August, a command granted after his exceptional service during the orcish raids.

Boom! Alexa heaved again to the complaint of overtaxed muscles. *Boom!* The demands of the drum were becoming too much. *Boom!* She nearly cried out in pain as she pulled once more. *Boom!* Desperate yells erupted from around her. *Boom!* One more time she pulled on the oar, as Ro let out a roar of defiance.

"Stop! Alright, bank oars lads!" Sergeant Prinius yelled as he walked to the rear of the ship.

She and Ro quickly brought their oar in and let it fall to the deck. Huge breaths accompanied the exhausted stupor they adopted. Nothing mattered but recovery, and it was several seconds before she heard the sergeant once more.

"Rangemaster! You said you wanted to see? Come and look!" Prinius's voice was filled with excitement.

Her official title brought her back to the fore and with a deep breath she stood, rolling her shoulders to try and loosen the overworked tissue. She would be sore the next day, but she *had* asked to experience these 'defensive measures' in their full glory, rowing and all. Complaining now would do her no good. She hopped up from the rower's benches and made her way down the center strake towards the sergeant.

He beamed at her, a small scar on his forehead, the only reminder of his contribution in the Battle for Elgion. Before that momentous battle had even begun, she had commanded the defense of Farney Ford, a successful blocking action that had culled the orcish numbers. Her success there had garnered her much respect from The Warriors of August, Sergeant Prinius chief amongst them. So, it came as no surprise the man was thrilled to show her a little of what he had been doing in the years since.

He waved for her to hurry, then turned towards the sea behind them, "Look!" He pointed to a pile of chum they had thrown overboard, now no more than a small splash of red on a sea of blue and white.

At first, Alexa saw nothing but a gentle roll of a calm sea, but then, a massive, scaled head, the color of moss, peeked above the water. Even from this distance she could hear the beast's jaw snap as it took in a mouthful. Successful in feeding on the treat, the lizard rolled back down under the waves, taking *at least* three seconds for all its body to follow suit, a slap of its tail finalizing its descent.

Sergeant Prinius chuckled, most likely from her slack-jawed look. "Right? These things are huge! I figure that that one was fifteen … maybe twenty meters."

Another deinocus—the official name for the massive crocs—burst from under the waves and chomped at the chum, rolling away with its prize intact. Then another. And another. And before long, it seemed every deinocii in existence emerged to take part in the free feast. They had, after all, lured the beasts away with three-quarter rowing speed and a small trickle of chum to entice them. With what felt like the attention of every predator of Deinos Bay on them, the trierarch had increased to a full speed row as they dropped hundreds of pounds of fish guts and animal offal overboard. A treat to those deinocii that had followed them away from the bay.

Now, as Alexa felt the strain of an hour or more of intense rowing, she took in the impressive sight. She wondered how any of the fishermen and women of Elgion could dare the seas knowing such creatures lurked within its depths. *Brave pioneers.*

She laughed aloud as a spray of saltwater hit the bow of the boat, soaking her and the sergeant. She needed this release—this escape—and she had secretly wanted to hug her old friend, Sergeant Prinius, when he had suggested, "Why don't you see for yerself Rangemaster? 'Sides a good taste of Melleas always helps clear me head."

She always wanted to see one of the many preventive measures in place to reduce the threat of the deinocii. Especially since her input on maintaining The Balance—that ancient code of the Ranger order—had been respected. Sure, they hunted the beasts in an attempt to cull their numbers, but so far this met with little success. The deinocii scales resisted all but the mightiest of spear throws, and since the creatures rarely came out of the water, they became a particularly difficult prey. Now, partly in honor of her order's wishes, and partly because they simply did not know how to deal with them physically, the deinocii threat was mitigated with controlled hunting and insane maneuvers like the one she had just been a part of.

"The fishermen will have the run of the Bay for at least three days now!" Sergeant Prinius yelled as he wiped the water from his face. "Eventually, these crocs' will get bored or hungry and make their way back to the richer waters near the coast. But 'till then? Smooth sailing."

Alexa nodded and was abruptly splashed by another roll of the sea. She felt unsteady on the rolling bireme, and she could feel the first stirrings of sickness now that they were in deep water, and she was no longer rowing for her life.

Sergeant Prinius laughed again, "Yer looking a little green around the gills! These warships handle like piss on the open water without speed. Best we be getting back to shore before too long." She unconsciously rubbed her shoulder at the mention of the return journey and Prinius laughed as he clapped her on the back. "Don't worry! We can catch the nor'easters that roar down from Melleas' Wroth. It will bring us right to the southern edge of the bay. Then it's an easy row back to port."

She sagged with relief, making the sergeant laugh even harder. He stomped away from her as he barked out orders to his crew, "Alright lads! We did what we came for. No crocs will be feasting on us tonight! Trierarch! Permission to hoist the sail!" After a confirmatory nod from the taciturn bireme commander, Prinius continued, "Hoist the sail lads, we are gonna catch a ride home!"

Alexa heard the sails slam down, and a sudden jerk yanked the boat southwards, forcing her against the rear rail of the bireme. She watched for a while, observing the feast of the deinocii and was happy to distract her mind from the guilt she felt.

Chapter Twenty-Three

Alexa

The sun hung low on the horizon in front of her, beckoning her towards home—towards Elgion. A small wind swirled amidst the calm waters in the Bay of Elgion. With a small, rotating contingent of rowers, they moved lazily along that southern coast. Stolidly marching towards the port, Alexa couldn't be happier. She was dead on her feet; hours of physical exertion had taken their toll. Her normally dark thoughts were subdued by intense labor, and the effort had left her depleted. Now, she wanted nothing more than to sleep.

"It's quite the sight innit," Roderick joined her on the stern, gripping the rail.

She didn't answer at first; just letting the golden light dance across her eyes as she took in the spectacle. A dazzling sheen amongst gently rolling waves, which was accented against rich green hills that bordered shallow beaches. Stands of hawthorn and oak scattered amongst windswept grass, ferns, and brush like small lords over hill kingdoms. "Yeah … it always is." His eyes were on her, but she didn't look. She couldn't stand the inspection, not now.

Still, he stared, and with an apprehensive sigh he ventured, "Rangemaster?"

It was his ploy, little Ro would always prompt her in such an innocent way, forcing her to recognize him. "Yes, Ro?"

"You alright? It's just that you seem … out of sorts. I mean; I get it. I heard what happened …"

It all came back then, but she was too tired, too exhausted to let the normal surge of anger from those thoughts grip her. She gritted her teeth and forced a response, "I'm-I'm fine." The lie made her feel even more hollow.

Roderick opened his mouth. She could hear the intake of breath, but he did not speak. Even little Ro didn't know what else to say.

"Port spotted ahead, trierarch!" A sailor with particularly keen eyes bellowed not far away.

The trierarch, a woman Alexa did not know, strolled to the stern, a few meters away from Alexa and Ro. Her hands were clasped behind her back, and her calm inspection of the truth belied her command method. Little to say, but when she did, it was to be heard. "Very well," the trierarch murmured, only loud enough for Alexa to hear. Then with a surprising force roared in command, "Sailor's, back to your oars! Strike the sail! Let's bring her home!"

A cheer rippled amongst the scattered crew as they raced to their positions.

"You heard the trierarch! Warriors! Back to oars," Sergeant Prinius echoed.

Alexa turned and jogged towards her bench, eager to drown her sorrows within the exertion once more. Though her shoulder wasn't *quite* as eager. Ro followed suit, no words needed to be said.

"Oarsmen! Ship oars!" Sergeant Prinius bellowed.

Alexa and Ro lifted their oar and ran it out the port until a copper ring, wrapped around the oar, slammed into the porthole, marking full extension.

"Drummer! Begin our count," Sergeant Prinius said and looked at the trierarch.

The captain inclined her head, "One half speed will do, sergeant."

"One half speed, drummer," Sergeant Prinius repeated at a massively increased volume.

The thud of the war drum boomed out over the deck, steadily finding the rhythm requested.

"Oarsmen! Row!" Sergeant Prinius called, and they all bent their shafts to the sea, and once again pulled to the steady beat of the drum.

They pulled towards home, and though she did not capture the minutiae of seamanship it took to bring the vessel to dock, she was silently impressed with the small calm maneuverings of the crew and their vessel—*The Malegost.*

Before long, Sergeant Prinius roared, "Boat the oars!"

They brought their ash wood oar back to its rest, and both her and Ro barely managed to stand against the creeping wave of exhaustion that threatened to claim them. Once her fatigue-blurred vision cleared, she glimpsed the red-haired ponytail of her younger sister, Bella. She was easy to spot amongst the browns and greens of the aging wood, and subconsciously she returned the eager wave from her scrappy, animal-enthusiast sister.

She tried not to stare, but the slow drift of the bireme as it bumped its fenders into its mooring gave plenty of time for anxious glances to dart back and forth. An awkwardness consumed her in that interminable wait, and her drifting, tired thoughts wondered why such an odd assortment of people surrounded Bella. A sense of foreboding weaseled its way into her stomach; one that was not alleviated by the sight of Amilicus, that handsome warrior that looked so out of place. Big news was coming, and she wasn't sure if she was ready for it.

The lumbering giant, Blythe, stood awkwardly in his typical uncertainty of what to do with his dramatic proportions, mirroring the emotions Alexa felt inside. There was the one-armed Godfrey who somehow always looked rugged. He was alongside the grey-haired and scarred Guard-Captain Vitrusian. With the distance shortened, she saw Amilicus looking rather sad, and those gathered around him stood at a rather rigid form of attention. Behind Bella was the stooped, green-scaled features of Hislock. His cloak was drawn over his head as he preferred when around many people. And lastly, there was a young man Alexa did not recognize.

The gangplank slammed home and the call from the trierarch sealed their voyage, "Vessel secure! Make good the stores."

Sergeant Prinius barked out commands to his Warriors and the ship turned into a flurry of commotion, but not one that Alexa and Ro were a party to anymore. She made her way to the gangplank, passing the trierarch.

"Thank you for having us aboard, trierarch," she said cordially.

The black-haired woman looked hard at the Rangemaster; her raven features seemed to bore into her. The smallest of smiles, one Alexa had been unsure the woman could even perform, forced old wrinkles back into place. "It was my pleasure, Rangemaster."

"And mine as well!" Sergeant Prinius cried out, unable to break away from his duties. "You should join us again sometime, and if not, join me for a drink at the Broken Flagon!"

Alexa beamed at her old friend and, whilst waving, replied, "Maybe I will, sergeant, but not before I force you to shoot a bow. We need to be … even."

"Alright, come to the Broken Flagon one of these days and we'll arrange it. Me and the crew are there at least for a bit every time The Malegost is in port."

She dipped her head to the trierarch whose smile had grown, then made her way down the steep wooden plank to the wharf below. They had berthed at the old wharf of Elgion and as she gained purchase on the old timbers, a scent she quite enjoyed whipped across her face, fresh pine and tar. Across the port, a newer pier was being built, and the seaside docks were growing alongside the community of Elgion, only one of the old warehouses was standing. The tradesmen that had run the other two opting for bigger, newer buildings. Now, the old ramshackle building looked out of place, flanked by two impressive storehouses. A few bunkhouses had also sprung up around the port, and another unknown building was coming into place, its frame looking like a skeleton amongst the living. *It'll be a town of its own before long*, Alexa thought.

"Went for a lil' fishin, did we?" Bella asked mischievously.

Alexa simply held her arms out for an embrace. It had been nearly three weeks since she saw Bella, and the departure hadn't been on the best of terms. Elira's death, particularly the manner of it, hung heavy on their souls. The two sisters fell into one another's arms, and for a moment they escaped their burdens. A small bit of tension loosened from Bella's shoulders, and the exhaustion Alexa felt pulled mightily on her eyelids. After a few seconds, and not wanting to fall asleep standing, she decided to grab her slightly smaller sister by the shoulders and hold her just within reach. She stared into Bella's hazel eyes, their green tinged irises holding some truth of how Bella truly felt.

There was pain, *lots* of pain. A sudden surge of homesickness washed over her as she recognized the similarity to Sophia in her twin sister's gaze, even though a gulf of immense space separated them. *How long has it been since they had seen Augustia? Five years?* It had felt like a lifetime, and now the strain of it was being acutely felt.

Bella, not wanting to mull over the pain yet, spoke with forced cheeriness, "Well, did ya?"

"Did I what?" Alexa replied.

"Catch anything! Ya big oaf," a genuine chuckle broke free.

"Oh! Right, um … no, but we did what we set out for. Ol' Prinius says the Bay should be clear for at least three days."

"I knew it. Ya didn't bring back a single fish for the rest of us. Blythe, didn't I say they wouldn't?"

The tall man replied, "You did ma'am."

"Tsk, tsk, tsk. Typical of ya," Bella said over a slowly growing grin.

Alexa shrugged and tried to make a face that feigned innocence. She was rewarded with a short bark of laughter.

Bella clapped her on the shoulder. "Come on, let's head on over to the shore. We … have a lot to discuss."

Through a sigh, Alexa relented though she felt the tiredness of the day weigh upon her.

Amilicus awkwardly fell in next to her as the motley crew made their way portside to the now cobbled road. "It's good to see you. You look … good."

Liar, she grinned and then felt a sudden urge to waste the rest of the evening away with the muscle-bound lad, but, seeing how that was becoming less and less likely an option, she just smiled in response. "Thanks." She leant in towards him and whispered, "What's this about?"

He sighed and replied with a murmur, "You'll see."

A small garden with some benches had been made for those who just wished to watch the sea, and the group gathered around them. The construction, simply for emotional needs, demonstrated how far Elgion had come. The smell of cinnamon and lady fern weaved itself between oleanders. Discordant with the smell of salted fish that wafted strongly on the breeze. Drying racks scattered along the coast evidence of its origin.

For a time, they looked around; none of them sure of what to say. So, Alexa broke the silence, anxious to know what caused folk like this such pause, "Well, what is it?"

A series of grunts and the clearing of throats issued forth until the young man, who up until now had been shuffling nervously, elected to speak, "I'm Sidon. From Xeeland. Your … friends save Sidon. Gulmavarn ogre. Oh, right, *hunnngry* ogre." The teenage boy spoke in halting Holliserrian, but his words, although clearly second hand, were clear enough.

Bella spoke irritably, "This here, as he has so rudely introduced himself already, is Sidon. And … well, he is a big part of the reason we are all here to see ya."

Sidon, not noticing the irritation of Bella, continued, "This Elgion? You mayor?"

The question had been directed at Alexa, and she laughed at the imposition, "No, lad. I am not the mayor. I am, however, the Rangemaster of Elgion. This is just her port."

Sidon's eyes grew wider, "Rang-Rangemaster!?"

She nodded in confirmation.

The boy jumped with excitement and before anyone could stop him, he launched into a series of questions. All of which was in his native Xetem tongue. Clearly, he knew of Rangemasters. This came as no surprise for the Rangers had guilds within all the major city-states of Telaea. An order that, although held loyalty to their patron, ultimately served *The Balance* first and as such had some cooperation between halls even amongst the most bitter of rival states. Sure, rangers *had* been used as weapons like everyone else, and probably would be used again, but they tended to have some form of kindred culture across the breadth of Telaea.

As the boy continued to speak in a flurry of excited questions, Godfrey made his way over to him. The old soldier placed his hand on the boy's shoulder, and, with sudden realization, Sidon stopped as he recognized his folly. Quickly, the boy—over reddening cheeks—repeated a word, "Surret, surret."

"It means sorry." Godfrey clarified, and with a look of fatherly care aimed at the boy, decided to apologize for him, "He's an eager lad but he means well. Shukop."

The last word was directed at Sidon who closed his eyes in relief.

"So, to the point then," Bella said. "We have had a chat with Guard Captain Vitrusian and the governor already. Sidon here is the sole survivor of the camp that those *bloody* mercenaries were here for. We found him about to feed the ogre he mentioned."

Alexa raised her eyebrows in question; not knowing if Sidon had misspoken. An ogre was worrisome, for that could only mean a human or humans had been interacting with a cambyad; a rather dangerous woodland faerie. Of course, that danger was only prevalent if prompted. Still, it was definitely a concern within the purview of the Rangemaster and now she wanted answers.

Bella sensed the question, "Yes, yes. I don't know how the beast came about, but I'm thinking ya might need to ask around." Bella glanced at the Guard-Captain, seemingly for reassurance about what she was going to say next. "The governor—" She trailed off; still hesitant.

In the pause, Alexa felt a pang of nostalgia for the old governor. One she had grown to like, despite his misgivings. In the aftermath of the Battle of Elgion, his true character shone, and it turned out his heart was as big as his stomach. His efforts to rebuild the fledgling community had given hope amidst the downtrodden. Unfortunately, he was forced into retirement by severe arthritis and gout. Across the Sea of Melleas, he served as advisor of sorts, one Sophia followed *very* closely. *She never liked the man*, Alexa chuckled inwardly.

The new governor, Governor Luna, was his opposite in every way. Cold and calculating, the Raven Matron—as some of her detractors called her—was a competent and effective leader, albeit one who instilled more fear than laughter. Yet, Alexa could not complain, the woman was a wizard with regional management and the appointment showed Augustia's investment into Elgion's success.

Amilicus broke in for Bella, sensing the difficulty at broaching the subject, "The governor has requested that Bella, Godfrey, and Hislock return with Sidon to Augustia. The, um, nature of this delicate situation needing a more *serious* escort."

Alexa's heart sank. She would be virtually alone, while her family was all back in Augustia. "Whe-when?"

"Tomorrow," Bella said with abrupt finality.

It was all a blow, and her mind swirled at the implications. She sat heavily on one of the benches. The smell of salt-kissed greenery greeted her abrupt descent.

Bella continued her reluctant monologue, "The governor and, alongside the agreement of Elgion's Keeper—" Bella paused and just barely under her breath murmured, "—*who should still be Sophia*—has requested that we take the orator Malfias and … and *you*."

There it was. The reason for this odd gathering and Bella's abnormal hesitancy. "Well, I can't jus—"

Guard-Captain Vitrusian interrupted her by holding up his hand, his iron mail coat clinking from the abrupt motion, "We knew you would resist, but I assure you that Elgion will be in good hands. Besides, it is common for Rangemaster's to check in with their main guild hall on occasion."

Alexa tried to take hold of her tempestuous thoughts, a rather difficult task amidst such abrupt, world-changing news. So many had been lost under her command, and she felt *cheated*, like her time here wasn't quite over. She looked around at the gathered faces, and even Amilicus nodded in resignation.

It was heartbreaking, but there was truth to the return journey. After all, the Guard-Captain was right, a visit to the Rangemaster's Hall in Augustia wouldn't be out of the question. Though she wondered if she even deserved the title. With her mind still reeling, she asked about what she *did* have a handle on, "What about the rangers here? Who will care for them while I'm gone?"

Guard-Captain Vitrusian smiled, the same smile from three years ago when she had knelt before him and her old Rangemaster, Erin Apararius. "They will be alright, Rangemaster. I will take proxy leadership, but I'm sure you have many hopefuls that could assist running the Hall in your absence."

She did not hesitate to respond. "Yes, there is a few. Ro here is eager but is still quite green."

Roderick puffed his chest out, the praise making him affect a position of attention at his nomination.

She continued, "There is also Gaston, who should be recovered from his injuries. He's a little hot-headed but *very* knowledgeable, and of course there is Elir—" She froze. Unbidden thoughts of her mutilated friend took over her psyche.

All of them there knew what had happened on the beach, and all of them shuffled uncomfortably.

Her mind went blank.

Sidon, unaware of the issue, interrupted, "Surret, what is problem?"

Alexa managed to look up and, with a wry smile, she replied, "Oh, nothing. It is, um, nothing." She pushed through the pain of loss, "Menias is also a decent choice, though I wonder if he would be happier without people around altogether."

Alexander nodded, recognizing her desire to not address the slip up, "Very well, I will use those you mentioned as my counsel."

"Well, now hold on. Don't I get a say in this?" Alexa protested.

"I'm 'fraid not. The governor was *quite* clear. That you—specifically you—needs to go," Godfrey said.

The Guard-Captain nodded, and Alexa looked around at the assembled people for their confirmation.

Blythe nodded, Hislock made a low rumbling hiss, and Amilicus was looking rather defeated.

When she glanced at Bella, she saw the same frozen horror that had gripped herself. Bella, after all, had been the first to spot Elira. In fact, she had taken time away from them all to process the horrific scene. The sight made her ask, "Well, what about the stables?"

"I got that taken care of mum," Blythe said empathetically.

"Th-the …" she trailed off, knowing that her protests would all be addressed. "It's just I-I—" Tears welled in her eyes, and she rubbed angrily at them.

Amilicus wrapped his arm around her shoulder giving her some small comfort.

Alexander spoke calmly, "We will take care of it all, Rangemaster. But you and yer sister need to see home—family. You have done enough for Elgion. It's time for Elgion to do something for you. Since the best we can manage is a break, well, that's what we will be giving you."

Godfrey chimed in joyfully, "And I heard tell of a vacation so 'course I had to come. Couldn't let y'all have all the fun!" He beamed at her and she couldn't help but chuckle. "There she is!" Godfrey said.

The released tension opening the floodgates, and a tear fell freely from her face.

Bella came back to them then with a distant voice, "You already heard that Hislock will be accompanying us. A 'mission of cultural outreach' Governor Luna called it. And well, Godfrey is basically the only ambassador to the saurians in all of Telaea. But … as for me and you, yeah, they say it's for this or that, but … *But*, I think we need to see home sister. It's been a while."

The emotion of the moment overwhelmed her. She stood abruptly, Amilicus's hand falling without resistance, and embraced Bella. She heard a soft sob escape, and the two sisters held each other against the horrors of what they had seen. Over her sister's shoulder, Alexa relented, "Very well. I guess we could see ol' Augustia again. But first!" She didn't finish; she didn't need to. Her glance at Amilicus told everyone what needed to be done.

The young man smiled ruefully, his own eyes welling with tears.

The assorted company shuffled awkwardly until Godfrey spoke up, "Come on guys, let's give these two some space." The group departed and, as the time crept on, the silence became vast. Like a dark sea separating ships amidst its waves.

"I guess … I guess this is goodbye," Amilicus finally said.

She burst into tears and plopped back down on the bench to hug him. With all her might, she squeezed the young man. She had been so enamored with him, so excited to see where their story would take them, but now it was coming to a close. She wasn't sure she was ready for that. Slowly, their embrace fell away. "I am sure that we will meet again. Pick up where we left off?" The words felt hollow the minute she spoke them.

He nodded, a smile that lacked his normal pearly white teeth. That small change told her that he knew what it was. "Yeah! Maybe …" He wrapped his arm around her, and together they sat on the bench looking out at the bay. "Ya know, I enjoyed our time together."

Alexa smiled once more and let her head rest on his shoulder. She would miss the young man she had grown to adore, but home was calling and she knew she was duty bound to return.

Part Two

Chapter One
Sophia

Sophia waited in an immaculate lounge, its hall decorated with finely wrought marble statues and gold trimmed pillars. A place of extreme wealth that served to tell guests *exactly* how rich they could become, or—if they were enemies—how much they would have to face. It was something of a mixed emotion; she normally spurned such gross displays of wealth. Yet, at the same time she couldn't help but feel *enamored* by the luxury.

"Thank you so much for coming," Master Eamon Salferesis said to a young man and woman, both immaculately dressed, both arm and arm. The lord of the estate had a voice that carried well in the domed space, even over the trickling waters of a centerpiece fountain. The woman, who had a scarf of elegant, drodang silk draped about her slender neck, placed a delicate hand on Eamon's forearm. Although her lips moved, her voice was too low to carry. *Not like the member of the Chosen's Wisdom,* Sophia reflected.

"I would be delighted!" Eamon replied.

The young man murmured something that warranted a gentle nod from Eamon and then he ushered his companion out rather quickly. By the rosy coloring on his companion's cheeks, which only served to make the pretty little brunette even more radiant, Sophia could only assume she had offered a more … intimate invitation. A familiar twist in her gut, and the usually infrequent emotion of jealousy struck home.

She sighed, and though she could be within the bounds of politeness to make herself known, she elected to just observe the member of the Chosen. He watched his guests depart, holding a look of pleasant contentment even as they had disappeared out of sight; just … staring after them.

It gave off the impression he genuinely cared about those he called upon and it made her heart skip a beat in anticipation of her own encounter.

With a sudden, almost unnerving twist of his head, he looked at her. It was as if he knew exactly where she had been the whole time. "Ah, Keeper Sophia Vollimosa! How grand it is for you to drop by!"

It was a curious way to phrase it. He had invited her to his estate within the Upper Bowl of the city, and she definitely didn't feel like she was 'dropping by' for a social visit. Yet, the phrase came forth and instantly she felt more alive; more *invigorated*. She stood, regretting having to leave the drodang-silk couch she was slowly melding into.

Master Eamon made his way around the fountain, holding his arms bent at the elbows with the palms up. "I hope that you weren't waiting overly long."

She replied with an easy smile, "No, no it was no trouble."

He returned the gesture and crossed the last few paces towards her with his hands still outstretched in welcome. "Ah! Then it *must* have been a long wait."

She cocked her head and brow in curiosity. His smiling face and open hands forced her—almost subconsciously—to offer her own hand to him in greeting. He accepted the gesture and clasped her hand gently between both of his own. With the slightest of bows, he made her feel like one of the Mandated—as if she rivaled Trelion III himself. As delightful as it was, her curiosity overwhelmed her, "What did you mean by that?"

Furrowed brows and then, like he had stumbled upon what she referred to, he widened them in sudden recognition. "Ah, yes! Well, if the wait hadn't been long, you would have outright said no. But you said it was no trouble. Therefore, you were accepting my apology instead of rejecting it. So, with that my lady I hope that your wait was … pleasant."

It was shocking that the slightest nuance tipped him off. After all, it *had* been nearly an hour, but with the constant stream of fresh oranges and grapes coupled with a delectable red wine, Sophia had not been neglected. In fact, they had offered her a piece of huckleberry pie, an immense luxury. Not only was it out of season but also the berry itself was only grown in Continens Hyclepius. Regardless, the tangy taste of the sweetened pie filling still clung to her mouth as she replied in earnest, "I am not going to lie Master Eamon. It was *delightful.*"

He let go of her hand and clapped, his powerful arms rippling in the sudden explosion. She felt a prickle of excitement as his face lit up into one of pure joy. It was a heady feeling, being lost in that genuine happiness.

"Come," He beckoned as he slowly let a palm fall upon her shoulder, guiding her to another room. "We have much to discuss."

She did not resist, and in her guilty thoughts, she even welcomed it. His powerful arms, coated in dark black hair, were hard not to notice, and his neatly trimmed beard shone with oil. Even the scent he carried was one of masculinity, a mixture of massage oil and a lavender-kissed musk. It was difficult not to feel the first pull of desires intoxicating effects, but she tried to remember: This man was first and foremost a politician. Secondly, he was a tradesman. And finally, she was currently spoken for. *Now if only my thoughts matched my resolve,* she lamented.

They passed through a set of twin bronze doors; different to the ones he had led his other guests away from. On the gleaming metal, intricate designs of the most agreed upon look of Ember, the dragon god, were carved. The gaze of that god of all gods was upon her, and a terrible pressure mounted while under the scrutiny of that powerful head. Especially since this rendition was given the four horns of temptation, curling and rather painful looking appendages. Myths and legends swore Ember grew them to remind themselves of their own fragility. In the shadow of such a depiction, she felt small and insignificant.

In that insecurity, the faintest of whispers started scratching at her mind. It was a common occurrence ever since her destruction of the Magi

Stone, the Deceiver's shard, and Ember *spoke* to her more and more often. Unfortunately, and as always with the gods, the words seemed like no more than indiscernible whispers. Ones that usually made her feel fatigued and sick after she strangled her mind for some sort of interpretation. Now, here in this opulent house, being led by the charming Master Eamon, she bade them leave. She just wished to enjoy this luxurious moment, and—frankly—the company of her host.

"How long have you lived here?" She asked trying to escape the whispers of the gods.

"Going on four … no, wait, five years now," He replied as he pushed open a wooden side door within the hall they were in.

She wanted to take in the multitude of art and sculpture that decorated the hallway, but all of it was happening so fast. She barely had time to formulate her next thoughts. "Just you?" As she crossed through the open door, she realized what that type of question implied. Her eyes closed in embarrassment and horror.

Master Eamon entered the room followed closely by a servant who closed the door behind them. With a smile, that somehow expressed her question was not offensive, he replied, "Unfortunately, yes. Though I have had much company, there is no … Lady Salferesis at present."

She bowed her head in acknowledgement, and hoped her cheeks were only slightly flushed.

"Come," Eamon gestured. "This way! We have the best vintage come straight from the Silver Bay. Would you like for me to fetch a glass?" Master Eamon beckoned to a set of red-silk couches that lay central to the room.

She made her way to the luxuriant furniture, guided by a skylight from above. The room was kissed by delicate rays of sun, and that exposure was used to grow vines and philodendrons that saturated the air with a rich, earthy texture. She felt like finding a pleasure read like the one she currently enjoyed, *Maiden's Folly*, and lazing the day away amongst the greenhouse-styled room. That was of course an impossibility. "Uh, sure. I could use a refresher."

"Excellent. Matthias, fetch us a bottle of the Argent Bay. The four-twenty-nine if you please," Master Eamon turned and found a seat on a separate couch from her own.

She couldn't help but feel disappointed.

Eamon spoke past her woes, "Can you believe that it's been four hundred and fifty-nine years since Augustia's founding? Truly, our people have come a long way from the nomads that we were."

"True, The Holliserian Fringe was no more than a backwater when we first came, but our people are resilient. Of course, it helps that we have never wanted for builders," She replied effortlessly.

"Truer words have never been spoken." Eamon dramatically gestured around himself, "Take this room for example. Such luxury encapsulated within our own homes. Remarkable."

"It is not true for all though," She replied, immediately regretting the slight chastisement.

"Yet another truth. One that I try to rectify. You were present at my arguments about the orphanage. I may live in splendor myself, but it wasn't always like that. I grew up on the Lower Bowl, right near the docks in fact!" He paused and looked over her shoulder as if he were lost in memory. "I can still smell the fish. It saturated *everything* in my house. No matter how hard my mom tried, she just couldn't get rid of that damned smell …"

Sophia was about to apologize when he spoke once more in a strong voice. It seemed unaffected by whatever dredged up woes from the past, "Still! I have done well for myself. Just don't doubt for a second that I remember where I came from. A knowledge that drives me to do right by the people. To give all those little Eamon's of the world the hope that they *too* can become whatever they set out to be."

A wave of guilt washed over her, and she stammered wordlessly. Normally, she would write such fancy speeches off, but she couldn't help but remember him at the Chosen's Hall as he argued in favor of an orphanage. *Maybe he was a man of his word,* and she felt slightly sick at having questioned that.

He must have noticed her regret and offered conciliation, "Oh, it is no bother. I am not offended. I deal with *all* of Augustia, but I find it is much easier to have that kind of reach when you don't have to worry about your purse."

His aura was palpable, and she struggled to not crumble under his scrutiny. Not in a way of fear, but in a way that belied his raw force, a commanding posture even amidst the comforts of an awfully luxurious couch.

Eamon's smile widened; it was infectious. Suddenly, he spoke again, "Did you know that those folks I just spoke to are looking to buy some Artstone? They pay me massive sums to obtain those … *Slivers of Truth.* Gods know how exactly they use them, but they do. I have heard rumors that they indulge in the gods' gifts to see a *truth* more beautiful than our own. Nonsense if you ask me, but it does pay well. So many Augustian marks, the likes of which the common man or woman would never see. It is how I have truly made my fortune grow."

"You trade in Artstone?" she asked, his dismissal of her regret easing some of the tension.

"Yes! It is all above board and sanctioned by your Bastion, I assure you," he said while leaning forward. He rested his elbows on his knees and clasped his hands together.

His tempo is relentless, she thought, a slight surge of energy coursing through her.

Eamon continued, "Of course, I trade in many things. Wool, fish, copper, drodang silk … I even got my hands on some coffee sales recently.

But there is nothing quite like Artstone. Those five hundred marks I secured for the orphanage? I am aimed to make that and then some from just last week's trades; no small amount of which coming from that debutante and her woefully-out-of-his-element boyfriend."

Her mouth dropped in shock. Five hundred marks was a fortune, and she had never considered how expensive the literal stones of the gods would be on a free market. "Fiv-five hundred!?"

He laughed, "That's right. Though I must secure the needs of the Keeper's first, free of charge. My contracts have given me much leeway in how to handle the, um, remaining godstone."

A sudden sense of worry grew within her. Artstone was a powerful hallucinogen, not a fun time for bored rich folks to 'see the real truth.' Chronic users were known to go insane if not cautious, and a frightening image of the young woman losing her mind in pursuit of Minollo's truth swirled in her thoughts. Not to mention the fact that Artstone, when accumulated in a bundle of shaped rods, could grant the user the ability to read minds. This factoid, granted to her by Gilbert, allowed users to see the truth of thoughts—of emotions. And here it was being sold on the free market. Her stomach cramped with tension.

Matthias, the servant, entered the room with a silver tray that held a pair of gold trimmed goblets, a tall pitcher in the middle. He placed the tray down on a low table that acted as a centerpiece between the luxuriant red couches and left with a graceful elegance.

"Thank you, Matthias," Eamon said as he poured a dark red wine into each goblet, offering the first to Sophia. Before he spoke again, he took a sip of his own and smacked his lips appreciatively. "Ah, that is truly an excellent vintage!"

The bitter notes of Silver Bay pulsed pleasantly. The warming flush of alcohol's embrace greeted her as she spoke, "It really is. Thank you."

"No matter! So, I can tell that this *sale* of godstones concerns you. As it should! But know that we have been selling the shards of the gods for many years now. Ever since the Mandated allowed it around … three-ninety-two. Yet, I feel your reservations. How are we going to protect ourselves when the untrained or—gods forbid—the malicious are able to so easily obtain these most powerful of artifacts?"

She couldn't help but agree and nodded as she took another sip. The richness of the wine staining the inside of her mouth, cleansing her palate of the huckleberry pie.

"Which is why I have sought you out. Well, the primary reason," He winked unabashedly at her, letting her know without a shadow of a doubt he was open to her desires.

She flushed deeply at the implication and hid her shame within her goblet.

He took a drink of his own and over the sound of metal slamming down on the silver platter, he spoke, "No, I have sought you out because I believe Augustia has overstepped."

He stood and clasped his hands behind his back starting a pace behind the couch. "How are we going to keep ourselves safe? Did you know I secured the purchase of some of Melleas's shards from Creos just two months ago? Their lodestone, one of the only ones that we know of on dry land, just being offered to the highest bidder! I can't help but wonder. If we keep selling these precious stones, will we not leave ourselves defenseless? Somewhere, someone—perhaps the Argolonians themselves—are securing these stones and preparing them for their dominion of Telaea. I would hate for Augustia to fall into that trap. So, there it is! I have sought you out to be my supporter. The people of Augustia know you. They have heard of your battle against Dolocius and they think of you as *incorruptible*. I need that sort of support if I am to make my case in the Chosen's Hall. I need you to help me secure Augustia's future. I need you to warn these *fools* of the dangers of just selling our godstone in farcical trade agreements! I need you—" He trailed off and let his gaze linger on her.

So enthralled by his passionate speech, his sudden lack of words caught her by surprise. His gaze made her tingle, and she sat up under the scrutiny.

Before it became awkward, he finished, "I need you to be my Keeper. My advisor as I push a new bill through the Chosen. What say you?"

"Um, I—" Sophia began.

"You do not have to answer just yet. But just remember that my aim is simple. Cease trade of godstone from Augustia."

It was an easy decision to make. "I can support you." Realizing how open-ended that offer was, she clarified, "But *only* in this."

Eamon cocked his head in question.

She struggled to say what she needed to, but with flushed cheeks she forced her way through, "I mean, I don't want to be some ill-trained fop that serves a household instead of a Bastion. Not some *courtesan*."

He smiled wickedly at her and smoothly glided into the seat next to her on the couch.

Her heart fluttered in response.

Delicately, he grabbed her hand and held it in his own, forcing her to look into his unflinching gaze. "Sophia, I will not misuse your talents. I ask for no more than what a friend would ask for. And I do not ask you to stray from the Bastion. Only for your help in this and *this* alone. I swear it."

The solemnity in which he delivered his promise was overwhelming, and she had to look away so as to properly consider his offer. Recent events looped within her mind, and she struggled not to reach out to him. To increase the extent of the touch he had already engendered. Guilty flashes of Gilbert's innocent face danced within her mind. Her eyes closed in an attempt to reaffirm her resolve. Slowly, she recovered from her desires and looked up at Eamon, nodding at him in the finality of acceptance.

"Excellent!" Eamon said as he clapped his hands once more, leaving her own hands feeling rather cold.

Chapter Two

Sophia

Birdsong echoed within her chambers, flittering in time with her eyelids. Her mind was thick as it slogged through the process of waking. The wine was definitely overstaying its welcome. Though it had had only been three glasses, two of which were slowly enjoyed over dangerously flirtatious conversation. That was the end of it, and she had left his estate with no more than flushed cheeks and wicked thoughts. Yet, the pulsing throb of the wine was there all the same.

With a sudden alarm, her slow rise became a jolt. Fear and anxiety were now paramount, and she worried if the brightness of the day coincided with potential tardiness to the daily meeting with Grand Keeper Chalepos.

The man was a tyrant; her punishment would be severe. She rushed to the small window of her loft and glanced at the courtyard below. Her rapidly thudding heart slowed a fraction; the statue of Grand Keeper Erica cast its shadow barely past the morning's mark.

Thank the gods for Grand Keeper Erica! Not the first time that makeshift sundial was useful, Sophia thought as she let out a sigh.

The excitement of an abrupt awakening faded, and her head throbbed in agony. She groaned as she—having slept in trousers and a light undershirt—pulled on her heavy Keeper's robe. The vestment lay near the small vanity she was allowed, and as she glanced at herself in its tiny mirror, she sneered in disgust. Ever since arriving at the Bastion, she had been forced to wear the garment, and looking at it now, after three … long … years, made her yearn for the days back in Elgion. Free, adventurous days which she could get away with the much lighter vest and cloak that still could hold all the tools of her order. An outfit even some of the Senior Keepers chose to wear, especially as the days got warmer. With fading spring and summer's first heat creeping up, the lighter design would be immensely helpful. Not for Chalepos though. The man wore that itchy, drab-grey robe like a badge of honor; like a big, ugly beacon of suffering to show how strong his convictions truly were.

Alas, there was little time to wallow in pity, and Sophia rubbed her gums with a small bundle of mint. A basin of water near her vanity—though lukewarm to the touch—felt refreshing as she splashed water on her face. Looking into the paltry pane of glass that served as a mirror, she undid her ponytail, smoothed out the more errant strands of her hair, and refixed it into the tighter knot she normally wore. With a grunt and a tug on her robe, she braced for the day.

*

It was warm already, and though they had just left the rains of spring behind, summer was walking in with full force. Remnants of evening's chill made small drops of dew cling to the flower beds near Grand Keeper Erica's statue. She rushed past the courtyard, brushing a hand on the raised platform in small reverence of her founder. Not wanting to risk the sound of the bell that told the world the day had started, she rushed towards the looming construction which held the Grand Keeper and his lieutenants, the Senior Keepers.

She was immediately bombarded by Monique's greeting, "Good morning, Sophia! It's a wonderful day innit?"

Sophia forced a smile. "Yes, it is quite wonderful."

"Here to see yer warden then?" The bubbly Keeper asked as she stood from her desk.

Sophia nodded, feeling her smile become more genuine as the infectious enthusiasm of the greeter gripped her.

Monique risked one more glance at her desk before crossing the room. Surely, just out of eyesight, a puzzle was being put together and

Sophia wondered how the charismatic woman could do such a hobby with the constant interruptions she had to endure. Still, Monique had gotten used to the routine of Sophia's morning arrival, and she walked to the door leading into the stairwell with no hint of annoyance or complaint.

Another nod as the door was unlocked and pushed open. Sophia managed to mumble a thank you in response to the bubbly smile that never seemed to waver. Monique never faltered in her cheeriness. *A little … unnerving*, Sophia considered.

"No problem, love! Have a good morning!" Monique responded enthusiastically.

With that, the door closed, and Sophia was left alone in the echoing stairwell. With a groan, she began her climb. Like every time before, it was a slogging, miserable climb up a vast spiral staircase. The landing of the seventh floor was never a shorter climb, no matter how many times she did it.

Drops of alcohol-soaked sweat coursed down her brow, and she wiped them away with her robe before knocking on the door. She heard the characteristic shuffling of her wiry warden as the man put down his study materials and made his way to the door. The sound of many locks disengaging echoed in the stairwell and with what felt like intentional slowness, Grand Keeper Chalepos unbarred his door. She was greeted by a wash of sunlight. A product of the many stone-arched windows dotted about his room.

"Ah, Sophia," he said with only the smallest hint of his normal disdain. "Hurry now, we have much to discuss!" He swung the door open wide and with impatience, beckoned to her to enter.

She crossed the threshold of the room and was left standing as Chalepos slammed the door shut, relocking all five locks of his door. The man hurriedly crossed the room to his desk which lay in the center of an open-plan laboratory of sorts. All around the edges of the room were desks, wardrobes, and cabinets filled with curiosities and books that seemed hardly contained by the furniture they rested upon. Dust motes hung heavily in the air, reflecting the rays of sunlight that danced about the room. The lingering scent of candlewax betrayed the Grand Keeper's activities. He had been up well before the sun; his untidied bed—that sat tucked behind his desk—the final evidence of his rapid rise from sleep and subsequent dive straight into his labors. *The man was relentless,* and she groaned inwardly at whatever inane tasks he had in store for her.

Keeper Chalepos shuffled past, mumbling irritably to himself. He rounded his desk, and—with a rather cold look—he beckoned for Sophia to come closer. She obliged and took up her normal position in front of the desk. She had learned long ago not to assume where to stand and always waited for his summons. As usual, he did not offer a seat.

Instead, he launched into his newest tirade, "I will need you to recopy one of my letters from yesterday. *You* managed to misspell a word written twice before, and I can't be having my records look so *shoddy.*" He shoved the letter in question across the desk. That was invitation enough to grab the document. He glared at her, whatever good humors he had at the entrance disappearing quite rapidly. The cause? An overly large 'X' lancing through the word 'cieling'.

She had misspelled it; *damn.* It was an audit of roofing practices amongst the masons of Milrest, an important grain processing village that rested along The Arms. The Grand Keeper must have lost his mind when he saw her misspell such a word for such a document.

Losing his patience at her survey of the letter, he continued his demands, "You will also need to copy a passage from *Keeper Kaldin's Agricultural Primer*, I can't be sure of its location but the mayor of Salcap, that pastoral backwater west of here, has asked for guidance on how to properly grow green beans. Best copy the whole section to be sure."

Sophia struggled not to scoff at the demand. It would not be a simple task, seeing as how the late Keeper Kaldin was famous for being long-winded. Unfortunately, Grand Keeper Chalepos was not concerned with the enormity of it and continued his barrage, "I will need you to take this bundle of Artstone rods and deliver it to a Master Falris Lupern. I believe you are acquainted with the man?"

Of course I am, she thought, but after her discussion with Master Eamon, she reeled from the request.

"Have you lost your wits!? Do you know the man or not!"

She shook her head, clearing it of hesitation, "Yes, Keeper. I know the man."

"I thought as much. Anyways, bring it to him. He should be at his estate, or—" The Grand Keeper glanced out a window to his left. "At this hour he's more likely down by the docks." Chalepos grabbed a fine leather wrap tied with infinite care and placed the satchel on the desktop. A faint clinking sound could be heard as the satchel rolled. "The price is already agreed, and I will know if he shorted us. Do not! Bother counting it." With the final sentence he fixed her with a malevolent glare.

He thought of her as an incompetent, a dunce. What was worse? He was obviously selling the Artstone bundle. Master Eamon had warned her of this type of trade, and though she had always felt strong convictions towards the use of godstone, Master Eamon had turned the matter into one of utmost importance. She struggled not to complain and luckily was able to offer a curt nod as a sign of obedience.

Master Chalepos gazed at her with a mixture of revulsion and curiosity. It was as if he knew she was up to trouble, and if he ever found out what it was, he would be mortified. His judgmental eyes finally dropped back to his desk and whatever inspection he had conducted concluded with a satisfactory result. Or not, it was impossible to tell with Grand Keeper Chalepos. His reedy voice rang out once more but with far less urgency. It was almost like he was speaking as an afterthought. "While you are at the docks, bring this contract," he absently placed another parchment on the desk and slid it towards her. "And give it to a Master Benard in the Trade Hall. It's to replenish our Maidenstone reserves … which are running low. Especially since your *friend,* at least I think he is your friend, had an unfortunate accident."

Sophia's eyes widened. Keeper Chalepos could only mean one person, *Gilbert.* Her mind raced at the possibilities and Chalepos's mouth twitched with the smallest trace of emotion; either a frown or a smile was impossible to tell.

"Anyways, Keeper Gilbert came back from his *vacation* with two missing fingers. Apparently, he danced with Melleas and got a little frostbitten. The story is that robbers or some such attacked him, and he had to defend himself." He paused and inspected his fingernails while leaning back in his chair. With a rather nonchalant tone, he continued, "I say, let Mosyneta discover the truth of it. We have Necrostone for exactly this reason, but *alas* I am not his warden." Chalepos looked up at her; his eyes searched her own, and in them she swore she could see a hint of humor.

"That is unfortunate." She said coldly. She secured the slowly curling parchment with the contract and added it to the bundle she now carried. "The gods can be fickle. Melleas most of all."

Keeper Chalepos scoffed. "You should know, yes?"

His derisive tone grated on her nerves, and her teeth ground under his continued onslaught.

"Keeper Gilbert is a promising member of our community. I would hate for him to become *tainted* by some of your more ludicrous thoughts. You wouldn't know anything about his unfortunate *accident,* would you?"

There it was. Her senior, her warden, suspected she had sent Gilbert in her stead to the Broken Stallion after he had implicitly rejected her own request. To be fair—the man was right. But still, she had hoped the ruse would be a little more effective. Of course, she figured there would be suspicion when the young Keeper left, and sure there had been a persistent pallor of doubt as soon as he had gone on his 'vacation' to see his family, *but* it wasn't out of the question for Gilbert to do so. After all, he did have familial holdings there. Now, a week on, Keeper Chalepos was still ruthless in his scrutiny. A scrutiny that would increase, especially after such an injury—*if it were even true*. One doesn't normally become injured whilst visiting the farmlands to the north, and the obvious use of godstone by Gilbert would make things *complicated*.

If they used Necrostone on him, then she and Gilbert were teetering on the brink of discovery. She knew there were options. They could try and use Artstone or even Embershard to corrupt the reading, but other Keepers would quickly know Mosyneta had been fouled, and their plight would worsen. No, her and Gilbert's best bet to avoid this dilemma was to avoid any further investigation altogether.

"No, Keeper. I do not know anything of this accident. In fact, I did not even know of his return until you told me just now. The injury was part of that news." An easy statement to make, since it was rooted in truth. She stood rigidly, waiting for the speculative glance of her warden to fade.

To her relief, the Grand Keeper relented, waving dismissively. With a heavy sigh, he spoke, "Very well, you have your orders. When you have completed the recopying of that letter bring it back to me. I am writing a missive on *Keeper Pulios's Art of the Forge* and I will need some copies made."

Her warden raised his eyebrows to her, waiting.

"Yes, Keeper." She said with the most neutral tone she could manage, though fury swirled inside.

"Alright, you are dismissed. Begone!" He shooed her away with his hand.

Her final look at her warden saw him bent over his desk; immediately diving back into his work. He was as callous and cold as they came. But

Sophia had to admit that he was a powerhouse of efficiency. Men and women that rose to the position of Senior Keeper, especially the vaulted title of Grand Keeper, did not get there through anything less than merit, and Chalepos brought a particular work ethic that shamed all but the most maniacal. Still, he was a right prick.

Chapter Three

Sophia

She couldn't wait to see Gilbert; couldn't wait to see if he was alright. Yet, she knew his duties and his *injuries* would keep him occupied. Regardless of how he got hurt, his first duty was to the bastion, not to her. A pang of worry threaded its way through her heart, and the lingering memory of his last touch graced her cheek, a gentle caress as they had said goodbye…

She bit down, her jaw flexing under the anger of impotency. It would do no good to sit and wait for *her* turn to see the young man, so she set about doing what she could to be useful, and that would start with Dunkeath and Olivia. They *had* to have news for her, and she opted to miss out on the bowl of milk, oats, and grain that was customary breakfast for the Keepers. Her stomach, all worked up in knots, would probably not handle food well anyways. With a nod to the squad of gate guards—provided by the Warriors of August—she left the twin oaken doors of the Bastion behind.

Dunkeath and Olivia met up with her as she made her way down Grange Street and towards the Lower Bowl; it was their usual method of rendezvous. The sight of the rapscallion known as Dunkeath and the bubbly former laundress gave her a sense of relief she had not expected. And, as they closed in on one another, she couldn't help but smile at the pair.

"You look in right spirits!" Olivia beamed.

Dunkeath, not able to resist a barb, added, "I didn't think you and Gilbert would git *reacquainted* so fast."

Olivia slapped the man's arm, but with no real force. The familiar look of friendship—verging on the intimate—blossomed on Olivia's jovial cheeks.

Though the reminder of the young man made her heart ache, she replied in good humor, "Aye, not yet, Dunkeath. But we have much to discuss, and I have much to accomplish. Walk with me."

The trio sauntered down the cobblestone street, passing commuters from the Lower Bowl destined to whatever trade or craft they pursued. The sound of horseshoes was a persistent cacophony that echoed all along the main thoroughfare of the Upper Bowl, the walls of which were a plethora of two- and three-story houses. Carts were strewn about the road and along its edges were a collection of scattered silos, giving the street its name, Grange Street.

In the gentle, summer morning, many of those carts were loaded with fresh vegetables, a good chunk of which would be preserved and stored. A repository of food that was held in accordance with the *Grange Law*. A rather well received piece of legislation that stated: The citizens of Augustia must give up one tenth of their crops to those stores. Many times, the action had saved lives. The preserved food, either salted or dried, acted as a buffer to starvation in the lean winter months. True, it was a tax, but it was a tax that rarely received complaints. An ironic thought as she passed the shouting vendors finding room within the forum. Their attempts at hawking their wares, reminding her of the straight tax on sales that received *many* complaints.

Sophia breathed in contentment as they passed the normal machinations of her beloved city. "So, what can you tell me?"

"Well ma'am, we can't *fully* show it here, but we definitely found what you were looking for," Dunkeath said with his typical gruffness.

She raised an eyebrow at him as a group of clarks bowed in respect to her. Their curtesy a formality as they raced to be the first in line for the ink, paper, and dyes that would be on sale at the forum.

Dunkeath attempted to clarify, "What I mean is—"

"What he means is that we have another one of those coded letters we found in the Lady's house," Olivia interrupted. Dunkeath took this as his sign to give up their find and handed a small metal tube with a wooden stopper at its end to Sophia.

Intriguing, she thought as she grabbed the tube, making it jingle as it disappeared into one of the many pockets of her robe. "What did it say?"

"We don't know. It was jumbled up like the last one," Dunkeath said with a shrug, having to dance to the side as a group of distracted women nearly bowled him over. The streets were becoming crowded and Sophia wished to make it to the docks before the second morning bell rang.

Olivia spoke hesitantly, "We were hoping you could decode it. Ya know like you did last time."

Choosing to ignore the fact that it was deciphering and not decoding, Sophia replied in haste, "Yes, yes, I can take a look, but what else. What happened to Gilbert? Why is he missing fingers?!"

"Ah, that there is a bit of problem innit." Dunkeath said matter-of-factly. "Ya see … we ran into a bit of trouble. Methinks that whoever *did in* the lady was suspicious of the very place you were. We was ambushed."

That seemed rather obvious, but she nodded towards him to encourage more details.

"Three mercenaries, Argolonian, tried to make off wit' our 'eads, but ol' Gilbert surprised us all. Not to mention the innkeeper who also had a couple of tricks up his sleeve," Dunkeath said with a grin.

"That's right, Gilbert did in one of the fellows with a bolt of ice—or something—that shot out of one 'dem stones. Melleas I think," Olivia said with the meagre confidence she displayed when discussing Keeper business.

Sophia sighed ever so slightly, knowing Olivia was becoming very knowledgeable about the stones to the point she rivalled many of Telaea's most predominant scholars. *One day the former laundress would grow in confidence,* she hoped.

They waited for a string of carts to cross in front of them before turning onto Harbor Street. The cobbles at the intersection of the two main arteries of Augustia were spattered with mud and debris, an eventuality for such a busy place. But no comment on the state of the road could be made for they had to jostle their way into the crowds, bullying their way alongside folks who responded to the first bell. As they fell in line with the morning traffic, Sophia tried to ignore the smell—sewer gas rising with the warming sun. The Augustian day was in full swing; its citizens marshalled forth by the ringing of the bells.

The quality of the surrounding buildings dropped with every meter closer to sea level; the excessive wealth of the Upper Bowl behind, and the homes and shops around them become utilitarian—cramped. It was a problem she knew not the answer for, and so marched stolidly on as a string of wharves and piers pierced the sea to her right. The harbor stretched along the coast, but the road to the Trade Hall—her goal—and its occupants were located east of the intersection.

The second bell rang, its brassy vibrations booming over the stones of the city, and the tempo of the crowds increased in fervor. Just as they felt as if they were to be swept away they turned onto Fisherman's Way, the street that would lead to the administrative buildings she aimed for.

Sophia picked up where they left off, "So, Gilbert got frostbit by Melleas?"

"That's what it seems like," Olivia replied.

Why in the gods would he use that fickle god? She thought with a wince. She resolved to ask him when they next met. "Well, this is all useful news. Good work you two," she shuffled off into a small alcove along the street to allow passersby to continue.

Her twin companions, or as Gilbert liked to call them, cronies, smiled at her in appreciation and expectation.

She never could find the appropriate words to thank them as much as she thought they deserved … still, she tried, "Truly, I appreciate it. Now, as promised, your pay." She pulled out her small bag of Augustian coins. She fished out ten silver coins and handed five to each of them.

"Thank you, ma'am," Dunkeath said as he stowed the coins away.

Sophia sighed as she saw the typical look of guilt on Olivia's features. The wealth more than the laundress ever could have made previously. "As I told you before, Olivia, I am paying for *skilled* labor, and that is what I am receiving. Don't you give me no grief. You are worth it."

Olivia opened her mouth as if to speak but quickly shut it when she saw the stern reproof of her employer; her friend. The happy-go-lucky woman smiled once more and tucked her coins away into a hidden pouch. Sure, the sums she had paid the two over the last three years strained her own funds, but she needed the extra pair of hands. Hands that were free of the constraints of the Bastion. She swore she would pay back the loan she had taken from her father as soon as she was able. For now, though, she had a mystery to solve and another missive to decode.

*

The dried kwamin melted in her mouth as she passed the Bastion's threshold. She had picked up the luxury, alongside some cinnamon, before heading back from her errands. A pang of emotion had stolen her reserve, as the dockside merchant advertised his goods, "Come, Keeper, grab a taste of the new world!"

His toothy grin had nearly made her walk away. After all, she understood the *tastes* of the new world better than most. Yet still, the sight of the dried fruit caught her attention. It hadn't helped that a trade ship fresh from Elgion and full of cotton, wool, and timber had brought back bitter memories. Under her weakened will, she had paid half a gold mark for a hefty bag of the fruit. The cost was exorbitant, and nausea accompanied the price, made worse by the loss of another fifteen silvers for three sticks of cinnamon.

Her emotions ruled her, and memories of Bella's excited letter, outlining the combination of milk, cinnamon, and kwamin as being an irresistible treat were in the forefront of her thoughts. Though she had tried the indulgence before, she needed a reprieve from her bitter thoughts. The loss of her Keeper's seat in Elgion still soured, and the sweet, desert-style dish might assuage some of her swelling anger. Besides, it was one of the only ways she could connect with her sisters, by tasting the experiences of their lives. A yearning took hold of her heart, as she thought of them over the sea.

Most likely, Bella had been the first to taste the sweet kwamin treat, and the reflection on Bella's character made Sophia smile sadly to herself. It wasn't Bella's way to capitalize on the sale of such a good; instead, she would simply share it with those she cared about. Now some other, greedier individual had latched onto the idea, quickly making the delicacy available to the old world. Whoever they were, they had to be rich by now.

Her eyes adjusted as she entered the dining hall of the Bastion. A strong surge of garlic gripped her senses, making her salivate. It was carried aloft by the heat of the kitchens and crowded tables. The dining hall was always a warm place to be, but in the afternoon of a sunbaked day, it only got worse. She shifted her damnable Keeper's robe, hoping a sliver of air would find its way through.

"Hey. Library, I will be there for two hours," a familiar voice whispered to her, startling her from her thoughts. Her eyes came into focus, and Gilbert, his young, handsome face soured by anxiety, stared at her.

Her face trembled as she recognized him and—with a flush—she replied much too loud for the evident secrecy he wanted to encapsulate, "Gilbert!"

He smiled at her, enjoying her obvious pleasure at seeing him. He placed his right hand on her arm. "Meet me in the library. Eat first though." He stepped back, and when Sophia nodded with what could only be a look of dumbfounded surprise, he smirked and walked out the door. A stark white bandage now gripped his left hand.

How would that look when it came off? Shame bit at her as thoughts of deformed flesh came unbidden. Many days at the clinic had exposed her to a multitude of injuries, and her imagination ran wild. With a deep, centering breath, she assured herself it couldn't be too bad.

Nature must have understood, for she was kissed by a cooler breeze that danced through the many open windows of the hall. Eager to get back to Gilbert and to *decipher* the message she had received from Dunkeath and Olivia, she crossed the room to some buffet tables. There, with ceramic plate and fork in hand, she realized how hungry she was. Steaming chicken cabbage wraps shifted into view and her stomach growled in anticipation.

"Hey Sophia, ya eating with us today?" Isabella, one of the two cooks for the Bastion, asked in her normal friendly tone.

"That's right. This looks delicious!" Sophia exclaimed and Isabella used some iron tongs to place two of the stuffed wraps onto her plate as well as a hunk of bread, typical with every meal. The wraps were bursting at the seams, and bits of rosemary and carrot fell to her plate as they settled. She turned to find a seat, and of the ten tables that could seat ten people a piece, there was still plenty of room. The hall was only ever filled during big events like The Day of Choice or Ember's Feast in midwinter. Sophia recalled her shock when she had been a trainee: nearly one hundred Keepers that called the Augustian Bastion home had gathered in the dining hall for Ember's Feast. Now it was barren in comparison. She scooted to a table in the far corner of the room, eager to avoid the attention of the nervous trainees that grouped together like a school of fish.

She dove into her cabbage wrap, a slurry of flavor washing across her tongue. Bits of garlic, onion, and carrot caressed her taste buds. The chicken, the backbone of the meal, was moist and she wolfed down her first roll with a voracious appetite. The sourness of her stomach now just a memory. She had to admit, *regardless of virtual imprisonment, they sure ate well.*

"Hey there, Sophia!" Monique said over a chuckle. "Looks as if ya haven't eaten in a month!"

Sophia was chomping on the second wrap, surprised by the sudden appearance of the bubbly Keeper. *I must look like a proper barbarian!* Sophia realized, as she felt bits of cabbage clinging to her bottom lip.

"Do ya mind if I sit?"

She shook her head as she chewed and held a hand towards the empty bench opposite her. With ill grace, she managed to paste down enough of her current bite to speak, "I'm sorry … I was starving!"

"Oh, don't be sorry to me, sister. I am not one to fuss over food," Monique replied while gently patting her stomach. The woman bit her own wrap and a satisfied sigh escaped through mouthfuls of cabbage and chicken.

"Its grand, isn't it?" Sophia asked, and Monique's expression said volumes to its taste.

No reply came, instead, satisfied grunts muffled forth over a bite of bread. *No reason not to dive back into my own meal.* Together they enjoyed the silence as they ate the savory food and, before long, Sophia had finished her wrap and was sipping on cool well water—bread in hand. Monique was not far behind. Sophia smiled in thought, *I can't think of anyone that would appreciate this treat more than her.*

With a grin she pulled out the bag of dried kwamin and cinnamon from her pocket, garnering an immediate, excitable response, "Is that what I think it is?"

"You want some?" Sophia asked mischievously, earning a slow nod. "I'll be right back." She raced over to the buffet line, catching Isabella's eye. "You wouldn't happen to have a couple of bowls and some milk, would you?"

Isabella eyed her suspiciously but did not wish to question the request. The cook nodded and disappeared into the stone doorway that led into the kitchen proper. In a few minutes, Isabella returned with two wooden bowls and a glass jar of cold milk, "I need the jar back."

"Of course, thank you!" Sophia said, and with childish delight she raced back to the table where Monique was idly nibbling on the last of her bread.

"Alright, Monique, I hope you're ready for a treat."

The Keeper's normally cheerful expression was morphed into one of zealous concentration—beads of sweat at her brow. It was a somewhat frightening visage. That was until Sophia recognized it as the *enthusiasm* that had engendered Monique's success. Carefree as she seemed—like so many others—passion appeared to be her pathway through life.

Best to not keep her waiting, Sophia thought as she split the bag into two equal portions, letting the dried morsels settle into the wooden bowls. Then she took the three cinnamon sticks and broke one in half. She wasn't sure what to do with the cinnamon, just like the last time, and she was still no wiser.

Opting for the safe course of action, she handed Monique's portion over, and the Keeper yanked the proffered sticks out of her hand. Quickly, Monique crumbled the sticks by rolling them in her hand. Small sprinkles of brown cinnamon drifted down into the bowl. Seeing the intensity in which the skilled connoisseur conducted the act, Sophia copied the action.

With the feeling she was on the verge of greatness—or they had reached some significant point in a ritualistic event—Sophia poured the cold milk with infinite care into each bowl. The dried kwamin bits bobbed in the liquid, and each of them stirred their mixture with a look of almost graven finality. Together they acquired a spoonful of Kwamin, nodded in expectation, and then tasted the divine.

It was cool and refreshing; the milk coating her tongue. The sweet spice of cinnamon caressed her taste buds until a spark of sour made itself known. As she chewed the softening kwamin morsel, a sudden explosion of flavor erupted. It was a cacophony of taste, and Sophia closed her eyes in reverential bliss. When she opened them again, Monique was beaming at her. The flavor obviously had the same effect on her companion, and without a word, the two started laughing in a sort of manic ferocity. One that can only be found in two souls that experience a joy of unspeakable potency together.

Chapter Four

Sophia

"Are you alright!" Sophia shouted before realizing the library was empty. Racing over, she wrapped Gilbert in a warm hug, made more potent by the delightful buzz of the kwamin dish.

Gilbert chuckled, "I'm fine, I'm fine. Though you might choke the life out of me yet!"

"Oh, Maiden's Blessings! Are you ok? Did I hurt your hand?"

Gilbert shook his head, "I'm fine. Don't worry. Besides I still have three of my digits," he said as he held the bandaged hand up for her inspection.

Her heart sank at the sight, empathy tugging at her previous delight. A flash of Master Eamon's charismatic smile graced her mind's eye. As quickly as she was able, she brushed it aside, firming her lips in slight anger. She stayed in his embrace, but at a distance that she could look into his eyes. He wore a brave face, and her heart went out to him. *To lose any part of your body, let alone something so often used for manipulation, that had to weigh on his conscience,* she thought.

Gilbert, confusing her firmed lips for reproof or worry for himself, spoke quickly to interrupt anymore fretting, "So, did you speak with Dunkeath and Olivia?"

Sophia nodded and, as the two found their seats at the corner table they were so fond of, she produced the stoppered tube. Her hands tingled slightly as the rolled parchment was removed from its protective covering. Carefully, she unrolled the document and secured the curling ends with some of the books Gilbert had been reading. Though the light of day waxed full from the skylight, she still brought a candle close, and together the two Keepers bent over the coded missive.

"Is it … is it another language?" Gilbert asked.

"No, it's a cipher. And this—" Sophia replied as she pulled out the cipher she had found with the help of the nocturne at Lady Aliana's house. She had not wanted to risk its discovery and so had kept it on her person since that day. "This … this is the key." She unrolled the cipher, fixing its edges with a few more of Gilbert's accumulated books.

$$c^1 \; n^2 \; v^3 \; t^4 \; f^5 \; r^6 \; u^7 \; w^8 \; s^9 \; e^{10} \; l^{11} \; o^{12} \; b^{13} \; a^{14} \; q^{15} \; k^{16} \; h^{17} \; x^{18} \; d^{19} \; g^{20} \; z^{21}$$

$$y^{22} \; i^{23} \; p^{24} \; j^{25} \; m^{26}$$

With the quick wit Sophia had learned to enjoy, Gilbert grasped the concept readily. "Ah, I see! it's a replacement cipher. Should be simple enough." The young keeper lent even closer and the two froze as their heads touched.

A wisp of Sophia's hair fell across his face. *It had to itch.*

Still, the young man did not move. Instead, he looked up at her without moving his body. His clear brown eyes searched her soul, and—at that moment—she had no room in her thoughts for anyone save Gilbert. The stark whiteness of his bandages caught her eye, and she couldn't resist, "Of all the gods, why did you use Melleas?"

He stifled a small chuckle and closed his eyes as if in penance. "I knew you were going to ask me that." He took a deep breath. "Look, we were in a barn. Barns are flammable. Ember is flammable. I figured burning the very building you're in wouldn't be the smartest move."

Her mouth opened slightly in sudden understanding; embarrassed by her own, reproving question.

"Yea, exactly. 'Course Melleas didn't like how I asked, and, so, they delivered the bill for their services." Gilbert held up his hand to accentuate his point.

"I'm sorry Gilbert! I-I didn't kno—"

"It's fine," He interrupted—affection on his lips. His eyes went to the letter once more. "Shall we?"

Full of surprises, aren't you? She thought with a flutter in her chest and resumed work on the cipher. With a quill and ink on the table from Gilbert's earlier work, and with a blank piece of cheap parchment, she and Gilbert scrawled out the decoded message.

> *If you decipher this, you must be Augustian and know about my little bird. We could work together. Augustia has someone trying to manufacture war to secure monopoly on the shards, most urgent. If interested, leave message under bridge outside of Harbor Gate. I will find you.*
>
> *-Bloodeye*

There it was again, that name, Bloodeye, she thought, and her mind dived into the new insights revealed by the letter. Whoever this person was, they were thoroughly involved in an ever-thickening plot. One that had eventually led to the double murder of a highborn lady and an unfortunate Lower Bowl citizen.

Memories of a particularly sad visit in which she visited the widow of Navin came flooding back to her. Navin, the poor eyeless victim that had started her down this path, had left behind a family. Understandably, his wife had been beside herself with grief, and she just couldn't understand why her husband had been murdered. After all, he had *only* gone out for a loan to save their newborn babe, Demetrius.

That young child had been the epitome of health when she had seen him. From first glance, you would never have known he had been struggling with a nearly fatal disease. Gentle questions about the child's recovery were all it took for a reluctant admittance about the events that led to the miraculous recovery. Apparently, Navin had left a large sum of coin behind from what the widow called 'investments.'

That had piqued Sophia's interest, for although it was not entirely implausible for a lower-class man to have such an 'investment,' it was *highly* unlikely. The payout of those investments had been delivered by a rather beautiful woman—per the widow's description—and that woman had explained Navin's 'insurance policy' to her. Coin to be paid out, a good chunk of which had gone to save their child. It was plain the widow took great comfort from the final act of her husband, and Sophia had left it there. Trying to reveal a more accurate truth would gain nothing. Even if it did, she wasn't a monster.

That interaction had clarified a particularly troubling piece of this puzzle: why this random individual was involved at all? He had been a messenger for Lady Aliana, a messenger who had been discovered and paid the ultimate price for it.

At least whoever had hired Navin had been good on their word, and Sophia took some solace from the memory of the widow clutching the legacy of a now dead father. Whatever message he had carried must have been so damning—so revealing—the culprits of this conspiracy were forced to act.

But who were they? Just today she traded in a bundle of Artstone at the request of Grand Keeper Chalepos. The bitter old man *might* be capable of such a heinous act. After all, the culprit—or culprits—knew the capabilities of Keepers and that they should cover their tracks. Chalepos would have been damn sure on how to prevent Necrostone use. He had also been rather adamant that she not go to the Broken Stallion Inn. *Perhaps that was to conceal the very missive she now read?*

Or it could be Master Falris Lupern, whose wife now lay cold in the ground, murdered for discovering her husband's dark deeds. Although the man seemed to lack the cunning to organize such a coordinated effort. *Perhaps it was a ruse?* As her mind raced over the multitude of individuals she knew who dealt in godstone, the picture only became more and more muddied. All of them were suspect.

Finally, her mind rested on one man, and her heart skipped a beat. He had warned her of the trade in godstone, he had called out their greed, and he had even proposed stopping the trade altogether—Master Eamon. But could she trust him? She didn't know. The rather powerful member of the Chosen, who had a flourishing trade empire, could easily have their will bent towards treachery. Those who dealt with so much wealth, no matter how frugal they lived, had a propensity towards corruption. Though that felt unfair as any form of evidence, she resolved to probe the man for signs of his involvement. Their regular meetings as they hammered out his bill to cease godstone trade would be the perfect opportunity.

In the meantime, she had a lead and a lifeline to the very informants Lady Aliana had died trying to communicate with. The thought sent a small shiver up her spine, and she shook to relieve the tension.

"Who do you think it is? Who do you think is trying to *manufacture* war?" Gilbert asked, leaning back in his chair as he obviously debated the very questions plaguing her.

"I … I don't know. There must be a hundred suspects, and that's just on the higher levels. It could even be a simple dockworker that's involved in this, working with a benefactor from Argolon or Xeeland, or-or … Ember's Breath! It could be any of the cursed city-states!" Sophia's voice rose in tempo as she became flustered at the sheer enormity of the case. She glanced around, recognizing her echo in the high walls of the library. Still, no other occupants came to peruse the knowledge held within. She sighed, and Gilbert placed a hand on her shoulder, helping her find calm once more.

It seemed that with every new lead, this back-alley murder only became more complex. Hidden missives guarded by nocturnes, gouged out eyes and tongues to prevent Necrostone use, shadowy informants hidden in far off inns, and now, corruption at possibly the highest levels of her government. *What more could this case involve?*

With that thought, a small pang of longing touched her heart. She wished she could share these details with Alexa and Bella. Those two—with their rustic frontier logic—would see some avenue or clue that she had missed; that she had somehow glossed over in her over-analytical review of the details. It was amazing. No matter how many times she poured over a document, Bella and Alexa would come along and point out the most glaring of errors. *Big picture and small picture,* she guessed. Alas, they were across the sea, and she would have to make do with herself … and well, Gilbert was here. *That's not so bad,* she mused deviously.

She furrowed her brow, settling on the only logical course of action. "One thing is for certain though. *We* are going to figure out what it's like to be Bloodeye's 'little bird'."

Chapter Five

Sophia

Once more she found herself in the Hall of the Chosen, its marbled benches feeling cool even through her robes. She did not sit in the gallery for observers—not this time. This time she was called as a witness upon Master Eamon's request. The excitement had nearly driven her mad, and she had struggled to find sleep the night before. Her restlessness made her vulnerable to the heat, and her body seemed to sweat profusely. It didn't help that they were near the middle of summer, and she was still cursed with heavy linen. The unfortunate apparel made her all the more thankful Grand Keeper Erica had opted for many high windows to let in the sea breeze. The gentle, salt-kissed air helped calm her nerves. That small reprieve from discomfort let her mind drift through the events of the last three furious weeks.

Every few days, she had met with Master Eamon to discuss the details of their bill. At first, she had been suspicious of the charming man, knowing he was as suspect as any other. Short of outright accusing him though, she had not found any fault in the man's manner. In fact, at times it seemed like he was a god's attempt to prevent the very thing she and the secretive Argolonian messages warned her of. His passionate approach to his work, including the very bill she had been called witness to today, made it hard to believe he could hide anything he worked on. The man was a force to be reckoned with. From the smallest detail to the macroscopic view of his trade empire, he was thoroughly invested. In all that time, she had not found a single link to him nor anything that would be considered untoward.

Even the two missives that had arrived at the drop outside of the Harbor Gate did not incriminate him. In fact, they might have even been speaking towards his character not against it. One line in particular played over in her head.

> *Though you should be wary of trust, there are potential allies in the city who could help you. We have worked with them before. Seek out friends but be wary of their intentions.*

At present, the only person coming even remotely close to a 'friend' was Master Eamon, unlike the other suspects: Grand Keeper Chalepos and Master Falris. Yet, those suspicions were shaky at best, and she could do no more than bide her time as she built up a relationship with Bloodeye and a case that would lead to more information.

She groaned at the monumental effort she had put into decryption work. The excitement of the first few cases fading faster than the promise of love from an unfaithful spouse. But in Bloodeye's most recent letter, he had opted for *significantly* more detail, including the fact his official title was 'Strategos' Bloodeye. Although—beyond that instance—he never signed his letters in that fashion, *smart*. The offering of his official title an effort to build rapport amongst a contact.

What Bloodeye couldn't have known is how meaningful the word strategos was to her. The word itself had her thoughts dancing towards the memory of an old tome, *Strategos Dante Stelios's Observations of War*. It was a time tainted with the shadow of Dolocius's deceptions, but still, it was a damn good book—full of insight and knowledge. She wished Dante had written down a guide on message decryption.

Unfortunately, the very nature of the subject meant little knowledge was recorded, and she had been forced to go at it with her own naivete. A fact that saw her nearly slapping Dunkeath when he had wished her luck before a particularly difficult message. Instead—and to Dunkeath's amusement—she had settled for a scornful glare, knowing the man risked his life being the courier of such secrecy. Still, it had taken her nearly an hour to fully decipher the message, and in her private thoughts—then and now—

she jokingly played with the idea of tricking Monique into unravelling the next message. *She did love puzzles after all,* she chuckled.

No, she would have to continue the grueling work herself. It wasn't so bad. She had gleaned valuable insights, such as potential allies … and threats. She just wished it wasn't so cryptic, the most recent message an egregious offender of the term.

> *This conspiracy has its roots many years back. War on the horizon if not stopped. We are from Argolon and even we do not know what government, if any, is involved. We do know that they are powerful and able to strike at their foes with blades and words. They have built up their power base and soon they will strike out for their ultimate goal. Be ready and please give us any details you discover.*
>
> *-Bloodeye*

"Are you ready?" A familiar voice asked in its normal charming tone, breaking her from her reverie.

She replied, a light smile gracing her lips, and without needing to open her eyes she knew to whom she spoke, "Yes, Master Eamon. I am ready, as I have been the last three times you've asked."

The prolific trader chuckled. "Ya got me there. *But* believe it or not, even I, the great and benevolent Eamon, Chosen of the People and Trader of the Seas, still get nervous."

She glanced at him, surprised at his calming humor. His charming banter always seemed to gravitate others towards his disposition, and she could see now—as she had over the last few weeks—how he had become a Chosen. Still, a little prick to his pride wouldn't hurt. "Humble, are we?"

"But of course, ma'am! I am the humblest of them all, don't ya know?" He grabbed the hems of his chasuble in the characteristic stance of a debater. A wide, toothy smile forming, typical of whenever he made a clever joke.

She decided to play along with his game. "Yes, you *definitely* are the humblest person I've ever met. Never have I came across one so great as yourself."

"Ah, now you finally see the truth!" He stood as straight as he could, effecting the visage of an overly proud individual.

She couldn't help but laugh; her cheeks flushed with the joy of the moment. As he recovered from his dramatic pose, Sophia found it hard to maintain his gaze. Gilbert had not been fond of the man, especially after she had finally introduced him. In her private thoughts, she knew why and she herself struggled to not consider the possibilities.

Before Eamon let his lingering gaze become uncomfortable, he spoke once more, "Now—as we practiced—I will call upon you after I deliver some boring epithet on the horrors of godstone trade. Then you will embolden my case with your own recollections of Dolocius and Magdris."

"Yes, yes, I remember. You just be sure to do your part, and I will do mine," she said playfully, teasing the man as he went over the details for the thousandth time. Truthfully, she was thankful he did, but it helped to trade jibes with a fellow intellect before such a momentous occasion. A jolt of anxiety bolted through her, not helped by the rapidly filling hall. Members of the Chosen's Wisdom and citizens of Augustia came in force to see the acclaimed bill Master Eamon had touted to the public *so* often.

"Hey," Master Eamon said with impetus, forcing her to look into his eyes. When he knew he had her attention, he spoke with the utmost calm, "It's gonna be alright." He smiled empathetically, and she felt a chunk of her fear melt away.

"Thank you." It was all she could do not to hug the man.

"Well, I best take my position. Good luck, and Maiden's Blessings to you, Keeper." With that, Master Eamon strode over to the two dockworkers he had also called as witness, leaving her alone on the marbled benches set aside for guests of the court.

Her lines jostled in her mind—over and over—and she struggled to keep her heartbeat from racing. A hissing whisper from a newly entered citizen caught her attention, and there Gilbert waved enthusiastically at her. Once again—present—like the rock he was. Her return smile and wave, as he made his way to the gallery above, felt as genuine as his affections. The sight of the crowded wooden platform though …

That filled her with dread, and they still had nearly half an hour to go. *They'll be pouring out into the forum before we even begin,* she bemoaned. Once again, she wondered why—in all the gods—she had involved herself in possibly the largest bill that had been passed in Augustia in a generation?

There wasn't much she could do about that now, and so she closed her eyes, going over the potential questions she could be asked. Tough interrogatives Eamon and her had practiced over and *over* again. In that meditative stance, time slipped away from her, and she had almost forgotten about the enormity of the crowds gathered.

A sudden booming call from the Master of the Hall, Master Balder, broke her calm, "Hear ye, hear ye, all present for this session come to order!"

She opened her eyes to an enormous gathering of Augustians. Suddenly, sweat, an inordinate amount, had accumulated on her palms. She rubbed them nervously on her robe.

"We will have order!" Balder's sharp tone lanced out and, almost as one, the murmuring and conversation died down to a low drone. The Master of the Hall scanned the gathered crowds and—satisfied with their compliance—nodded. "Today, we have a most *intriguing* proposal. One that we surely all know of by now." His voice was strong, and each word was spoken slowly but clearly.

The impetus on pronunciation gave her time to wonder if Eamon had somehow convinced the man to call the bill 'intriguing'. It was an obvious bias, and it would see them start off on a good footing. Although, she wondered about its legality.

The slow murmur of disapproval that rippled through the Chosen let her know the answer, though Master Balder chose to ignore the complaints. "Today we will hear Master Eamon," The man gestured to Eamon, who stood on the Chosen's ampitheatre. He waved to the gathered people; his face beaming with delight. "We will hear this Chosen as he proposes a new bill, one he has deemed *The Godstone Decree.*"

An excited whisper rippled through the gallery, and Sophia smirked lightly to herself. They had worked on that title for a long time, concluding that its catchy sound would serve to garner more support. *They had been right.*

The Master of the Hall gestured to a group to his right, "Representatives of Augustia's citizens, selected by the People's Will, are allowed to interject." Twenty citizens—all Augustian proud—sat in reverential silence, the gravity to represent the common man and woman heavy on their shoulders.

Sophia hoped those present today, chosen by lot to serve for one year, considered the duty an honor and not an obligation. After all, The People's Will did have the power to overturn the Chosen's Wisdom, but only if they stood unanimous. If they were resentful of their duty, any flowery language or disturbances to their schedule could find them voting in reprisal not in logic.

But Eamon had reassured her. The People's Will had not exercised that power since the end of The Five Points War. Instead, they served more as the electoral branch that would see the confirmation of the Chosen's Wisdom, the true power of Augustia. Of course, the Mandated, alongside High Magistrate Trelion III, held ultimate sway, but that was for another time.

After the People's Will were recognized, Master Balder gestured towards her and the two dockworkers. Under the scrutiny of the city, she felt herself shrink in fear.

"All those seated to my left have been called Witness to today's events, either for their expertise or for the arguments of our Chosen."

Her heart thudded painfully in her chest.

"And now I hand the floor over to Master Eamon."

The debate had started, and no manner of preparation could keep her heart from pounding like a drum of war.

Chapter Six

Sophia

"Thank you, Master Balder! A voice of the gods, as always," Eamon said to the sound of laughter.

The Master of the Hall took the light teasing in stride and sat in a chair at the front of the Hall. It was the closest thing to a throne in that place, and only because Augustia learned long ago that their debates needed a firm hand to guide them from turmoil.

Master Eamon crossed to the center of the hall, standing centered on the sunburst heraldry of the Augustian sun. He grabbed his chasuble—the gleaming gold of its edges contrasting beautifully with its stark white cloth—and waited for silence. Even then, he waited for a second longer, building the anticipation until even some of the Chosen leaned forward to hear him. *He's a master at this,* Sophia grinned.

"My dear Augustians, welcome! Welcome to this glorious hall of ours. This monument to our might, to our combined struggles, and to our *democracy.* Through our strength and passion, we have built a city that reaches across the very sea! Together we have done wondrous things, and the world over knows of the golden glory of our city, of *our* Augustia." He paused then, having the whole of the crowd's attention. Then he dipped his head as if in disappointment and began pacing amidst the heraldry of their city. "Yet, there is a dire threat to our achievements. One that we have allowed to *fester!*"

A murmur of shock emanated from the gallery, and Sophia felt the excitement buzz from the gathered masses. "Yes, we have been blind— my people. As glorious as we are, we are still human, still flawed. Even *I* have fallen victim to this newest of curses."

Suddenly, he looked up at them all, scanning the faces around him. His voice rose in tempo, "I call to you now for action! We *must* stop the trade of our most precious resource … the godstones."

The hall erupted at his proclamation. Though he had advertised this bill, Master Eamon and those who knew of the details had not divulged them to anyone. No, they wanted it to be a surprise. If they let slip early, those diabolical traders of the very shards of the gods would only gain more time to muster a defense. The enraged shouts of many of the Chosen—primarily those who profited from godstone trade—were proof of their successful secrecy. Nearly a minute went by as shouts from around the Hall echoed, until Master Balder took a stand and thumped the ground with a metal staff. The effect was instant, and the ringing boom quietened dissenting voices.

"Master Eamon has not ceded the floor, nor has he run out of his allotted time! All of you must come to order or see yourself escorted by the Warriors of August!" With that, the two ceremonial guards, donning clubs at their hips, stepped forward. Their own sunburst heraldry caught the light that drifted from the high windows. Sophia glimpsed the many guards that hid in the recess of the Hall, ready to retain order—with force if necessary. The threat was not idle, and the citizenry, including the Chosen, fell silent with little protest. With a nod to Eamon, Master Balder took his seat once more.

"Thank you, Master of the Hall. Like I said, our people are passionate!" The crowd laughed apprehensively; their humor slightly soured by the recent pandemonium. "But in all seriousness, it is paramount that we cease trading away our very link to the gods. Yes, it is profitable. Oh, trust me *I* know!" He smirked at this, earning another, more confident ripple of laughter even from amongst the Chosen themselves. "It is profitable because it is abused. We all know how the elite indulge in Minollo's sight, allowing the god of art and beauty to twist their vision. Is this the kind of use our founders envisioned? Did Grand Keeper Erica desire for us to use the shards of the gods in such a way?" He let the questions hang in the air, playing on their morality.

"Do you not think it better to hold onto the things of true value? To not squander them on the fancies of some wealthy man or woman with too much time on their hands? As Minollo is quoted as saying, 'What greater beauty is there than the truth?' I ask you this now—not as a god—but as a mortal. What truth is there in simple money, in simple marks? *None!* Not when compared to the truth of the gods!"

A roar of approval boomed over the hall; Master Eamon's supporters within the Chosen were the loudest amongst them. Balder only had to tap his staff once to resume the order he had already threatened to obtain.

"I propose that all godstone trade be ceased within the year, and that we put an indefinite ban on all future trade. In recompense to our traders, and to those cities friendly to us, I propose new agreements with terms favorable to all. Today, I ask that you allow this bill to move forward. I ask that you assign a commission of Chosen delegates which can help me finish the drafting of this bill for approval by the People's Will and—gods willing—review by the Mandated's Justice. I have brought witnesses, two dockworkers attesting to the gratuitous loss of godstone, destined to ports *far* from here. And a Keeper! One we all know well. One who has personally dealt with the malice of our more *malign* gods."

The eyes of the raucous crowd fell upon them, and Sophia's mouth became suddenly dry. She swallowed hard under their scrutiny. It had been no secret she had incinerated a Magi Stone, that shard of The Deceiver, Dolocius. It was so well known that upon her return to Augustia three years ago, some had hailed her as a hero. Others, like Grand Keeper Chalepos, considered her a fool to have fallen into such a trap. Though there had been no celebration or trial—save for the convention of the Keepers senior members—the city had reacted to her tale. Plays and performances

257

within the theatres of the Lower and Upper Bowl had belted out dramatic retellings of her struggle, and she had become something of a local legend. Now, although the excitement around her story had faded with time, she was once again the center of everyone's attention. She wasn't sure if she liked it. Not then, and she *knew* she didn't like it now.

"So, my fellow Chosen, People's Will, I look forward to hearing your arguments. Master of the Hall, I cede the floor." Master Eamon Salferesis crossed the marbled floor and sat upon the front bench, the sound of applause echoing along with his steps. Many of those Chosen seated near him patted him on the back whispering words of encouragement.

It had been a good start, Sophia thought

Master Balder stood and surveyed the room for any who wished to argue the point. Sitting next to Master Falris, a lithe woman sprung up from her seat. She stood erect, like a soldier receiving an inspection.

So much like Alexa, the stance of a soldier, Sophia reflected.

The Master of the Hall recognized the sturdy woman, "Master Aranos, would you like to speak?"

Visibly swallowing, her only sign of nervousness, Master Aranos replied, "Yes, Master Balder I would like the floor."

"It is yours," Balder said, beckoning to the oval mural on which Eamon had stood.

She gracefully made her way to the floor, and it was plain the woman had some athleticism. An immaculately dressed bun held long brown hair securely in place, and everything from the woman's gleaming chasuble to her stoic poise, even while descending the marble stairs, told of a woman who sought perfection. *No denying her martial past with that display,* Sophia mused.

Master Aranos reached the floor and spun in place with a smile at the gathered crowds. Whatever fear she had swallowed away, gone. "Esteemed members of the Chosen, honorable representatives of The People's Will, and citizens of Augustia, thank you."

The formalities delivered, Master Aranos began to pace much like Eamon had done, though Sophia could see a stiffness within the Chosen's gait.

Aranos continued, "By now, we are all accustomed to Master Eamon's *delightful* speeches." A ripple of laughter spread through the seats of the Chosen. "But we must see through to the truth of the matter. Why are we considering the disbanding of godstone trade? Why would we close ourselves off from the shards that cannot be found within Augustian lands? Why are we afraid of our friends and allies?"

Master Eamon shot up from his seat as murmurs of agreement blanketed the crowds. Balder and Aranos both recognized his desire to speak. And Eamon waited for their recognition, instead of blurting out his desired interjection.

Master Balder asked tentatively, "Yes, Master Eamon?"

"If I may, Master Balder," Eamon waited for the slightest of nods. To the audible groan of the woman who still held the floor, Eamon spoke, "By *friends* and allies do you mean those Argolonians who broke our armies at Argentios? Not once—but twice? Do you mean those brutes who slaughtered our kin and whose very borders creep ever closer to our heart? Is that who you speak of?"

Master Aranos narrowed her eyes, "I speak for all the Holliserian people. City-states like Lucidicus and Creos, who lent their aid during the very war you speak of."

It was a good reply, but the damage had been done. Master Eamon had sowed discord, and a grumbling sound of malice rumbled through the stones of the Hall. It had been sixty-four years since war had gripped the people of Argent Bay, and almost everyone there still had a living relative who had suffered during the Five Points War. The Argolonians were not loved within Augustia, only tolerated.

Master Eamon replied, "Yes, those city-states *did* lend their aid. One of which is under our stewardship and would *not* be blocked from trade, godstone or otherwise. I guess you misunderstood me, Master Aranos, I plan to keep the holdings of Augustia—within Augustia! I also plan for Lucidicus, Ember's Breath! Even Xeeland to obtain far better trade agreements with us. Ones in which we can offer the luxuries of the new world to them! This is not some rebuke of friendship, it is only a practical step towards security. Where *we* control the might and power of the godstones! Let us not forget what those outside of Augustia are capable of … I doubt any of us want another rebellion like we had at Creos."

Master Aranos was plainly at a loss, the ill-fated rebellion, known as the Harrowing of Creos, still soured many Augustian opinions. It would be hard to disagree with safeguards from such a danger; hard to argue against trying to prevent a similar massacre. The crowd was growing restless, until it looked like an idea had struck her. Master Aranos and her eyes filled with sudden passion. "Master Eamon, is it not true that your most profitable enterprise, save for godstone, lies in the trade of wool?"

Master Eamon paused, his face full of suspicion. With measured slowness, he nodded.

Aranos pressed the attack, "Ah, as I thought. And who amongst our *friends* would you say deals in the trade of wool the most?"

Master Eamon opened his mouth but did not speak.

Aranos had struck a vulnerability, and she capitalized. "Oh! The great Master Eamon at a loss for words! Never did I think I would see the day. Let me tell you, people of Augustia, it is Xeeland. One of those cities he just named as a benefactor to his *proposed* new trade agreements. Be prepared my good citizens, for I can only imagine the charters being rewrote in *his* favor! Furthermore, the very god he quotes … 'What greater beauty is there than the truth?' That is one we would be cut off from in this ludicrous notion of protectionism. Yes, my good people, what *Master* Eamon fails to grasp in his desire for wealth, is that Augustia has no known seam of Artstone within our … what did you call it?" Master Aranos snapped her fingers as if she just remembered the word, "Holdings."

It was a masterful stroke, and Sophia's heart raced as she wondered how Eamon would recover from the blow. The rebuttal by this bold woman felt almost personal. Suddenly, the ominous warning found in the Broken Stallion Inn echoed in her thoughts as she remembered the dire warning from it.

> *Augustia has someone trying to manufacture war to secure monopoly*
> *on the shards.*

Master Eamon did not take long to find his response. "You have a good point, Master Aranos. Yet, what *you* do not recognize is that we are not without the beauty of Minollo. From the rods held within the Keeper's Bastion to the very seam that my people discovered just weeks ago, we are blessed with the bounty of every *last* one of the gods."

The crowd erupted into chaos. Even she had not heard of this development. Sophia's mind raced at the implication. For years, Augustia never quite held a secure source on all the godstones. *Ember's breath*, she nearly cursed aloud. One of the main reasons for Augustia's desire for control of Argentios in the Five Points War was its ready access to the largest Embershard deposit within the Holliserian Fringe. Now Eamon was suggesting that they had resolved the issue.

Well, nearly resolved it; they would still be woefully short on some of the gods' stones, but if he was telling the truth, they would have secured a source—albeit meagre—for every one of the known deities. *But, what seam had his people discovered?* She pondered. This could be a manufactured truth to deflect Master Aranos's very valid points.

Evidently, the people of Augustia felt the same and were now in pandemonium at the announcement of a new link to the gods. Every discovery of those shards was cause for celebration—every loss a blow. If this were a lie, Eamon risked losing everything. Even banishment, if there was no seam … *No, he had to be telling the truth,* she told herself.

"People, people," Eamon called out, gesturing to the crowds for calm. Slowly, they responded to his plea, and when the clamor had fallen to a gentle rustle, he spoke, "I assure you that this new seam will be shared amongst us."

"Where is it?" Master Aranos asked venomously.

Eamon shot his opponent a glance, and for a second Sophia could see unadorned malice in his eyes. It felt wrong coming from the normally affable man, and a tiny whisper of worry crept through her subconscious, though it had yet to find a voice.

Master Eamon recovered with his normal smile, "I have contacts in Continens Hyclepius, that new world named so after the Maiden, who I have sent far and wide in search of fragments. Ever since Keeper Sophia's discovery of Maidenstone near Elgion I have been desperately scouring the new world for traces of our most benevolent lords." He gestured to Sophia, and the crowd stared at her once more.

It was true, she *had* discovered a new cache of Maidenstone, that healing rock which—like all the godstones—faded or broke with frequent use. Large quantities were needed to stock up the stores of Augustia, and Sophia had obliged back when she had been Elgion's Keeper. Now, the gratitude and satisfaction of those days were a thing of the past, and she faced the combined gaze of Augustian's citizenry.

A prickle of sweat broke free from her brow before Eamon took advantage of the attention upon her, "I ask you now, while we are considering the gods themselves, to hear my witness, Keeper Sophia."

She did not know how to respond to the summons, even though she had prepared mercilessly for this very moment. Sensing her uncertainty, Master Balder, with a raised brow, asked, "Keeper, would you like to stand? Address the crowd?"

Sophia gulped then nodded to the Master of the Hall as her heart leapt in her chest. Apprehensively, she stood and glanced over at Master Eamon. The member of the Chosen's Wisdom smiled while dipping his head ever so slightly, sending out his support in an unseen wave of communication. The subtle gesture reaffirmed her resolve in their combined mission, and the familiar certainty of Master Eamon's good intentions propped up her courage.

With a timorous voice she began, "People of Augustia. Th-th-thank you for allowing me to speak here today. As you all have certainly heard before, I have dealt with the … uh, intrigues of the gods, and, uh, it was not pleasant." She felt her confidence grow as the crowd responded with the tiniest ripple of laughter.

"I dealt with that deceiver, Dolocius, and struck him down in his ambitions." Her voice rose in tempo, her own memories of the events galvanizing her passion. The crowd murmured. "I have aligned with Master Eamon on this bill, *The Godstone Decree*, for I see nothing but the truth in it. Our people risk destruction if we let the shards of the gods run amok. I know how far those … *lords* will go to gain power over us. Magdris, that Crimson King, was allied with Dolocius on that fateful day. The day an orcish horde attacked Elgion, and, at the height of their power, only the pity of the Maiden and the strength of Ember saved us from destruction. I tell you now that we must be vigilant over the shards. Not use them as tokens to gain more wealth! Trust me on this."

Just as they had practiced, Sophia paused. The crowd held their breath. *If they didn't believe me before, they do now,* she thought with zeal.

"Our Keepers have significant caches of those shards we most risk the loss of. We have stores of Artstone, Necrostone, and of course … Embershard, the very lord of gods who gave me the power to defeat Dolocius and his corruption!" The noise of the crowd grew in response, and she had to nearly shout to be heard. "Our risk with this endeavor is small, but our gain? Great! If we trade away our advantage, we risk destruction. I implore you, members of the Chosen's Wisdom, representatives of The People's Will, and citizens of Augustia, pass this bill here and we *will* safeguard our future!"

The hall erupted into chaos, and from across the floor she saw Master Eamon smile wickedly at her. She blushed at the attention; she had done well. All their planning and preparation had been worth it, and a great weight fell off her shoulders. The crowds echoed her triumph, and once more Master Balder had to silence them with a thunderous crash of his staff. Reluctantly, the people of Augustia came to order, allowing the Chosen to fall into debate once more.

With her duty done, she could not focus on what was said anymore. Her adrenaline had been spent, and she sat heavily on her seat as the session droned on around her. For days, almost weeks, she had been preparing for this moment. Now her part was over, and she felt like melting into the marble with relief.

Several minutes passed alternating between Masters Aranos, Eamon, Falris, and even Kylos, who was always ready to counter Eamon's charismatic proposals. The members of the Chosen met with raucous applause and cheers that echoed amongst the high walls of the Hall. The dockworkers had been summoned, and their nervous voices played their part, frightening the crowds with tales of godstone-filled crates being shipped to far off lands. Even in her unfocused state, Sophia knew the advantage lie with them. Yet, in the end, Master Balder had to call the vote and no amount of preparation or passionate speech could override that.

A silence, eerie in its tangible presence, fell over the Hall as two hundred members of the Chosen's Wisdom stood and formed a line. Upon receiving their chasuble, that vestment of responsibility, members of the Chosen's Wisdom were also given two metal disks, one silver and another gold. The golden disk would indicate a vote for yes and the silver for no, a tradition nearly as old as Augustia herself.

The Chosen approached a clay jar that sat atop a table near Master Balder and dropped their metal disk within. The sound muffled by a cloth wrap used to hide the shine of the disks. It was a small measure to prevent retaliation from those who observed the voting, and indirectly to prevent influence on the votes of those proceeding the voter.

Of course, Master Eamon was quick to find a spot near the front of the queue, and when he added his vote to the jar, he turned to the waiting Chosen and smiled. It was a reminder of who they voted for, or who they voted against. A sound strategy, but one that made Sophia feel ill at the prospect. She would be glad to be rid of politics for a while after this.

She forced herself to focus on her breathing as the steady sound of a jar filling with cloth wrapped disks echoed. *Tink. Tink. Tink.* Finally, the vote came to a close with the last Chosen dropping their disk into the jar with a flourish.

Master Balder surveyed the people of Augustia, and with little ceremony struck the jar with a small hammer, breaking it asunder. The disks spilled out over the table with a few clattering to the floor below. It was a dramatic scene, and one that gave Sophia a small sense of pride in her city—in her people. No matter the situation, those two hundred disks represented the citizens' right to power.

The two guards that flanked Master Balder were quick to respond and moved to pick up the errant pieces of metal. Two members of the representative contingent of the People's Will approached, and, alongside Master Balder, took turns counting the disks. It was a painfully slow process, especially considering the anticipation that buzzed within the hall. The second member of The People's Will had even started counting aloud. When he stumbled over his own accounting and had to restart—to groans within the gallery, Master Balder whispered in his ear. The man flushed with embarrassment and restarted his count. Only the faintest movement on his lips.

In the damnable waiting she tried to affect a visage of calm, of one not prone to fidgeting, but it was a challenge. Sure, she had prepared herself for the outcome of the vote, either bad or good, and knew to show too much emotion would not reflect kindly on her status. To her surprise, she caught Master Eamon staring at her, and, as she returned the glance, he winked at her. It was all she could do not to giggle at the flirtatious gesture, and suddenly she was aware of Gilbert's attendance within the gallery. She prayed to the Maiden the poor man had not seen the act. Unfortunately, Master Eamon drew the eye.

Her thoughts were interrupted by a sudden shout from Master Balder, "The People's Will and I have come to a final tally!" The Master of the Hall stood and paced forward a few steps.

The man liked drama, Sophia recognized.

"We have counted sixty-eight silver disks," immediately the crowds erupted into pandemonium. Everyone knew before it was even said, who had won the vote, but still Master Balder screamed the tally out, "and one-hundred-thirty-two golden disks! *The Godstone Decree* will move for approval by the People's Will!"

She barely heard Master Balder belt out the effects of the vote over the cheering of the crowds. Everyone there had felt invested in the proceedings, and it was plain the citizens of Augustia were sympathetic towards Master Eamon's arguments. *They act as if they had won themselves,* Sophia allowed as a genuine smile graced her lips. In the energy of the room, she couldn't help but stand.

A dockworker clapped her on the shoulder, "Great work, Keeper!"

"Yea we did right by 'em today," their partner said.

She laughed, unable to contain the joy she felt, and began to clap in recognition of their success.

"I told you we could do it!" Master Eamon bellowed at her, having weaved his way through the thickening crowd.

To her astonishment, he hugged her in his massive arms, picking her up as he squeezed. As he placed her back to the ground, she was flush with excitement. She hadn't asked for the embrace, but she had to admit … she didn't mind. Once more she laughed in sheer joy.

"We have secured Augustia's future!" Master Eamon belted out over his own laughter.

"Ah, that was *exhilarating*," Sophia said through panting breaths.

"I told you that you would love it! There is no better place in the world than the Chosen's Hall and being basked in the attentions of Augustians!" Eamon grabbed his chasuble, and this time he was *not* mocking his own importance.

Maybe he had earned it today, she figured, but still, she couldn't help herself. "Still *so* humble I see."

The big-armed man roared in appreciation at the jest until his attendant, a man in a purple waistcoat, whispered in his ear. Sophia had seen the thin man as a persistent shadow to the member of the Chosen wherever he went, and she felt a small tug at her heart as Master Eamon was yanked away to speak to some other, more important individual.

"Sophia!" Gilbert cried out.

She turned to see the young man shoving his way through the bustling crowd, and she winced as he nearly fell over one particularly stubborn individual. True, he wasn't as agile or as athletic as Eamon, but his genuine smile made her heart melt ever so slightly.

"Sophia, what a great job! *You* were amazing!" He yelled as he held his arms out to hug her.

She smiled back at him and allowed herself to be wrapped in his gentle embrace. "Thank you, I was so … nervous!"

Gilbert laughed, "I bet! I would have been beside myself. Still, you were great! I even saw Grand Keeper Chalepos smile after you had spoken."

She felt a strange wash of relief at that news. She didn't expect that man to approve of anything she did—especially this. Apparently, she had finally done something right in the old man's eyes. *Finally.*

Gilbert, having pulled her away so he could look at her, must have sensed her disbelief and spoke once more, "It's true. Ember's Breath, its true! The man let loose a smile." He stepped back a pace, bumping into a woman who cursed at his clumsiness. "Sorry," he apologized. Then with a playful grin he held up his hand, "On the Maiden's honor I tell you the truth!"

She laughed with unadulterated joy. She hugged Gilbert, noticing he was only slightly taller than herself. Not like Eamon, that man seemed to tower over her. Still, she squeezed with affection, and—for a time—they just sat there. Surrounded by crowds of excited Augustians. Truly, it was a glorious moment.

One that should be bathed in a feeling of bliss, but slowly, a small hollow formed within her chest. The whispers of the gods felt anxious—almost angry. They never spoke aloud, not even now, unless she sought them out, but their persistent murmurings had taken a turn for the worse. The normal drone of their aura was wreathed in dread and dire premonition, and a vague emotion began to blossom within her core. It was a deep-seated *wrongness*, and somewhere inside her conscious, she buried a warning of things to come. All she could do was pray to those ever-present whispers that she had not been the cause of their anxiety. It had little effect.

Chapter Seven

Bella

Bella still remembered her first, terrifying voyage across the Sea of Melleas, a month and half long journey fraught with peril. One she wasn't quite sure she wanted to relive. Unfortunately, that choice had been stripped from her, and now—once more—she felt the bob and weave of Melleas's torments. She did try to call herself lucky, seeing how she managed to keep her lunch down unlike so many others, but that was a difficult call to make.

After all, she couldn't shake the feeling of existential dread. During good weather, she could see for what felt like forever, a circumstance she almost wished would not occur. In that boundless horizon, all anyone could see was the roll of the sea's waves, tumbling ever onwards until they gave way to the curve that dipped the horizon out of view. The fear of being set adrift in that wash of blues and whites plunged her into a near panic on her worst days. And on her best days, cursed her with thoughts of her own insignificance against the backdrop of such vastness.

The alternative to that awe-inspiring horizon was a darkened sky interrupted by the rise and fall of raging waters. On occasion, even this far south of the strait known as Melleas's Wroth, the sea could turn into a froth of angry waves. It was the after effect of the strait; weather forced into a tempestuous temperament. Still, it was better than trying to navigate the strait itself. That relatively narrow passage between the old and new worlds was lethal, and many explorers had tried—and failed—to chart a course through its winding chain of broken islands. So instead, Augustian sailors learned to cross well south of Melleas's Wroth where the wind had been becalmed to a tolerable level, though it extended the journey's distance considerably.

That increased distance gave the captain many more chances to check his maps and his astrolabe; Bella's fear of becoming lost following in lock step with the captain's own level of certainty. Only Hislock's presence around the squat sailor helped her maintain some semblance of patience. She wondered how many times she had watched Hislock be shown some minor adjustment of the astrolabe, some whispered words of description, all followed by some scrawl on the map?

The captain's expressive face tended towards concentration when Hislock was there to be taught, and Bella was glad for it. It was a much better sight than the small moments of fear written on his face. Lines of minute panic whenever the astrolabe refused to divulge its secrets. With a student, the captain's confidence seemed more concrete, even when they had to readjust the astrolabe multiple times. Fortunately, Hislock was fascinated by the okenavis and its many marvels. So much so he had even roped her into trying to learn the astrolabe's secrets, but its complex weave of lines and glyphs were maddeningly convoluted.

The device reminded her of Sophia, who, on their first journey, simply said, "It's to chart us against the stars, which stay bound in the sky relative to us. How to use it? I don't know, but I bet those who do probably spend a good part of their life mastering it."

That mastery had enthralled Hislock and the lizardman spent many of the days on the sea in deep conversation with the captain. Well, it was more like clipped words complimented with exaggerated body language. Still, the captain seemed more than eager to divulge his secrets to a fellow enthusiast. Much to her relief. She had worried they would revile the saurian, but Hislock's affable nature and terrifying athleticism had earned the respect of those old-world natives.

Now, as they stood at the bow of the okenavis, she smiled at her gecko-like friend who was about to see her home city. Godfrey was there, but only because he was glad to be done with the—as he put it, "Gods damned voyage!" The poor man had vomited for three straight days when they began their journey. It wasn't until he managed to stomach some fermented cabbage, a requisite food for any long sea voyage, that he took a break from his time at the rail. Only able to subsist on meagre rations, Godfrey looked as ragged as ever. The normally kempt hairs of his beard running wild and taking on a whiter hue than normal. To her left, stood Alexa, who held a contented smile as they neared the Augustian port.

"I can almost smell it from here!" Bella roared over the splash of a wave as they tore through the final breakers of the sea. Augustia's port had a shallow approach to its natural harbor. Twin peninsulas of land were dotted with torchlit towers, warehouses, and drying racks. The stretches of land reached out to greet them as they pulled through the shoals. Once they crossed the threshold of those arms, the waves would die down as they entered a deep lagoon that held Augustia's rich trading port.

"You mean the smell of piss and feces?" Alexa asked with a grin.

"Yes, but also the smell of *home*." The two laughed, their excitement palpable, and Alexa clapped her on the shoulder. It was good to see her sister in good spirits again. The first couple weeks of the voyage had become quite tiresome with Alexa crying over that sop back in Elgion. *Amildo or Amicus or something like that.* The worst of that heartbreak seemed to be over; although Bella still saw her sister clutch at a little wooden figurine, a keepsake from a lost love. *Thank the gods*, she thought, even though she knew the young warrior seemed a decent sort.

They ripped through another wave to the sound of the rowing drum: the captain had ordered the single rowing deck and sails at full speed. A necessity so that they could get through breaker waves or risk becoming capsized. And today the crossing that separated the harbor and the open sea was as perilous as ever. *The power of Melleas was never one to disappoint,* Bella mused. Another wave crashed into the side of the okenavis, and it was easy to see how even larger vessels could flounder.

Godfrey groaned, "One more damned curse from that bastard god!"

"Who is bastard god?" Sidon asked to the groans of Godfrey.

"Don't repeat that lad," Alexa intervened.

Even Hislock laughed, his typical, rattling chuckle showing his delight at Godfrey's comical misery.

"There are no bastard gods, Sidon. Godfrey—as is typical with him—is being a nuisance." Bella gripped the shoulder of the young lad and pulled him towards the railing to stand next to her. "Godfrey, we're almost home, now stop yer whining!" She roared as salty water splashed her face.

"Thank the gods! I never want to be on this damned ocean again."

"Why? I like this—how you say? *Damned* ocean," Sidon mimicked.

Bella sighed as the boy once again repeated the worst words and phrases they uttered. She settled on redirection. "It is something isn't it?"

Another splash on the bow; another spray of cold salty water. Sidon and even Orator Malfias, the diplomatic envoy who had a habit of sneaking up behind them, yelped with elation. Bella couldn't help but laugh as Alexa joined in with a whoop of her own. Her heart was filled with excitement as she turned back to take in the view, water running down her face. They fell down another trough of the breaker waves—pummeled by its intensity.

Then, without warning, they were simply gliding along placid waters. They had crossed the twin peninsulas and a bellowing horn from the shore denoted their arrival. A new ship had come to Augustia's shores, and Bella felt a pang of nostalgia. In the quieter days of the past, she would watch ships enter the harbor with her dad. She wondered then—as she did now—if the horn blower's throat ever got sore from the constant employment. After all, the harbor was teeming with ships, and Bella felt alive with glee.

"Strike the sail!" The captain roared, and the okenavis slowed, coasting to a pleasant cruising speed. The captain laid their course towards a large pier that darted out into the lagoon.

Bella looked up then at the Bowl, that ring of hills that looked like a moon, and her breath caught in her throat. She had not realized how beautiful her city truly was. White marble halls and homes dotted the upper hills, looking like little pillars of light amidst the browns and greens of vegetation. Running like rivers through those islands of gleaming white were wide cobbled streets that crisscrossed the city.

She traced the lines of the stony roads until she was looking towards her childhood home. It had been a comfortable spot, nestled between the Lower and Upper Bowl just to the east of Grange Street, that main artery of the city that split like a river around The Chosen's Hall. That monument to humanity's greatness, with its gleaming pillars strung along the outer walls and its massive clay tiled roof that seemed to dominate the surrounding area. Even from the lagoon, its features were clearly visible, and Bella likened it to a central plinth amidst a sea of traders and craftsmen. A myriad of folks made their shops within the forum that surrounded the structure. Of course, the Keeper's Bastion and the Court of the Mandated towered over it all, but the Chosen's Hall felt more *commanding,* more central.

"Rowers! Quarter speed!" The Sergeant of the Deck bellowed as they neared the pier.

The okenavis slowed under her and she had to grip the rail to not lose her footing. When she looked back up at the city, the visage of The Lower Bowl dominated her view. A cacophony of wooden and stone buildings ran between the shoreline and the base of the hill only stopped by the harbor's footprint. It was the sad part of Augustia, the stratification of humanities wealth was so plainly displayed. *No wonder so many were eager to travel to the new world,* she thought.

"Rowers! Bank oars!" The captain had steered them expertly, and hemp and cloth fenders gently bumped against the pier. Lines were thrown to workmen along the dock, and they scurried to and fro, securing the ship for landing.

Hislock hissed, forcing her to glance towards him, and she saw astonishment on his face.

"Quite the sight, isn't it?" she nudged him.

He slowly turned to her, his mouth agape, showing the sharpened tines of his teeth. "Human build strong."

Bella replied as Alexa chuckled, "Yes, we build strong. This here is Augustia. My home, and *you* are welcome to it." She gestured with an open palm, sweeping the breadth of the city.

The gangplank thudded against the dock below and Godfrey wasted no time. "Let me off of this damn thing." He nearly pushed a sailor aside as they crossed in front of him with a bundle of wool. The old veteran stumbled down the ramp, fell to his knees, and kissed the wood below his feet. *Always one for drama,* Bella mused.

"Oh, thank the gods that's over. You hear me Maiden? Thank you! Ember? Thank you! Even you Melleas, thank you!" Godfrey held his one hand up in his closest attempt at prayer, and Bella thought she could see tears well into the man's eyes.

Truly, he hates the sea, she sympathized.

"Your friend is not one for the water," the captain said.

Bella chuckled knowingly, "Yea, you should see him on a horse."

The stout man let out a bark of laughter. "Typical of grey-haired veterans I suppose. Stubborn in their ways, but I wouldn't want to cross that axe of his… Anyways, I wanted to wish you all well on your journey. And-uh-I-uh—" the captain, unsure of how to deliver his gift, handed over a compass to Hislock.

The saurian looked down at the gold trimmed device and back up at the captain. Suddenly, he cocked his head and hooted towards the sky. With a grin he grabbed the compass, capering backwards like a child at Ember's Feast.

The captain smiled sheepishly. "It's for-uh-you and your *people* when you want to try and navigate. Ya know, like we talked about."

Hislock stopped mid-caper and fixed the man with a serious glance. With the utmost care Hislock annunciated his words, "Thank you, friend." The saurian reached out his free hand to the captain, and the two clasped each other's arms.

Bella jumped slightly as Orator Malfias's voice emanated from behind her shoulder, "Rangemaster, Stablemaster, I will take my leave and meet you two at the Ranger's Hall tomorrow as we discussed. From there we can go to the Court of the Mandated together. Have a pleasant reunion."

"Thank you, Orator. Enjoy your time with your family and be sure to try Bodie's Kabobs!" Alexa replied.

Orator Malfias laughed, "Yes, yes, I will try them, Rangemaster. I look forward to our next meeting." With that, the robe-drenched man, whose head was shaven bald and polished to a glistening sheen, nodded towards the captain.

"Orator Malfias, thank you for your counsel," The captain said.

"Please, captain. It was *my* pleasure." Finally, the orator looked towards Hislock. Malfias seemed to ponder the scaled sentient being for a while, long enough for Hislock to straighten under the scrutiny. "Hislock; honored friend! Your people do us great service in sending you here as an ambassador. I will speak to the Mandated and the Chosen to see if we can return the favor. I think it is high time for a diplomatic mission of our own."

Hislock nodded, "Thank you … friend. We, and Great Saurusss, see fo-forward to you."

The orator bowed to Hislock; then he was off, flanked by his bodyguard.

The captain addressed the rest of the gathered passengers. "Right, I will have the crew bring your luggage. Truly, it's been a pleasure. Rangemaster, Stablemaster, Sidon ... Hislock." The captain then pivoted on his feet and set about wrapping up the affairs of his latest voyage.

*

They wound their way through claustrophobic alleys, hemmed in by two- and three-story buildings. Bella watched as Hislock's head swiveled mercilessly. The saurian tried to take in every sight, every shout, and every clatter of city noise. Of course, a sentient bipedal reptile had drawn the gaze of the souls they crossed. One old lady working on some sort of soup had nearly fallen over as the saurian walked in front of her. Fortunately, Hislock did not seem to mind or even notice. After all, he was an explorer at heart, and he was filled with joy at so many new things to see.

It was late afternoon by the time they arrived at Harbor and Grange Street's intersection. Bella's stomach rumbled as they were greeted by the smell of city flavors, especially with so many vendors preparing their wares for the dinner time rush. Even after so many years, Bella could pick out one of her favorites. Chicken, fried in olive oil, all homegrown and all delicious. Other scents, including the more unfortunate smells of the city, greeted them as they made their way up the hill. But her hunger tricked her into ignoring those *distinct* aromas. In so doing, she could focus on the more dominant smell of food. Honey-drizzled, laepous legs with asparagus, stewed beef and lamb on rice, fresh bread buttered with the products of local cows, and, a particular favorite of her childhood, honey-sweetened, plum cakes baked to a crisp perfection.

"Gulmavarn," Sidon said suddenly, his old tongue slipping out.

Bella smiled "I'm hungry too little one."

"I am not little."

Alexa reached out and ruffled his hair, prompting an angry glance. "No, you are not. It is just a turn of phrase, Sidon." The words must have gone some way to assuage Sidon's wounded pride because he stood a little straighter as they started their climb up The Bowl.

Alexa had agreed with her that they would hit the forum first, preferably bringing a treat with them as they wound their way to their childhood home. Not to mention, they *had* to take in the sights of their old city after so long away. The planning had made her curious about Godfrey's own ambitions, wondering if Grace—the mother he had referenced on occasion—was still within the city. Instead, the man had become rather quiet as she brought it up, and she decided not to press the issue. So, the company wound its way up the hill through the steadily growing crowds, many pockets of which stopped and stared at them. Fingers were pointed and gasps were heard as they looked upon the green, scaled saurian amongst their number.

Surely, these people had heard of saurians by now? To be fair, they had probably never seen one. Hislock—to his credit—did not take offense and, being a warrior, stood proudly; it was as if he were on a victory march coming home.

"In time they will get to know ya lad," Godfrey said, evidently of the same mind.

Hislock hissed in response.

"They must be having a clinic day," Alexa said while pointing up the hill.

Of course, Alexa stands erect. Not even pretending that this damned hill phases her, Bella thought. Then, a better—more welcome—thought hit her. Through the steadily increasing strain of her muscles and the heat that accompanied the warming summer day, her excitement grew.

Alexa must have had the same idea, because her brown eyes were looking right at her. Together the two belted out the same word, "Sophia!" Almost as one they quickened their pace, knowing their Keeper sister would definitely attend a clinic, that old service provided by the Bastion to the community.

Sidon, not trying to hide the difficulty of the climb like the rest, shouted over shortened breath, "Wait up!"

But Bella pretended not to hear; vigorously stomping up the last hundred meters alongside Alexa. As they crested the climb to the space flattened for the forum, they scanned the gathered peoples. There were lines of sick and injured. Folks who came out once a month to receive the blessings of the gods from the messengers themselves. And there she was, Sophia, a proud and regal Keeper.

"There," Bella said as she smacked Alexa's arm and pointed. Their sister was in the middle of making a small girl laugh while the parents nervously waited as treatment was administered. Alexa and Bella rushed over.

"Now, you be a good girl and take this brew every night," Sophia said. She prodded the girl's stomach with a finger, earning a giggle. "OK?"

Over her own laughter, the girl responded sheepishly, "OK." The girl was about to hop out of the seat when her eyes became serious. "Keeper?"

Sophia responded with a smile, "Yes?"

"Can I … become like you one day?"

Sophia's smile widened until Bella thought it might crack her face in two. The overjoyed Keeper responded, "Why, of course my dear! I was just like you once, and I had dreams of talking to the gods. But!" Sophia shifted her tone to a more serious one, gaining the girl's utter focus. "*You* must be strong, and *you* must stick to your studies. Not everyone can hear the whispers of the gods, but the gods do tend to favor those who work hard. Understand?"

The little girl nodded sternly, and Bella felt a small shiver through her nerves as she saw a reflection of herself—of her sisters in that little girl.

"Alright, run along now," Sophia said as she gently pushed the girl back towards her parents, who muttered a thousand platitudes.

"What you got for some old friends?" Bella asked mischievously.

Sophia, who had been staring after the girl and her family, stiffened. Sharply, she turned to them and her lips pursed in that strange emotional mix that accompanies a long-awaited reunion. As she stood, her heavy Keeper's robes upset the small stool that sat in front of her, and her face melted into tears. She paced over to them—arms outstretched.

The three sisters embraced, and emotions flowed freely. Sophia's sobbing voice barely heard over muffling cloth, "Welcome back!"

"You two look alike!" Sidon interjected, looking back and forth between Sophia and Bella.

The sisters laughed, and Bella, her face propped over Sophia's shoulder, responded, "Yes, Sidon. That's because we are sisters!"

"I know, but you and this one look even more alike!"

"It's the hair," Sophia said as their hug broke apart. She grabbed her autumnal red ponytail wrapped in silver bangles and displayed it to the young man. Sidon nodded, satisfied with the explanation.

"This here is Sidon, and he—as impertinent as he is—is one of the reasons we're here," Alexa introduced him.

Hislock and Godfrey took this opportunity to step forward and be recognized.

"Welcome to Augustia, Sidon," Sophia said formally. She then bent a crooked smile at Godfrey. "Godfrey, I see that you are … What happened to you?"

"It's that damned sea ma'am, I hates it. I will be right as rain in no time, just you wait."

"Ah, I see. And Hislock! How good it is to see you again," Sophia looked around suddenly, scanning the gathering crowds. They had come to see what made their stern Keeper so vibrant. "They've been treating you well, haven't they?" Sophia asked as much to Hislock as to the people around them.

Bella laughed and chose to respond for her friend, "Yes, they have. Save for the stares of curiosity, we've been treated well enough. Hislock here even made a friend of the captain—gave him a compass."

Hislock displayed the gold-trimmed treasure with delight and then spoke in his rasping tongue, "Friend give treasure!" The saurians rather loud retort caused a gasp amongst the surrounding people.

Bella heard the cries, "He speaks!"

Another, "It-it-it's a talking lizard!"

She even thought a woman fainted as her yelp was abruptly cut off, "Gods above! Never ha—"

It was almost comical in a way, but Sophia was having none of it and she turned to the crowds once more, fixing them with a stern glare. Their Keeper sister had to have grown accustomed to large groups and how to deal with them, and, as Sophia swept her gaze over the people, she spoke, "All of you! There is nothing to see here! Go about your business!"

Reluctantly, the crowds dispersed, murmuring and whispering to themselves about the curiosity they had witnessed. Satisfied her order had been obeyed, Sophia clapped her hands together. "You all must be hungry! Alexa, Bella, mom and dad will be *so* happy to see you! Come on now, clinic is wrapping up for the day, and I have time to grab some supper. How about we head home?"

"I couldn't imagine a better plan," Bella replied as utter joy rippled through her.

Chapter Eight

Bella

It was just like Bella remembered—a stone structure with a clay tiled roof, small wooden framed windows dotted along its outside, and a wrought iron fence jutting off to the north and west until it disappeared out of sight. The *cluck cluck* of chickens emanated from behind that iron fence. Little fiends that scoured their patch of Telaea for anything to eat. Only her dad's wattle fencing kept the chicken's domain of dirt from expanding, a fence he had been *so* proud of. She still remembered her dad slapping the top of his first section of wattle he ever made only for it to immediately fall over.

"Shit," Bella murmured to herself.

"I beg to differ, I think it looks pretty nice," Sophia joked.

She chuckled, "No, no, just … remembering dad cursing up a storm whenever he had to build something."

Alexa chuckled before chiming in, "Yea he was all pride and pomposity when he finished, but before then … *woo* he was a right tempest."

More memories flooded in, and she found the words flowing. "You remember how mom would pull us away so she could distract us with *treats*?"

"Of course I do, that's the only time she ever tried to sing—it was atrocious!" Alexa said to a chorus of laughter.

Sophia said with some emotion, "Yea, I actually kind of like those memories. It showed our parents as flawed—as human. Most days I thought of them akin to the gods themselves, but on those days … Those days, I recognized that they were just like us."

Hislock had been listening in on the conversation and apparently could not contain himself anymore, "Bellaaa, you parent live here!?"

Bella nodded in confirmation.

Hislock jumped excitedly. "Gooood, I much like to see such strong breeds!"

"Don't … don't call 'em that," Bella responded.

"I hate to break it to ya—" Godfrey started, but she interrupted him by shooting up a warning hand. The old man grinned at her mischievously.

Not wanting to give the old veteran a chance to tease her further she offered, "Well, we made it this far. Shall we?"

Alexa nodded, her face becoming stern, much like it always did when she was nervous and trying to hide it. Bella didn't blame her; it had been nearly five-and-a-half years since they had seen their childhood home.

Sophia knocked loudly on the solid wooden door, a small wreath of juniper and local wildflower hung over its frame. She was studying the wreath when suddenly it was ripped away; bits of juniper scattered. Her breath caught. There in the threshold of the door was her mother, Mira Vollimosa, a tall proud woman with dark black hair, brown eyes, and a kind, rounded face that sat upon a healthy, albeit slightly portly frame.

"Ooooh," Was all Mira could manage. It was a characteristic noise of her mother, an utterance she used whenever she couldn't handle the excitement. Bella watched as her face went from neutral placidity to one of unbidden joy. "My babies!" Without warning, Bella was wrapped in her mother's arms and squeezed alongside her sisters. All three of them somehow still fitting in their mother's embrace. "Ooooh, my beautiful girls!" Her mom said over quickly made tears.

She couldn't help herself, the soft, joyful sobs of her mother unleashed her own emotional dam, and the tears burst. The nerves for this reunion gone in an instant. Her mother flushed away any anxiety, reminding her this was—and always would be—a safe place for her.

Mira let her mama-bear hug drop and she took a step back, studying them. Her face glistened with tears that mixed with some sort of light coating of lanolin, and amidst the oily mixture was a countenance full of pride.

"You two look like you have grown! Come on, yer dad will 'bout have a heart attack." Mira was about to step back to admit them inside, but suddenly she recognized Godfrey, Hislock, and Sidon standing at a respectable distance away. "Oh, I didn't see ya there! I'm sorry, you must be friends of my girls."

Godfrey stepped forward and dipped his head towards Mira, "Yes ma'am, we are. The saurian behind me is Hislock, the boy is Sidon, and I … well, I am Godfrey. You have a lovely home."

Mira blushed slightly at the compliment before Hislock darted forward, making a space for himself between the sisters and their mother.

"Oooh," Mira grasped her chest and took an involuntary step back.

Hislock didn't seem to notice his rudeness and spoke to the wide brown eyes of Mira in his raspy voice, "You mother of Bellaaa?"

Bella felt a slight tickle of anxiety at the strange action and heard a muttering apology issue from Godfrey.

"Yes …" Her mom said uncertainly.

Suddenly, Hislock grabbed Mira by the shoulders and let out a sort of bark. "You ssstrong breed! I happy to ssssee you."

Bella wasn't sure how to respond to this, and, like her sisters, stood stunned at Hislock's familiarity.

Thankfully, Godfrey came forward and placed a hand on the capering lizardman's shoulder. "I'm sorry about that ma'am. He … he, uh doesn't *quite* get our customs."

Her mom laughed with only a hint of nervousness, "That's alright! Hislock is it?"

The lizardman stopped and stood as erect as he could, which, due to his natural stoop, was still about thirty centimeters shy of the present company. He hit his chest with his scaled fist and nodded at Mira.

Her mom laughed, causing some consternation for Hislock, but she didn't notice the irritation because she was now looking at Sidon. The boy stood—looking broken—his head downcast. "Hey there, lad," she said gently.

Sidon only kicked at the stones beneath his feet, and Bella reckoned her mother was wise to the pain that Sidon tried to hide. He had just lost his father after all, and such a warm reunion amongst family would be tough on a young man.

"Would you like to come in and try one of my honey biscuits?" Her mom asked.

Sidon stopped mid-kick and, though he did not look up, gave the slightest of nods.

"Excellent!" Mira said as she clapped her hands together and stepped to the side. "Any friends of my girls are friends of mine. Come on in and have a bite to eat!"

They entered her childhood home and were instantly awash in the smells of her youth. The warmth that seemed to constantly blanket every room was still there, and the smell of homemade cooking, which was currently some sort of chicken-based dish, brought her back. An unbidden smile crossed her lips as she, alongside the rest of the group, took off their shoes in the small mud room they were in, surrounded by the outfits her dad preferred. Heavy fabrics able to sustain long periods of abuse and a plethora of shoes that ranged from working boots to simple slippers. Her dad was best described as an academic, but he liked the simpler, more efficient garb of those who worked with their hands.

As if on call, she heard that familiar voice. "Ah! Alexa! Bella!" Skorin rushed over to his long away daughters, picked up Bella due to proximity, and squeezed like his life depended on it.

"Ah, dad! Yer gonna ruin me!" Bella said with a smile on her lips. Even though he wasn't much taller than the vertically inclined sisters, he had scooped her up with ease. She smelt the familiar musk of her father and returned the hug with enthusiasm before he let her drop back down to the ground. He repeated the action with Alexa, albeit with *slightly* more difficulty. Bella noticed that his brownish blonde hair was trending towards grey and balding, and it looked like he was opting for a permanent five 'o'clock shadow that gave him a trace of gruffness.

As he placed Alexa back to the ground and with a smile as wide as the sea, he spoke, "My girls … my beautiful girls! Ho-how are you?" Strong emotion forcing the slightest of stammers.

Bella didn't know what to say, and all Alexa could manage was a playful chuckle. The emotion that welled inside of her brought the horrors of what she had seen to the fore. She tried to push them away, to speak, to tell her father how much she had missed him, but the words would not come.

"Come, Come! Let's have a seat. Your mom is making chicken with rice, and it smells *delicious!* You too young man," Skorin said with a glance towards Sidon. Her father beckoned with his hand as he walked towards the dining room. The whole of the company followed suit down a narrow hallway that opened into a kitchen area. A table lay just past a stone island that fronted the kitchen.

Mira scurried in behind them, checking the inside of a stone oven aglow with a reddish light. "No one told us you two were coming home! We would've prepared!" Her mom was yelling at this point because she was busy stirring a pot of rice on the heated stovetop. It all reminded Bella so much of the past. Yet still no words would come; instead, her mind flashed images of a mutilated Elira—a torn Godwin. She shook her head and glanced up to see her dad studying her—concern plain on his face. She went to open her mouth, but she could think of nothing to say.

Thankfully, Alexa was not at such a loss, and Bella dipped her head as she heard her sister speak. "We had to leave right away, and any message would have travelled as fast as us. Sorry, mum."

Her mom whipped around, steaming pot held in both hands. As she placed it down on the stone island, she talked through the white mist, "Now, don't be sorry love! I'm glad yer home; just … a surprise is all." Mira finished stirring the pot and was about to check on her oven when a new development forced her to stop.

Bella chuckled to herself as she saw her mom give Godfrey a menacing glare. He had not sat with the rest of them and was apparently attempting to help her mother in the kitchen. The one-armed man involuntarily backed a step and held up his good hand in an attempt at placation. Mira spoke with a waspish tone, "And just what do you think you are doing?! Trying to steal a bite?!"

"N-n-no ma'am, I just was trying to help is all."

"Help? Help!" her mom huffed dramatically. "This here is my space, and I don't need no help. I can manage just fine by myself, *thank you* very much. Ember's Breath, I run an apothecary; this? This is child's play!"

"S-sorry," Godfrey managed to mumble, and retreated away from her furious glare.

Mom never let anyone in her kitchen, Bella mused.

Godfrey did a sort of stumbling fall into one of the wooden chairs that surrounded the table. It was a lesson they had all learned in one way or another, and the three sisters along with their father held knowing smiles.

Her dad spoke with mirth in his voice, "Don't worry, sir, she only gets that way in her kitchen. She will be stuffing you full of honey biscuits and sweets in no time."

Godfrey, looking a little bit shocked at the hard rebuff from Mira, replied, "I-I just never … well, let's just say … I see where yer daughters get their spirit from."

Mira barked out a laugh from over the stone island, and, without ever breaking stride in the food preparation, spoke proudly, "I always said, 'don't ever get in the way of a Vollimosa woman!'"

Skorin nodded at Godfrey, showing truer words had never been spoken. Her dad continued, "Hmmm, I didn't catch yer name, sir, but you must be Godfrey. The girls have all written about you. I believe some thanks are in order. What with helping Bella here get out of that awful situation with the orcs."

Mira stopped suddenly, "That was you!?"

Godfrey nodded, though he was oddly quiet.

In that silence, Mira rounded the stone island and with outstretched arms—ones that made Godfrey wince in anticipation—spoke, "Come on then! I believe a hug's in order."

Godfrey obeyed, standing in time to be scooped up in a momma-bear hug. Mira grunted as she spoke, "Thank the Maiden you were there! From what we've heard it took all of you together to make it through."

Godfrey, who had been released from the embrace, muttered, "Yer welcome, ma'am."

"Just stay out of my kitchen, ya hear?"

Godfrey nodded vigorously, looking like a young boy who desperately wanted to please his mum. Mira went back to preparing the food, and he sheepishly sat back down in his seat.

With smiles infecting the Vollimosa family members, her dad refocused their attentions towards Sidon, "What's yer name, lad?" Sidon's eyes widened at having been asked a question. His sheepishness from outside somewhat diminished, but, in combination with his language barrier and the recent commotion, he too looked at a loss of words.

Sophia answered for him, "His name is Sidon, dad, an—"

"Let the boy answer for himself," Skorin replied with an upheld hand. That familiar paternal parentage baring its teeth. Bella felt a pang of nostalgia at seeing her father in his normal routines. Discipline was paramount, and Mister Vollimosa was a master of the craft.

"Sidon." The boy said at a whisper, forcing her dad to lean forward.

Her father held his hand to his ear; plainly showing either he didn't hear or was pretending not to so the boy would speak with pride.

Sidon took the hint and repeated himself, although this time at a shout, "Sidon!"

Skorin leaned back in his chair, noting the trace of anger that had leapt from the young man. "Sidon, is it?"

The boy nodded.

Skorin returned the gesture, and for a few seconds, just looked at the boy. Bella nearly shook her head as she saw the same disciplinary temperament her father had always used. The silence would do its work, and most of the time, whoever was being *taught* knew when they had made a mistake. A mistake that would become apparent either through their own conclusion or from the stern disappointment of their father's countenance. The small flush on Sidon's cheeks told Bella the trick was working.

"You wouldn't happen to be from Xeeland would ya?"

Sidon sat up straighter in the chair and replied, "Yes, I from Xeeland."

"I knew it!" Skorin said as he slapped the table. "You see—that name is in several texts I have read from Xeeland scholars. You know what it means?" Her dad leaned forward excitedly. His academic curiosity piqued.

Sidon let a small smile slip and with more eagerness in his voice responded, "I-I think it mean sea, or something like that … Maybe fish?"

Skorin nodded vigorously, accepting the answer for what it was. "I see. Well, Sidon, I am a bit of goof when it comes to names. My daughter's names all have meaning. Alexa here means defender of humanity." Skorin held a hand towards his eldest daughter, and Alexa smiled in return. Her posture a little straighter than before.

He repeated the gesture towards Sophia, "Sophia means wisdom, and I couldn't have been more right about that one!" Another smile and another, near-imperceptible change to demeanor.

Then he gestured towards Bella and her heart quickened, suddenly nervous. He did not speak immediately, causing Sidon and even Hislock to lean forward. "Bella, it means beautiful." The two curious onlookers were about to slide back into their seats, disappointed, when Skorin continued with a hand and finger, held poignantly upwards. "*But*, beauty goes far beyond physical appearance. Beauty in a finely wrought piece of art, beauty in a masterful sword stroke, beauty in a woman who cooks like the Maiden herself!" Her dad was rewarded with a guffaw from her mom, but Bella could see the charm had worked, a smile fresh on her mother's face.

"Beauty in all things *if* you just know where to look. So, ya see, Sidon? All names have meaning. And though some—like yer own—just mean 'the sea,' and others—like Alexa—are more complex, they *all* carry weight. Carry permanence of purpose. How you wish to carry that weight is up to you, but know that when you were named, someone put a spark of hope inside of you, a spark of belief. You understand, lad?"

Strong conviction took root within the boy, and he nodded solemnly, telling Skorin—beyond a shadow of a doubt—he understood the meaning behind the words. Hislock seemed enraptured, and though Bella knew he couldn't understand everything, the saurian hissed as he nodded.

Skorin took a liking to that gesture and smiled at the lizardman, which prompted Hislock to give his own name, "Hissslocke."

"Skorin," her dad replied. "My own name means early or quick. My parents were comedians and named me because I was born earlier than I was supposed to. Pray, tell me, do you know what your name means, sir?"

Hislock looked at him and then towards Bella. He had not understood all he asked, and Bella, having to translate for her friend, finally found her voice. "Dad, he didn't quite understand. You will have to be more … simple with yer words. He is a quick study, but Holliserian is a hard language for his tongue."

Her dad bit his lip and locked her in his sights. Her chest thumped faster as he studied her. Emotions swirled amidst the demons of tainted memory. Slowly, he nodded at her, but she knew he saw inside of her—he saw the pain. He was good at that—good at picking up on their changes in demeanor, those little trifles and big moments that altered the course of one's life. Yeah, he was always quick to figure out when *something* had happened. That familiar scrutiny made her reflect on the changes wrought upon her soul.

After a time, Skorin spoke, "Very well. Hislock, my name means quick. My parents wanted to laugh when they named me," Hislock's own hissing chuckle made Skorin smile, knowing he was understood. "Do you know what yer name means?"

Hislock nodded vigorously. "Hisslocke mean *hold* the line. Me issss warrior. Fight!" The sudden slap of Hislock's fist into his other made Skorin jump.

Her dad's cheeks became ruddy. "Well, I see they were right to name you so!" The two looked at one another, and happiness gripped them both. "Come now! You *must* tell me about your people!"

"Oh, Skorin leave 'em be. At least not 'til they've had something to eat," her mom chimed in as she swiveled around the table with heaping plates of chicken and rice. Sidon's face lit up as Mira placed a full plate in front of him, but before he could dig in, she smacked his hand. Then she went to grab the remaining servings, yelling over her shoulder, "Not until we've thanked the gods for this!"

The table was served rapidly, and Mira found her seat at the other end from her husband. "Sophia, could you do us the honor?"

Sophia nodded, and Bella could tell that in the years her sister had been returned home, this was a common occurrence amongst them.

Sophia bowed her head and spoke, "To the gods, we thank you. To Hercurius for your speedy deliverance, to Mosyneta for your unflinching knowledge, to Olkanestus for your stalwart structures, to Minollo for teaching us of beauty in all things, to Melleas for teaching us to respect the sea, to the Maiden for your mercy, and to Ember, the lord of the gods, for your wisdom in keeping us all safe. Thank you."

They all repeated the platitude to the gods, and with a cheerful beat, Mira resumed, "Now lad, you can dig in!"

Sidon did not hesitate and shoved a steaming spoonful into his mouth. They all laughed as he desperately tried to cool the steaming bite with little luck.

As Bella took a bite of her own rice infused with shredded chicken, she felt a wave of sadness washing over her. The taste of her mother's cooking brought memories of childhood in abundance. The feeling of warmth that came with those memories, especially compared to recent events, was overwhelming. Tears threatened her eyes, and she forced another bite to dissuade them from falling.

She chewed on the delicious morsel and looked around the table. Friends and family were gathered, and her heart felt heavy with longing for older, simpler times. Happiness and sadness in equal measure. Finally, she looked up at her father who—to her surprise—was looking back at her. With careful slowness, his jaw working the food, he leaned back and nodded at her. His eyes saw the truth, and she could see the hurt it caused him. For all the world, she wished she could just be happy on this reunion, but it would not come.

The orc chieftain's malicious grin while imprisoned, the blood drenched field after the battle for Elgion, Godwin's dead, cold eyes, and the mutilated bodies of Alexa's rangers—it was all too much. She could not overcome those thoughts; she could not just … go back to the way it was. She wished for his sake and her mother's she could just be that little girl that had made them laugh, that had made them smile. That happy little girl. She wished they could all live in that moment once more. A single tear coursed its way down her cheek. Thankfully, only her father saw it.

Chapter Nine

Bella

"Hey there Bell Bells," her dad said solemnly, interrupting her thoughts. She had found that quiet spot she remembered as a child. That small patch of land behind her parents' house—amidst the clucking of chickens. Bella would sit there for hours looking at all the happenings of life that surrounded her. Bees and butterflies fluttered amidst the breeze, trying to grab a taste of the lilies and daisies that filled the flower bed. Small pill bugs and ants would crisscross the patio, emerging or diving into the green grass beyond the edge of the concrete. All the while, the sounds of the city carried on relentlessly. A world of noise—barred away by a wrought iron fence.

"Hey," she replied distantly, her eyes squinting against the setting sun.

"Ya know, I don't have to ask, but I will anyways. What's got you all messed up?"

She closed her eyes, not sure if she could handle the pain of opening those emotional scars.

Her dad must have sensed it, and he placed a calming hand on her shoulder, forcing her to choke back tears.

Painfully, she tried a reply, "I … I just—" She slammed a fist against her knee, sudden anger coursing through her. "I-I don't know dad!" A sob escaped and she had to grit her teeth to choke it down.

He didn't reply, letting her grind out some of the anger—some of the emotion at the memory of her recent trauma. Finally, she fought back the tears and Skorin tried once more, "I, or anyone for that matter, can't help you unless we know what's got you in its grips."

It was *too* much, the dam broke, and she fell into his arms—awash in sorrow.

He shushed her, rubbing her shoulder in empathy, and for a time he just let her cry it out.

Slowly, she regained enough sense to try and speak—to explain, "It-it's just—" another sob. "It's just the things I have seen …" Her eyes closed as all the horrors of the last three years raced in front of her mind's eye. "The things I have seen *haunt* me. I just wanted to come back home. To be back home with you all once more, but even now I can't! I just can't—" She let herself drop into his embrace once more as visceral sobs wracked her body.

Like before, he didn't reply. He knew she needed to let it out; to let it *all* out.

She swallowed hard and pressed on, "I've tried! I've tried *so* hard to keep it altogether, but maybe …" She sucked in a breath through clenched teeth. Finally, she voiced a nagging thought, an undesirable emotion that she just couldn't let go. "Maybe I'm just a coward!"

"You are *not* a coward," her dad responded immediately, having to nearly yell over her violent sob. "Listen to me! You are not a coward and never have been. Not a one of us lives without fear, and you, more than most, have seen your share. I have read the letters—the reports. I can't say I know what you've been through. Emotionally, that is, but I at least know what you've been through physically. None of us! And I mean *none of us* would come through that unscarred."

She nodded at him, but she had to ask; she had to know, because it gnawed at her. *How had so many others seen war and death and were able to just … carry on?* "Grandpa … he-he, uh, fought in the Five Points. Why wasn't he all messed up?"

Her dad grabbed her by the shoulders and held her upright so he could stare into her eyes. When she had focused on him, he spoke as seriously as she had ever heard. "He *was* messed up. I know because I saw it. He just never, and I mean *never,* let the outside world see it. I think … I think that's what killed him in the end. He died young, his heart gave out and …" She saw her dad's eyes grow distant in memory. He broke eye contact, looking out toward the chicken pen. "I always wonder if he would've made it further, if he would be here even now if he had just addressed the scars he carried."

Her face was covered in drying tears and she felt her cheeks crackle slightly with the salty crust. No new sobs escaped, and she was able to speak more clearly, though her voice was becoming hoarse, "He always seemed *so* happy though."

Her dad laughed wryly, "Yeah, that was yer grandpa. He would've never wanted you girls to see his pain. He was a stubborn bastard. A good man—" he shook his head before he continued with some aggression in his voice, "but Magdris's Teeth was he a stubborn one!"

Bella laughed at her dad's sudden admonishment of her grandfather. It wasn't something she had ever heard him describe, and in that revelation, she felt a bit better.

The old man laughed, and as they dealt with emotion of the highest caliber, he squeezed her shoulder. The force of which was enough to make her scoot towards him. A dog barked from somewhere close by and the sound of a man shouting for it to be quiet echoed through the streets. Together the two sighed; the pain of freshly opened scars working its magic.

Neither spoke right away, instead opting to sit there in silence, basking in the rarity of compassionate company. The warmth of the summer sun radiated into her bones, and her heart slowed for the first time in months. A tension she had not known was there, released. Although she knew it would come back, that she would have to face it again and *again*, here in this moment, she felt a reprieve.

Finally, her dad broke that silence, "So, ya see Bell Bells. No one comes out of such a thing without scars. Just promise me something."

She looked at him, and his own face had the telltale rivulets of tears that had woven their way towards Telaea. She nodded solemnly.

"Promise me that you *will* talk about this. That you won't let it fester."

She had to tighten her jaw to not burst into tears again. "I promise …"

He pursed his lips in a forced smile. "Good … good. Also, you need to look after that boy. Sidon was his name, right?"

She nodded.

"Yeah, that boy has some scars himself, and it might do the two of you some good to go through your recent traumas together."

She blinked in surprise at the request. Not only because of its simplicity, but also since she could see the truth of it. People always worked better through trauma when they could commiserate together. Frankly, she was lucky she had someone to relate to. Someone to confide in within the very group she travelled with. Stern or no, the old man knew a thing or two. She smiled at him for the advice—for all he had done.

"What?" he asked with a smile of his own starting to form.

"Nothing, jus-just thank you dad. I-I love you."

"I love you too, and … I will *always* be here for you. You can bet on that."

*

"So, you are telling me that not only is Magdris involved in our lives once more but also this boy—this Sidon—is the only survivor of a mercenary attack on a mining camp?" Sophia asked, incredulity souring her voice.

Alexa shrugged her shoulders and tried to gesture with her hands held outwards, but her right hand slammed into one of her dad's bookcases. Her older sister was not used to being crammed into such a small room with so many people, and frankly neither was Bella.

"Well, do we have any information about these mercenaries? Where they're from? Who they work for?" Sophia pressed.

"They might be Argolonians. Bastards are always itching for a fight," Godfrey added sourly.

"Hmmmm, I don't think that is the case. The Argolonians have been the very people trying to stop this nonsense," Sophia replied.

"You sure of that? How you know they ain't jus' using you—us for their own gain?" Godfrey asked with a logic Bella couldn't fault.

"You make a good point, sir, *but* I can't just run off hunches. No matter how aggressive Argolon has been in the past, as far as I can tell, they are acting in interests that align with our own. So, do we have any other details about this … group of cutthroats?"

"No," Alexa replied, shaking out her hand and scooting away from the bookcase. "Well, save from the fact that they had a couple of Caprix with them, and that they were willing to sacrifice some to save the many. Rather cosmopolitan group fighting for ideology I reckon."

Sophia sighed, ruffling the ledgers and accounts stolen away from Sidon's ravaged expeditionary camp. A leather satchel, full of valuable information, had been spirited away by a frightened young man from what could only be described as the most horrific event of his life.

The boy was courageous at the very least, Bella thought.

"Well, these documents you brought—thank you by the way—do reveal *some* truths. Whoever it is—probably an Augustian—gave these poor folks valuable reconnaissance to where the most likely godstone seams lie. Now, and it seems ludicrous, but as far as I can tell, this same individual employed the mercenaries to slaughter the very people they gave confidential information to!" Sophia huffed, looking exasperated by the explanation she gave.

It did seem insane, but Bella found when dealing with Keeper nonsense, insanity was a common factor. She just wondered when Sophia would recognize that.

"I will have to try and find how it is linked, but for now we must discuss these *bloodstone berserkers*." Sophia finished.

Three figures stood behind her Keeper sister, crammed against the back wall of the study, looking like they were the henchman of some gang leader. Dunkeath and Olivia Bella knew well, but the third figure, a Keeper whose name was Gilbert, was a first-time introduction. The man apparently was Sophia's *friend,* and Bella had audibly scoffed when she had introduced him, earning a look of malice from Sophia and some sort of puppy-dog-in-pain look from the brown-eyed *boy.* The unbidden—and very recent—memory made her wince, and she couldn't help but glance over at the meek looking figure.

From beneath his short crop of black hair, he did not return her gaze; instead, he looked as if he were contemplating the secrets of life. His hand, which was holding his chin in a sort of philosopher's pose, shot away from his face and he spoke in time with the gesture, "They must be working for this *traitor* inside of Augustia." Gilbert bit his lip and looked towards Sophia, eager for her thoughts.

Sophia indulged him, "Hmmm, that is the most likely case, but we can't *assume* that to be true. Whatever is happening I am glad that you two are back. I think it was wise for Governor Luna to send you back here. Though I don't have any answers for you, how about I tell you what *I* know? That might help us get to the bottom of our ... potentially combined mystery."

Bella, who had managed to snag a chair that was pushed against the front left wall of the room, nodded, and Alexa gestured with her left hand as if the floor was all Sophia's.

"Very well, so—as you already know—I have been a part of some rather *disturbing* murder cases. Well, these cases are undoubtedly linked, and—" Sophia stopped mid-sentence as if a new thought struck her. "Gilbert, can you um ... shield us?"

"Certainly," Gilbert replied as he fished out a bundle of rose gold rods from his robes. Bella recognized it as Artstone and the irony of using the very stone that seemed to be at the heart of this mess was not lost on her. Especially since Sidon had been a member of an Artstone mining expedition. Gilbert raised the rods in front of him, and he muttered a phrase, "Minollo, I ask that you shield us from unwanted eyes."

Golden sparks fizzled and popped from atop the rods, and Bella felt that all-too-familiar- feeling of a god's presence, an omnipotent shadow that soaked the air she breathed. The hairs on her arms raised, and, much like she had felt in the forests of Mossgrave when some predator lurked, she had the distinct sensation she was being watched.

"Minollo, I thank thee for the protection. We will use this reprieve to better ourselves in the pursuit of perfection," Gilbert finished and rapidly the bundle of rods became inert once more; Bella swore they were fractionally smaller than before.

She wondered how the god of art had anything to do with truth and shielding from spies, and evidently her puzzlement drew Sophia's eye.

Her sister—always one to offer an explanation—allowed a faint smile to crease her left cheek, and the academic in her launched into an unsolicited description. "Minollo seeks truth in all things. Most of us associate that concept with art, which is this gods predominant field, but Gilbert here knows better. Minollo deals in *all* truths in *all* things. Though we are essentially asking them to hide our own truth, some very smart Keepers learned that Minollo is quite accepting of … dramatic reveals. Giving the artist time to create in peace before they have to show the world. *And* when you involve Minollo, they *will* force you to show the world what you have asked to hide. Fortunately, if we succeed, that won't be a problem."

Bella spoke, the words coming out before she had time to think on them, "I prefer when *you* talk to the gods."

Sophia chuckled, "Sister, Gilbert is quite capable, and frankly he is more attuned with Minollo than I. My godstone seems to be Embershard, and that is no small thing. Trust me, I *am* involved whenever the gods are."

Bella nodded, though she felt uneasy. The pervasive feeling of Minollo's 'shield' put her on edge, and she was none too happy. After all, a relative stranger had placed that shadow over her. Still, if Sophia trusted him, then so would she.

Sophia looked around at the scattered papers, searching for some hint to remind her where she had left off. Abruptly, she snapped her fingers. "Right! So, the two murders are undoubtedly linked. A poor lad from the docks had been hired by Lady Aliana to deliver *something*. I, and some others who are still quite sore about a certain lack of trust, imagine that whatever was in that *something* held a damnable secret that would have solved this case long ago. Of course, our quarry did not let that happen and they killed two poor souls, gouged out their eyes, and deeply slit their throats all to prevent us pesky Keepers from digging for the truth."

"Ember's Breath," Godfrey, who stood to the side of Bella's chair, muttered to himself.

Sophia continued with a conciliatory glance at Godfrey, "Don't fret, good sir. When we investigated the lady's home, we found a missive!" A yellowing piece of parchment that looked rather worn crackled as it was held upright. "Dunkeath, Olivia, and Gilbert here pursued this clue. *I* was not allowed to attend thanks to my *warden*." Sophia stopped for a second, clinching her fist in obvious anger.

Bella still couldn't wrap her head around the fact that Sophia was demoted to a more junior rank. She had always been such a strong presence—such a knowledgeable figure—that it was difficult to imagine her being thrown back in with the novices. Bella reckoned that that was how her and Gilbert had met, and she thought—quite maliciously—that she had found solace in a less than suitable man. A thought that turned rapidly into guilt, he *had* been there, and she couldn't fault him for that.

Sophia continued, "Regardless, these three uncovered more to the story. Finding a letter that had been given to the innkeeper for safekeeping. Within that ciphered missive we have learned that Argolon's agents are hot on the trail of a conspiracy. One that has its roots right here in Augustia!"

Alexa folded her arms, and Sophia must have noticed something akin to disbelief, holding up a hand towards the Rangemaster—almost in placation, "I assure you that we are not being led astray, and, if we are, I am taking … precautions."

"Ain't that the truth," Dunkeath piped up, and was rewarded with a smack from Olivia. "Ow, I was jus' saying!"

Bella had to hold back a chuckle from the scene. She liked the former laundress and the rascally Dunkeath. Even in light of Dunkeath's rather *crispy* shoulder. Bella felt somehow comfortable with the two *cronies*, like they were almost … family. It was easy to see why Sophia had brought them into her employ.

Sophia sighed, but, being satisfied with Olivia's secondhand rebuke of Dunkeath, pressed on, "Regardless, I have been in contact with these *agents*. And we have narrowed down a few choices of who could be involved in this plot. Some good news though! Me and a Master Eamon Salferesis were able to push through a piece of legislation that should slow down their plans, *The Godstone Decree*." Sophia leaned back and puffed out her chest.

Bella snorted as she thought, *Ah Sophia, always a little boastful.*

Sophia did *not* appreciate the gesture and shot her a menacing glance. "As I was saying, these individuals are most likely involved, and evidently they have a reach across the sea; what with the news you brought me of mercenary raids." Sophia seemed distracted for a second, before a new thought hit her. "That definitely fits with what the Argolonians have told us. Strategos Bloodeye said 'they are able to strike with blades and words…'"

Gilbert nudged Sophia gently and she shook her head bringing herself back to the present, "Right! Fortunately, we have narrowed it down to a few suspects. Master Falris Lupern, the husband of Lady Aliana, and a prolific—albeit rather stupid—tradesman. Master Aranos Ferillo a former commander that served alongside Master Falris and a discrete individual who has been rather … difficult to learn anything about—save her nickname, The Iron Hand." Sophia sneered as she spoke of the former commander.

Even Bella had heard that title, a legend amongst the Warriors of August, and more than a few drunken soldiers had invoked her name for luck in their dice rolls.

Sophia pressed on, "Though I am loathe to admit to a Keeper being corrupt, I have been party to too many clues indicating my very own warden, Grand Keeper Chalepos, to be able to deny him as suspect as well. There is also Master Eamon himself, though he holds a fairly strong alibi, seeing as how he championed *The Godstone Decree* and all. Still, Gilbert has assured me that the man is not beyond suspicion, and frankly I am inclined—or maybe forced—to agree." Sophia smiled at a rather reproving Gilbert.

Bella could see some form of inside joke there.

Sophia continued, "Still, the man has a way about him that could lend itself to being rather … deceptive. Best keep an eye on him."

Bella couldn't help but notice the slight flush that blossomed on Sophia's cheek, and, to her amusement, she also couldn't help but notice Gilbert's jaw tense in anger. *I am going to have to meet this … Master Eamon,* she thought with bemusement.

Sophia droned on about the potential for other suspects, ones hidden in plain sight, but Bella did not hear the words. Instead, an intrusive memory consumed her focus, a game of Trelido in the holds of the oke-navis they had travelled in. Well, it was more like many games in which she had lost twelve whole silvers to those greedy sailors. Still, there it was in her mind's eye, the croaking voice of that old crusty sailor amidst the toss of the dice, "I wonder who ol' Master Eamon will be swiving next, seeing as how his ol' mistress bit the dust. Ah … Lady Aliana, she was a right beaut' that."

"It has to be Master Eamon!" Bella exclaimed suddenly, interrupting a now rather perturbed looking Sophia.

Her sister fixed her with a look of irritation, "And what makes you think that?"

"Because he was having an affair with Lady Aliana. Somehow during their lover's rendezvous, the Lady must have found out about his secret, grew a conscience, and tried to make it right. Well, that got her in a right mess and now she's dead and buried. Well, most of her is buried anyways," Bella explained.

With raised eyebrows that bordered on amusement, Alexa asked, "And how do you know all that?"

"Easy, I just listened. Sailors, soldiers, and just about everyone for that matter does an awful lot of talking when yer playing dice. Specifically, when yer about to lose to a gods awful forest play in Trelido."

Even Sophia couldn't help but smile at this revelation. She leaned back and crossed her hands in thought, obviously mulling over what Bella had just told her. "How have we not heard of this?" Dunkeath and Olivia both just shrugged their shoulders in response, and Sophia shook her head. "This could very well just be sailor's gossip but it's too risky to just ignore. I will have to follow up on this … maybe do a little prodding on our sup-posed ally. Good work, Bella, and … thank you."

Bella wanted to scoff at the platitude, feeling like it was too much of a superior complimenting their subordinate, but she shrugged it off. This was Sophia's case and frankly it was Sophia's demeanor. "Not a problem, boss. Question I have is, what does he stand to gain from passing this ... what you call it? *Godstone Decree?*"

Chapter Ten
Rollo

"Owen! Come on in now lad, time for some supper!" Rollo called his son, wiping the dirty sweat that had accumulated on his brow. Their crop of winter wheat had come in full, and his small family had been hard at work for the last week, hacking away at the hearty stalks. His wife, Matildy, was already at home and would have laid out a nice summertime meal. He could picture the sliced goat cheese and day-old bread alongside a hearty helping of blackberries. If they were lucky, she might even pull out some of those grapes she had gotten from the Farmer's Market in Tritimon.

"Alright son, that's good enough!" He tried again, feeling his stomach suddenly tense with hunger. He cursed silently to himself as he recognized the hard work ethic of his first and only child. It was possible the boy would work until the sun dropped if left to his own devices. Finally, and much to his relief, Owen stopped his hacking and turned to look at his father. Before he lost the opportunity, Rollo beckoned emphatically and let what white still remained on his teeth flash in the setting summer sun. "Good lad! That's a good lad!"

Owen looked like the epitome of a farmer, and his dirt-covered face made Rollo swell with pride. Him and Matildy had done a good job with the boy, and a familiar longing gripped him; *what if they had one more child?* How much more pride and joy he would experience, getting to taste little moments like this with twice the frequency. Raw joy—purest in its forms—doubled, as he would get to watch not one, but two children witness life anew like he had done so many years ago. Unfortunately, Matildy had nearly died from the first baby, and he loved her too much to even broach the subject with her. "I bet you're starvin'! Come on, yer mother might pull out the grapes. If'n we're lucky."

Owen grinned, and Rollo smiled back. He thought he might strain the muscles in his cheek with the intensity of it. *Ember's breath, life was good.* He placed a calloused hand on his son's shoulder and steered him down the hill towards their homestead.

That was when he saw it, a small cloud in the sky above Tritimon. But it wasn't right. The grey, billowing formation looked like it touched the ground. Besides, there wasn't a single other cloud across the whole horizon. He would know; he had been sweating in it all day.

"Is that … is that smoke?" Owen asked with slowly widening eyes.

The words spoken aloud, and Rollo's mind made sense of the display before him. *Tritimon was on fire!* "Come on lad, let's get back to yer mother!"

The two raced down the slope, trying not to trip over the stubble of their harvest. Rollo could see it was coming from multiple sources and knew this wasn't a simple house caught fire. His heart sank, figuring the most likely scenario was an attack, possibly trolls or even worse *raiders*, a re-sparking of the old rivalries between the city-states.

He looked at his own home—no sign of smoke or fire, and he felt a small glimmer of hope. They were a few kilometers out of town and anybody wanting to take a piece of theirs would need to mount some fairly hefty hillside. If they could get Matildy and load up the pack horse, maybe they could make it into the mountains before anyone came calling. Still, it was far too close for comfort and Rollo had barely held his weapon over the years. Even then he had only ever practiced with it, a simple spear he had been given for being in the August Highway Road Guard as a youth.

Owen was at least fifty meters ahead of him now, his young legs powering down the hill and over the obstacles that lay before them. Rollo heard a scream; a lump dropped into his stomach. *That was Matildy's voice.* He watched in horror as she burst out the back door of the homestead. He could hear his dog, Melkor, barking and knew whatever made his wife scream was *not* friendly. Something, or someone, was already on their way to raid them. *Why?* Tritimon was an Augustian backwater with little more than some grain and a few garnets. It didn't make any sense; they had been at peace for years.

"Mom!" Owen yelled, prompted by a woman on horseback—her face covered by a skull mask—who rounded the side of the house. His son was still three hundred meters away, and Rollo could see the writing on the wall. Matildy would be cut down in front of her son, and they could do nothing to stop it. Then he felt a spark of hope as Melkor burst out the back door, bounding after the stranger. Surely, his loyal hound would die, but maybe it would be enough to let them get away? Maybe it would be enough time to get his spear?

"Owen, ge-get my spear," Rollo called over his faltering breath. They were so close, but he was getting old, and his stamina was very nearly gone, especially after working under the hot sun all day. Rollo heard a pained yelp and glanced at the rider just in time to see her double back, trotting over the corpse of his hound. *Melkor ...*

The shock was raw, but he could not stop. Not with this bloodthirsty fiend galloping after his wife, his son.

"Mom!" Owen cried out as he reached his mother. They slammed into one another, embracing for what might be the last time. Matildy was frantic and Rollo could hear incoherent sobs breaking free from her lips. He hadn't the time to console her; besides, Owen was with her. His only focus was getting his spear; its metal tip gleamed in the sun as it leaned against the back of his house.

"Get up the hill!" He yelled at them as he ran past.

"Ro-Rollo!" Matildy cried after him, but it was too late; he was committed. He glanced to his right and saw the rider in all her bloody glory. He didn't know much about the history of the city-states, but the outfit of an Argolonian was easily recognizable, even for him. The gleaming bronze shone brightly as the warrior—apparently finished with the slaughter of

Melkor—kicked her mount to a gallop and towards him. Fear gripped him, knowing this killer was coming, but he stayed true to his course. He could make it to his spear—*just a few more meters*. His heart pounded and his knee felt like it was going to give way any moment, but he pushed on.

He pushed on until he slammed into the mud siding of his home, leaving an imprint in the outer wall. He couldn't help but curse at himself, *it'll be a pain to fix that*. The sound of rapidly approaching hoofbeats interrupted his worries. He ripped the spear away from the wall and swung it around, taking up the only stance he knew; spear held straight in a two-handed grip.

He had made it just in time. The rider's mount reared at the sudden blade that challenged it. Rollo felt a sudden surge of anger course through him; he felt elation; he felt eager. *Was this-was this the battle joy he had heard of?* The warrior's courage that came to those in the middle of a fight. If so, it sure did taste a lot like blood.

Then the warhorse plunged back to Telaea and the rider urged her mount into a side canter. Rollo jabbed his spear forward once more, trying to ward them off. A sudden impact reverberated up the shaft and he brought the weapon back to a guard position. To his horror, the blow had shattered it, and the spearpoint dangled limply; held together by what few fibers of wood remained.

The sudden onrush of sound made him snap his eyes up. The raider—hidden behind the skull of another—was bearing down on him again and he jabbed his blade forward in a desperate attempt. The impotent weapon crashed harmlessly on her armor, and he felt a rending agony gouge into his neck. A heavy iron blade buried itself into his throat. He felt a heat course down his chest. He shuddered, and with a gasp fell to his knees.

Sound eked through to him, drowned against the backdrop of what sounded like rushing water, he could make out the heavy trod of a warrior's boot. He almost smiled, knowing the delay might give his wife and son the time they needed.

Everything felt weak—like it was draining away. Just minutes ago, he had felt such joy, and now it had all been ripped away. His eyes drooped but he *had* to see; he *had* to know if his family would make it. He hoped against all hope that they would. The raider's shadow loomed over him. With what little energy he had left, he forced his eyes open for one last look. Behind the deadly menace, he saw the white of Matildy's bonnet flash briefly as it faded from view.

"Brave lad, Magdris is gonna *love* you," the raider murmured from beneath her skull mask.

Rollo shuddered once more and fell forward, allowing death to take him. His last thoughts were of his dinner table; the laughter of his son and wife; the taste of grapes fresh from the market.

Chapter Eleven

Alexa

Alexa breathed in deeply as the rich, log-cabin smell of Augustia's Rangers Hall pervaded her senses. It was a smell that lingered in her memory, a piece of her core self, made so by the frequency with which she indulged in it. Pine and oak, heated in the summer sun, alongside the rangers' efforts to dry game and livestock swirled into a mixture rich with the sensibilities of the forest. The bittersweet memories of her youth and a sort of gnawing sensation had made her dread this necessary visit. However, four days after arriving in the city, she found herself within its confines, regardless of her apprehension.

She had delayed as long as she could, taking a few days to recuperate alongside the others, a necessity after their long sea voyage. A requirement to rekindle old bonds and remember others lost across the sea. Yet, she had grown restless in that three-day hiatus. Thoughts of Amilicus would flash in the quiet hours of the dark, ravaging her sleep with fever dreams. Her only solace was a small wooden figurine—a ranger he had carved for her. She clutched it now, sending a small prayer to the Maiden. At least her dreams had been of him, and not Elira or Matthias.

The last few days had been an emotional time, starting with Bella divulging her trauma to their dad on the first night. Alexa still remembered the look of raw relief on Bella's face, a raw tension gone after her and their dad had talked. It was like Bella had been holding onto some insurmountable pain, only to be granted a reprieve by the bonds of family, and—for a moment—a taste of her old happiness.

They were still the strong wholesome parents she remembered after all, even with their faults. *Man, it's good to be back with family,* Alexa thought with a smirk, especially after how Bella, Sophia, and herself had ended their second night back. Strong drink with copious talk, the three of them crying together into the wee hours of the morning. It had been a necessity—one that allowed Alexa and Bella broach the subject of the horror on the beach. Though Sophia had not been a part of that horrific day, like any good sibling, she listened to their stories. Perhaps in the guise of that truth, each sister was finally able to approach the terror of that day, and Alexa—although still raw from that emotional turmoil—felt better than she had in weeks.

That swell of emotion had given her the courage to speak more with her mother and father, and she had told them how she felt adrift amidst the sea of responsibilities laid before her. Together they had offered advice and comfort, telling her the platitudes one would expect from loved ones. That too was needed—necessary. Yet, in the end, she knew she would have to find her validation in the cold and unforgiving realities of the harsh world outside. She would have to prove herself to those unrelated to her and to the hardest critic of all … herself.

Those thoughts had led her here, ready to start that terrifying journey of purpose once more. Led her to a pale spot of light brown pine that reminded her of the wilderness demonstrations she had seen as a youth. There Alexa had encountered her first moment of awe. A demonstration of the tameability of a hawk as well as the rending potential of its claws. It was there she had heard firsthand accounts of ogres and trolls, orcs and goblins, bandits and rogues, and she figured those stories were a bit less fabricated than the stories her dad had told her. It was there she fell in love with the outdoors, or at least the idea they sold. Now, many years later, she walked in nostalgic memory of those early years fully fitted as the ranger she had always wanted to be. Yet, she did not feel the happiness she had always dreamt of.

Instead, a hollow void—outlined in suffering—inundated her, drowning her in a despondency she could not overcome. Elira was dead, Matthias was dead, and she had been responsible. She had been the Rangemaster that had delivered them unto their deaths, and now, right where she had started her journey, she felt as unworthy of the title as she had ever been. Questions of validity plagued her mind. *How can I even call myself a ranger—let alone a Rangemaster? How can I carry on with such tremendous failure on my soul? Am I really cut out for this?*

"Ranger," a neutral but weighty voice interrupted her thoughts. She had been staring at the pale patch on the floor, and, at first, she wondered if it was the ranger pair that had let her in.

No, this cadence is different. She turned abruptly to see the source of the voice.

A short, bald man wearing the forest green of the ranger's cloak approached, his face unreadable. The man had no hair whatsoever on his face and the skin glistened—not with sweat, but with a healthy sheen. His brown leather boots padded softly on the wood, and she realized if he had not called out to her, she would have never known of his approach.

The man stopped a respectful distance away and studied her. She went to open her mouth in greeting, but he shot up a hand for silence. The gesture was lighting fast, and Alexa was stunned into silence from the sheer force behind the move. With her mouth slightly ajar, she stood—unmoving. She allowed the neutral features of this seemingly unimpressive man look her over. It felt like a deception; the outward display hiding a force, a power. "You must be Rangemaster Alexa Vollimosa, recent leader of Elgion's Hall."

Alexa nodded, and the man swept towards her. He stopped centimeters away, and intense blue eyes bore into her. She felt so small even though he was at least thirty centimeters shorter than her. The man had an intensity about him.

"I am Prime Master Epiklos, and the Orator Malfias told me of your pending arrival. It was good that you brought the Xeelander back here.

The Mandated, including the High Magistrate, were pleased that you took the situation seriously. Elgion, I am certain, was left in good hands?"

Alexa was taken aback, she had expected to have to explain her presence. "I-I, uh, yes I left martial affairs in the hands of the Guard-Captain, a very capable man."

"Good, walk with me, Rangemaster," the Prime Master said, and moved towards a set of double doors before she had time to respond, forcing her to catch up. "Tell me, how does it feel to lead?"

Alexa was once again taken aback; the man's question was abrupt, especially since it dealt with such serious premises. "Well, I, uh, I don't know—"

Outside of the double doors, Prime Master Epiklos stopped abruptly. He turned to her and fixed her with his intense blue eyes. "You do *know*, Rangemaster. Now, please stop with the bluster and enlighten me."

She swallowed hard, made nervous by this man—the leader of all of Augustia's rangers. "I am sorry, Prime Master. Frankly, it does not always feel good, sir."

His eyes softened slightly, and he nodded before stepping onwards. The rear of the Ranger's Hall was much like Elgion's: training grounds, a courtyard surrounded by rest benches, and walls that gave privacy from outside eyes. To the north, the stone wall that ringed the city blocked their view. If they were to gaze over that rampart, they would see vast rolling farmlands that stretched away into the horizon; instead, they saw naught but the grey of shaped rock.

Prime Master Epiklos weaved his way along a path made of large flat stones, breathing in the scent of a peony that grew within one of the many flowerbeds. "I have heard of your *endeavors*. The Orator Malfias was quite thorough. I do hope you are not offended by my prying, but you are one of my charges. One that was promoted rather quickly."

He glanced at her, wanting a response. She tried her best not to stutter. "No, no, sir I am not offended."

He smiled at this, and for the first time she felt a little more at ease. His teeth were stark white, and she could see he was not unused to happiness.

Maybe the man was just intense because he had to be, Alexa surmised

"Good, it is unfortunate that we are deprived of Rangemaster Erin Apararius, but I have been told that you are a suitable replacement. So, with that in mind, back to the answer you gave me, 'that it does not always feel good.'" He stopped and ran his fingers along the leaves of a fern that dangled over a hanging clay pot. "I am inclined to agree."

She had to hold back a laugh as he turned and smiled at her, a knowing smile that spoke of shared pains.

Epiklos moved on, rounding a path that wove behind the straw training dummies—fortunately, not under use. "I have another question for you, do you *wish* to lead?"

Alexa responded almost immediately, her penchant for authority forcing her to give the answer she thought he wanted, "Yes, of cou—"

Once more the Prime Master surprised Alexa with his hand shooting up for silence. "Answer truthfully. It has been ingrained in us to believe leaders are the best amongst us, but that is simply not true. Plenty of folks are capable of great things and *not* capable of great leadership. Not all of us are meant to lead, and that is not a shameful thing. Look amongst the very gods themselves. Only Ember is lord above them and even then, we believe he struggled with the task. So, once again, do you wish to lead?"

She bit her lip, and looked inside, searching for the truth he sought. "I—" she started to speak but the words did not come.

The Prime Master waited patiently for her response.

Truth be told, she was uncertain if she did want to lead. She felt like a failure in that regard, and she had not necessarily enjoyed the job, stressing over the smallest of details. Of course, she had thrived as a Rangemaster, but she had never truly asked herself if she *wanted* to be a leader. "I … I honestly don't know, Prime Master."

He nodded and gestured for them to walk on. They dove into a series of arches covered in vera arcus, a vine that bloomed in brilliant pinks and reds in spring. *Elgion would definitely need to add some homely touches to their own hall,* she thought as she imagined the vines in full bloom.

Epiklos spoke once more, "I remember when I first led. I thought I was the *absolute* worst. Supplies went unaccounted for, reports went unfiled, and rangers … rangers died under my command. I blamed myself for each and every one of those failures."

The Prime Master was silent for a time, his hands held clasped behind his back. Their unnerving steadiness hidden under a cloak that billowed in the light summer breeze. "It took many years to ask myself the same question I am asking you now. Of course, my answer was yes but I realized then that no one had ever bothered to ask me—not even myself. So, I have a solution for us both."

He glanced at her as they finished their circuit of the courtyard and started on another. "I am sending you as escort for the boy back to Xeeland. You will take two rangers, Mikael and Mishanda, they are currently getting supplies from the markets. This next part I would make an order, but I can't force it; they are not my charges. Still, I would highly recommend that you take those who came with you. More often than not we travel with those we trust the most, yes? You understand my orders?"

"I do, Prime Master. We can leave right away," Alexa responded.

He smiled wryly, "Well, take your time with this one. With a nominal command you should have plenty of time to *think* while still remembering how it feels to lead. Do you understand?"

She did, he was asking her to explore herself. To truly come to grips with the question of her future. It was a smart play. "I do, Prime Master."

"Good," he said pleasantly, and they walked on, rounding a corner of the path. She was unsure if she had been dismissed, so, she continued to walk alongside the modest man. He took his time with things, stopping to observe a fluttering butterfly. The pause in the action gave her the courage to speak once more but as she opened her mouth he started again, "I have heard of your most recent losses Rangemaster. Ones that trouble even me."

She swallowed hard, the memory of Elira and Matthias coursing through her mind. She worried he was going to chastise her; punish her for such a reckless loss. With gravel in her voice, she grumbled, "Yes, it was … troubling."

His face twitched slightly, and he furrowed his brows, "Yesterday, and today, were filled with talks of what to do about these *developments*. The Mandated, the Chosen, the very leadership of Augustia has taken this matter at its most serious and trust me, Rangemaster, we *will* get to the bottom of this. Some even say that your sister, Sophia, will get there before us."

Alexa was stunned. Not only was the man not blaming the deaths of Elira and Matthias on her, but also he knew far more than she had been led to believe. Sophia had explicitly told them her investigation was no longer ordained, but if the Prime Master knew … *Ember's breath*, the odds were good that many others knew. She felt a knot in her stomach, and the play of worry on her face made the Prime Master laugh.

"Don't fret, Rangemaster, I have seen your sister. We all have. Anyone that tangles with that Keeper is a fool, but it is hard to keep something like an unsanctioned investigation a secret." He stopped as they ended their second circuit, and he looked up at her. His eyes unblinking. "Trust me, there are those who wish to see her succeed. Just … right now, it is a rather *delicate* game. But that is beside the point. I must talk about you once more, before you can go."

It was Alexa's turn to furrow her brows. *What else could the man have to say?*

"The death of those in our command … it's always painful." For the first time, it was the Prime Master who looked away, his head bowed in some painful memory. "And from what I have heard, your most recent loss was quite *tragic*. With that in mind, I *need* you to hear this." He looked back up at her, his gaze once more unflinching. "Mistakes are not what define us. You made a call, and though it was the wrong one, those that follow you obeyed your commands because they trusted you—they believed in you. Their deaths may be from your orders, but their deaths are not ones to regret. They knew that you would not throw their lives away, and if they didn't, they would not have followed you. *This* is what I have learned of leadership in my time, and this is what I am passing onto you."

The look in his eyes told her he was about to say something meant for only a select few, "We are given a *terrible* burden: those who follow us … trust us, even though they know they might die due to our decisions. But just like ourselves, they know that sometimes these decisions must be made if we are to achieve our goals. Have you not given an order that could have led to death, but instead gave you victory over some evil? Have you not sent off those under you to some near certain doom only for them to triumph? I have, but of course, we always remember the failures the most. That is just human nature; that is just how the gods decided we should learn to grow. So, if you choose to remain a Rangemaster, keep this lesson close to your chest. For it will see you through the worst of it. Do you understand?"

Alexa opened her mouth and closed it. Once again, she was at a loss for words. The man was a force, and she felt nigh exhausted delving into his mind. He had pinned her to a board and carved out every vulnerability as if they were butcher's cuts marked in ink. Slowly, and under the intensity of his blue-eyed stare she responded, "Yes, Prime Master."

Epiklos nodded and beckoned towards the double doors that led into the hall. "Good. Well, you best get a move on, Rangemaster, Mikael and Mishanda will be returning soon. Also, I am quite certain that the fidgety saurian that you have waiting outside is ready to move as well."

Alexa couldn't help but chuckle at this. The Prime Master knew everything, even those who had come with her. She smiled at him and dipped her head in recognition of his efforts and respect for his leadership. She strode towards the doors and on to her newest mission, feeling better than she had in a while. It wasn't perfect, but it was a start.

Chapter Twelve

Alexa

Alexa started at the sudden sound of racing hoofbeats on cobblestone. A lone rider galloped by, yelling, "Augustia has been attacked! Augustia has been attacked!"

A fearful glance shared with Bella—the words full of terrifying implications. *Attacked by who—where?* Questions that would change the very fate of their existence. Mikael and Mishanda shuffled nervously. Unsure how to respond under the authority of their new, temporary leader, who was rather uncertain herself. Echoing her turbulent emotions, Godfrey let loose a heavy sigh, and Hislock snarled.

"What is matter? What is *attacked?*" Sidon glanced around at his companions, all of whom looked a tad bit more frightened than he was accustomed to.

"Attacked means someone fought us. Means war," Godfrey replied with the distant tone of a veteran remembering old wounds.

Sidon's eyes widened until his sclera dominated his face. Fortunately, Bella took pity on him and offered words of reassurance, "It's alright, lad. That's not happenin' here, and no, I doubt there is any *war.*" With the final word, she shot Godfrey a glare.

He only shrugged in response, and—to tell the truth—Alexa was inclined to agree with his assertion. Augustia and all of the Holliserian city-states had been at peace for many years, but a sudden attack like this? One that warranted a frantic horseman dashing through the streets to yell out a warning. Now that—that was probably the prelude to war, she sighed as she hefted her pack onto her back. Fortunately, they had all been outfitted for a journey, not knowing what the visit to the Ranger's Hall would entail.

"Let's head to the forum, and see what's what," she said with as much calm as she could muster. Godfrey and Bella nodded in silent agreement and her newest charges, a pair of green rangers that looked almost like twins, fell into a loose formation behind her. Their packs rustled with the movement.

She shot a glance over her shoulder, and they stiffened at their commander's sudden attention. They were both short relative to her one-hundred-dred-and-eighty-centimeter frame and had a crop of brown hair shaven on the sides. Mishanda's was slightly longer in the middle than Mikael's, but still—it looked like they had a finely trimmed hedge on the top of their heads. She had heard of this style, this 'faux hawk.' Seeing it in person made her realize she was no longer the youngest generation; she was drifting out of touch. Of course, it didn't help she had been overseas nigh on six years; regardless, it was still a shock.

She dipped her head imperceptibly, and the pair blinked brown eyes back at her. They seemed like siblings, save for the fact she saw them locked in a rather intimate embrace when she had found them in the larder. At least, she hoped they were not related—not after seeing that. The scarlet flush on Mishanda was just now starting to fade, and—by all the gods— Alexa hoped it was brought on by non-related relations.

She set off down the hill to the echoing cry of the lone horseman. The city steadily became a turbulent, chaotic mess around her. People had heard the errant call, and come out to investigate. Shop keepers abandoned their stores to stand on their stoops and small children raced underfoot. The poor and rich alike crammed into Grange Street, shoving their way towards the forum—towards the leaders of Augustia.

It stank. The smell of people, sewage, and filth, a smell she hadn't realized existed within the city when she was younger. Now—returned from her foray in the fresh air of Elgion—she couldn't help but notice.

Amidst that unpleasant aroma, it was easy to remember why she had wanted to leave in the first place.

Yeah, the marbled halls and shining cobbles delivered a sense of awe and prosperity that spoke to somewhere deep within her soul, but when you looked closer, you could see the cracks in the stonework. Trash and filth accumulated in dark corners of the streets, beggars and homeless pined for a pittance, and the stark contrast between the ragged poor and the opulent rich made her grit her teeth. Now, as the denizens of the city poured out into the street alongside her, those faults in the city's makeup were blatantly obvious.

They rounded the side of The Chosen's Hall, and a finely dressed fool aimed to push a messy-haired child. She was ready to curse at him—to bark obscenities at the ingrate, when she heard a voice. Even from here, over the din of people shouting and shoving, Alexa could hear it plainly. It was rich and authoritative, but not in a threatening way, more like a strong, guiding hand in a tempest.

"People of Augustia! I am sure you have heard, as I have, that our dear people have been attacked!"

She could see the source now, and there standing atop a smattering of crates was a tall muscularly built man with the chasuble of a Chosen hastily draped about his shoulders.

"But do not fear! I know; I know … that is a lot to ask, but when have the people of this fair city ever shirked from a hard task?" He was rewarded with scattered shouts and applause.

The crowd was still gathering, and some had not noticed his speech. Yet Alexa could see many, including her own group, had stopped to listen in.

"Never! From the days of Grand Keeper Erica, we have been strong! We have been mighty!" Even more shouts were heard this time, and she could see this fellow was well versed in the art of rousing a crowd. She wished Sophia was there with them. She would be able to tell her every-thing she needed to know about the leaders and politicians of Augustia … and who to trust. Alas, the duties of a Keeper were relentless, and she had to return each morning to the Bastion, duty bound to fulfill her obligations.

"What I tell you now is important," he paused, waiting for more of the crowd to be baited to his hook. "Augustia *has* been attacked, and it was by Argolon herself, though they tried to hide themselves behind cruel masks rent from the skulls of the dead!"

A murmur of dread rippled through the crowds. A lady near them cried out, "Maiden preserve us!" And Alexa had to plant her feet to not be jostled by the flurry of movement within the crowd.

This leader now held a good chunk of the city within his grasp. "I have confirmed this with Master Aranos, who, alongside the brave scouts of the Warriors of August, managed to sight the foe that dealt this terrible blow! Tritimon, a defenseless homestead of farmers and miners, has been ransacked—its people slain!"

The crowd jostled even more, and Alexa heard Hislock bark in his saurian tongue. The unmistakable grunting of a person being shoved. She turned to see Mishanda grimacing, a person reeling back with their nose in their hands from her upright elbow. Alexa narrowed her eyes at the ranger, wondering if she should chastise her, but the immediate downcast eyes and look of shame told Alexa the lesson was already grasped.

"Calm people! Calm!" The leader gestured for them to breathe in … and out. Alexa felt a tangible wave of tension flow away from the populace.

"We are not without tools to fight this threat. We are not helpless. Augustia is strong, and I, Master Eamon Salferesis, will ensure that you do not suffer the same fate as our brothers and sisters in Tritimon!"

The crowd roared at this, and Alexa struggled to keep sight of the focal point of their celebration. Another member of the Chosen, a woman with a curly bob of black hair, yelled at him, jabbing a finger in obvious indignation.

"Who does he think he is?" Bella echoed the woman's thoughts. Alexa had to agree; this Master Eamon was overreaching. Nonetheless, the crowd did not seem to think so. The jeers that pulsed from the center showed their disdain for the chastising woman.

"People! People! Master Kylos is only passionate about the city. Just as you and I are! She *is* an Augustian, and her counsel is wise. We must band together to survive the coming storm and that means we must be malleable, willing to listen to those who have our best interest at heart." This seemed to placate the female Chosen, who must have known she did not have the support of the people. *If anything,* Alexa thought, *this Master Eamon was throwing her a lifeline, keeping her from the angst of the mob.*

Eamon nodded curtly to the dissenting Chosen and swept his gaze back over the crowd. "To that end, I, alongside Master Aranos, who—although doesn't always agree with me—will stand with me to face this threat—" Master Eamon gestured to a rigid woman of military demeanor that stood behind him to his left.

The woman nodded once, her face stern and unreadable.

Eamon continued, "After all, a threat to Augustia is a threat to all of us, regardless of our politics. With that in mind, we have already sent messages to the Mandated to ask for emergency powers. We will use these powers to retaliate *and* to deliver those who harmed us to justice. The Argolonians, oh … the Argolonians will see that Augustia has teeth!" The man bared white enamel and clenched his fist, giving emphasis to his own call to action.

The crowd erupted into a cacophony of emotion. Raw, primal yells—swept up in the maelstrom of vengeful desire.

He waved to the crowd once more, asking for silence. They were enthralled by this man. And, as his face took on a graven expression, those around Alexa leaned forward subconsciously, hanging on every word. "People … *my* people! I have more news to share with you all." He paused and Alexa watched as a lady stumbled forward, seemingly so lost in the moment she had lost her balance.

He chewed his lip, letting his eyes grow distant. With a hollowness in his tone, he carried on, "My best people tell me that a mine near Tritimon had just uncovered a new seam. A cache of Minollo's stone, that blessed Artstone, unlike any we have ever seen. And that, to me, makes it quite clear why Argolon attacks …"

A pregnant pause settled over the waiting populace, and then—then his head snapped forward and he fixed the crowd with an intensity that forced some to recoil. "They want our godstone! They want to take what is ours, by right! Oh, but we will not have that, will we?!" The people grumbled angrily in agreement, echoing the very cadence of Eamon's voice. "They want to take our conduit to the gods for their own. And, I hate to tell you, 'I told you so.'" He paused, flashing a smile at them, his intensity gone in an instant, replaced by a look of good humor. The crowd laughed, prompted by Eamon's change in tone.

After the laughter died to a whisper, he continued, "I couldn't be happier about the work we have done with our latest bill, *The Godstone Decree*. Maybe they had heard of our latest policy, maybe they wished to weaken us before we could grow too strong. Who is to say?" He paused, allowing the crowd to hang in anticipation. "Regardless of their motivations, they have attacked, and we … we *will* respond!" He punched the air, and the crowd erupted.

Over the shouts of his audience he bellowed, his voice just audible over the roar. "Finally, I will say this! People! People!" The crowd was still ecstatic, but he managed to wrangle some control before he pressed on. "Master Falris and I can assure you that Augustia does not lack for godstone! Though he may be my greatest competitor in trade, together we have a common interest in mind—Augustia! And together we have used that common interest to secure the shards of the gods themselves for our city. So, not only will I be asking the Mandated and High Magistrate Trelion III for emergency martial powers, but also, I will be asking for a committee to oversee the use and acquisition of new shards."

"There it is," Godfrey grumbled, his own tone contrasting against the cheers of the crowd. Godfrey was not alone in his doubt, a few amongst the gathered throng hesitated, uncertain if Eamon's last request deserved the raw, primal praise of before.

Alexa turned to the veteran; a questioning look wrought upon her face.

Godfrey returned it, his heavy brows strained with concern, "The man could ask for the world at this point, and they would give it to him."

Even so, Master Eamon didn't give the people much time to argue against his latest proposal, launching into the next portion of his address. "So, I will march into the Chosen's Hall and—gods willing—I will see off those fiends that dare raid our land!" He stepped down from his crate, immediately flanked by a huge brute with a face so heavily scarred that, even from this distance, Alexa could see the lines. The behemoth of a man barred any approach to his lord and then, with purpose, Master Eamon Salferesis marched straight to the steps of the Hall. The big man did not need to shove; people parted, almost desperate to be out of the way. The Chosen's steps were followed by thunderous applause; a roar of adulation that threatened her hearing. As she watched him disappear, she realized Godfrey was right, if Eamon had asked, they would have given him the world.

Chapter Thirteen

Alexa

They escaped the chaos that followed. Crowds, so wrapped in fervor, posed a serious risk of injury, and Alexa did not need to order her company to leave. With a glance, they understood, retreating up the hill from whence they came. They chose the hill, not for any particular reason other than its relative safety; a place to regroup. As they trudged up the cobbles of Grange Street, Alexa shouted, "We *must* find Sophia! This—this is insanity!"

There was no response, just a few grunts as the group powered onwards. They too were wrapped up in the commotion, not out of fervor. No, their urgency was brought on by fear; fear of what had unfolded. Alexa wondered at the loyalties of Master Eamon, and she knew the others felt the same way. Well, save for the naivete of her newest companions, Mikael and Mishanda. They were ignorant of the danger the city faced; ignorant of the knowledge Sophia had entrusted with the rest. Alexa envied them for it.

All three suspects Sophia had named were involved in this latest development, and whatever plan this elusive enemy had in mind was obviously now in motion. *Maybe they were all in on it?* She shook her head, not in disbelief but in shock at the sum of it all.

When her vision refocused, she saw the perimeter wall of the Keeper's Bastion, the pinnacles of its buildings looming over them all. Towering over the city, atop the highest summit in the land, stood the Keepers tower. Its only rival being the Court of the Mandated, which was built as a fortress first—squat and strong—and *not* a monument to the gods. Her awe of the structure kept her as stunned as she ever had been. Then anxiety gripped her insides, because not even this place of academics, this bastion for the gods' messengers, could be considered safe. After all, even Sophia's warden, the Grand Keeper, might be involved. It was a terrifying thought, one that would involve so many of Augustia's governing officials. She shook her head again, subconsciously denying the gravity of it all.

A panicked voice echoed from their right. Along the upper road that ran along the summit of the Bowl, aptly named Summit Way, trotted Gilbert, his face flush with exertion. "Hey! Hey, there you all are—" He had to stop, doubling over to suck in deep breaths. "I … I have been loo-looking all over." A couple more heavy breaths and a lackluster wave of his hand to show the scope of his search. "Sophia is gone. Taken prisoner! I don't know why, but one moment she was meeting with Chalepos and the next … well, the next moment she was being escorted away in chains, looking like she was nigh unconscious. Her robes and amulet stripped!"

There was a sharp intake of breath from Bella, and Alexa felt another shock pummeling her already battered spirit. *Her sister in chains? Impossible.* But even though she had just met this man, the despondency that gripped his normally meek features told her everything she needed to know. *They needed to act, but how?*

She looked around at her companions, desperate for ideas, but to no avail. Then a flash caught her eye, and from the darkness of an alley between two large estates, she saw Dunkeath, his lanky arms gesturing for them to come over. Alexa relayed the command to her company, "Come with me."

With a rush they charged into the alley, rounding a tight corner in pursuit of the gesturing Dunkeath. For a terrifying second, Alexa dreaded she led them into an ambush; daggers and knifes would appear from the recesses of the alley and bathe them in bloody ruin. Those fears quickly subsided when she saw a very troubled Olivia pacing back and forth within the shadows of the streets far side. Here the walls of the larger estate buildings were tall enough to block the afternoon sun. The sight of the normally affable woman chewing on her fingernails and muttering to herself wasn't a much better feeling than prior, but at least she knew she wasn't about to be stabbed. Also—while she was trying to be optimistic, she now knew Gilbert was telling the truth. On the other hand, if she wanted to be pessimistic, well … she wouldn't consider that until there were more answers.

"What's happened?" Bella squawked in irritable question.

Dunkeath, who had hardly waited for the company to follow his gesturing, fell in beside his normal companion, "Bastards tried to kill us!"

Olivia stopped, snapping a frenetic rage-speckled look towards the group. "That's right—they must've figured we knew too much. Too bad for them though," Olivia grinned malevolently, pulling out a still bloody dagger from her trousers.

"Wouldn't be our first scrap," Dunkeath offered. "'Sides we are some damn hardy pioneers. Frankly, it's a bit insultin' just sending the two for us now that I'm thinking of it."

Alexa, tired of the chaos of recent events was desperate for clear cut solutions, "Answers, you two! We need answers. Where is my sister?"

Dunkeath closed his eyes, and when he reopened them, she saw a different man than ever before.

Alexa had figured this man had morphed into someone of quality based on Sophia's letters, but now, in the light of the chaos before them, it was plainly written upon his face. His purpose, his loyalty, and his scruples were the kind Alexa preferred, and she was glad he bent those talents too their purpose.

Dunkeath spoke, "We don't know fer sure. But we do have a plan, one that we wanted to get you all involved in first."

Olivia, who still bit at her fingers, added, "Right, so as our enemies grow desperate and try to knife us, our friends do as well. Ya see, after we survived our tumble, a little orphan boy delivered us a message, right to the door." Olivia's eyes shot wide, and she nudged Dunkeath. "If'n they knew where we were, then you can bet the enemy did to."

Dunkeath nodded, deciding to pick up the conversation, "You're probably right. Anyways, you all know about the Argolonian agents Sophia was talking too?" No one spoke, but the chorus of nods gave Dunkeath the answer he needed. "Right, well them folks want us to meet at Minollo's Flagon. We would have went, but we wanted to get Sophia first. When we saw Gilbert running all in a huff, well, we figured that the worst had happened."

Olivia dropped her head, and Alexa watched Dunkeath put a calming hand on the portly woman's back. "It's alright, love," he said.

Olivia bobbed her head up and down and sniffled quite loudly before adding, "Well, we were right scared after the attempted stabbing and all and we needed a breather. So, we decided to wait and see."

Alexa saw the shame in Olivia's eyes—in Dunkeath's. The two had essentially hid, their courage faltering at the gates to the Bastion, but she could hardly blame them. An attempt on one's life, especially after adrenaline fades, can be paralyzing. "There's nothing to be worried about friends. You've done well," Alexa said as she looked into their eyes.

A small measure of their confidence returned, evident in a straighter posture.

Alexa turned to the two rangers under her command, their faces contemplative, "Mikael, Mishanda you know the way to Minollo's Flagon?"

Mikael's knowing grin, and Mishanda's slap of Mikael for said grin told Alexa they probably knew it *too* well, but she didn't have time to inquire, nor—now she thought about it—did she care. "Good, can you take us there? Away from the main roads?"

Mikael glanced at Mishanda, and together the two dipped their heads towards her.

"Great! Now lead the way and keep your eyes out for an ambush." Before they turned to their task, Alexa grabbed Mishanda's shoulder, emphasizing her next words upon the young ranger, "You are the watcher correct?"

Mishanda nodded, anxiety and uncertainty competing for her face in equal measure.

Alexa clarified, "Treat this just as the wilds. You understand?"

The young woman, bow now unslung and within her grasp, nodded solemnly. Mikael affected a slight crouch as he took up his guardian's spear, and with one final nod to their leader, they dashed south towards the docks and Minollo's Flagon.

*

The race through the city, though quite eventful, hid no ambushes. No more daggers came for Olivia or Dunkeath. They did receive plenty of concerned glances from the old and infirm who weren't able to be a part of the celebratory mood that gripped the streets. The people of Augustia were enamored by the dissonance whipped up by Master Eamon, and as such were still chaotically celebrating in the streets around the forum. Not yet making their way to those establishments that would offer them inebriation to accompany their insanity. With nary a crowd in sight, Alexa and her crew managed to make it inside Minollo's Flagon with no upsets. Unfortunately, it was stifling inside, the summer sun turning it into an oven.

It was a circumstance of the tavern's popularity, for "The Flagon", as the locals tended to call it, was clearly visible to locals and travelers alike. That circumstance meant it had no shade for most of midday and through the afternoon. Instead, Minollo's Flagon sat at the apex of a city block that jutted out towards Harbor Street and stood like a monument at the intersection of not just two, but *five* roads. Truly, the tavern took the idiom of 'location, location, location' to heart; because of that, it suffered in the midday heat, but at night—when it mattered—the place was always busy.

The tavern keeper creaked down from his loft, sweat glistening on his bristly cheeks. He looked like he was ready to demand that the group depart, until Alexa flashed an Augustian mark in front of him. The pouch of funds, given to her by the Prime Master, was already being used for what was expected to be its main purpose … bribes.

Though they both knew what it was for, she couldn't help but place an order, "Something to quench our thirst. Nothing intoxicating."

The man grumbled, flipped the coin in his palm a couple of times, and then rushed off. He returned a few minutes later with a young woman that looked like his daughter and mugs full of chilled grape juice. The first taste was a shocking refresher for the situation they were in, and many of the group muttered thanks. The young girl, terrified of Hislock, squealed in fright as the lizard-man hissed his gratitude towards her. She bowed her head—her cheeks a deep crimson—and mumbled an apology.

Godfrey smacked his lips in appreciation as he slammed his mug down, bobbing his head at the surly tavern owner and the now mortified lass. The two glanced at Alexa and, with a gesture, she gave them the leave to depart.

The tavern keeper paused in his race to be away and managed to mutter, "Let us know if ya need anything, I make a rather delicious honey mead."

Alexa replied with her own pleasantry, "Ok, will do sir."

The two fled, glad to be away from the strange group. She wondered how Sidon would have responded to this mess, the thought giving her a momentary smirk. Alas, he was with her parents, kept safe by the relative anonymity of the location and the watchful eyes of her mother.

For a long minute, the group sipped at their juice, biding time until whoever was supposed to meet them arrived. Alexa clarified her own thought, *that is whoever is supposed to meet Dunkeath and Olivia.*

As she tasted the bottom of her mug, Alexa noticed an elegant woman approach them from the dark side of the tavern. The only indication of where she came from lie within the faintest whisper of a breeze.

Possibly a side door? Alexa surmised.

The woman's head was shadowed in a dark green cloak and her clothing was of a fine make, hints of silk woven in its embroidery. A glint of metal danced in Alexa's peripheral vision, and she heard Bella gently unsheathe one of her daggers. Mikael gripped his spear tightly, making a rubbing noise that complimented the tension. Mishanda—to Alexa's pleasure—had stood and taken two steps back. She knew their watcher saw a threat and was preparing to fire upon it. The lady sighed and pulled the cloak from her face, and even Alexa was stunned by the beauty she saw there.

"I didn't think you would bring an army," the lady spoke, her attentions directed towards Dunkeath and Olivia. The two had to turn in their seats to look at her.

Dunkeath let slip, "Ember's breath …"

Olivia slapped his shoulder, and he immediately looked away.

The lady smiled conciliatorily towards Olivia. High cheekbones flexed with the gesture. "Still, you are here, and we have much to discuss. The luxury of secrecy has abandoned us." The lady placed a hand on Godfrey's left shoulder. There was folded cloth in place of his missing arm, and as he looked at her, she smiled. "May I sit?" Her words were like honey, and Alexa felt a small twitch of envy.

"You can sit wherever you like, ma'am," Godfrey replied with such a serious expression it made Bella scoff. The lady squeezed in between Godfrey and Olivia. The benches of their table nearly filled with people. Alexa looked at Mishanda and gestured for the alert ranger to sit. A smile graced Alexa's cheeks as she watched the ranger unstring her bow. *Good girl.*

"I'll be brief. Time is not ours right now," the lady said at a whisper, and then sat upright pulling out a tiny mirror and pretended to touch up her nose. She saw the woman's eyes dart to and fro, using the mirror as a tool to scan her surroundings. She tucked away the mirror and leaned forward, a silver bangle around an immaculately tied ponytail jingled slightly.

At a whisper, the woman continued, "Our mutual friend, Keeper Sophia Vollimosa has been taken. She had sent us correspondence exposing Master Eamon as the most likely of suspects, and upon our advice and your friends here—" she gestured with a delicate hand towards Dunkeath, Olivia, and Gilbert. "She went to speak to one we thought safe. One who could get us into a position of power within Augustia. We were wrong. Whatever transpired there led to her capture and, coupled with his rather *passionate* speech in the forum, I would say that Master Eamon has put all his cards on the table."

Bella shot a glance at Alexa, and Alexa could see pain in them. After all, it had been Bella who had named Master Eamon as the most likely suspect. *She's blaming herself,* Alexa sighed internally. She *had* to say something, "You didn't know sister. You didn't know that would happen."

The woman looked back and forth between the two and let a crooked smile crease her cheek. "You must be her sisters. For once, I see that the rumors are true."

Alexa furrowed her brows as she returned the woman's look.

The elegant lady clarified, "Well, ladies, the people of Augustia know of you three. The three Vollimosa sisters—not to be underestimated. Seeing as how the smallest of you was ready to stab me with a dagger," The woman's eyes locked onto Alexa. "And how you command not only the room but also the people within it. *And* that your sister is the only known Keeper to overcome the wiles of Dolocius … I think it's safe to say that the rumors are true. You are most definitely *not* to be underestimated." She smiled at her as she leaned back.

"Enough flattery," Bella said coldly, tucking a dagger, Alexa thought was concealed, away. The woman smirked in response.

Alexa chimed in, "Who are you? Why are you helping us?"

Gilbert joined in on the offensive, "How did you know Sophia was captured? How did you know where to find Dunkeath and Olivia?"

"Ah, another Keeper, our odds get better and better," the woman said in response to Gilbert, though her countenance held a thinly veiled tone of malice. Quickly, she glanced to her left and right and then straightened before speaking formally, "I am the Mistress Elgana, heir to the House of Elgan in Argolon, and liaison to our *interests* in this city. You may know him as Bloodeye. Pleased to make your acquaintance. As for knowing how and where, well let's just say I have many little eyes and ears in the city. I also happen to know how to use one of these." She held out a bundle of dazzling rose gold rods.

Gilbert whispered in awe, "Artstone. You, You're a Keeper?"

The woman laughed, "No, no, not like the ones you have here or in the bastion in Argolon. No, I am just a collector who happens to hear Minollo's voice."

"A whisperer then," Gilbert said accusingly.

The piercing blue eyes of the woman fixed Gilbert with menace. Alexa silently applauded the man, who—although was trembling—returned her stare without flinching. "You are not the first person to mistrust me; the Lady Aliana didn't either. And because of that, the very evidence we could have used to solve this kerfuffle could have been exposed weeks ago. Instead, she decided to trap the damned documents so that they could only be seen by Bloodeye, a costly distrust I have been trying to clean up ever since. Now, yes, I *am* a whisperer, and yes, I am not sanctioned. I hope that this … fact won't dissuade you from making the right choice."

Alexa wracked her brain for Sophia's debrief on the events of the conspiracy and recalled mention of a poor dockworker, dead and broken now.

She also vaguely recalled a lesson on whisperers. On rare occasions, people managed to speak to a godstone without the appropriate training of the Keeper order. *Infinitely dangerous and infinitely worrisome.* Still, this lady seemed like she wished to help and—for now, courtesy would do them no harm. "Alexa Vollimosa, and this is my sister Bella."

Mistress Elgana smiled tightly at them both, recognizing the effort put forth. She spoke with a similar tightness in her own tone. "If you are worried about our intentions; if you think that I might be in bed with the enemy, well … then you are smart. But, let me assure you, I, along with House Perigoss, have been investigating this plot since …" Elgana paused, counting on her full red lips in silence. "Well, since I was able to hear a particular interesting bit from Minollo themselves. You see, when your plot involves a god who despises lies, it's hard for that god not to share all your little secrets. Apparently, this plot has been in the works for years now, and we are … fortunate to be here at its climax."

Gilbert piped up, "Minollo, you spoke to them? What did they say?" His tone carried more iron than Alexa thought he had, and she noticed how the pretty woman's flattery had little effect on him.

This Keeper has some teeth, and some loyalty, after all, she mused

"What greater beauty is there than the truth?" Elgana replied matter-of-factly. "House Perigoss and myself are quite capable of speaking to the gods and though I can't just hand you some *thing* and say, 'look I speak the truth.' I can assure you that our interests are aligned. With that in mind, let me give you this … 'blood and bone, sinew and stone, beware the coming woe.'" The mistress paused, her eyes pursed tightly. Blue, cerulean eyes opened, a mollifying smile accenting their emotion. "We want to save your friend, your sister, the Keeper who stands the best chance against the coming storm."

Gilbert nodded to Elgana, and, as he leaned back, he looked at Alexa, "I have heard that same phrase whispered for some time now." A sudden haunted look crossed the brown eyes of the Keeper, and he had to shake his head to force himself onwards. "Artstone is my most attuned godstone and all I can say is that she at least knows what Minollo has been saying. As for the rest," He shrugged his shoulders, as if to say he couldn't find fault in her story.

She was inclined to agree. "Listen, we know time is short. So, for lack of not being able to vet you fully we are going to trust you. *But* let me say this. If you cross us, you will quickly find out why the Vollimosa sisters have a reputation."

Bella, as she always did, played her part beautifully. The sound of metal echoed in the tavern. Bella's twin daggers were displayed with such sudden force that Elgana couldn't help but flash a momentary sign of fear.

The woman put her hand to her chest and then as she recovered, chuckled. "My, my you are a sight. I assure you, Rangemaster, Stablemaster, I will *not* cross you." She looked at them each in turn as she used their title, pouring as much reassurance as she could into the look. Alexa relaxed slightly. *She is an ally—at least for now.*

The Mistress Elgana grinned, "Now, I know where your sister is. Fortunately for us all, it's not that far away."

Chapter Fourteen

Sophia

Cold—bitter, relentless cold! A moment of sheer panic; her heart racing; her mind adrift. *Where was she?* Water coursed over her face. Instinctually, her hand rubbed at the intrusive liquid and flicked away the worst of it. *That explained what brought about the plunging temperature*, a thrown bucket of water. She strained to focus on her surroundings, her mind groggy from whatever had claimed her consciousness.

With a groan, Sophia pulled herself upright, making out small flickers of dim candlelight—little blurs of yellow. Whoever had woken her was giving her blessed time to recover her faculties. Not that it was a welcome thought, but still, she was able to try and reclaim some of the lost time, a skill she unfortunately remembered from her dealings with Dolocius.

Last she recalled, she had decided to divulge the truth to someone within the higher echelons of the Keeper's Bastion. It had felt like the only course of action, especially after Bella's candid admission of Master Eamon's affair with Lady Aliana. Coupled with the ledgers and letters brought by Sidon and Bella from the ravaged Xeelander outpost, the evidence mounted against the charming Chosen. If it *were* him, the bastard had given reconnaissance information to the Xeelander expedition, only to have them slaughtered by his own mercenaries. It seemed like a stretch, but there was no other explanation at present. And their time felt like it was running out. She had been forced to act quickly, which always led to mistakes. Even her final message to the Argolonian contact, detailing the newest evidence, came back with a simple reply.

Seek friends within the Bastion, one we think is true and who holds the door.

-Bloodeye

They were right, she needed allies within her city, someone with power and influence that could help her parse out the purveyors of the godstone plot. Echoing the letter's sentiments, Gilbert, Dunkeath, and Olivia counseled that she seek out the one individual they all thought uncorrupted: Monique the Keeper. Monique, beyond being well-versed with the gods' gifts, had many connections obtained from the duties of her station. *They had never been more wrong,* she sighed heavily in memory.

The bubbly Keeper had been so ready to be her confidant, so eager to hear Sophia's urgent request for an audience, it should have been a warning. Yet, the woman was so inviting—so safe. Sophia had followed her into her private chambers, accepted a refreshment no questions asked, and watched in horror as Monique's face had shifted from inviting host to malevolent fiend.

"Hemlock and raspberry, lightly dusted with some Epidus blossom! It's a wonderful combination that's rather delicious and … shall we say, cathartic?" Monique had toyed with her, unveiling her deception as Sophia sunk into a paralytic stupor. She had tried to reach for her Embershard amulet, but Monique simply tutted, holding up her Seastone in kind, "That won't work here Keeper. Especially not in your state." A malevolent grin as the triumphant Keeper tucked her cerulean stone away. "Did you like the tea though? People tend to forget that us Keeper's dabble quite heavily in alchemy, and, well, I have been trying to get the taste of this particular brew *just* right. Not too heavy on the Epidus blossom? I find it's earthy musk can be a bit *overwhelming.*" Sophia had drifted ever closer to unconsciousness before her eyes had felt too heavy to lift. She heard the deceptive woman say, "If it's any consolation I *did* like you. There's nothing personal here, but … well, orders are orders."

The possibility of Grand Keeper Chalepos's corruption had blinded her to the truth. Now, that ignorance had delivered her to the enemy. *What a fool she was—a cold, miserable fool.* A light skiff of cloth, now soaked, was all she had to protect herself from the elements. Whatever those may entail in this musty place. A shiver ran through her as she brought her knees to her chest.

"Ah, there you are! Finally awake!" A familiar voice called out, and in the shadows of her vision, she saw a large blur step to within a meter or two of her.

The figure was broken up by some sort of vertical bars, the image hard to reconcile in her mind—that was until clarity returned to her vision. Some sort of jail cell, and there, staring down at her from the other side of her enclosure, was a man she had thought to call friend. A man who had spent so many days and nights with her, perfecting what she had thought to be the foil for the godstone plot. A man who must have grown weary as she challenged him with little barbs and interrogatives time and time again; her natural academic inclination had not allowed her to rule him out completely. Not until she could prove it without a doubt. In his agitation, he apparently had decided to end her time as his pawn. She felt like a fool, and Master Eamon Salferesis stood looking all the more triumphant for it.

"Now, now, why so glum? You were right! You figured me out and all your little suspicions are proven correct. I *am* the one you seek!" Eamon spread his arms wide like he was handing himself over to her mercy. "Course, I couldn't just let you ruin all I worked for. Years of work! Down the drain? No, thank you!" He stood near the bars, grabbing onto them so he could poke his face through.

The man was taunting her, gloating in his victory, and all she could do was suffer through it. It made her sick. *How could she have been so blind?*

"Oh, you still worried about ol' Monique? Yeah, she is a right beaut' that one. Able to let me in on *all* your little Keeper secrets; all while being so … damn … likable! She's a magician that one, no doubt about it. Turns out, denying such a talented woman a Senior Keeper position for *so* long doesn't bode well for morale," Eamon pushed away from the bars, and nonchalantly looked at his nails. Without a care in the world, he dropped a truth that made the betrayal undeniably believable, "Well, that and the fact that Magdris might have a way to make a barren woman … shall we say *fertile*. Poor girl. It must have been so terribly lonely after her last husband. He went off to father sons and daughters with some highborn bitch. Ah well, such as life."

Sophia didn't respond. Besides, there wasn't much she could say to change her fate. Instead, she shook her head in disbelief before drooping it in defeat.

Eamon did not relent. "Oh, that reminds me!" He snapped his fingers. "Magdris, save from giving lonely divorcees second chances, also has a particular fascination with *you*. Turns out … the gods tend to take notice of those who harness power such as yours." Eamon dropped his voice a few octaves and leaned forward like he was letting her in on a secret. "You remember how you incinerated a whole slew of orcs alongside a shard of The Deceiver himself." Eamon tutted. "Yeah, that is one impressive feat—one that is hard to ignore."

He came back to the bars and poked his head through. "You see, he wants you *so* bad that he helped me enact this little plan of mine." Eamon swept a hand over the cell. "I get the people of Augustia to stem godstone trade; I concoct a little conflict; I obtain emergency powers; and, in a gnomish second, I now have all of the godstone I could dream of."

His eyes widened suddenly, and he effected a look of raw excitement, "Oh, oh, oh, you will love this! You see, we found a particularly juicy trove of Artstone not far from your little *village*." He sneered before letting his face turn into a grin of raw malevolence. "You will *have* to tell your sister that I am dreadfully sorry about her rangers." He clicked his teeth, "*But* they did try to stop my people."

Sophia could not hold back any longer; she charged. Her limbs were still weak from the hemlock draught, and she was much too slow to catch Eamon unawares.

The man backed away with exaggerated fear. "There she is! Still got a little fight left in you I see. Don't worry, I'm sure your damned siblings are finding some way to use that cursed boy to their advantage. Unfortunate that he survived … he's going to be so traumatized after watching such a slaughter."

"You're a monster!" Sophia yelled. Vivid descriptions by Alexa and Bella came to life within her imagination. A little boy terrified and alone ripped from his family and friends. All because of this man, this *demon*. It was too much, and even her Keeper's reserve faltered at his callousness.

His grin twisted to a mockery of empathy, "I grew up in the slums ya know? A poor ratty little orphan who had to scrounge for scraps by the docks. Not like you with your *perfect* life and your *perfect* family. No, I … I had to make myself. I had to earn this!" He poked at his chest forcefully, and it was his turn to charge the bars. He slammed into them, making her fall back with the sudden force of it.

She shuddered.

Eamon breathed deeply. "I digress! Ya see, the way I reckon is that not long after you toasted his disciples over in Elgion, he got to work … through me. No, no, no!" He shook his head in response to her look of horror, evidently reading her terrifying thought—*possession*.

"Not like some sort of corruption. But through, let's say … a deal. I spent many hours alone, in the dark, with this!" From within his tunic, he produced a bundle of Artstone rods, and even in the gloom, Sophia could see they were waning in power from heavy use.

"I never was a whisperer or anything, but one day ol' Minollo starts talking to me. Truly beautiful to hear the *Slivers of Truth*, they came clear as day. Ya see, him and his brother Magdris want to work with *me*. They saw my ambition and wanted to reward it. The gods do love drama—and tri-umph!" Eamon danced back a couple steps and spun like a ballet while holding the bundle of rods.

He looked at the rose gold amethysts lovingly and tucked them back into the recesses of his clothing. "Why am I telling you all this? Simple, Minollo told me to. You probably already know but they tend to like it when you tell the truth of your schemes. Minollo will hide things for you for a time, but on the condition that we eventually reveal the truth. I am not about to incur the wrath of more than one god." He pointed at her then, and she knew he spoke of her attunement with Ember.

"Magdris, well at least the messages relayed through Minollo from Magdris, assure me that you and your little dragon are quite helpless to stop this," he said as his face contorted into a rictus of malice. "So, long story short, Magdris who is working with Minollo saw that I wanted to create a monopoly on godstone trade—to gain the power so denied me as a youth. In turn Magdris wants *you*, and for that price I get the boons of not one but *two* gods to make my empire." His eyes grew distant, and he looked lost in thought.

She sucked in shaky breaths, and seconds ticked away as this madman dreamt of the empire he wished to make. Suddenly, his eyes snapped back towards her, boring into her soul, "But first, I need to take care of some things! So, I hope you don't mind if I leave you here in the care of my *associates*."

From the shadows stepped a wiry looking man wearing a purple waist-coat, a man she had seen so many times before around the Chosen. Ap-parently, his duties went far beyond what she had originally thought.

"Timon here may not look like much, but he is one wicked son of a bitch! Man *insisted* that we gouge out the eyes and cut out the tongues." He clicked his own tongue in morbid irony. "It was quite a shame to have to do that to such a beautiful woman, but hey!" Eamon backed away from the bars holding his hands out like it couldn't be helped. "Sometimes you have to crack a few eggs."

She stepped up to the bars grunting in frustration. Unable to find words through the anger.

"Alright now, you be good Sophia. Oh, and for what it was worth— I had fun around you." Eamon winked at her and disappeared into the shadows. She heard his steps ascend some sort of stairs, and she took that small tidbit of information as an outline of her surroundings.

Timon introduced himself, "Ah, Keeper! Magdris's teeth, it was hard trying to get you off our tails. I know you're not having the best time right now, but I … I am having a blast! It's rather thrilling getting to *formally* meet you!" Timon paused, waiting for a reply. When none came, he continued, a look of mock indignation on his face. "No one ever suspects the servants, a truth Master Eamon knows *all* too well." His eyes took on a glossy look before a wicked grin split his lips, "Ah, well. We are gonna have *so* much fun—now that you're here!"

From the recesses of the room appeared two more figures: one a scarred brute and the other a woman who held a wicked looking dagger.

Sophia's heart sank in despair.

Timon spoke again, his voice reedy and thin even within the small space, "What's the matter? Gnomes steal your tongue?" He stepped towards the bars, bringing himself to within centimeters of her. "That's ok, soon you won't need to worry about it. Everything will be … alright." He patted her cheek with a hand she had not seen moving. He then pivoted on his foot and walked away, a dry chuckle on his throat. The man snapped a finger and pointed at the brute. The scarred behemoth brought her a small wooden bowl filled with some dubious looking grains.

"Enjoy!" Timon said before all three disappeared into the recesses of the room.

They may not be visible, but they *were* watching her. Not able to hide, she forced the lukewarm food down her throat. The small heat sending a sliver of pain through her jaw. *You aren't the only clever one,* she mused.

After all, she hadn't gone into her meeting with Monique blind and dumb. She wasn't a *total* fool. Her rear left molar gone—replaced with a small bit of Necrostone. *It's always wise to have redundancies,* she thought as she remembered Gilbert yanking the molar free … the only pain he ever had caused her. She choked down a smile, for Mosyneta, that god of memory, had captured it all. Every *little* detail. *Now, I just have to get it into the right hands.*

Chapter Fifteen

Bella

Bella crouched against the wall; her muscles fatigued beyond measure. Her thighs and calves warned they would fail at any moment. To be fair, she *had* forced them through darkened alleys and shadowed avenues on a mad dash back up the Bowl. What was to be a day of relative leisure had turned into one of mayhem, and now—like any sensible organ—her muscles were rebelling against the brutal change of pace.

She envied Sidon, who would undoubtedly be back with her mother and father getting fat on sweetened honey cakes. The lucky lad hadn't even been roused to prepare for the original plan, a journey to Xeeland to return him to his countrymen. Instead, the world had been turned upside down, and ever since Eamon's speech in the forum, Bella and her group had been going nonstop.

Alongside Mistress Elgana, the company had delivered themselves to an opulent estate on the western edge of the Upper Bowl, and now they had paused to regain composure. After Bella managed a few heavy recovery breaths, Alexa ordered Mikael to act as a stool for Mishanda. The two rangers were turning into an observatory as the rather muscular Mishanda peeked over the seemingly unguarded wall. While Bella waited, she glanced to the rally point Mistress Elgana had retreated to—an alley veiled in shadow.

There was still suspicion there, brought on by a dramatic change in appearance in front of their very eyes. All that recently golden-haired lady had to do was just whisper to her stones, sending Gilbert into a flurry of excited questions. It wasn't until the woman had placed a finger to his lips that he stopped, never answering one of them.

In place of the woman they had met at the Flagon, a short, dark-haired, buxom woman whose pale features seemed to blend in with the shadows had appeared. Wild magic from a whisperer—*Dangerous.* To make matters worse, the shapeshifter had refused an offered blade. Instead, she simply held up her hands, and Alexa—their de facto leader—did not press the issue. Her sister after all, knew a reluctant fighter could get them all killed. Still, Bella wondered why this *spy* couldn't be bothered to help.

Regardless of the transformative woman, Alexa, the two new rangers, Hislock, Godfrey, Dunkeath, Olivia, Gilbert, and herself had readied themselves for battle. Now, in the moon-less night, they launched an assault on the small walls of the estate, dwarfed against the backdrop of the city's ramparts.

At a hissing whisper, Mishanda spoke to her commander, "No guards nearby, Rangemaster, we are safe from prying ears and eyes … for now."

Alexa clicked her teeth. With what incidental light, primarily from the torches and candles of the surrounding city, Bella could make out Alexa's lithe frame crouched against the wall. The assorted company rallied around the Rangemaster, whose torchlit eyes glanced at each of them in turn.

Alexa whispered, "Alright, Gilbert, work your words. What can Minollo tell us?"

"Right," Gilbert replied and pulled out his Artstone bundle. It was so like the one Mistress Elgana had, the one she had used to morph her appearance. "Our *friend* isn't the only one with a connection to Minollo," he snarked before closing his eyes. While holding the rods between his hands, he started murmuring. The godstones fizzled as small sparks flew upwards before popping like miniature fireworks. The noise, albeit miniscule, made Bella wince even though she was assured it was a necessity. Gilbert had said he could scout inside, but the closer he got, the better the vision.

It felt like a long time before the Keeper opened his eyes, "hmmm, it seems like there is others who can speak to the gods in there. I am … well, my vision is obscured. Good news is that I found Sophia, or at least her *thoughts*, she is the only one I *can* see. It's all just shadows and shapes to be honest."

"Where," Alexa interrupted before the Keeper could explain further. Bella smirked; they were both well-versed in the over-explanatory nature of Keepers.

"North side; down some stairs; a basement maybe?" He offered. "I can't really make out who's all in there. Minollo shows me shapes, but they could just be fragments of left over feeling and emotion." He shrugged apologetically, "Could be twenty guards—could be none."

Alexa sighed while placing a hand on the Keeper's shoulder, "Thank you, Gilbert, I know you have done your best. We know where she is, and that's all we need." The Rangemaster offered a forlorn smile, and then turned to Mishanda, "What's it look like on the outside?"

"I see one rather sleepy looking fellow at the front. Nothing else."

"Alright, Hislock, I have seen your kind work. Can you take him out *silently*?"

Hislock nodded as he let out a small hiss.

"Good, we will follow you in. Once we breach the front door we need to move quickly. Our only hope is speed. Whoever is in there needs to be neutralized before they have time to wake." Alexa breathed in heavily, before adding, "Let's just hope Eamon isn't expecting us. Since none of us have been in there before, any ambush would be catastrophic. If it looks like we are going to go down, retreat the way we came and find Mistress Elgana. She should be able to hide you from their reprisal. Are we clear?"

Scattered shuffling and murmuring were the only response.

Alexa nodded to Hislock. The saurian leaped to the top of the wall with ease and slithered over the side. His agile nature leaving no trace of his movements save for the faintest scraping sound. This was the hard part, the waiting. Bella's heart thudded in her chest, her body tensing for the fight to come. *How many fights had she been in? How many lives taken? How many lost?*

"He's done it," Mishanda whispered, and Bella gripped her dagger hilts tightly.

"Alright, let's go save a Keeper," Alexa said, risking a bit more noise to give some confidence to her voice—to them.

Mishanda was first over the wall, already perched on Mikael's splayed hands. Alexa stood by Mikael's side and slapped the back of each of them as they took turns being boosted by the guardian ranger. Bella followed Olivia, and she had to scramble at the top of the wall as Mikael nearly pushed her past the precipice. A few desperate scuffling footfalls slowed her descent on the far side, and she was able to ease her landing. Godfrey nearly fell into her as he too was tossed like a feather by the surprisingly strong ranger.

"Ember's breath, that lad has some oomph," Godfrey said as his hasty descent caused him to bump into her. They backpedaled together and re-gained their balance before crashing into a rather spiky-looking hedge.

"Yea, the bastard nearly threw me clean over," Bella replied, and she saw a flash of slightly yellowing teeth. Godfrey's presence was comforting, although she worried for his safety. He did, after all, have a missing arm. Still, that insistence gave her courage.

No missing arm is gonna slow me down, she imagined him saying.

Alexa was now over the side, and Mishanda boosted her so she could reach over the wall and pull Mikael over. They were lucky the wall, which stood about two-and-a-half meters tall, was only a preventive measure and not a true, defensive construction.

Hislock met up with them in the small garden they occupied, scaped with steppingstones and immaculately manicured flower beds. Bella could make out colors now as a wash of torchlight backlit the scene before her.

The lack of guards made her uneasy, and she let her mind slip into the maw of fear that was ever present.

"Did you hear anything, Hislock? See anything?" Alexa asked apprehensively.

The saurian shook his head, a look of worry, not easily distinguished on his scaled face, developed. Bella assumed he too was feeling the wrongness of this place, of this raid. Yet, they had to press on, and the company scuttled forward on crouched legs, trying to muffle their approach. They took up two breaching lines on either side of twin, bronze-rimmed, oak doors that fronted the house. The lone guard's body lay past a marble pillar, and Bella could see his face, half lit in a cross beam of torchlight. His eyes were still open, and the pale blue orbs stared outwards toward a world they would never experience again. She shuddered.

A sudden clang echoed from the inside of the estate. The doors had been breached, and Alexa abandoned silence, "Go! Go! Take them quickly!"

Bella tensed her grip on the twin daggers—blades of hard iron made as a present by Elgion's blacksmith—and charged. Austere white marble, near blinding relative to the darkness outside, beckoned to her like a lone light in the dark. She had nearly breached the door, the sight of a cascading fountain ahead, when a whizzing sound whirled up. One she had heard before. Dunkeath let out a simple groan and crashed to the floor.

"No!" Olivia wailed, dropping to his side.

She nearly fell, as the two made an obstacle. "Get out the doorway!" She stumbled and reeled back, a cracking sound pinging off the marble in front of her. "We have to move him!"

The laundress nodded, and together they grabbed his tunic, pulling him by the shoulders behind a gold-trimmed pillar on the north side of the entrance. Her, Gilbert, Hislock, and now Olivia and Dunkeath were hiding behind its bulk. The others fell in behind its twin to seek cover from the deadly missiles. It had been as they feared—an ambush, and the company was pinned down.

"Oh no, oh no, oh no," Olivia repeated in frantic desperation. Blood thick on her hands as she groped around Dunkeath's head.

Bella couldn't worry about him now; his fate was with the gods. A fate they would all face if they did not deal with this threat. Although they would miss the two fighters, especially Olivia's beloved short spear, *Bertha*, it couldn't be helped. Gilbert was rummaging around in his Keeper's robes, looking for ways to heal.

Bella looked over at Alexa to see her sister mouth one word, "Caprix."

That was where she had heard it before, the whirring. It was the twin goatmen that had so harried their raid on the beach back on Continens Hyclepius. They were here, or at least ones similarly trained. Another whirl, and a crack sent a splinter of marble crashing against the back wall. Bella winced at the destructive force. It would be a far cry for Dunkeath to survive such a blow.

Mishanda risked a shot as she side-stepped from the southern pillar. The ominous whirring sound spoiled her aim; the echo of an arrow clattering off stone told them of its failure. The goatmen were at the far end of the large foyer, occupying two small galleries that protruded from the north and south walls. The door they had breached was on the western edge of the building. Another stone cracked against marble.

"Ah, shit," Mishanda cursed as splinters of stone scored her face.

"Relax ranger. Small targets; small misses." Alexa said with a fortifying control that helped calm Bella's own ragged nerves. From across the gap between the two pillars, Alexa relayed her orders. "Now, Mikael, Hislock I need you to advance on my word, throw your spears when you get close. Bella, Godfrey advance behind them and get underneath! Me and Mishanda will distract."

Bella felt sweat break out as a flood of adrenaline coursed through her. This was the moment, the shaking trembling fear before impending doom. She gritted her teeth, and, though she did not hear, she saw Alexa's mouth open in a simple bellow, "Go!"

She let out a shuddering breath through clenched teeth, watching Hislock bound forward. She would follow; her course laid out before her: To the left of the fountain, past a red drodang-silk couch, and over open ground until she made it to the far wall, just past a single oak door. Alexa and Mishanda both stepped out of cover and drew their bows towards the enemy. They were taking their time, *small targets; small misses.*

Seconds crawled by, and Hislock took three leaping steps that felt like an eternity. That was enough; that would allow her to slip by without being targeted.

She broke from cover and watched twin arrows arc against the vaulted ceiling above. Their feathers looked like waterfowl against a backdrop of fountain-induced mist. She did not watch their progress, instead refocusing on her goal. Hislock's tail swept back and forth, balancing him during his desperate charge. They were close now, and the ominous whirring—that damnable sound—wound up once more. Hislock stopped, having reached a spear throwing distance, and Bella skirted by him on his left. A grunting noise could be heard, and the sound of an impact against flesh greeted her as she slammed against the northern wall.

She took in a breath; one she had not known she was holding. A caprix suddenly slammed into the stones next to her, forcing a yelp from her heightened senses. Their body now a meter away, a saurian spear protruding from its chest. Bella, her heart near bursting from the unexpected noise, charged towards the impaled foe. She had learned from harsh lessons; unless an enemy was truly dead, you never, *ever,* let down your guard.

She dove to her knees at the caprix's side, plunging her daggers towards them. The goat man did not move as her blade sawed into his throat.

She did not hesitate and pushed the second dagger into flesh. *She had to be sure.* Still, no response. She screamed in anger and agony—the first challenge overcome.

Blood sprayed across her face from the retracted dagger, and she surveyed the progress of the others. Mishanda lay on her side, next to a still firing Alexa, a small dark pool gathering at her head. *Lethal bastards*, she moaned. She looked at the second gallery and watched as the caprix dodged an arrow. Mikael raced to grab his spear at the far east side of the gallery, and Godfrey …

Well, Godfrey was staring straight back at her. He looked concerned; concerned for her. She growled at him, and the expression broke him out of whatever trance that gripped him. The veteran sidestepped from underneath the gallery, changed the grip on his axe to a throwing stance, breathed in, and hefted the weapon towards the back of the Caprix. It was a good throw, and through the small gaps in the wooden rail, the blade struck true. It buried itself deep into the enemy's back side.

The goat man howled in pain, and their instinctual reaction was to arch upwards, grabbing at the offending object. That was their final mistake; Alexa's next arrow took him in their throat. His howl cut off abruptly, and, with an eerie slowness, he toppled over the side of the rail and onto the stones below. Bella blinked as she watched their left leg snap as it made contact with the ground. The rest of the body rebounded slightly off the broken bone before rolling over it to its final rest on the marble floor. The silence that followed was tantamount to her feelings, and evidently the others as well. There was no need to make sure this enemy was dead.

"Mishanda!" Mikael cried out as he raced towards his fallen range mate. Alexa beckoned towards her, Godfrey, and Hislock. The veteran yanked his thrown axe free of the caprix corpse, meeting them at the fountain.

It had not gone well. Mikael and Gilbert were working on Mishanda, and Olivia was left holding a still unconscious Dunkeath. *Two of them down for two of theirs*, Bella cursed inwardly.

The Rangemaster allowed the group some heavy breaths, ragged against the constant droning of the cascading fountain. "We still have fight in us." Alexa said with conviction, and Bella believed it.

Another round of heavy breaths, Mikael was brushed aside by Gilbert as he invoked the power of a gleaming Maidenstone shard, that most potent of healers—the god, Hyclepius. The anxious ranger, seeing he could no longer assist, meekly approached the regrouped company. Alexa nodded at him before growling her next orders, "We still can win, and we can *still* save Sophia. We knew what this could mean, we knew the risks! Our sacrifices will only be in vain if we fail. Now, let us ready up and show these *bastards* who they are dealing with!"

Hislock let loose a primal fury of sound, and Bella bared her teeth maliciously.

"You gods damned right ma'am," Godfrey echoed their sentiments.

Alexa surveyed the situation, "Alright, Olivia … Olivia!" The shout necessary to try and break the now sobbing woman free of her emotions. "Olivia, he may yet survive, but you *have* to listen!"

This broke through, and with tremendous effort, Olivia swallowed a sob and slowly inclined her head to the Rangemaster. She held the now bandaged head of Dunkeath in her lap, a red stain soaking through to stain her trousers. Another sob before she composed herself. Eyes fixed and ready to receive orders.

It gave Alexa pause, but her sister had seen battle before and knew what needed to be done, "Olivia, he may yet survive. Gilbert has tended his wounds, and we are about to find the best damn healer I have ever known. Take heart!"

The laundress—to her credit—only had to scuff at her face once before taking a calming breath.

Alexa continued, "We *have* to press on. I need you to stay here with Dunkeath and Mishanda, look after them. Understand?"

Olivia nodded.

"Good," Alexa said as Gilbert, who had gently laid Mishanda's head against a bundle of cloth, approached them.

"Mikael. Mishanda will survive. The Maiden has assured me."

"Thank the gods!" Mikael replied.

Gilbert smiled before offering more, "Though, she will be shy of some teeth on her lower jaw. The bleeding came mostly from the disruption there." Mikael dipped his head, a smile still forming against the relatively light news of what had seemed a dire situation.

Alexa mouthed a question to Gilbert—a name, "Dunkeath?"

The young Keeper shook his head slowly, and Bella's heart sank. She had not liked the man when they first met, he seemed a scoundrel and a liar, but after hearing of Sophia's journey over the last three years, she couldn't help but feel sorrow. Sorrow emphasized by an utterly despondent laundress who had seemed so full of life.

Alexa seemed to process the news before continuing, "Now, for the rest of us, we need to stick together. These bastards are deadly." Her sister looked around at her remaining command. "Gilbert, you said basement; north side, correct?"

The Keeper recalled his interaction with the god of beauty before piping up, "Ah, yes! North side—seems to be down some stairs. It's all a bit foggy. I can't make out individuals just the idea of them. It seems like … it seems like I am being blocked from a full vision. Be wary of enemy Keepers, or whisperers. No telling."

"Got it! Mikael take point. Let's all see where that door leads." Alexa pointed at the lone oak door on the northern side of the hall. The mutilated corpse of the goatman was not far from it. Bella shuddered as she fell in behind Godfrey.

Chapter Sixteen

Bella

She focused on her breath—slow and steady. They made their way down an opulent hallway. Rich, red carpet graced the floor below and plinths adorned with statuettes and curiosities of immense wealth were placed liberally along the walls. They passed several doors, each one holding the potential of death, and Bella had to force in calm as they looked for any sign of a basement entrance.

"There," Gilbert hissed. It was a simple door like any of the others in the hall, but Gilbert's god-touched gifts must have told him something they could not see.

They stacked against the wall, and Alexa took up a firing position. She was ready to shoot through the threshold of the doorway the minute it opened.

With a nod from his commander, Mikael, with his left hand, pushed the door and it came open; unbarred and unlocked.

Bella followed behind Godfrey, who in turn followed behind Mikael as the young guardian entered the doorway.

A sudden explosion of noise. The door came slamming back, pinning Mikael against the stone wall and its heavy oak construction. The young ranger cried out in pain as the door recoiled backwards on its hinges. He slumped to the ground, impeding the others' progress.

Alexa fired an arrow through the gap, and a nearly inhuman growl emanated from the darkness beyond. The Rangemaster pulled Mikael free of the doorway, nodding to Godfrey to pick up the charge.

The veteran soldier whispered back to Bella, "Here we go."

She followed him, calmly stepping just centimeters behind as he pushed through the door and into darkness. Godfrey responded to an unseen threat and darted to his right before slashing his axe in a downwards cross swing—another growl of pain. Bella could make out a silhouette in the gloom, a massive brute half-hidden by the door. She knew what to do here; she had fought oversized fiends before. With a tuck and a roll, she swept under the enemy's guard and came out behind him. One meaty arm swung like a wrecking ball, but it was too slow. She darted in with one of her daggers. The blade punched into flesh, and she ripped it free before the towering brute could grab her. Air swept by her arm.

Godfrey slashed his axe across the man's back, causing him to howl in pain before swinging his arms back around in a blind rage. The big man was fast for his size, and Godfrey took a glancing blow to his shoulder, forcing him to reel backwards.

Hislock's spear, lightning quick and deadly, brutalized the man's chest.

It was a mortal blow, and now that Bella's eyes were adjusted to the dim light, she saw the brute as he recognized his death. He was almost childlike in his pleading innocence. A small shiver ran up her spine as he fell to his knees. She sliced her dagger into him, under his collarbone—straight into the heart.

A meaty thud resounded in the dark room. The man's bare chest slapping into the landing they perched upon. *They had to be on the right path. No one would put such a goliath here without good cause*, she assumed.

"Hislock! Take point! Mikael's arm is broken," Alexa ordered.

The saurian hissed and carefully stepped onto the stair that descended into the gloom below. At the base of it was a rough stone wall and a ninety degree turn to the left. Flickering torchlight pulsed shadows and illumination in rapid succession, giving their destination an ominous appearance. Bella pressed forward, urged on by the desire to secure her friend's back.

Slight hesitation, and Hislock stepped down to the bottom landing, twisting to the left with his spear outstretched. No immediate response, and Bella followed behind him with Godfrey, Gilbert, and Alexa in tow.

A glint of iron to her right, a shadow on her periphery. She shot up her dagger to deflect the blow, the singing ring of iron-on-iron.

"Magdris's teeth," the attacker muttered. She must have known her time was measured. A saurian spear and Godfrey's axe took her on the left and right simultaneously. She was a hardy looking woman, but she had been given no time to respond to either blow—her blade caught against Bellas. She watched the woman smirk at her, her face cast in shadow and then … light, before falling backwards in a heap.

"Bella!" a cry came from the far side of the room. There she was, *Sophia*! She looked tattered and torn in a thin skiff of white cloth, but Sophia's voice held firm with a warning, "There is another!"

The light disappeared, blown out by some unseen force. Bella breathed nervously. A woosh of air whizzed by her, pulling a yelp from her.

A grunt from Alexa, and the sound of sword on sword.

"Ember! Give us light!" Gilbert cried out, and in the palm of his hand, a small flame flickered into existence. The light started to expand, but then she saw it.

A thin man in a purple waistcoat appeared seemingly out of nowhere to slash a sword down at Gilbert. The blade, wielded by one who evidently spent little time with them, struck Gilbert's arm with more of a hammer blow than a slicing strike. The Keeper cried out as Ember's light faded and died.

Her eyes were useless now. The temporary light having blinded her to any night vision she may have gained.

Gilbert groaned.

"He's using Quickstone!" Sophia yelled into the darkness. A clang of a body on metal, and Sophia's voice was minutely closer. "Watch for teleports! I think he travels dimensions." When no immediate attack came, the Keeper offered solace with slightly more calm, "But he can't hurt you until he comes back to ours."

A sinister laugh grew. It felt distant; like it was from another room, another place. "Very good, Keeper, but that won't save your friends. Not all of them!"

Hislock cried out, and Bella's heart skipped. She hoped, even in this absolute darkness, that the natural night vision of his kind would save him from death. The sound of grunting and a spear being used like a club made her ease.

The muffled voice permeated the dungeon, "You see, I *could* leave. I could just walk away, but when you have the business of a god to attend to. Well, I think you understand—don't ya Keeper?"

She felt it before she knew he was there. A crackling energy from behind, and she spun to meet the attack. A blade swished past the top of her scalp, narrowly missing her due to her tendency to crouch while dancing with her blades. A grunt of pain was her reward, and she knew one of her daggers had slashed him.

"Ah!" The distant voice echoed from some unseen place. The coward had dived into his pockets of unreality, and all she could do was pivot in place, jumping at shadows. Seconds passed, the huffing and puffing of the company's breath somehow reassuring in the dark that blanketed them.

"Ember! Give us your light," Gilbert risked illumination once more, and when his image flickered in view, she saw he was cast in a skim of icy blue.

A hollow reedy laugh wheezed in response, "Very good! You … you learn fast, don't ya? Ah, well, we can dance in the light."

Gilbert spun to greet some unseen presence, but no one came. No attackers leapt from the ether. Instead, they were left in silence, left to glance around at the walls which held threats unknown.

"Gather up!" Alexa commanded, and they moved to obey. Being back-to-back would render this form of assault near harmless.

Bella nodded at Godfrey and moved towards him, wanting that old veteran at her own back. Her eyes widened in horror as the enemy swam into view, a blade lancing out. His lack of skill shorn up by luck, and though Godfrey tried to twist away, it was too late. The sword pierced his throat, and the blade—so forcefully thrust—jammed through his esophagus and rested against his lower jaw.

"Godfrey, No!" Bella wailed in desperation. *The bastard had taken him, had taken the life of a good man.*

Reprisal came in full measure, but not from her. She was too far away. Hislock darted forward, taking the purple waistcoated man in the torso. The fool had tried to pry his blade free, but in his lust to kill, he had lodged it too deep. Now, he scoffed in disbelief as a spear protruded from his upper abdomen. Alexa finished him, slashing her sword across his throat, a mist of blood dropping the curtain on the Quickstone-whisperer.

Godfrey gurgled as red frothy liquid dribbled down his chin. He fell to his knees, the sword finally dislodging with a clatter to the stones.

Bella raced over, sliding to his side. She grabbed him gently from behind so as to not let him fall ungracefully.

He looked up at her, recognition of his death and her sorrow in equal measure. She felt his hand grace her cheek, and though he choked, she swore he tried to smile. A spasm rocked his body, and she let him drop closer to the ground. Not because she had wanted to, but from the dead weight that strained against her arms.

"Godfrey … no, no, no," She whimpered. Tears flowing fast and free.

The old veteran choked again and went to open his mouth, the ruined esophagus making it nigh impossible. Still, the crusty old bastard persisted, and Bella leaned in to let him say his final piece.

"Yo-you tak—" Another splutter as the blood welled in his throat. "Take care of yerself. Yer the stron—" he choked again and she gave him precious seconds to clear his throat. Finally, through spluttering, wheezing breaths he forced the words out, "Yer the strongest person I know."

She burst into sobs and sat upright to look at her friend. This man who had seen her through the worst time of her life and back. She caressed his brow with her free hand smiling at him.

He managed a half grin, though the effort hurt him. "Oh, and watch that boy. He … he needs you," she heard him whisper. The silence from the others giving weight to his words. Another spasm, this one unrelenting. He tried to cough, to clear his throat, but to no avail. The death throes were too intense, and Bella couldn't hold him upright any longer. He fell. Her guiding hands prevented the sword from causing him more pain, and as gently as she could allow, he was laid to rest upon the cool stone floor. A final spasm, and then a rattle of bloody, mucus-filled breath.

All she could do was weep. All she could do was silently say goodbye to Godfrey—Warrior of August, ambassador to the saurian tribes, ruffian and vagabond, and most of all, a damn good friend.

Chapter Seventeen
Sophia

Sophia burst out the cell door as Gilbert unlocked it. For as much as she wished to embrace him; for all the moments of quiet contemplation in which he dominated her thoughts, she couldn't—not now. Instead, she rushed to Bella's side, desperate to comfort her grieving sister. The blow had been fatal, and no manner of god or otherwise could save their old friend. She offered a hand to Bella, who, flanked by Alexa on her right, let out an odd, sad chuckle at the gesture. The hand was wet with blood, and Sophia gripped it tightly, desperate to let her know she was there.

All three were on their knees around their slain friend. In that odd wake, they sat for a time, trading sobs and sorrowful glances at one another.

It was Alexa who broke the wordless reverie, "He was a damned good man."

Bella coughed on a massive sob, the words hurting and helping her in equal measure—in that bittersweet way of memory. She watched the red ponytail, so much like her own, bob up and down as Bella nodded furiously in agreement. "Yes, yes he was."

They laughed, and for some unknown reason they let loose. The words just seemed so … true in that moment of grief. The sort of clipped barking chuckles common with overwhelming loss. It made Sophia think of him, of Godfrey, trying with ill luck to help their mother in the kitchen. His look of fear as she scolded him so genuine … so pure. "Mum is gonna miss him."

This time they laughed, a true hearty laugh.

Hislock joined them then, not in laughter, but instead kneeling next to the human he had called friend. She wondered then how much of a bond the two had formed over the years. One steeped in an interaction with Hislock's kind no other human had known. Bella being the closest rival in that regard, but still, not a worthy contender.

With infinite care, Hislock grabbed Godfrey's axe and placed it in his hand. The scaled hand gripping tightly to ensure the body would hold the blade unto death. Hislock murmured something to himself and looked up to nothing, obviously sending a prayer to the gods. His reptilian eyes looked at the sisters then, "Heee was bessst human. Strong, warrior!" Hislock slapped his own chest. "Great Saurussss will guide him."

Sophia nodded to the noble lizardman, trying not to offend him by showing too much curiosity at the term. *'Great Saurus?' There was only one god that would fit that moniker.*

Alexa blurted out, as if in memory, "Sophia! Dun-Dunkeath he … he is in the entrance hall. You could still save him."

Her heart became icy cold as worry wracked her mind, *Dunkeath was down as well? How many had fallen to try and save her?* She nodded and though she was weak, she leapt to her feet, looking to her ranger sister to guide her.

Alexa rushed up the stairs, and she desperately clambered up behind. They dashed into a hall, one she had walked down in better times. Sophia had not been conscious when they brought her here for her imprisonment. Now, as they raced by, she saw scared faces of servants glance out from behind doors. One timid face partially blocked the view of a room she recognized, the very room Eamon had used to broach the idea of *The God-stone Decree.* She scoffed in irritation at the betrayal but quickly regretted it as her breath failed her. She pressed on with gritted teeth.

They burst into the entrance hall, the sound of calmly flowing water discordant with her feelings.

"Keeper! It-it-it's you! You're alive! Thank the gods!" Olivia cried out, and though it looked as if the former laundress wished to hug her, she remained immobile. Instead, she looked forlornly down at Dunkeath as if to guide Sophia to his prostrate form.

Sophia did not hesitate, and though dizziness washed over her from ill treatment and a desperate dash to his side, she pressed on. She banged her knees hard on the stones as her strength faltered. She watched, desperate for a sign…

There, there it was! *A breath*! It was shallow and far between, but it was there. She sighed in relief. *There was still a chance.* "Gil—" She tried to yell, but her breath was gone, swaying as she looked around for Gilbert.

He placed a hand on her back, a steadying grip that gave her strength. "I've got it right here," he said knowing she needed Maidenstone. The gleaming white rock a balm against the desperation she felt.

"Good," she managed to say, and then gripped the stone still held by Gilbert. She paused, feeling his knuckles under her touch. Desperately she looked into his eyes, trying to convey all that needed to be said. His brown eyes blinked once, and she saw understanding there. She saw him firm his jaw, and she knew—that with his help—she could give it her all.

She turned to the prone figure, a bloody red bandage like a beacon to his wound. She held the Maidenstone upright and began the chant. She needed the god of healing now! The bandage could be changed after. "Maiden! Grace us with the boon of your mercy!" Her voice did not falter, not now, not even against the looming sensation of fainting.

"Maiden! Grace us with the boon of your mercy!" She implored. And as her strength faltered, she felt the presence. That all-too-familiar sensation of the gods. A gentle caress slid over her cheek, and a tear slipped free.

A whisper, as clear as she had ever heard, graced her ears and her ears alone. "Sophia Vollimosa, you are one to watch. The gods know you, and they … they vie for your *talents*." A wind whipped around them.

"Maiden's blessings," Olivia murmured in awestruck recognition.

The goddess continued her personal monologue, "I will save your friend. I will grant you my boon, but only because you kissed him with Ember's fire once before; otherwise, he would be beyond saving. My power is too weak here, unless through my lord's *gifts*. But, before I do, know this, Keeper of the Stones, my bloody sibling is on the march, and you are too late to stop them. They will burn your world to ash, unless you can rally Ember's children. As my errant sibling Minollo would say, 'blood and bone, sinew and stone, beware the coming woe.' Now, be blessed and reunite with your friend!"

She felt a surge of energy course through her. The hands clasped upon the Maidenstone, wracked with turbulent forces that arced towards Dunkeath. She held herself as rigid as she could against the storm, feeling the blessing drain into him. Then, the stone crumbled, its bits turning into chalky paste in her hands. Relief flooded her as the spell was cast, and she allowed her arms to fall to her side. Her muscles utterly spent. The swirling breeze from unknown realms died down, and she felt tiny flecks of cooling water. A mist whipped up from the fountain settled back to Telaea. She opened her eyes and looked upon a welcome sight.

"Hey there, Keeper," Dunkeath said with little sign of pain or struggle, a knowing grin on his face.

She laughed. The damned grin was still just as irritating as it had ever been. Her laugh died to a shuddering chuckle as the weight of Telaea became too much.

Fortunately, Gilbert was there to ease her fall, and before she let sleep claim her, she reached into her mouth and jerked out the false Necrostone tooth. She handed it to him; his horrified expression made her chuckle. She forced herself to speak, to pass on some of the burden of the future, "It's got everything we need to take these *fiends* down. But first, use it on that bastard in the purple coat. Find out where Eamon is. The Maiden …

The Maiden says we are too late to stop him, but maybe we can prevent further damage."

He nodded slowly at her, the gravity of responsibility dawning on him. She reached out a hand to hold his cheek and smiled. He was a good man, a good friend, and a good Keeper. She knew he would do the job right, and without another word, she let sleep claim her.

The End

Epilogue

Magdris

The void had been dark and cold. Too long had Magdris been away. Too long had they travelled the stars—alone. Now their goal was at hand, and Magdris hungered to be rid of this formless existence. Through the eyes of their disciple, their vision was narrowed by the iron slits of a raven crowned helm. That bloody-minded thrall who only wished to please them. A thrall whose mind was a cacophony of delightful brutality. Truly, a child of war destined to serve Magdris; to serve them in their conquest.

Magdris had tried once before, through the rough skin of the barbaric children known as orcs. Their crude worship of Magdris's power, disgusting in its simplicity, had been a beacon to them in the dark. Unfortunately, the brutes were cannibals and little smarter than the creatures of the wilds. Little smarter than Epidus's own charges—pathetic little things they were. That plan had been foiled by a bulwark against the assault. A *Keeper of the Stones*, as the humans had called her, and even though Dolocius had their talons sunk into her, she overcame. Magdris's deceitful sibling failed once again, and alongside the Keeper's damnable sisters, they both had been thwarted. The pain of being cast out by Ember's fiery tempest still irked Magdris. Although, it had been some comfort to know Dolocius suffered immense agony. Their form now cast to the void until it could take some semblance of being once more. That could be millennia.

In lieu of Dolocius's failings, Magdris would succeed. Especially now the Keeper was captured, locked away by the deception of the foolish, power-hungry human known as Eamon, a puppet easily swayed by greed and the promise of power. Oh, how fruitful it had been convincing Minollo to play their part. Magdris's art-obsessed sibling loved the drama of 'mortalities stage.' Now it was time to collect, for Minollo was not an ally, just a tool.

Magdris, from their detached formless view, looked out over the burning Argolonian village. The sights, the carnage, it was all so … wonderful. It had not been a battle, but a slaughter and though Magdris did not revel in death for death's sake, it had been too long since a proper bloodbath slaked their thirst. Now the screams of the damned as they were impaled on spikes caressed Magdris's wicked thoughts. The burning thatch of a villager's home complimented the chopping blow of an executioner's axe. A woman's head, too weak to be a worthy sacrifice, was severed by the blow.

It was all so *delicious*. They breathed in, or at least what went for breath in this shapeless form. Now, the moment they had been waiting for was here, and they buzzed with excitement at the prospect. Enough blood had been gathered, enough carnage. Starting with the massive war known as The Five Points and capped off by these bloody punitive raids. Yes, Magdris could take shape once more; they could take an avatar. It couldn't be the bloody handed mercenary—the 'Strategos'—they used as their eyes, regardless of how excellent of a servant they were.

No, the Strategos's reputation in this realm would not suit their needs. It couldn't be Eamon; he would be outed as a traitor soon. The fool didn't understand Minollo, soon their sibling would force the truth out, and not to just the one he had fooled. No lie could be held by Minollo's deceptions for long. Every act must end with the beautiful truth, and Eamon's act was over.

There was another, a fool who—though she had resisted at first— now fully bought into Eamon's lies, one who could purge themselves of wrongdoing. One who was known as *The Iron Hand*.

Without a word, Magdris urged their thrall away from the carnage. The battle was won, and these bloodstone berserkers no longer needed their commander. Now it was Magdris's turn. Silently, the mercenary approached the mounted leaders, politicians assigned to the punitive raid by Augustia's hand.

"Fine work, commander," Master Eamon said. "Though we *must* dispense with the … um, torture."

Master Aranos nearly leapt out of the saddle in agreement, "Yes! We *cannot* do this! We must let who still lives go. Th-this is wrong!" Magdris nearly laughed aloud through his disciple. The Iron Hand's mind was wrought with conflict, and her emotions were delicious as they oozed from her.

She felt sick at the thought of being deceived by Eamon—the thought she had been used to slaughter innocents.

Magdris knew she had been suspicious from the moment Eamon delivered her to his waiting company of oddly familiar looking mercenaries. The lie of not having enough time to rally the Warriors of August *just* convincing enough. That trickery had her accompanying them on their hasty march away from their city-state, giving them credibility on their quest for what she thought was simple revenge. Oh, how exciting it was to see her recognize how wrong she had been.

Magdris chose not to hear the politician's pleas and issued a command. With fluid motion, the mercenary, the strategos, drew his sword, stabbing upwards at their former master. The blow was quick and true, and Eamon's face fell open with shock. There were no words, the blow had burst his heart, giving him no time for final moments. Magdris would spare the fool of torment in this life. The only prize for his *service*.

Master Aranos started, "Ember's breath! Wha-what are you doing!?"

Magdris coursed their energies through the thrall, watching the scene from above. The mercenary's head ratcheted upwards, and blood from nearby corpses surged into him, giving Magdris the power to speak their cursed oaths. "Master Aranos!"

The Chosen's eyebrows shot up in fear and awe, she kicked the sides of her mount to try and flee. It was too late. Two berserkers approached from behind, grabbing the reins.

"Master Aranos, you are now mine! Your foolish bid for power is over, and now all that you have wrought will be reaped … by me." Magdris delightfully soaked in the terror of their victim.

The woman whimpered in fear and tried desperately to flee, even going as far as to draw her sword. The blade was arrested in her hand as a tendril of bloody sinew gripped the arm. The impaled bodies served as conduits for lashing tentacles of Magdris's power.

The blade dropped and more tendrils ripped free from the now wailing bodies. Master Aranos was pinned from all angles and pulled free of her saddle. The bloody tools brought the helpless Chosen in front of the enthralled strategos. With a blank expression, that thrall, that Argolonian warlord, opened his mouth. A fountain of blood poured forth.

Magdris laughed in ecstatic delight, as their energy coursed into the vessel. Soon they would feel once more. Soon they would be free!

Master Aranos could not resist anymore, and her body went rigid as the slithering blood coursed its way into every orifice, replacing her vitae entirely.

And there, there it was! They were free! And oh, how they reveled in that sensation. The punishment of Ember, who had soured their victory so long ago, was undone. Now they were free to walk the worlds once more. In that freedom, they knew of one place they must go. One score to settle that had started not far from here—just a sea away.

Master Aranos, who had fallen to her knees when the tendrils let her go, rose once more. Her eyes had taken on a new sheen, their former blue, almost-grey hue now approaching a cerulean, unworldly tint. She rubbed her jaw; rough skin scratched her calloused hands. The god looked down upon their new body, and saw the lines etched in their skin. The work of years carved into flesh, now theirs to command.

Master Aranos, Magdris, curled her fist and brought it upwards. It was time to speak to *her* children. It was time for war. "Captain, we will scour this land of its *filth*, and when we have sewn enough blood into the air. When I have grown strong enough, we shall find that bastard Ember, that self-proclaimed lord of gods, and bring … him … low …"

Book one of Gods Adrift.

SHARDS
OF EMBER
MITCHELL LECOULTRE

The Glossary to the Gods

Grand Keeper Erica

In support of our mission to settle this new land, this 'Holliserian Fringe,' I believe it best to dedicate some time to the particulars that might fall through the cracks. Primary of which *must be* a clear definition of those inhabitants of the shards, those gods of our realm. For too long, the tyranny of Xetemian might has held sway over our concepts—our ideas. It's to the point that some of our people believe in some rather ludicrous thoughts. For example, a gentleman the other day told me, "That Hercurius is likely to join us because of our surplus of food."

That's right? This man believed Hercurius himself was a gnome! Preposterous.

Even worse was a run in with a lady the other day. A member of our brave pioneering expedition who asked me if the father Hyclepius would help cure her of a rather nasty boil. I thought my ears had been blasted clean off, because I figured I can't be hearing this right. *The father?* But no, she was utterly serious, she called The Maiden, the most benevolent of gods, the *father …* absurd. So, taking into account these shackles of ignorance thrown upon us by that husk of an empire, I seek to change this alarming course.

Therefore, I order that this glossary to our gods be distributed amongst our peoples at every availability. After all, a clear and concise understanding of those who hold sway over the very forces of nature is a crucial element to the success of any venture; city-building or no. So, without further ado, I present you my abridged glossary to the gods! May it shield us from Xetemian insanity.

Dolocius (The Deceiver): In line with their trade, Dolocius holds many names: Sorrowstone, Magi Stone, or even Devil's Bargain. All of which alludes to the sinister truth behind this trickster, that Magi Stone is not to be trifled with. **Never, EVER,** use a Magi Stone! It may seem a beautiful object, a precious gem, with a beautiful azure coating hiding an inviting purple glow, but every instance of its usage has led to tragic downfall. The user's mind being torn asunder by the malefic manifestations of Dolocius. Though no surviving Magi Stone user exists, there are records from those who damned themselves by delving into the stone's sinister embrace. Heightened perception and a sort of *opening* of the mind's potential are common effects of the stone, though at a great cost. These tolls … these costs the stone takes fit with the deceiver's history, for Dolocius is believed to be the architect of the Shattering. That event we know so little of, that led to the very shards that grace Telaea.

I could spend pages warning you, dear reader, of the dangers of Dolocius but I will leave you with this quote.

"We walk amongst the Shards of Ember with only deceit to blame."

-Grand Keeper Madrios

Dolocius adores the trickster, the deceiver, and the schemer. The god of deception does not just wish to lead their victim astray, but they wish to see a well-laid plan come to fruition exactly as they desired.

Hercurius: Also known as Quickstone, Hercurius, is most attuned with our tiny friends, the gnomes. We all have heard the stories of gnomes guarding a cellar or a pantry, but the method seems to be a bit blurry. That blurriness also curses the Keeper cadre, but I, and many of those who will deliver this pamphlet to you, believe that our gnomish companions have learned the secrets of near instantaneous travel! A miracle granted by a combination of their size and a natural race-born affinity to the patron of

Quickstone. Unfortunately, this theory is insanely difficult to prove since the gnomes are loathe to give away their secrets.

As for the rest of us, Hercurius bestows its users with increased agility and speed. Caution must be exercised! For many athletes have torn muscles and ligaments when ingesting the stone. The god may give us their supernatural speed, but they don't give us the bodies to match!

Hercurius, constantly in a rush due their job as messenger to the gods, prefers the company of the restless and the adventurous. They hold the principles of the expeditious delivery, the vagabond's journey, and the wandering heart in highest regard.

Ember: Inhabitant of the Shards of Ember or Embershard. Lord over all the rest, and owner of the common curse word, "Ember's breath!" Portrayed as a large, scaled beast with four limbs, two wings, and four horns that grow in a spiral fashion from a skull of immense proportions. Ember is known to be rather temperamental but if caught in the right mood (much like any lord of our *own* realms) can grant the user immense power, typically in the realms of fire. When heard, this god is an authoritative presence that demands respect. There is no denying Ember's lordship over the other gods, although some postulate that the shattering is due to rebellion against this god. Ember holds respect, honor, and loyalty in high regard.

Epidus: Though there are rumors to the existence of a godstone for this god, none have ever been recorded. Much like their patrons, animals and beasts, Epidus remains on the periphery of humanity's grace. The only reason we even know they exist is through the rare occurrence in which a person is cursed with Epidus' whispers. Afflicted individuals are known to shed all forms of civilization, retreat into the wilds, and live out their lives as hermits. Wherever they die, Epidus' Blossom grows in full bloom. Epidus hold creatures and beasts of the land as paramount.

Magdris (The Crimson King): Inhabitant of the cursed Bloodstone. Of all the gods, this one is innately the most ruthless. Though many believe the gods are incapable of good or evil, myself included, this god definitely aligns itself with humanities traditional definitions of evil. Those who have attempted to commune with Magdris tend to go mad with bloodlust and end up 'berserking' on friend and foe alike. Any instances in which users of The Crimson King's boons are not instantly killed usually end with some story of wanton bloodshed and murder. Some of my colleagues believe that during the shattering, Magdris was the chief warlord of the faction in revolt against Ember. Magdris holds the honorable fight, warfare, bloodshed, and predatory behaviour in highest regard.

The Maiden (Hyclepius): Inhabitant of the Maidenstone. A benevolent god that often appears as a gentle breeze. Capable of assisting healers with even the direst of cases. When you speak to this god and SHE replies, many report a caring presence most often described as their own mother's voice. Truly, the most compassionate of gods, and the most well-known. As such I will not dive as deeply into her gifts, for even the lowest of servants knows how to invoke the Maiden. Just a simple plea for help can bring her soothing touch to your door, although not in as tempered a manner as a Keeper. The Maiden holds love and compassion as her highest principles.

Melleas: God of the sea and inhabitant of the Seastone. This is a difficult god to understand, and Melleas's apparent mood shifts cause its usage to be near random. I have noticed that those who do use Seastone tend to be exceptionally aligned with the sea and struggle to use any of the other godstones. Seastone can produce shards of ice or sudden freezes of small areas as well as torrents of water. In some cases, it has been used to becalm a small pond or river ford in windy weather. Melleas holds the sea, travel, and the irascible nature of water in high regard.

Minollo: Inhabitant of the Artstone. For many years, Keepers wrote this god off as no more than bacchanal celebrant. Recent revelations have shown that Minollo is capable of *so* much more. A few Keepers have managed to 'see the truth' as it were and visualize objects and people over great distances and through walls just within their minds. Minollo has also been shown to hide certain truths from people but every foray into this deceit has ended with some form of dramatic reveal to the truth. This is one god that I, and my colleagues, are keeping an eye on. Much like the art they represent, Minollo holds truths for everyone that looks. Minollo holds art, creativity, truth, and beauty in the utmost regard.

Mosyneta: Also known as Necrostone, Mosyneta encompasses the realms of memory and knowledge. This god was believed to be the recorder of all the history of our universe and is said to have a library that contains all memories to have ever existed. With that being said, I must implore our dear people to temper their fearful explanations of this stone. *No, Necrostone doesn't raise the dead!*
Instead, it is an artifact of the stone's method of action. You see, Mosyneta literally drags whatever memory we wish to revisit through the original vessel that experienced it. As you can imagine, this has led to some instances in which a dead individual has been *questioned* and their body, as corrupt and decayed as it is, being used as the conduit of the god's message. Truly, a frightening experience but one that I can assure you is completely safe. Mosyneta holds memory, cognition, and knowledge as their highest priorities.

Olkanestus: Inhabitant of the Forgestone. If any god holds the honor of patron to our new city, Augustia, it must be Olkanestus. In my years overseeing the construction of our new home I have been visited by this god on many occasions. Firelight vigils in which I query the supernatural with the problems of construction. True to their name, for they hold no obvious gender, Olkanestus is able to devise the most illustrious and efficient of solutions to engineering problems and more. Olkanestus is a curt, almost-grumpy voice that speaks in a way that each word matters. This god holds building, engineering, and innovation in high regard.

About the Author

Hello there! My name is Mitchell Lecoultre, but you can call me Mitch. I am, most proudly, a dad to three wonderful daughters, aged nine, six, and six. Yes, that means I have twins! My daughters, my wife, and I reside in Oklahoma where I work as a clinical laboratory scientist, helping physicians treat those who are burdened with diseases such as leukemia. I was born and raised in a small town in northern Idaho where I was raised by a loving family. I learned to love nature and respect the simpler joys of life and thus am more at home with campfire wisdom than cocktail etiquette. When I turned eighteen, I was unsure of what to do in life and, although I was enrolled in college, I joined the US Army instead. I served with honor as a cannon crewmember from 2006-2010. I will however admit that my time deployed overseas, in support of Operation Iraqi Freedom (2007-2008), transformed me, vanquishing the older, simpler me. After I finished my term of service, I got married to my beautiful wife, Vanessa, and we went to college at the University of Idaho, where I received a B.S. in Molecular Biology/Biotechnology. I have employed that degree to moderate financial success and am using it now for my current job. I enjoy hiking, walks with my loved ones, miniature painting, video games, reading, well-made television and YouTube content, and audiobooks.

If you would like to read more, support the author, or just stay informed check out the links below!

Website: mitchelllecoultre.com

Amazon: Mitchell Lecoultre (Follow the author). Be sure to leave a review for "The Godstone Decree."

Goodreads: Mitchell Lecoultre. Please leave a review!

Instagram: Mitchell Lecoultre

Facebook: Mitchell Lecoultre Author

Email: mitchleco@hotmail.com

Thank you!!!

Sneak Peak for book three of *Gods Adrift*

"What makes the green grass grow!?"

"Blood! Blood! Bright, red blood, strategos!" Dolus's corps yelled back at him.

"And what fertilizes that grass?" He continued the chant; the mantra that he had been so familiar with years ago.

"Bones! Bleach dead bones, strategos!"

Like his strategos before him, he implored his corps to greater volume, "What? I don't think those bastards in Augustia heard you!"

"Bones! Bleach dead bones, strategos!"

"That's better!" Dolus grinned with malicious intensity. "Now, corps! Prosochi!"

He paced down the line, hands clasped behind his back. The sight of so many young men and women, so many Argolonians ready for war, made it impossible not to feel a bit proud, no matter how green they were. They were the warrior-born of Argolon and they would make their home city proud—Strategos Dolus just needed a little time.

He stopped at the center of the formation, and, with practiced efficiency, swirled to prosochi himself, the position from which he would give all his commands. "Corps! Relax."

The new group of recruits loosely placed their hands behind their backs, legs spread to a more comfortable position, and their eyes remained—as always—ever forward.

With intentional ferocity and speed, Dolus wrenched one of two javelins from his back. The short spear, designed as a lethal throwing weapon, felt slightly cumbersome as he grasped it two handed. "This! This is to be your newest friend. Magdris's teeth! Probably your only friend from the looks of you all."

A light chorus of laughter rippled through the corps. They loved it when he mocked them, and eager grins flashed white in the ruddy morning light. *Fatherless whores would slap their own mothers to please me.*

Dolus lunged the javelin forward to demonstrate its killing potential. It was a beautiful thrust, and the heavy iron point whistled in the air as it came to a stop. "With this blade you can become an asset to Argolon; you can become a weapon. *Maybe* ... just maybe ... some of you can finally rise above the level of putrid cock stain that you are to something of value."

Strategos Dolus let the javelin rest by his side, while the corps stifled laughter. Before they could bask in the humor, he scoffed at them, pouring a baleful glare upon anyone who had a trace of happiness. One recruit looked as if his eyes were going to pop out from his skull; *sometimes it's damn hard not to laugh.*

It was all part of the game, and he couldn't let them know that he was in on his own joke. No, they *had* to believe he truly thought that they were the 'maggots of Argolon', the 'scum atop a sewage pond,' or even the simple yet effective 'troll turds.' Yet, the truth was, eighteen years ago, he remembered a day very similar to this one, when he was mocked by a grim-faced woman. Her face had more scars than a butcher's cutting board, and he nearly lost his bowels whenever she laid her murderous eyes upon him. Eighteen years of hard discipline, grim soldiery, and sometimes absolutely hilarious insults.

Now he would need to use all of that soldiery; all of that warrior's skill he had mastered over the years to turn these young men and women into weapons of war. He had to do it soon, because Augustia—the rotten bastards of Magdris that they were—had attacked, butchering a village with a savagery even unheard of during the Five Points War. Now he would have to equip this newest generation to revenge that insult, and, hopefully, relight the fire in himself for that fight.

"This weapon is a killer! From up close ..." Strategos Dolus marched a few paces to his right. The eyes of the recruits intent on his every move. He stopped, glanced at the straw target, and hefted the javelin into a thrower's stance.

He had planned this very demonstration, a testament to the power and skill of an Argolonian warrior. If he messed up the javelin throw though ...

He couldn't delay. Confidence must be his, and with one deep breath he fell into the rhythm of the throw. Three quick steps, a lunge, and then, his hips and shoulder flung the javelin like a machine of war. Its heavy iron point sliced through the air. A puff of straw exploded from the target, and he let his lips curl in satisfaction.

"And from afar! Of course, you maggots are nowhere close to learning that most effective of skills. So, we will start with getting comfortable. You will learn the feel of your javelin. You will understand her weight, her curves, her balance. By the time we are done here you will know that piece of wood and iron better than you know your own privates!" Dolus looked around at the assembled soldiers. Most of them were grinning, awed by the demonstration, and, in that giddiness, pliable to his crude humor.

"Yes! That includes you, Kymon." Dolus roared, making the young man, who had been the most animated of the group, blush in fear and embarrassment. "It's a miracle that you play with that thing of yours so often." Strategos Dolus let a malicious grin ripple across his weather-worn face and marched in front of the young recruit. "I mean ..." Dolus held up his gloved hands and left a tiny gap between his index finger and thumb.

The corps erupted into laughter, their discipline failing utterly at the well-timed joke. Even Dolus struggled not to laugh at the infectious humor. Yet, he couldn't, not in front of these ... puke-stains. "Go fetch my javelin, lad."

Kymon darted off, glad to be away from the torment.

Strategos Dolus returned to his position at the center of the formation, taking his time so that Kymon would have time to return with his weapon. Dolus grabbed the offered spear and held it upright for all the corps to see. "This is just one weapon our enemy fears! This is the javelin of Argolon, and starting today you will learn how to wield it. Starting today, you will learn how to wield the might and legacy of your forebears, of the shields of Argolon. Today, you will start your legacy!"

He thrust the javelin into the air once more, its point singing alongside the roar of the young recruits. They all cheered now, overwhelmed with the eager, near-suicidal, enthusiasm of youth. They would need it, because soon they would all be going to war. Strategos Dolus hoped that all of their javelins, swords, shields, and enthusiasm would be enough.